THE LONG DISTANCE MEN

by

SEAN MAGUIRE

The mysterious history before history, the blank slate of knowledge about ourselves before Jericho, has licensed our collective imagination and authorised the creation of primitive Edens for some, forgotten matriarchies for others. It is good to dream, but a sober, waking rationality suggests that if we start with ancestors like chimpanzees and end up with modern humans building walls and fighting platforms, the 5-million-year long trail to our modern selves was lined, along its full stretch, by a male aggression that structured our ancestors' social lives and technology and minds.'

Demonic Males: Apes and The Origin of
Human Violence, Richard Wrangham and
Dale Peterson

When one has not had a good father, one must create one.

Frederick Nietzsche

For my mother, Patsy Maguire

CHAPTER ONE

Hugh Gallon pushed through the heavy wrought iron gates, their austere design softened by ornate shamrock motifs embedded into the otherwise forbidding metal work, and ambled up the driveway that lead to his parent's house. Despite the ash grey of the skies above and the hard chill of the day, the early morning birds were cooing optimistically from within the thick lining of trees that shouldered the broad expanse of tarmac before him. He nestled his chin into his chest, lowering the crown of his head in an unconscious effort to mitigate the effects of his most recent growth spurt which had propelled his body onto the cusp of manhood. He was now well over six feet tall and had yet to come to terms with this sudden increase in height and as a result had become uncharacteristically self-consciousness in the company of his sixth - form peers, boys whose own surges had either not yet begun or had failed to yield such dramatic results.

As he approached the house, he half-consciously fended off the vague traces of physical discomfort that constitute a hangover for an eighteen year old and instead attended to the more pressing matter of how he was going to explain the recently acquired blood spatters that dappled his shirt, their once livid scarlet now dried into orange-brown smears across the white, crumpled fabric. His mother would be furious, of course; it wouldn't matter to her one jot that he had done the right thing in the course of acquiring them. His father would inevitably bleat out his usual ineffectual reprimands which would be answered by Hugh's undisguised indifference in response; after all, it is difficult to respect a man who one does not fear. His mother's wrath on the other hand, was an altogether different matter; her reprimands had something of the lash about them.

He cast his mind back over the events of the previous night which had lead to the current rather inconvenient state of affairs in an attempt to frame his behaviour in the most favourable light for when the inevitable interrogation came. It had been an excellent house-party, there was no doubt about that, and even the participants who hadn't secured the exam results they had hoped for had at least been able to drown their disappointment in an ocean of cheap wine and even cheaper tinned beer.

He and his friends had begun the evening in the bar of the local golf club and had eventually moved onto to Richard's house, the venue for the night's shenanigans. Richard's parents were holidaying in France for a couple of days and they had, after a prolonged period of negotiation which had involved Richard attaining A-level grades his parents had thought improbable, reluctantly given permission for him to hold a party at their home providing certain conditions were strictly observed. One such condition was that no strangers were allowed to attend, a requirement which had proved difficult to enforce given that the party had been eagerly anticipated for weeks and word had inevitably spread. Hugh was hoping above all that it might provide him with an opportunity to progress the physical side of his relationship with his girlfriend, Jane, although this hope was tempered with some pessimism. Nonetheless, he was prepared to rely on the possibility that a few glasses of wine might dissolve her Catholic restraint and much to his surprise he had eventually managed to persuade her to leave the melee of the lower floor of the house and go with him into the privacy of one of the bedrooms, but she was insistent that they would do no more than kiss.

Just at the moment he had embraced her and had brought his lips to her's it had started: unintelligible shouting and roaring exploded from the floor below, followed by a heavy crash. He felt Jane's body stiffen in his arms and he looked down to see her eyes open wide in alarm. In a rush of over - optimism he told her to remain where she was and he had darted through the bedroom door and sped to the top of the stairs. He surveyed the scene unfolding before him in the hallway below. The large, heavy bookcase which had stood next to the front door had been toppled and a small crowd had gathered around Richard as he was being hoisted into the air by his throat by an unknown young man, a stranger to all in the house.

The stranger was flanked by two equally unfamiliar young men who glared menacingly at the adolescent party goers who stood aghast, transfixed by the events unfolding before them. Hugh had read the situation quickly: clearly, they were gate crashers who had not reacted well to Richard's refusal to give them entry and one of them was about to take out his disappointment on Richard's face. Hugh had

3

momentarily turned to Jane who was now stood at his side, partly for permission to act and partly for forgiveness for behaviour to come, but his unspoken request had failed to register in her horrified mind. He had leapt down the stairs before punching the first interloper squarely on the jaw using his forward momentum to leverage the blow, sending the intruder reeling through the still open doorway. The second intruder, caught out by this unexpected turn of events, immediately released Richard, who fell to the floor in an ungainly cluster of limbs and torso, and turned to face Hugh who, now amidst the crowd, could not draw back his fist a second time to strike this new target. Instead, Hugh had launched himself at the stranger, the force of his fifteen stones driving the hapless bully to the ground. Hugh was first to his feet and he grasped the intruder by his shirt collar and drove his fist into his astonished face sending a spray of blood out into the world as the stranger's nose crumpled under the weight of the blow.

Upon witnessing this dramatic turnaround in his gang's fortunes the third young man turned and made a hasty escape through the front door, helping the first of Hugh's opponents to his feet, and they both sped off into the night. Hugh had looked down at the groaning man at his feet and, grasping a fist full of his hair, dragged him through the door, indifferent to his moans of pain. Richard scrambled to his feet and rushed to join them, adrenaline whizzing through him, and circled his proxy - beaten foe and began shrieking with all the vigour of newly minted courage that the police had been called and would be arriving in minutes. Hugh released his grip and the man stumbled to his feet, blood streaming from his nose, and staggered off down the driveway without so much as a backwards glance, abandoning his former courage as if it were a treacherous ally.

Hugh turned around to face the open door and the assembled party goers let out a loud cheer of approval. He had blushed slightly and lowered his head to disguise his evident discomfort and walked back into the house, friends, acquaintances and strangers alike slapping him on the back in congratulations. He turned to Richard who was now stood rigid in the driveway, his eyes wide and glazed, his face ashen, contorted into an expression of fear and dread. 'Bloody hell, Richard', Hugh had said, 'you'd better sit down mate.' He took Richard by the shoulders and guided him through the door. Richard collapsed onto the bottom stair and tried to collect himself, to restrain the tremors that ran through his body. After a minute or so he looked up at Hugh.

'That was bloody awful'. His voice was strained with anxiety and he turned his eyes to the floor. A moment or two passed and then he looked up at Hugh. 'How can you be so calm?', he asked incredulously.

'I don't know', Hugh replied, his self – consciousness returning. 'You know me, that kind of thing doesn't bother me. I suppose it should, but it doesn't.' He raised his hands and looked at his fingers; they were unmoving, steady. What he didn't tell Richard was that he felt exhilarated by the experience, that he had relished such encounters for as long as he could remember.

'Your shirt's covered in blood', observed Richard as he raised himself from the stairs, his composure slowly returning 'You'd better get it cleaned off', and they headed down the hallway towards the kitchen. Hugh received more congratulatory handshakes and slaps on the back as they went, news of the brief confrontation now transforming him into the champion of this clutch of relieved adolescents. By the time they entered the kitchen drinks had been handed to them and Hugh had given in to the repeated requests that he give a blow-by-blow account of what had just taken place. The blood stains on his shirt had pretty much dried out and been forgotten by the time he'd finished the third re-telling of the tale.

Hugh came to a stop five or six yards from the door of his home. The car his father used for the morning commute was still in the driveway confirming that he was still in the house, probably eating breakfast. His mother would have been sat at the breakfast table with him. It was unusually early in the morning for Hugh to be up and about, but Jane had left the party at midnight and what little sleep he had managed to snatch after her departure was spent on the lounge floor, all the beds having been taken, and he'd left for home in search of greater comfort as soon as he had been awoken by the morning sunlight streaming in through the French windows. He wanted his bed, but he didn't want to take the risk of entering the house and having to endure his mother's reaction to the evidence of the previous night's antics now painted across his shirt. As he speculated on whether there might have been an old T-shirt or pullover of his in the garage, the front door opened and his father appeared.

'Bloody hell!', he sighed in exasperation as he saw Hugh stood there and quickly pulled the front door closed behind him. 'What the hell have you been up to? Look at the state of you!', hissed David Gallon as he strode towards Hugh, trying to keep his voice low without compromising the rage that informed every syllable of his reprimand. He was squared up to Hugh in a couple of strides and then he snatched a fist full of Hugh's blood-speckled shirt and looked from this to Hugh's face. 'Fighting again, eh? Like some brainless thug, eh?', he scolded.

The scene would have looked strange to a casual observer. At five foot seven David was considerably shorter than Hugh and was an all-round smaller individual. Hugh was wider across the shoulders and deeper in the chest even at eighteen, despite the padding that David had instructed his tailor to discretely insert into his suit jacket to suggest the presence of a much bulkier frame beneath the elegantly cut fabric. It was only on the very hottest of days that David could be persuaded to remove his jacket.

Hugh tried to explain the events of the previous night, but David was having none of it. 'Get into the garage and wait there for me', he ordered. 'I'll go back in and get you a clean shirt. I am not going to put up with your mother's ranting about this for the next week; I've got far more important things to deal with.' Hugh stared at him, his indignation rising. 'Don't just stand there glaring', spat David and turned and walked back to the house. Hugh heard him call out to Kate, Hugh's mother, that he'd forgotten something, before the door closed behind him. He waited in the garage for a minute or so before his father entered and threw a shirt at him. 'Put that on and give me that rag you're wearing. I'll dispose of it at the yard', he said and waited impatiently for Hugh to comply, conspicuously raising his wrist to check his watch. Once Hugh had extracted himself from the offending shirt, David had snatched it from him and, before exiting the garage, he turned to look back at Hugh: 'how many more times is this going to happen, eh? Fighting like an animal?', and with a dismissive shake of his head strode to his car without waiting for a response.

Hugh watched him leave, sighed lightly and slowly shook his head at the impotence of his father's anger, before walking through the door that lead into the outer recesses of the kitchen. He was relieved to note that his mother wasn't around. As he turned on the kettle and waited for it to boil his thoughts drifted back to Jane. His only regret about the events of the previous night was that they had occurred just at the time she might have loosened her otherwise iron self-control. He hazily contemplated what might have been but was startled out of this blissful reverie by his mother's voice as she entered the kitchen.

'Hello', she said, a startled note in her voice evidencing her surprise at his unexpected presence at such an early hour. 'What are you doing up so early? Not like you when you've any choice in the matter.'

'I've just got in', he replied. 'I've been at Richard's house all night, the party, you remember'.

'I'd no idea that you were going to be out all night. I'm not sure I like that. You didn't call.'

'I thought I'd told you', he said casually as he made his coffee.

'I knew you were going to a party, that's it', she replied testily.

Richard picked up his cup and walked off in the direction of the stairs. 'And where are you going now?', his mother called after him.

'Bed. I'm knackered', he replied without turning his head to face her.

'Language!', she snapped in reply. 'It's only just gone six and your best approach the day is to go back to your bed? I can tell you now young man, I'm not going to put up with this for the rest of the summer', she continued to a now absent Hugh. She turned to make her own drink. She disliked beginning the day in an irritated state of mind.

7

CHAPTER TWO

The train pulled into the station and a stream of impatient passengers spilled out into the bleak, grey dampness of the early morning. Conspicuous amongst the crowd was a tall, powerfully built man, his hard, chiselled features belying his recent entry into middle – age. He stopped for a moment and shuffled the backpack slung across his broad shoulders into a more comfortable position before moving along the platform with the silent menace of a prowling jaguar, unimpeded by his fellow travellers who instinctively diverted their own paths away from his, something deep within their ancestral brains responding to the elemental danger amongst them. He came to a stop, oblivious to the bustling throng around him and pulled up the collar of his weathered moleskin jacket and dug his heavy hands into the pockets of his faded corduroy trousers. He raised his chin slightly as if sniffing the air and glanced around him, his bull head turning slowly in a lopsided arc in deference to his missing left eye, an absence marked by roughly stitched leather covering, its straps fastened in a bulbous knot at the back of his head. He raised his hand to adjust the makeshift eye-patch as if to remind himself of his purpose here, his thick, calloused fingers surprisingly deft in the touching of it, and he snorted quietly in a rebuke to the now unfamiliar skyline of glass, steel and concrete.

The memories came to him in pulses of revelation, breathing rhythmically through his smouldering rage, gently restoring its vigour. The pain he carried with him in his wanderer's soul was newly hatched that night almost twenty years ago and he shuddered inwardly at the recollection of its youthful ferocity and how it had almost crushed him, how she had almost crushed him. Yet with the passing of the years he had learned the mastery of it and how to put it to use, and now here he was, back where it had first found him.

At his weakest then he had staggered through the night lost in a dream of drunken despair, unaware of the street or the city or the world that contained him, thinking only of her and the destruction that she had wrought, she who had revealed to him a new world life of joy, of hope and of love only to mock the revelation as she cast it aside, a disposable thing unfit for purpose, her purpose. He had been young then, he had trusted her; he had been a fool to do so. He had rationed his foolishness with the care of a miser sheltering hidden gold ever since.

It had been that same night that they had pounced, that night of unrepeatable weakness. He was almost grateful for it, the physical pain. 'There he is. Get it done', he had heard barked out from the darkness behind him as he reached out in his drunkeness to steady himself against a crumbling wall on the derelict street. He raised his head, his eyelids heavy as lead, knowing instinctively that the call was for him and swayed in his stupor as he looked around him unable to focus through the rumours of light. He tried in vain to raise his fists in defence against the onslaught that he knew was to come and a voice awakening within him cursed their disobedience. Then it began. He was felled by a heavy chain coiling around his skull like an iron snake, its head whipping viciously into his eye, crushing the eyeball in its socket like a grape under a hammer. Then a pic axe handle came crashing down on him, then another, then another. White lights flashed before him like lightning bolts as tried to right himself, no pain yet, nothing but dull thuds against his flesh and bestial grunts filling the air. Then as suddenly as the brutality had begun, it had ended.

He lay on the cobbled street struggling to retain his grip on consciousness, his body unresponsive as he tried to marshal his mutinous limbs in a vain attempt to shield himself against blows yet to come. The filth embedded in the ruts between the cobble stones seeped into his nostrils as a huge figure casually pushed his way through the circle of men gathered around him, each amongst them cackling at their own savagery. The giant lumbered towards him silhouetted against the lamp – lit night, his face shrouded in darkness. 'Your time in this city is done, d'ya hear me?', he growled down at him. 'If you're still here this time tomorrow there'll be more of this for you', and with that the colossus brought the heel of his boot down onto his head sending him reeling into unconsciousness.

He awoke the next day in a hospital bed, the circumstances of his arrival a mystery to him, and he discharged himself four days later ignoring the protestations of nurses and doctors alike. He had gone from the hospital directly to the railway station and taken the first train out of city, his body half wrecked, and spent the next two weeks recovering in some nameless, flee-infested doss house with his youth as his only physician, knowing that although his body would recover from this onslaught, the damage that she had wrought would endure until his final breath.

That was twenty years ago, time enough to build a life for some, no more than a pause for breath for others. Now he was returned bearing scars in greater abundance than he had departed with, each one of these accounted for in vicious retribution, all but those that had been marked upon his flesh here, then; and now a reckoning was due. He breathed deeply of the morning air and tightened the strap of the backpack and re-joined the crowd as they made their way towards the station exit, his enormous fists clenching rhythmically in his pockets, marking out the time of the beat of his brutal heart.

CHAPTER THREE

The legend 'Gallon Civil Engineering Ltd', embossed in bright yellow lettering on the wide green doors of the waggon, glistened under a momentary wash of pale sunlight as it came to a muttering stop halfway down a row of mill-blackened terraced houses in one of the less well to do parts of the city. Its horn trumpeted through the thin, quiet air of the early morning causing the sidling birds to scatter into precautionary flight from their perches on the guttering above. The driver, a grizzled, grey- haired labourer in his sixties, immediately bridled, startled by the noise he had created and quickly silenced the engine as if in response to an unspoken rebuke.

'He's late', said Gene, the driver, to his mate whose sinuous frame was bent almost double in the passenger seat, his forearms resting on his knees and his head bowed, the sour odour of stale beer rising from him like a sickly heat. He barely raised his head to look at Gene and with an upwards flick of his eyebrows acknowledged the observation before returning his gaze to the mud-caked floor of the waggon. 'You don't look so good yourself, Mick', said Gene.

'Maybe not', his workmate replied with some irritation, 'but I'm here, aren't I', as if his mere attendance at his job of work was in itself an achievement that warranted commendation. Gene silently acknowledged that it wouldn't be worth the trouble to ask Mick to get out of the van and give the door of the house a rattle and that he, as the ganger man, had no business chasing a man to do a day's work when he hadn't the enthusiasm to get out of bed himself, so they sat in silence waiting for the emergence of their errant workmate

Gene shifted his position in his seat in order to secure an angle which would better allow him peer through the half-drawn curtains of the bedroom window above in the hope of identifying some movement within. There was none. Even if Frankie was late out of his bed, a vigorous shake of the bedroom curtains would usually indicate that he was up and about and would soon tumble out of the front door, dishevelled perhaps, but ready for the day's labours. But this morning, nothing.

'This is no good at all', muttered Gene under his breath, his irritation growing with the passing minutes. He hit the horn again, more as an expression of his growing annoyance than from any hope that it would rouse his overdue workmate. He immediately regretted it and cursed his temper. It was 6:15am and his better judgement told him to be wary of using the horn any more than necessary at this time of the day in case he woke anyone in the adjoining houses. This reluctance was not born of a heightened sense of civic responsibility, but rather of the knowledge that the company telephone number was emblazoned across the driver's door panel. He didn't want to take the chance that a disgruntled neighbour, used to a more leisurely start time to the day, might telephone the company office protesting that their sleep had been prematurely interrupted. Jones, the senior agent with the company, and Gene's boss, was a man whose temper was easily roused and Gene knew that he would relish the opportunity to chastise him, particularly if he was in the right, not always a requirement for Jones when it came to abusing the men under his charge.

'Bugger him', growled Gene under his breath and reached towards the keys dangling from the ignition, but before he had chance to kick the engine into life a flicker of activity in the bedroom window caught his attention. No sooner had he turned his head to investigate than the curtains had been whipped back and the windows thrown open with enough force to rattle the cheap frames against the brickwork of the building's façade, once again sending the skittish birds up into the air. The frames bounced back almost hitting the woman's arms as she leant through the casement, resting her palms on the windowsill. Any concerns that he may have had about the level of disturbance that the horn may have caused quickly disappeared as she began bellowing at them with a complete disregard for the previously peaceful slumbers of her neighbours.

'The bastard isn't here; hasn't been here all night', she bawled down at the waggon. 'And you can tell him when you see him that I'm not fucking stupid. I know where he's been!'. She continued in this vein for some minutes, her temper building into a spluttering crescendo of fury as she leant ever further through the window causing the grubby housecoat she was wearing to fall open revealing the deep gulley between her now partially uncovered breasts, a display she did nothing to counter. As her temper appeared to peak, she suddenly paused and fell silent absorbed in thought and then disappeared into the hidden recesses of the room.

'Jesus Christ, he's been at it again', said Gene, his shoulders bouncing slightly with mirth as he turned grinning at his mate who responded with an indifferent grunt. Gene quickly spun around as the woman re-emerged from the window holding what appeared to be a large bundle of clothing.

'Tell him to go fuck himself', she bellowed down at them stripping items from the multi-coloured wad of fabric in her arms and hurling them to the ground below as if underscoring each syllable with an act of rejection. Within minutes she appeared to grow tired of the obvious inefficiency of this approach, not to mention its dwindling dramatic force, and instead raised the remainder of the bundle above her head as if to cast it to the ground in one fell swoop. Then something appeared to catch her attention on the stretch of pathway behind the waggon and she stood motionless momentarily distracted, her housecoat hoisted by her raised arms revealing the full dimensions of her low-slung breasts, vein-ridden and pendulous. The driver followed her gaze along the street behind him and wound down his window to better see the object of her attentions, shifting his position in the seat with a muffled grunt.

Frankie Conroy was ambling casually along the pavement, his shoulders hunched up to his ears as a buffer against the early morning chill, his emerald – eyed good looks still evident despite the wearying effects of a long day of drinking and a long night of little sleep. He nodded his head in acknowledgement to the driver who, once recognised, retreated smiling into the cabin now ready to swap an early departure for the comedy of the confrontation about to take place between the soon to be ex-lovers.

'And there he is, the dirty fucker. Don't be thinking you're getting back in here, oh no, because you're not,' shrieked the woman spitting out the final negative with elaborate precision and hurling the remains of the bundle to the ground. Frankie neither acknowledged her insults nor chose even to glance in her direction which served only to ratchet up her indignation. Instead, he causally gathered up the clothing strewn across the footpath and walked unhurriedly around to the passenger side of the waggon and jauntily hopped in, greeting the occupants with a smile.

The ongoing tirade now appeared to be taking its toll on her neighbour's rest as an adjacent window flew open and an equally dishevelled head poked through and added its voice to the clamour outside. 'Will you shut the fuck up Mary, its six in the fucking morning, you dozy bitch!', exclaimed the neighbour, utterly disregarding the fact that she too was raising the volume of the day.

Frankie, now comfortably settled into the sanctuary of the waggon, became a matter of secondary concern for Mary as she re-directed her attentions to this new target. The exact contents of her response to her neighbour were reduced to an indistinct crowing for the occupants of the waggon as the driver wound up his window, started the engine and slowly pulled out from the curb, leaving the bluster of neighbourly discontent behind them.

Gene glanced down at the bundle of clothes piled unceremoniously on Frankie's lap and, as he shook his head in quiet exasperation, his attention was drawn to the patent leather shoes on Frankie's feet, gleaming in the half-light of the cab. He looked Frankie up and down, surveying his workmate's outfit of pressed slacks and starched white dress shirt. 'Jesus Frankie, you're dressed for a night out in a dance hall, not a day's work in the track!', Frankie ignored him and continued to fumble around in the bundle finally looking up and tutting.

'Jesus, Gene, no boots!'.

'Would you want to go back for them?', replied Gene, smiling. Frankie duly ignored the question and instead nudged the man sat next to him.

'What do you reckon Mick, would I be in full compliance with the health and safety requirements applicable to an excavation operative?', he said struggling to maintain a faux official tone of voice and raising his shiny leather shoe for inspection by his indifferent workmate. Mick, whose posture had barely altered since Gene had picked him up that morning, grunted indistinctly. 'Dog rough, I suppose?', said Frankie, indicating Mick with his thumb as he glanced at Gene.

'Rough enough', said Mick as he raised his upper body to an erect position, stretching his reluctant back muscles. 'O'Grady locked us in at half ten and we couldn't get out until half two.'

'Locked you in, eh?, mused Gene. 'I wouldn't imagine you protested too much. How many stayed back?'

'Oh, a dozen or so,' replied Mick with little enthusiasm.

'Fighting in lumps?', enquired Frankie.

'Aye, it was lively enough towards the end', grunted Mick reluctantly then turned once again to face the floor as if wearied by the exchange.

Frankie turned his attentions back to the collection of garments piled unceremoniously on his lap and frantically rummaged through them with growing unease. 'Jesus, there's no working clothes here at all Gene', he said finally, shaking his head in disbelief. 'You'd have thought that if she was going to fuck a man's worldly goods out of the window, she'd at least be thorough!'.

'Well, you might want to stay out of the way when we get into the yard. You don't want The Heifer catching you dressed like that', cautioned Gene.

'Fuck him', said Franky indignantly, 'stood up there on his perch bawling and shouting like he was some kind of big shot', his previous good humour evaporating and leaving a disgruntled silence in its place. It had been said more than once that the mere mention of Jones' name could suck the joy out of a children's party.

CHAPTER FOUR

After a drive of fifteen minutes or so through the still streets of the city the waggon pulled into what had once been the site of an old textile mill, long since demolished, and now home to Gallon Civil Engineering Ltd. The yard was approximately a third of an acre square and housed the site office which was little more than a rough assemblage of two large portacabins one sat atop the other and connected by an external timber staircase.

Stored next to the office in thin skeletal frames of grey steel were batteries of six- meter long pipes awaiting entrenchment beneath the streets and roads of the city by the men who scurried hurriedly around the yard carrying jack hammers, dragging compressors and loading their waggons with sundry tools, all eager to get out on site as quickly as possible and begin their day's labours. These were price-work men, paid by the meter dug and measured, and time was just another enemy to be outrun.

Arrayed around the perimeter of the yard in ragged dunes sat hillocks of sand and heavy stone aggregate piled next to vaporous mounds of steaming tarmac. The morning breeze swirled around and amongst them combining the acrid reek of glutinous black bitumen with the devilish exhaust fumes of waggons revving impatiently in their eagerness to depart, creating ribbons of malodorous cloud which hung menacingly in the air above the yard, toxic to body and soul alike.

The centre space of the yard was reserved for the waggons and the storage of the huge air compressors that powered the heavy, unwieldy jack hammers used to break open the ground and to chisel out the trenches into which the pipes would be laid,

Despite repeated attempts by the management of the firm to install some kind of workable system for the organised entrance and exit to and from the yard the place remained steadfastly chaotic. Waggons shunted about trying to find their own paths heedless of the wants of those around them. As a result, the yard was as raucous as a steel mill: blaring horns and rumbling engines, the crashing of aggregate being loaded onto enormous grab waggons, the bang and clatter of heavy equipment being manhandled onto the back of sundry vehicles, and woven through this raucous pandemonium, the rough, hectoring voice of Jones stationed on the gantry of the staircase outside the door to the upper office. There he stood barking out curses and instructions to the men below in pulses of anger and frustration, bullying, threatening and cajoling them out of the yard.

Jones was a man who rarely went unheeded. His 23 stone frame indicating in no uncertain terms how long it had been since he had last wielded a shovel or a jack hammer, his enormous bulk not easily accommodated within the confines of the trench. He stood in striking physical contrast to the men dashing about the yard below who, by and large, had been made lean and strong by the demands of the work at hand. The shovel men were spare and wiry from the twenty tonnes of muck, stone and rock they prized out of the ground each day. The hammer men, butcher's block sturdy with heavy shoulders bunched above broad, strong backs sculpted by the eight stones of rattling steel that was the pneumatic jack hammer.

But Jones was no panting lump of a man. He would often make a show of his physical strength by striding up the timber stairs to the upper portacabin with a jack hammer or some other heavy piece of equipment straddling his shoulder, ignoring the creaking timbers underfoot. In truth he carried his weight well, its excesses distributed across his six foot five frame in a more or less proportionate manner except for his paunch, which the uncharitable claimed gave him the look of a cow on the brink of calving. And so while he encouraged folks to refer to him as 'The Bull', his detractors, of which there were many, preferred to refer to him as 'The Heifer', although he was seldom referred to in these terms within his earshot. Jones disliked more or less everybody on the more or less correct assumption that everybody disliked him. This was one of his rare instances of valid insight into his own character.

It usually took around an hour from the arrival of first cohort of men before the last of the waggons finally cleared the yard and Jones would not quit his position on the gantry until the final vehicle had trundled out through the gates. His patience was as fragile as porcelain and would shatter at the slightest interruption as to what he saw as the proper order of things, sending curses down upon the heads of the dawdlers below despite the inescapable hurly – burly of the morning exodus.

Jones surveyed the yard through narrowed yes and, satisfied that it had been cleared of men and vehicles, turned and entered the main works office. The interior was large enough to house five desks, but the mass of technical drawings, route maps and associated paraphernalia lining each wall seemed to compress the internal space and made it appear smaller than it was. Three site agents, Jones' immediate subordinates, occupied desks nested around the far end of the cabin. Sat facing them at the other end of the office was David Gallon, his diminutive frame ensconced behind an elaborately designed oak desk, still brooding over his encounter with Hugh less than an hour earlier.

The desk was utterly out of keeping with the tattered interior of the office. It had been salvaged many years ago from a local bank prior to its demolition at a time when it possessed all the sombre gravity of an Edwardian banker's self-regard. This world of polished elegance now long gone, the interior of its current home was instead decorated with a thick layer of dust carried in underfoot from the yard outside. The yellow - grey dust particles which coated the interior like glimmering velvet were fine enough to be lifted by the slightest of breezes; a mere footfall would scatter them like airborne mites sailing through the shafts of sunlight that cascaded in through the gridded windows, coating the ornate carvings of the desk like a mould. The Irish tricolour fixed to the wall behind David's desk had faired no better and was itself discoloured by dust particles now stubbornly embedded into the fabric of the flag.

David Gallon was second generation Irish as were many of the men who worked for the firm. The remainder of the workforce was comprised of Irish immigrants of varying lengths of residency in England, from men fresh off the boat eager to make their fortune to those who had been in the country for decades watching their children grow in a foreign country exposed to their ancestral homes only on annual trips whose frequency inevitably decreased with the passing years. The flag was one of David Gallon's few acknowledgments of the cultural mood of the yard.

This bleak northern city had been a destination for Irish immigrants for over two hundred years attracted by the flourishing textile industry that had once defined the city on the national stage, but whose decaying infrastructure was now little more than an emblem of the city's failure to adapt to changing times. While the women had gravitated towards work in the mills, the men were pulled across the water by the insatiable demand for workers willing to meet the cruel demands of building the canals, roads, tunnels and utilities that tied city and country together. It was the first of these grand national projects, the navigation canals, that in the late eighteenth century christened these rough-hewn men from across the water, these navvies. They had travelled across the Irish sea bringing with them a hard, half-savage culture born of brutal rural poverty. Shorn of educational opportunities, this was a culture that held few options for those with brains, so instead lauded a man for his physical strength, his capacity for work, his appetite for the fight and the drink, a culture in which the pub was as much a proving ground as the job site. As a result, it was world of rough, stoical men for whom the capacity to work and to drink and to fight were the most direct routes to gaining the respect of their peers.

These migrants had been restricted by their own poverty and the suspicions of the natives to the grim rows of damp and decaying terraced houses which surrounded the now decrepit mills situated in the city's southern reaches. Time had allowed the community to shape their environment to satisfy their own needs and requirements: Catholic churches and schools, raucous pubs, clubs and dance halls had stamped an identity on the area which marked it out as different from the city of which it was a part, as a community unto itself. While there had been periods of deep mistrust and animosity between the native population and what were perceived as interlopers in days gone by, the permanence of their presence and the gradual increase of intermarriage between the two communities had softened these internal urban borders. Nonetheless, Irish migrants and their descendants remained wedded as if by natural law to the pick, the shovel and the trench and it was only a lucky or a gifted man who could escape the tribulations of a line of work that once engaged with was quickly transformed into a form of life defined by hardship and the grim pleasures of the bottle. The lucky ones were those that married and stayed married, but they were in the minority. Most of these navvies were itinerant workers moving from city to city either chasing work or running from sin and were never in one place for long enough to settle anywhere but in the nearest public house, the 'long distance men' as they were known.

This flow of immigrants from across the water had always been consistent, but every generation or so had been given fresh impetus either by economic catastrophe at home or an explosion in demand in England for men born with callouses on their hands. One such cry resounded across the Irish Sea in the aftermath of the Second World War when for the first time opportunities for advancement had begun to present themselves for those with a mind to take them as the task of rebuilding the country fell to the Irish. One such man was Patrick Gallon, David's father, who arrived in England as a fifteen-year-old in 1947.

Patrick Gallon, now dead for over a decade, had built GCE through a steady, but consistent expansion and, as the financial rewards of his efforts began to accumulate, he had sought to insulate his only son from the hardships of immigrant life. To this end he had ensured that David had been provided with the opportunities that had been denied to him by the sullen poverty of his own childhood.

As a youth David Gallon had attended the same schools as many of the local lads who had earlier filled the yard, but as his father's coffers filled, he had been parachuted into the local fee-paying school. David had proved to be a diligent rather than an inspired student and the respectability of his examination results reflected this. He progressed through school smoothly enough and entered a middling university eventually qualifying as an accountant and had then gone on to enjoy a reasonably successful career as a reliable and diligent tax consultant for a mid-size local practise.

Nonetheless, despite this escape from his father's world, David Gallon retained a sense of dissatisfaction with himself within his chosen field. He could not escape from the knowledge that his father's intentions in encouraging him towards a white-collar occupation contained an implied recognition that he didn't have the toughness to survive within the rough world of the pick and the shovel, that he wasn't *man* enough to survive in this environment. Most of the time David was able dismiss this characterisation of maleness as juvenile and reductive, but only most of the time. Gallon Senior, for all his ambition for his son, had spent most of David's childhood and adolescence casually eroding David's self-esteem, chiding him for his slight physique, his prissiness, his fearfulness, qualities generally referred to by Gallon Senior in scathingly unfavourable terms.

'Jaysus now, another one of his fuckin' delicacies, eh? You'd think you think there was a young girl trying to get outta him', his father would exclaim whenever he witnessed one or other of David's several foibles, half-joking, half-not. David had heard reference to his supposed 'delicacies' on so many occasions over the years that the word had lost all meaning to him and had become little more than a slur of sound signalling his father's disapproval and disappointment.

The most devastating of these myriad incidents had come when his father had dragged him to the local GP's surgery demanding to know why David hadn't yet entered puberty when so many of his peers were deep into their own transformations.

He had sat in silence in the doctor's surgery while his father had insisted that David be prescribed medication which would accelerate the progress of his son's physical development, smashing his fist down on the doctor's desk when this was refused and then berating him as if a perfectly natural hormonal sluggishness was entirely of the doctor's doing. In response, the doctor, visibly cowed, had stuttered a request that they both leave his office. David's father had risen to his feet, his temper barely under control, and had pulled David out of his seat cursing the now terrified doctor as he dragged David to the door. Before leaving his father could not restrain himself from once again turning to bawl at the doctor who was scrambling for the telephone on his desk.

'Look at the cut of him', he said looking down at David, 'he's got more fucking delicacies than a new-born lamb and you do fuck all about it! You useless bastard', he roared bitterly. David stood in silence next to him, the colour drained from his face, utterly confused, utterly humiliated. Then he began weeping, silently weeping. His father had looked at him and let out a groan of exasperated disgust before once again grabbing him by his coat and pulling him through the surgery door which rattled on its hinges as his father slammed it shut behind them. David was seventeen.

His father's insults were made all the more incisive for the boy given his father's obvious maleness, a quality which both fascinated and repelled David in equal measure. As he moved through adolescence, he had learned to deflect his father's slights by silently characterising him as little more than a transplanted rural thug, a brute from another land, another world. Yet beneath this characterisation it was never an entirely settled matter for him as to whether this brutishness was a quality not to be admired. So, when his father died, and common sense dictated that David should sell the business and move on with his own professional life, to the surprise of many he instead took hold of the reins of Gallon Civil Engineering Ltd.

David had persuaded himself that his business acumen and financial skills would consolidate and enlarge upon his father's success, and this was just what had happened. He had gone on to make a very satisfactory living out of Gallon Civil Engineering, enough to secure a comfortable life for himself, Kate and Hugh and to achieve a certain standing within the community. His fortunes had been further favoured by the emergence of a new system of fibre optic communications which required protective ducts to be installed beneath every footpath in every city in the country and it was the navvy, either Irish or domestic, who was to undertake this mammoth task. GCE was perfectly situated to exploit this opportunity in its home city and the money rolled in. The early 1990s were proving to be a lucrative time for David Gallon.

More important for David than mere money in the bank was that his success had exceeded that of his father's and given him some grounds at least to rid himself of the corroding sense of failure that ran as rivulets of self-doubt through the bedrock of his character. His wealth had come to act as barometer of his masculinity, a proxy for the rough physicality that had acted as currency in his father's world, as the means of calibrating a man's worth. David would always be a pauper when measured against this yardstick, but his money told him that him he could run with the rough-hewn men that populated this world, that he could be one of them, that he could come to dominate them.

Yet he was no fool. He would not allow the whispering imp that sat on his shoulder repeating his father's causal insults to cause him to stumble idly into folly. His first act as boss was to promote the thug Jones from the trench and let him act as a buffer between himself and the men. The imp would occasionally remind him that Jones' presence was clear evidence that he himself didn't have what it took to gain the respect of the men and in a fit of petulance David would lash out at the uncomprehending Jones, persuading himself that by wielding power over Jones he was wielding power over the men that Jones himself had intimidated into obedience.

22

Jones lumbered towards David's desk. 'Andrews and Brown are missing, still drunk somewhere no doubt', he muttered his voice emptied of all anger and informed instead with a generalised sense of disappointment as if the absent workers were disobedient children who were beyond the pale of chastisement, hopeless cases who even he could not cajole into right attendance. In taking this approach he hoped thereby to absolve himself of responsibility for this lack of discipline amongst the men, instead attributing their failure to an irredeemable weakness in human nature.

It was crucial to Jones that David did not see the absence of these men as a reflection on his ability to command obedience from them, that David continued in his belief that Jones was the dominant figure in the yard, bar none. In reality, Jones took such mischief as a naked affront to his authority and made himself a promise to deal with the miscreants accordingly. There was little security of tenure in this line of work and Jones was well aware that his current position, not to mention any hope of advancement, was dependant on his remaining tethered to Gallon's good graces. He could name three or four men just out of the yard that morning who had previously held positions of authority within other firms who were now relegated back to the track, an unwelcoming and unforgiving destination after the relative comfort of the office.

'Well, we can't sack them', said Gallon, 'we need the men, especially with the next phase in the build starting next week. Put a notice up in the yard saying that from now on any absentee workers will be charged for the hire of the waggon and tackle for the day they skive. Might get them out bed.'

'Get them out of the pub, you mean,' added Jones. 'Aye, we can give it a go, good idea David. Anyways, I was half expecting a new gang to start this morning, John Lynch and his mates. I know him from below in Brighton, he's a good worker, been around for donkey's years but he hasn't shown up yet for some reason', he said returning to his desk.

'Probably got on with another firm. Good men are hard to find at the moment', replied David distractedly as he peered down at a set of technical drawings on his desk.

Jones turned to the agents clustered at the other end of the office with a look that enquired as to why they were still there and not out on site. They immediately broke off their conversation and arose as one and, after exchanging a few brief words with Jones, left the office.

'Now then', said Jones turning to David, a clear note of apprehension in his voice, 'I heard this morning that Danny Greene is working alongside Lynch. I don't know if it's right or not, but I thought I'd better tell you in case you bumped into him in the yard in the event that they show up later.' Jones attempted to deliver this information as lightly as he could, but knew that this was unwelcome news for both of them, him in particular, and that he would be held responsible for its portent.

At the sound of this name David Gallon immediately stopped what he was doing. 'What?!' he barked incredulously at Jones 'Danny Fucking Greene? Here?' his anger rising as he began to grasp the full implications of the news. 'Are you out of your fucking mind? Why the fuck would you set him on? I mean, are you looking to get the shit kicked out of yourself or just make an ass out of me, which of the two?', he roared at Jones who stared down at the floor of the cabin like a guilty schoolboy, unable to confront Gallon's accusing glare, barely able to bear the weight of the reprimand.

'Look', said Jones raising his eyes almost imploringly, but still unable to confront David's gaze. 'I had no idea that Greene was with the gang when I set them on, I mean, it's been nearly twenty years since he was around here, why would I think he'd be with that gang out of the hundreds of long distance men we've set on over the years? Paddy Lynch called me looking for work, why would I ask who was in his gang? I mean, who would give a fuck about that?'.

'You. Of all people, you should give a fuck', replied David, his initial shock subsiding with the recognition that Jones did have a point. A moment of silence passed as David grappled with the practical implications of the news. 'Who told you Greene was with Lynch?', he asked, a semblance of calm returning to his voice.

'Tony Deegan', replied Jones, noting the change in Gallon's tone. 'I was talking to him in the yard this morning about Lynch coming up knowing that they were mates down below in Brighton a few years back. He mentioned that Greene had been working with Lynch, that's all. I mean, it was a few years ago. You know what gangs are like, they could've parted company ages ago. I just thought I was doing the right thing by putting you in the picture, that's all. Anyway, Lynch hasn't shown, so fuck 'em, eh?', he pleaded in mitigation, an uneasy smile playing across his face. David stood up and walked to the mesh covered window of the portacabin and peered down into the yard. A heavy silence hung over the office.

'Well, it would've been embarrassing for me if that bollocks had appeared in the yard, but it would've been positively dangerous for you, eh?', said David, turning an sinister glance towards Jones.

'I don't give a fuck about him', replied Jones tersely. 'It'd take a tougher fucking man than Danny Greene to cost me a second thought. I was thinking more about you, the gossip, the muck – raking, all that stuff about your lad coming up again. I mean, I know how it bothers you.'

These disguised stabs at David's sensitivities were Jones' only way of striking out at David in response to his casual assumption that Greene would pose a threat to him. More fool David for letting me know his weak spots, thought Jones. More fool David indeed. There had been much talk within the community of Hugh's paternity at the time of his birth; aged matron's checking calendars, lads speculating in tap rooms, Patrick Gallon's disgusted glares finding David across the dining table. Jones knew all this, everybody did, but it wasn't until a company Christmas party several years ago during which David, uncharacteristically drunk, had taken Jones into his confidence, deep into his confidence. It was then that Jones had learned the truth of David's relationship with his Father, with Hugh. Jones had awoken the morning after the party with a gratifying sense of satisfaction. David's tedious, self-pitying ramblings had given him an insight into the fragile nature of his boss's masculinity and with that, his vulnerabilities.

David refrained from addressing Jones' remarks and collected himself. 'It would have been better if you'd have checked first before setting them on perhaps', he mused, ushering in a change of subject and allowing a silent moment to pass to underscore the diversion. He turned from the window. 'Danny Greene, eh?', he murmured lightly in an effort to gloss over the rawness that the mere mention of the man's name had exposed. 'I didn't know him to be honest. We were in different worlds. I saw him around once of twice, that's about it. He was just a thug from what I remember, bit of a brute. I'm surprised he's still alive given his lifestyle. I mean you and your mates sent him packing in some style, didn't you'.

'I'd have half expected him to have been found in a ditch with his head battered in years ago. He had a bad attitude', replied Jones pouncing on David's observation, now eager to dampen his boss' indignation and validate anything that he might say.

'Wouldn't have surprised me either', said David returning to his desk. 'He was a bit of a tough guy in his day though, I heard,' deliberately understating the facts.

Jones scoffed inwardly at David's use of the term 'tough guy'. 'He's watched too many films', he thought to himself.

'Everybody could fight at that age though, eh?', said Jones light-heartedly. 'It was just what we did, a bit of sport between the lads.'

'I preferred backgammon', said David dismissively and returned to his desk.

Jones looked down at him, his lips curling slightly in an expression of mild disgust. He turned and crossed the office to his own desk.

'Anyway, they didn't show, so it's neither here nor there', he remarked sitting himself heavily into his chair before briefly glancing at David to gauge his reaction before quickly averting his eyes in case he was caught out doing so. As he turned his eyes from his boss he was sure he saw a venomous glance whipping out at him from behind David's desk.

CHAPTER FIVE

The waggon pulled up on a quiet cul-de-sac and Gene clambered out quickly followed by Frankie. Mick eased himself out of the cab and stretched elaborately before clambering onto the back of the waggon and rummaging through the toolbox. He pulled out an empty bucket, eased himself stiffly onto the ground and wandered off towards one of the semi-detached houses that lined the street in the hope that one of the residents might fill the bucket with water. Gene began placing road warning signs at the entrance to the cul-de-sac, while Frankie began arranging the heavy - duty plastic barriers along the footpath to create a walkway for pedestrians, hemming in the seventy or so meters of pathway on which they would be working area during the course of the morning.

Mick duly found an obliging resident and headed back to the waggon, the contents of the bucket sloshing onto his trouser leg. He placed the bucket on the ground at the side of the cab and pulled off his T-shirt and dumped the remaining contents of the bucket over his head. He straightened up, shook his head like drenched dog and ran his palms over his scalp to plane off what remained of the water and reached into the cab, fumbling under the passenger seat. His hand reappeared clutching a large, dark brown bottle. He unscrewed the top and guzzled the entire contents in one draught, letting out a sigh of satisfaction. 'Right', he said to himself, 'ready to go!'.

'And about time too', muttered Gene as he passed him dragging the air compressor which powered the jack hammer in his wake.

Frankie had unloaded the tools necessary for the day's work and had laid the jack hammer on the footpath at the point where they were going to start digging. As Gene was connecting the hammer to the heavy air hose attached to the compressor, the grab waggon pulled into the avenue and began to unload its consignment of sand and aggregate onto the side of the road.

'We should get the hundred metres in today, that's if the rain holds off', said Frankie. They both raised their eyes thoughtfully to a sky flushed with a forbidding grey wash, both men silently noting the inky scarves of cloud above them.

'I can feel a dampness in the air', observed Gene. 'We'll open up to the end of the barriers and see what it's like then.' He nestled the top of the hammer into his inner thigh and nudged the blade with the inside edge of his boot etching a line down the surface of the tarmac footpath. Having scoured around 20 meters into the surface of the footpath he turned around and chiselled another line running parallel to the first to set out the edges of the trench they were about to excavate.

As he approached the waiting Frankie, Gene lifted his eyes from the track he was marking out and glanced at Mick who appeared suddenly reinvigorated as he laughed and joked with the grab-waggon driver. 'The cider seems to be doing its job', scowled Gene as he brought his heavy shoulders to bear down onto the hammer, twisting and turning the blade, flicking up a narrow sheet of surface tarmac and loosening the freshly exposed ground beneath. Frankie looked at him impassively, shovel poised. 'I had to knock the gobshite up again this morning and how many times has he missed this month?', asked Gene rhetorically, his irritation evident. Frankie tore into the loosened earth in silence, acutely aware of his own sins that very morning. He emptied the opening meter of the trench and hopped down into the space he'd made, ready to hurl out the rocky debris that the hammer blade had shaved off the dense, clay-drenched aggregate that made up the face of the trench.

The skill in using the jack hammer lay in breaking the solid, compacted earth into a pile of loose material on the floor of the trench which would then be thrown by the shovel-man into a waiting wheelbarrow. The contents of the wheelbarrow would then be dumped in a pile for the grab waggon to remove at various points during the day. The jack hammer was heavy, cumbersome tool and it required considerable upper body strength to use it effectively, particularly given that the hammer-man would be wrestling with its bulk virtually non-stop for eight or nine hours a day. A different kind of strength was required for the shovel-man. The trench was a narrow space, perhaps a foot across and foot and half deep, and adjusting legs and feet to this confinement placed a great deal of stress on the calves and lower back. In addition to this was the effort of lifting a shovel loaded with rocky debris from the floor of the trench into the waiting wheelbarrow, a nine-hour test for biceps, shoulders and upper back. Once a length of trench had been excavated, the six-meter-long ducts would be placed onto the floor of the trench, each one slotting into the one behind it, before being backfilled with sand and stone aggregate, compacted and then finally sealed with a thick skin of heavy tarmac, leaving a black scar down the length of the footpath, meagre evidence of the intensity of the days labours.

They worked on determinedly for an hour or so rarely communicating to one another above the dense mechanical pulsing of the jack hammer reverberating around the narrow confines of the cul-de-sac. They hit a good stretch: the ground was earthy and soft, which meant that the hammer man's job was an easy one. When positioned correctly the blade of the hammer could cut behind the trench face and required only the lightest flick of the wrist to lift the tip of the blade as it hit the base of the trench and loosened the debris into a small heap for the shovel man to hurl into the waiting wheelbarrow.

The hammer man drove the pace of the work when the ground was yielding and this usually meant that there was no let up for the man in the trench, soft ground being a rarity which must be exploited. Frankie had immediately fallen into a rhythm that was fluid, quick and focused, driven by an economy of effort refined over years in the track. They made good progress and their spirits were high despite the darkening sky above them.

An hour or so of this saw five or six tonnes of excavated spoil and around forty meters of track dug out behind them. Gene finally relaxed his grip on the hammer trigger. 'So how're the dancing shoes doing?', he asked grinning down at Frankie who wiped the sweat off his face with the palm of his hand.

'They'll be right enough as long as it keeps dry, but they won't be much fit for dancing after this carry on though', he replied leaning on the handle of the shovel and lifting a leg from the trench and resting his foot on the footpath to more carefully scrutinise the state of his shoes.

'He gets on my nerves that man down there', said Gene nodding towards Mick.

'Aye? From what I hear I don't think we'll be seeing him around for much longer. He's waiting on a cheque, tax rebate. Once that's in his paw he be gone till it's drank', said Frankie. Gene scowled and turned to look down the track.

'Hey, Mick', he bawled. Mick looked up from laying out ducts in the virgin trench. 'I hear you're waiting on a big cheque'.

'Aye', answered Mick, his back to Gene.

'You'll be going into semi-retirement for a while, I suppose?'

'Full retirement with a bit of luck from the gee-gees', replied Mick.

'And when's it due?', enquired Gene.

'Hard to know. Should've landed last week', he replied finally glancing in the direction of his two workmates.

'Did you notice any day labourers in the yard this morning?', Gene asked, looking down at Frankie. 'The sooner we can get shut of that gobshite the better. I wouldn't have set him on in the first place if anyone else had been around. Good men are hard to find these days'.

'Good men are always hard to find', replied Frankie.

'Aye, I suppose so. I don't know why that bollocks just doesn't split his money down the middle and hand half to the bookie and half to the landlord. It'd save him a lot in time, disappointment and hangovers.'

'I didn't notice anyone around the yard this morning, but then again I wasn't looking. There's always a few lads loitering though.'

'Aye, after the big money, eh?', replied Gene sarcastically referring to the myth common about the city that because it was price – work there were fortunes to be made.

Frankie smiled up at him from the trench.

'If only they knew, eh?', he said wistfully.

'So, where's the lie down tonight?', enquired Gene. 'I wouldn't expect the one this morning'll be keeping the place next to herself warm for you.'

'Mary? No, you might be right there. I'll be OK. I've another on the boil', replied Frankie grinning as he swung his resting leg back into the trench and made ready to continue work. As he bent his frame to the shovel, he felt a droplet of rainwater soaking through the back of his white dress shirt, then another. 'She's getting ready to come down', he said surveying the darkly marbled sky, silently welcoming an early finish to the shift. He'd had plenty of drink the day before himself and precious little sleep to go with it, being otherwise preoccupied by the demands of his new girlfriend, but he was far more adept than Mick at disguising the effects of such excesses.

Gene followed his gaze heavenward. 'Ah, it'll only be a shower,' he said, winking at Frankie, fully seized of his mate's eagerness to get off site but not wishing to indulge it, and proceeded to position the hammer at the head of the trench. The harsh pneumatic rattle of the hammer dispatched the suburban silence and marched Frankie's attention back to the task at hand.

The droplets became a shower, but they continued digging. The shower matured into a downpour, the shirt across Frankie's back now transparent revealing the thick matrix of muscle beneath the sodden cloth. They continued digging. After ten minutes or so Gene made a dash for the waggon and returned carrying two waterproof jackets, noting with some annoyance that Mick had already donned his. He passed one of these to Frankie who removed his saturated shirt and slid on the stiffly fibred jacket. 'Let's hope the council man doesn't pole up before we get to the end of the track, eh', said Frankie referring to the official whose remit was to monitor street works on behalf of the local authority. They laboured on under the downpour for the next hour or so, the rain showing no sign of abating and the leaden hue of the sky sapping the colour from the street. Mick ambled up towards them, his hair stuck to his head, a sullen look on his face. Gene quietened the hammer as he joined them.

'Jesus lads, are we not going to sit this one out in the waggon?', he asked his tone dismal and defeated, the salutary effects of the earlier draught of cider having long since worn off.

'Why we would we do that? Do you think that we might get wetter than we are now if we don't?', replied Gene dismissively, his mind now made up about his workmate. Mick retreated, mumbling incoherently to himself.

What do you think?', enquired Gene looking down at Frankie. Puddles were beginning to form in the already sodden floor of the trench and small rivulets of rainwater were streaming in from the footpath. Frankie's feet were wet and cold, and he was struggling to find any purchase on the slick bed of the trench.

'If I was bothered about the wet I'd get a job in a factory', he replied looking up at Gene and smiling, droplets of rain running off the tip his nose and his light auburn

31

hair darkened, clinging to his scalp like a glossy pelt. Just as Gene was about to kick the hammer back into life a small, sign – written local authority van pulled up on the road beside him and the driver wound down his window.

'Still out?' From a meter distance Gene felt a draft of warm air escaping from the interior of the vehicle.

Gene looked at the young council inspector stonily, reluctant to state the obvious. 'We can't have you digging in this weather Gene, the stone aggregate won't compact right when you're back filling, you know that. A few lads have gone back in already.'

'There's plenty of fellas that want nothing more than a drop of rain on Monday. They can hear the doors of the pub swinging open over the sound of the hammer', replied Gene, barely managing to disguise his annoyance at the unwelcome visitor's arrival.

'That maybe so, but the rain's in for the day and I'll be condemning any track that's dug from here on in, which means that you won't get paid for it, so I'd get piped up and backfilled sharpish if I were you. The tarmac waggon is on its way around to you, so you might want to get cracking', he said.

'In for the day, eh? I can tell you exactly when the rain'll die down', stated Gene, his tone becoming friendlier.

'So, you're a weatherman now, eh?', replied the council inspector with undisguised sarcasm.

'No, not at all, but I can say with the certainty of many years of experience that it'll stop five minutes after we get packed up and leave the site', he replied, his weak attempt at humour designed to placate the youthful arrogance of the inspector. It wouldn't do him any good getting on the wrong side of the official, rain or no rain. The inspector chuckled lightly.

'No one's stopping you from sitting it out in the waggon once you've got that bit of track sorted out. Who knows, it may just be a shower'. As he said this, another vehicle pulled up behind him and a GCE site agent got out of the driver - side door.

'How are you Gene? Bad start to the week, eh?', and he turned to look at the inspector without waiting or a response from Gene.

'You've told them to pack up?'

'I have', he replied.

'I'm telling all my gangs the same thing', he said barely attempting to disguise his ingratiating tone.

'The week's knackered', said Gene his irritation apparent as he reluctantly disconnected the hammer and hoisted it onto his shoulder and strode off towards the waggon. Frankie had already begun helping Mick to start backfilling the trench, the ducts having already been laid. 'You'll be off site in hour Gene?', the site agent called after him, his tone half query, half instruction.

'We'll be off site in half that time. The pub's been calling to this gang since this morning', replied Gene tersely. The council inspector wound up his window and retreated into the warmth of his vehicle unable to fully comprehend the belligerent resilience of these men.

CHAPTER SIX

Hugh was awakened by a loud banging on the front door of his parent's house. He laid motionless in bed waiting for his mother to respond to it, but as the knocking continued he reluctantly acknowledged that she mustn't be at home. He dragged himself out of bed and pulled on a pair of jeans that lay in a crumpled heap on the floor and quickly glanced at the clock on the bedside table. Twelve o'clock. He walked down the stairs on unsteady legs, rubbing the sleep from his eyes and opened the front door. Richard walked straight past him towards the kitchen collapsing his umbrella and leaving a trail of water droplets behind him.

'Good morning to you too', said Hugh sarcastically to the empty doorway and turned to follow Richard, closing the door behind him.

'What. A. Night!', exclaimed Richard as he turned the kettle on and opened a cupboard to retrieve a cup, his back to Hugh.

'Yeah, it was fun', replied Hugh slumping into a chair. 'Do please feel free to make use of any and all kitchen appliances, comestibles.....', he continued, maintaining his sarcastic tone.

'Do you want one?', said Richard turning to Hugh and holding up an empty cup. Hugh nodded.

'I'm only going to say two words to you', continued Richard turning back to the job at hand. 'Jennifer. Hartely'.

'Really?', replied Hugh, trying to disguise the note of scepticism in his voice. 'Did you, erm....do the deed?', he continued, his eyebrows raised, a smile playing across his mouth.

'Of course not. She's a St. Anne's girl remember, but we did get rather affectionate after I was massively assaulted in my own home earlier in the evening. I think it was probably a combination of wine and pity. Anyway, I'll take what's given mate.'

'Massively assaulted, eh?', repeated Hugh sceptically. 'Who were those blokes anyway?', continued Hugh.

'God knows, just some local louts. Picked up the news of the best house party of 1991 on the grapevine, I suppose. Thanks, by the way. They'd have kicked the shit out of me if you hadn't been there. I mean, where were my other so-called friends when I was being dangled by the throat by some random gorilla bent on home invasion?', he said passing the now filled coffee mug to Hugh.

'Well, they were big lads', replied Hugh.

'Older than us too', continued Richard. 'You were very impressive, I must say. Saved the day and all that. What I want to know is where does it come from, all this derring- do? I know you've grown over the past eighteen months or so, but you've always been taller than us all. I mean, I should know, I've known you long enough. But its not even that, not just your size. You don't get intimidated. Remember Nigel Williams? He was in the sixth form, you were thirteen. You punched him all over the playground. Where do you get it from, and can I have some? I mean, your dad's not like that, not at all.'

'I don't know. What can I say? I just can't abide bullies for starters, I suppose', replied Hugh. 'And that's an understatement about my father. Maybe it was my grandfather. His genes could've skipped a generation. I know he was a bit of a wild one. You remember him, surely. I was never away from his house when I was a kid. He was knocking on a bit then though of course. No, definitely not from David, although you wouldn't think so the way he talks to me. He caught me coming home this morning. Gave me a right bollocking. You know, the shirt. I'm pretty sure that if he thought he could get away with giving me a slap he would.'

'Ah yes', replied Richard. 'We never did get that cleaned off, did we. Why didn't you tell him what happened? I mean, you were just sticking up for me, what's wrong with that?'.

'Whenever has he given me the benefit of the doubt, eh?', replied Hugh dismissively. 'He was stood in front of me this morning out there', continued Hugh nodding towards the driveway, 'calling me a thug and God knows what else and I'm looking down at his scrawny little frame. I mean, I've never really noticed before, but he's a small man. I'm twice the size of him. You know it occurred to me that I could've just knocked him on his arse. God knows there were plenty of times when I was a kid that I'd would have loved to. I mean I wouldn't; I never would, but I've never seen him getting aggressive with another bloke, not like he does with me.

How're supposed to have any respect for a bloke like that? He's just a dick head, to be honest.'

'Yes, well. Your father has given you bit of a hard time', said Richard sympathetically, but don't they all?'

'Anyway, having said all that, he did get me off the hook with Mum, albeit reluctantly. She'd have lost it if she'd have seen another bloody shirt. The last time was bad enough.'

'What did Jane say? Was she all-a-flutter at your newly acquired hero status?', asked Richard, smiling conspiratorially.

Hugh laughed. 'No, not at all. She doesn't like that kind of thing. It bothers her. Frightens her a bit.'

'Well, she is a bit prim and proper. Gorgeous, of course, but all very above board. She's in for a shock or two when you go travelling, I would've thought. You know, the real world and all that.'

'Yeah. That reminds me. I've got to get a supermarket job sorted or something if I'm going to pay for the trip, and quickly. It's telling my mum and dad that's going to be the problem. I'll have to put that off for a couple of weeks until he calms down a bit. Mum wasn't very pleased with me staying out all night either, so God knows how she'll react when I tell her I'm going away from for twelve months. You'd think I was just a kid', he concluded, shaking his head.

'Yes, it will need to handled with some care. Anyway, we've got a round of golf booked, remember? Will you please get yourself suitably attired?', asked Richard and Hugh rose from his seat and wandered upstairs to get dressed.

CHAPTER SEVEN

The waggon pulled up outside 'The Harp' public house and Mick immediately leapt out without so much as acknowledging his work mates. 'Jesus, now that's the fastest I've seen him move all day' observed Gene as Mick disappeared through the doors of the public house. 'Where will I be collecting you tomorrow?', he continued looking at Frankie.

'Just across the way, I'm hoping', replied Frankie, nodding towards a block of flats on the other side of the road, a grin sweeping across his face.

'And who is the unfortunate girl, might I ask?', replied Gene.

'Jenny from the behind the bar in there', said Frankie, gesturing towards the pub with this thumb. 'That's who I was with last night, and I gave a pretty good account myself even I do say so.'

'I'm not interested in any of that nonsense talk', said Gene flatly. 'Anyway, what if this romantic scheme of your's doesn't work out?', he asked, dragging out the syllables of the word 'romantic'.

'Don't worry yourself about that. You've never known me miss a day's work have you?', Frankie pulled the passenger side visor down and shaped his hair in the small mirror affixed to it. 'Are you going to try an odd one, take the damp out of your jacket?', he asked.

'Oh no. I'm straight home. Cora'll be waiting for me, besides the tap room of 'The Harp' holds no secrets for me', Gene replied smiling ruefully.

'Hold on two minutes', asked Frankie who hopped out of the waggon and rummaged under the seat and retrieved an old sack that he'd taken from the yard that morning and shook the dust from it before cramming what remained of his wardrobe into the bag. 'I can't go in there with an arm full of clothes. The boys will think I've started taking in laundry.'

'You might earn a bit more money that way if the weather doesn't pick up', quipped Gene. Frankie grinned. 'Don't go stone mad with the drink today, remember she'll be expecting a performance off you tonight, you know, for your keep', cautioned Gene gravely. Frankie nodded, recognising that the caution was uttered to ensure that he was ready for work on time the next day rather than his competence as a lover. With that Gene pulled away leaving Frankie alone on the pavement, a solitary figure stood in the rain tying off an old, oil-stained sack containing the entirety of his worldly possessions.

The taproom was large, unfussy and clean and, thanks to the weather, full of customers whose shouted conversations competed with the even noisier fiddle music playing in the background. There was an odour of earthy dampness in the air which told a tale as to the common employment of the male patrons. Frankie acknowledged a couple of customers on the way to the bar and caught sight of Mick out of the corner of his eye sat with his wife at the far end of the room. Her presence suggested that Mick's cheque had arrived that morning and his wife, knowing the consequences of the rain, would have recognised that a half-shift was pretty much inevitable and had wasted no time in getting the good news to him.

As Frankie was musing on the likely consequences of this development a tall, shapely, blond-haired woman approached him from the other side of the bar, doe-eyed and pink-cheeked, and although there were other customers waiting, she ignored them and directed her smiling attention to him.

'How are you Jenny?', he said winking at her mischievously. She smiled back at him knowingly by way of an answer as she pulled his pint.

'I see you made a brief visit to work today', she chided. 'I didn't tire you out last night then?', she whispered as she passed him his drink.

'Just warming to the task', he replied, 'how about a rematch tonight?', he continued in equally low tones as he passed her his money.

'We'll see', she replied laughingly, her eyes lingering upon him as she turned to walk towards the till. 'I'm finished at four. We can talk about it then.'

Before she had chance to ring in the money, Mick appeared at Frankie's side. 'Hang on Jenny, let me get that', and he turned to Frankie smiling.

'So, the cheque's arrived', asked Frankie.

'How do you know?', quizzed Mick.

'Well, two reasons', replied Frankie. 'In the first place, the misses would only be here if she had news that couldn't wait to tell you and second, you're not a man who makes a habit of spending money on drink that isn't going down his own throat, so I imagine that this buying spree was an attempt to soften a blow. Anyway, you're too late, as usual. It's paid for.'

'Well, I'd be no good anyway. I just wouldn't be able to focus knowing that the cheque was sat on the mantelpiece untended to, like.'

'You could always stick it in the bank for a rainy day', said Frankie.

'But it is a rainy day', said Mick peering out through the window, confident that the argument was won. Frankie looked at him and slowly shook his head. 'So you're leaving us a man short, eh?'

Mick looked down at the floor. 'There's always plenty of lads in the yard of a morning looking for the start, aren't there', he suggested.

'Aye, and the most of 'em better men than you too', replied Frankie dismissively. 'I'd keep out of Gene's way if I were you. He's old school, doesn't agree with a man abandoning the gang just because he's a few quid ahead.' A look of apprehension appeared on Mick's face and he scuttled off to re-join his wife.

Jenny was serving the customer next to Frankie and was within earshot of the exchange. As she handed over the drink and collected the money, she turned to Frankie. 'If you're looking for another bloke there was a fella in here today looking for work, big bloke, wearing an eye patch. He didn't say much. A bit scary looking, to be honest. He was talking to Paddy Mitchell. It seemed as if they knew one another.'

'Really?', replied Frankie, 'thanks for that love. Give me another pint for Paddy when you're ready. Where's he sat?', he asked. She nodded in the direction of the far corner of the room and waited for Paddy's drink to arrive before threading his way through the crowd to where Jenny had indicated he would find the old timer.

'How are you now Paddy?', exclaimed Frankie settling himself down next to a wiry old man whose creased, mottled face broke into a wide, yellow-toothed smile as he greeted Frankie with a nod of his head.

'I'm damn good Francis, and yourself?'

'I'm well. Here, take this', he replied, passing Paddy the fresh pint.

'Jesus, you're a gentleman indeed. Rained off, eh?' he observed, slurping the pint and wiping a thick residue of ivory foam from his upper lip, revealing a stained and tattered shirt cuff beneath the sleeve of his crumpled jacket. 'In my day nobody bothered about a bit of rain, you know', he said glancing out at the downpour drumming against the window pane. 'There were plenty of sites where you'd get run off for even noticing it', he continued gravely, looking around the table for confirmation from his aged associates huddled over their beer and receiving enthusiastic grunts of agreement in response.

'Jesus, these men now think their badly done to if the rain messes their hair', added another stoking further murmurs of disapproval from the nodding crew of superannuated navvies. Frankie smiled indulgently and turned to Paddy.

'We're a man short and Jenny tells me that there was a bloke in here today looking for a start.' Paddy turned eagerly to Frankie, relishing his new-found relevancy.

'Indeed there was, and a good man too if you keep on the right side of him. Haven't seen him around this city for 20 years though. Do you remember Danny Greene, John?', he asked, directing his question to one of his companions. Frankie recognised the name immediately but kept his own counsel allowing Paddy and the assembled company the opportunity to share their reminiscences.

'I do indeed', he replied letting out a low whistle and shaking his head. 'He's some boy alright. A hard man. I knew him here years ago, but I crossed paths with him, oh, fifteen years ago down on a job in Kent. I'd keep hearing tales about him though around and about. Bit of a hand full that lad.' Paddy interjected, eager to regain centre stage.

'Aye, he was in here alright. I nearly fell off my chair when he walked through the door this morning. I recognised him right away, though he's an eye short of the set since I last saw him'.

'Well, we all know about that, don't we', added another member of the group, his tone hushed and conspiratorial.

'Well, no, we don't now do we, not for certain', interrupted Paddy, 'and I'd be very careful about telling those kinds of tales if I were you', he scolded. A chastened hush descended on the table.

'He could handle himself, but he was a nice enough young lad when I think back. He got an awful kicking off some crowd here for reasons unknown', he said looking pointedly at the recipient of his recent reprimand, 'and he left the town altogether after that I heard. His name would crop up from time to time though, fighting this one or that one. Ah these young lads', he said plaintively, shaking his head at the sad inevitability of it all. 'He'd be fighting for money and that kind of carry on, I heard. A dangerous game for a one-eyed man you would've thought, but he seemed to do alright at it. I mean. You never heard of him getting beat.'

'The opposite', offered another of his companions. 'I saw him fighting a huge travelling fella about ten years ago down on a site down in London. He was like a fucking bull. Jesus, it was pure carnage. Carnage I tell you. He made an awful mess of the big fella. I heard he got five grand for it.' The company murmured in awe.

Paddy looked askance at his companion once again indicating his displeasure at being temporarily supplanted as the centre of attention and sank into a brief period of silent contemplation before finally adjudicating on the matter. 'You'll be alright with him', he pronounced sagely. 'He's been around long enough so he'll know the work back to front and he'd be busy man.'

'Aye, I think I recognise the name', said Frankie casually. 'Is he due back in here tonight?', he enquired.

'Aye, I believe he's taken one of the rooms upstairs, so you might have to wait around for him for a bit though. Awful job, I know, sat in a pub with nothing to do but take the head off a few pints', he said winking at Frankie.

CHAPTER EIGHT

Gene drew up outside a smart looking semi-detached council house. The front garden was neatly dressed in an array of brightly coloured flowers and the small lawn was nicely trimmed by an obviously keen hand. He clambered stiffly out of the waggon closing the door behind him and briefly inspected the back of the vehicle to ensure that there were no tools left exposed to tempt the local thievery and then quickly surveyed the garden before unlocking the front door and entering the house.

'Hello Cora, its only me', he shouted from the bottom of the stairs. As he did so a frail looking woman emerged smiling from the kitchen to his right.

'My God love, what're you doing downstairs?', he exclaimed, startled to see her out of bed. 'Has the woman not been to attend to you? You shouldn't really be downstairs on your own, you know. What if you slipped or had a fall or something?', he said, clearly concerned.

'Oh yes love, she's been. Rained off?', she enquired listlessly and sank down into the nearest armchair, her face etched with weariness. Gene quickly crossed the small area of carpet separating them and knelt on one knee in front of her.

'Are you sure that you're alright love? What're you doing downstairs anyway?'

'Oh, I just fancied a cup of tea, that's all Gene', she said tiredly, her eyelids slowly closing and her breathing speeding up, familiar sights and sounds to him.

'Well, you've no need to worry about that now', said Gene jovially, 'your manservant has arrived home from the fields and is waiting upon your every instruction', he said smiling jovially in an effort to lighten the mood and with it her obvious discomfort. She opened her eyes and smiled weakly at him. He stood in front of her. 'Come on now love, let me get you up the stairs and back into that warm bed. I'll bring your tea up for you after.' He scooped her up from the chair noting how little effort it took, like cradling a small child in his arms, and she nestled her cheek between his neck and shoulder.

'Oh, you're a good man Geney, I think I'll keep you', she said smiling up at him without opening her eyes. She winced slightly as he turned rather quicker than she had anticipated. 'I'm sorry love', Gene said, unsure of what he had done to prove her discomfort.

'How's your appetite? Can I make you anything to eat?', he asked.

'No, I'm fine love, thanks. The lady made me a slice of toast, but I nodded off after I ate it and when I woke up my tea was cold.'

'Only a slice of toast?', I don't know if that's enough Cora. Are you sure now that you don't want me to make you a sandwich?'

'No, I'm fine love, really', she replied wearily.

He carried her up to the main bedroom of the house and gently laid her in the bed, tucking the sheets in tightly around her tiny frame. 'Are you sure, It'll only take a minute?'

'No thanks', she replied. I'm just not hungry.'

'You shouldn't be outside in this weather at your age, you know Gene', she continued and closed her eyes as she sank back into the pillows.

'Oh, I'm just an old donkey with a donkey's hide, you should know that by now love', he said tenderly as he swept to one side a loose hair that had fallen across her brow before sitting down heavily in the bedside chair. He remained there watching her until a change in the rhythm of her breathing suggested that she had fallen asleep, and he pushed himself out of the chair and moved towards the door.

'Are you going Gene?', she asked without opening her eyes, a hint of alarm in her voice.

'Not at all darling. I'm just going to get myself a cup of tea and my paper and I'll be right back.' He walked heavily down the stairs and into the kitchen and flicked on the kettle. His newspaper was lying on the floor below the letter box and he bent down to pick it up, casually throwing it onto the work surface as he pulled a mug from the cupboard above into which he dropped a tea bag. He flicked the kettle on and as he did so he caught sight of a framed monochrome picture of himself and Cora set in a small niche above the kitchen counter.

The photograph had remained on the small shelf for so long that for years he had barely noticed its existence. He reached up and took it down, blowing off the thin layer of accumulated dust which seemed to glow in the damp light that seeped in through the kitchen window. It had been taken what seemed to him like a lifetime ago, not long after they were married. They had taken a day trip to the coast and had been persuaded by a beach-front photographer to pose. Cora had draped herself extravagantly over Gene in a gleeful mess of affection, her head thrown back, her eyes tightly closed and her mouth wide in an almost audible paroxysm of laughter. Gene's smile was tight and awkward, constrained in self-conscious deference to the photographer's presence, yet his eyes were fixed on Cora's face, glistening with an enfolding light, unassailable in its absolute nature.

He stared at the photograph for a moment or two and laid it face down on the kitchen top and placed his palms flat on either side of the frame and bowed his head, his eyes closed. His heavy shoulders pulsed with tiny spasms as he tried to restrain the tears that promised a dull, easy relief, but which he would not countenance. The whistle on the kettle screeched out and he detached himself from the emotions threatening to make a mockery of his self-control and finished preparing his tea, picked up the mug and put the newspaper under his arm and returned upstairs.

Jenny came out from behind the bar holding a drink and settled herself down beside Frankie who curtailed his conversation with the old-timers and directed his full attention to her. 'Bet its nice to take a weight off after being on your feet all day, eh?', he said cheerfully.

'It's not as much fun as being on your back all night, that's for sure', she replied, cackling at her own joke. Frankie obligingly laughed along with her.

'You're in no rush, are you love?', he asked. 'I'm waiting for that lad to come back, the long distance man.'

'Long distance man?', she asked, a puzzled expression on her face.

'That bloke with the eye patch, the one that's taken the room. A 'long distance man' is what we call a fella who roams from city to city following the work, no cares, no troubles, just the open road in front of him. A bit like me, a bit of a vagabond', he said smiling at her. 'I'm a long distance man myself', he reiterated, stroking her thigh with increasing hopes that Danny would walk through the door sooner rather than later.

'Oh I'm in no rush', she giggled, 'but if you carry on with that, things might change', she continued glancing down at his hand before giving him a saucy wink indicating pleasures to come.

CHAPTER NINE

David stepped out onto the gantry to do a quick headcount of the compressors in the yard and, contented that all the plant was accounted for, re-entered the office. 'Look, I'm going to head off home now', he said to Jones as he arranged some papers on his desk. 'When the agents get back, make sure that they're all up to date with their paperwork. They don't get to sneak off just because it's raining. They're getting paid, so they'll do the full shift', referencing the fact that the agents were salaried men, unlike the men in the trench.

'Sure', said Jones. 'I've got them all out doing snagging lists anyway.' He knew that while a wet day could cost the gangs a few hundred pounds, it would cost Gallon a good bit more. He expected him to be ill-humoured and he was eager to adjust his behaviour around this despite knowing that David Gallon was wealthier than any man in the yard could ever hope to be, any man except himself of course. For despite the fact that Jones had crossed the threshold of middle-age he still had the ambitions of a much younger man, a man with considerably more time ahead of him to realise such hopes and expectations. The reality was that if there was a time when Jones was capable of being independently successful, then this had long since passed, not that he would have acknowledged it. He had persuaded himself that the right opportunity just hadn't crossed his path: if it had've done, a man with his intelligence would certainly have recognised it for what it was and would have exploited it to its fullest.

He had an opinion of himself not uncommon to men of unimposing intellectual ability: because of the limited range of gifts nature had bestowed upon him, he believed that any limits he encountered within himself in this regard were absolute, that the limits of his intelligence were the limits of intelligence per se. He was certain that the guile, cunning and acumen at his disposal exceeded that of any man he might be expected to contend with, not recognising that, to the extent that he possessed these qualities at all, they were merely a smeared reflection of those that someone like David had at his disposal. Unable to recognise his own limitations, he could not acknowledge that these might be transcended by others; for him, there was no intellectual space for them to occupy. He was one of those unlucky souls whose essential foolishness caused them to believe that they were the smartest people they knew.

David finished tidying his desk and made his way down to his car, a mid-range every-man vehicle, selected specifically because it did not advertise his wealth to the men in the yard. He had a vehicle at home which he used for personal purposes which did more than enough of that. He wasn't overly concerned about the loss of revenue resulting from the rain, this was just a cost of doing this kind of business, but he had to appear as if it mattered to him because it certainly did matter to the men in trench, and he felt that he had to display a semblance of participating in their frustration. Nonetheless, he had been knocked off his stride and it was the news about Greene that had done it. Here was a problem narrowly averted, he mused anxiously, but one which he nonetheless had been forced to consider. The fact of the matter was that even if it didn't happen today, it could happen tomorrow, anytime in fact. He didn't want to have to think about that eventuality and he had spent a good part of the day convincing himself that he didn't need to.

Gallon pulled into the driveway that snaked up to his expansive, mock-Tudor home and clicked a fob to open the double garage doors, parked the car inside and made his way into the house through rooms which were obviously the domain of a home-maker with an over - abundance of both time and money.

Kate was sat on the sofa in the spacious, well-furnished lounge dressed in three-quarter length slacks and a simple but expensive cotton blouse, her legs drawn up beneath her. She looked up as he walked into the room and offered him a casual greeting and turned her attention back to the magazine she was browsing. 'Rain stopped play, eh?', she enquired.

He sat down in a large armchair facing her and selected a newspaper from the rack beside the fireplace. The room was filled with a soothing quiet, disturbed only by the gentle patter of raindrops on the windowpanes, the grey skies outside creating a premature twilight within the room. He looked over at Kate, angling the newspaper in such a way as to disguise the fact that he was observing her. He wanted just to look at her, to focus on her beauty without the distraction of conversation. This was one of the few remaining pleasures that he was able to extract from his marriage, Kate's emotional remoteness from him now well entrenched within the rhythm of their lives.

She had barely altered in twenty – years, he thought. She was still as lithe and as slender as a dancer, her golden-hued complexion radiating health and vitality, her blue-black hair cropped at shoulder length, stylish and unfussy. He watched her read and couldn't help but sigh quietly as her brilliant aquamarine eyes drifted across the page. He had fallen for her the first time he had seen her. Everybody had in those days. It was as if she had come from a world of money and expensive things, of elegance and sophistication, but of course she hadn't. Her's was a world of toil and hardship and quiet desperation, but she had a fire within her which had propelled her beyond the grim circumstances of her birth, a fire which could scintillate and allure.

In the beginning he had never for one instant allowed himself the indulgence of believing that she would be interested in him romantically, girls like Kate never were, but when she did occasionally acknowledge him at mass he was overwhelmed with carefully disguised joy and excitement, dissecting the brief moments that made up their encounter for days afterwards.

He would return home from university on the weekends merely to attend Mass in the hope that she might once again notice him, perhaps even speak to him, prompting concerns at home about his apparently intensifying religious commitment, but he readily acknowledged to himself that he was simply one of her countless admirers, and one of the least conspicuous of them at that. He learnt to deal with the bitter fruits of disappointment, but by far the most painful blow came one horrendous Sunday morning when she had entered the church hand – in - hand with a young man who, to David, appeared to embody all the physical attributes which he had so often been told that he himself was lacking.

The stranger was tall and muscular, his sapphire eyes blazing defiantly under a shock of black hair, his face not exactly handsome, but resoundingly male. David watched, his heart fragmenting, as Kate and her young man walked through the church drawing admiring glances from the old women who, whispering and nudging one another, directed admiring glances at the couple as they took their seats far down the aisle and out of David's sight. It was too much for him. He had got up and left the church, appalled by the recognition that deep within him there had been hidden an echo of a hope.

He had skulked out of the church cursing not Kate, but instead the young man who had accompanied her, cursing him for his ruggedly handsome face, his wide shoulders and broad back that tapered down to a narrow waist; cursed him for being everything that he himself was not. He strode along the street, his pace increasing as imagined pictures of intimacy between Kate and her man began to force their way into his mind serving only to increase his anger and frustration and shame. Then he had done a foolish thing.

Approaching him on the pathway was a lad of about fourteen, tall for his age perhaps, but still smooth-chinned and walking with the gait of a boy. David half-decided to alter his path so that his shoulder collided with the boy's as they passed one another. The lad, not expecting David's change of course found himself ricocheting off the wall of the church building. David shrugged his shoulders and quietly snorted in a gesture of what he took to be domination. It took the boy a moment or two to collect himself.

'What the fuck was that for?', he called out to David who continued walking, a sense of unease growing within him at the rashness of his actions now that the boy had refused to cower. David didn't answer, but instead increased his pace slightly. The lad was not satisfied by his silence and sprinted past David and turned to face him.

'What the fuck was that about?', he repeated in his boy's voice.

David had not thought through the consequences of his attempt at bullying and was now growing increasing anxious at the lad's confidence. He had assumed that the size and age difference between them would have allowed him to burn off his petulance at the kid's expense and continue with his day with a much needed, albeit meagre, confirmation of his masculinity.

'I'll not ask you again', said the kid his eyebrows knitting together in an expression of juvenile anger.

'I err, I didn't notice you', said David half-smiling. 'I lost my footing, that's all', his natural cowardice now reasserting itself, and all too clearly.

The kid stared at him briefly, a look of contempt spreading across his face, before executing a technically excellent three-punch combination into David's body. David immediately crumpled and lowered himself to one knee as he gasped for breath through lungs that felt as if they'd been perforated. The lad, Paddy Flynn, a very promising junior boxer, glanced down at him to confirm that there would be no retaliation and proceeded on his way.

David turned his head and watched the youth depart before groaning as he tried to raise himself to his feet. He leant against the wall of the church as he tried to normalise the rhythm of his breathing all the time watching the kid disappear down the road as if nothing had happened to interrupt his stroll. Tears of frustration and self-loathing welled up in David's eyes as the image of Kate's lover, his face as alert and as full of menace as a jungle predator, once again pressed itself into his mind in a revolving juxtaposition with that of the fourteen-year-old boy that had so recently humbled him. Almost twenty years on Paddy Flynn now worked for GCE and had long since forgotten the incident. David still recalled it with a burning sense of shame.

He had not returned to the church for almost a year after that day, not until he was compelled to attend the funeral of an uncle. The deceased, his late mother's brother, had been a well-known figure within the wider Irish community and David had expected the service to be well-attended and so it was, the lives and deaths of members of this community being woven together like the strands of wool in a Galway shawl. It came as no surprise to him then when Kate entered the church with her father who was sporting a black-eye and, judging by his gait, not entirely sober. He felt a rush of relief to note that that she was otherwise unaccompanied.

He had trained himself to dispel all thoughts of her after the calamity he had witnessed here a year before and his subsequent humiliation at the hands of a child. Not only had reality mocked the vanity of his hopes, but the entirety of the distance between what she wanted and what he could offer had been made clear to him. It was a distance he could never hope to traverse. While he had learned to think about her less often, the tedium of the service coupled with the overwhelming power of her very presence in his vicinity had compelled him to steal furtive glances at her across the nave throughout the course of the service. She had been standing up for a

50

hymn and had turned and looked behind her to ensure her space on the pew was clear before sitting back down when she had caught him staring at her. He had immediately flushed a deep scarlet. She had held his eyes and smiled the most radiant smile that he had ever seen as she resumed her seat. David had almost collapsed down onto his. He could barely breathe.

He had spent the remainder of the service in a state tantamount to euphoria, his thoughts racing to answer an endless stream of questions as to the significance of her smile. The Mass passed by unheeded by him and he had to be nudged in the ribs several times by his father to observe to required procedural niceties. Finally, it came to an end and the mourners dutifully filed out of the church and gathered in small groups in the street outside idly chatting, confirming the location of the wake, discussing the merits of the deceased, the quality of the service.

David had waited with his father outside the church as Gallon Snr had talked enthusiastically with people who David didn't know, his euphoria slowly subsiding to be replaced by thoughts of his own foolishness in resurrecting the demon of hope that he had spent the better part of a year trying to conquer. Just as the self-recriminations were finding their voice, there she was beside him.

'Hello David', she said quietly, 'I'd like to offer you my condolences for your uncle's passing.'

He stood there in silence, looking at her uncomprehendingly.

'Are you Ok?', she said, reaching out to touch his arm in a gesture of sympathy. 'I can imagine it's been a difficult time for you all', she continued, misinterpreting his silence. He looked down at her hand resting on his forearm and then turned back to her desperately trying to master himself and say something, anything.

'Look, you probably don't want to talk at the moment. I can understand that', said Kate, a note of compassion threaded through her voice, her eyes lowered. A moment passed in silence. Then she reached into her handbag and pulled out a pen and a piece of paper and began scribbling before holding the note out to him.

'Here's my phone number. I know that you're away at university and stuff and you're obviously having a good time as I haven't seen you around for ages but give me a call if you need a shoulder to cry on, well, you know, if you want to talk about your loss.'

And that was it. They were married six months later at that very church. Kate was David's first girlfriend.

Kate reached up to turn on the lamp that stood next to the sofa and as she did so she caught David looking at her, a strange expression on his face. She raised her eyebrows in silent interrogation.

'Where's buggerlugs', he replied immediately falling out of his reverie and collecting his thoughts.

'He's in his room reading, I think', Kate replied nonchalantly, the soft light from the lamp bathing her in a golden glow.

'Well, I don't know if I can tolerate him idling around the house for another three months', he replied tersely, wanting to escape from the yearning that was building up inside him.

'Oh, leave him alone', she said with tired exasperation, her default tone of voice when defending her son against the years of subtle, thinly stated criticism from her husband. 'He's just been through a very intense period, what with his exams. You should know how that feels. And more to the point, he's done well. Give the lad a break.' Yet despite this defence she remained mindful of the morning's events. She had already decided that she was going to make it clear to Hugh that she simply would not accept him staying out all night and sleeping away the best part of the day, though she was biding her time for the appropriate moment. David needn't be involved in that conversation, she thought.

Kate had been a hard task master when it came to matters of study and exam preparation and she was not going to let up just because school had come to an end. Lads of Hugh's age needed structure she believed, particularly given that he would be living independently once he went off to university in a few months' time.

A silence descended onto the room. David knew that he could only go so far in offering any kind of criticism of their son, though he believed that he saw much to be critical of, his idleness being a case in point.

'Up in his room reading', thought Gallon. 'Up in *my* room, in *my* house, more like.' Then an idea occurred to him.

'I'm thinking of giving him a job with one of the gangs until he starts university, might give him a sense of the other side of life, what real physical work is', he suggested tentatively fully expecting her to respond with indignation at the suggestion that her precious boy should harden his hands amongst the hoi polloi, amongst the men whose labours provided her with the comfortable lifestyle she so cherished.

She placed the magazine onto her lap. 'Hmmmmm', she sounded thoughtfully, evidently giving some consideration to his proposal. This wasn't what she was supposed to do, he thought. She was supposed to dismiss the idea immediately and so confirm to them both that she coddled him, insulated him from the harsh realities of the real world. He began to get a little concerned.

'That might not be a bad idea, you know. It might give him a sense of perspective. Plus, the good weather's around the corner, so he wouldn't be out in the cold. And it would put some money in his pocket too', she continued giving voice to her thoughts before looking squarely at David. 'It's a good idea', she said conclusively, 'well done'. While Kate was protective of her son, her maternal sensibilities did not extend to cosseting him, despite David's views to contrary.

She was a child of that life herself. Her father had been an immigrant navvy too, though he had not enjoyed anything like the level of success of David's father with whom he had arrived in England, along with three other friends, at the age of fourteen. Joe Hanlon, Kate's father, had been smart, charismatic and likeable, but he had been doomed to a life of failure by his fondness for drink and his appetite for grand schemes and ill-considered manoeuvres designed put him in the money, a small number of which had proven successful, but most of which had failed catastrophically sending him careening back to the trench and increasingly prolonged bouts of self-doubt and depression. He had finally succumbed to the grim solace of the bottle following the death of Kate's mother, but not before taking satisfaction from the knowledge that Kate had married well, a matter that he had been gravely insistent upon from her childhood recognising within himself the likelihood that his repeated failures as a provider would require mitigation.

Perhaps more importantly though in his later years he had Hugh, the new centre of his world. Kate in her turn had held out great hopes that her father's relationship with her son might have provided him with fresh incentive to take a different course as his life progressed towards its conclusion. Indeed, for a time his deep affection for the boy had appeared to stave off the more dramatic excesses of his fondness for the bottle, but the damage had already been done.

Hugh and his grandfather had spent endless hours together. Joe had always relished an audience and he could not have found a more attentive one than that he found in Hugh. He had a knack of communicating directly to the boy that belied the age difference between them. Hugh had laughed more in the company of his grandfather than he had with anyone else, and it was abundantly clear that Joe adored him. As Hugh grew older, they would disappear for hours together and Joe would regale him with tales of his past exploits, both real and improvised, giving the characters who inhabited these stories an almost mythical status in the young boy's world. Joe had made an indelible mark on Hugh's young mind, so that it was with a sadness that transcended her own grief at the fact that Kate had to inform Hugh that his grandfather had passed away. Joe O'Hanlon had died when Hugh was 11 years old, astonishing his peers that he had made it that far, but in so doing he had broken the young boy's heart.

Kate stood up and walked to the foot of the broad, stylish staircase which swept up to the upper floor of the house and called out Hugh's name.

'Yes?', came the muffled reply.

'Come down here a minute we want to have a word with you'. Hugh emerged from his bedroom looking dishevelled and bleary eyed, running his hand through his raven black hair.

'What Mum?', he mumbled drowsily.

'Come down, your father and I have an idea for you to consider.' Kate returned to the lounge.

'Sleeping no doubt', observed David dismissively. A moment later Hugh ambled into the lounge and collapsed into the sofa next to his mother and awaited the reason for the summons.

'Your father's got an idea for you', she informed him, turning to look at David. 'Let him deal with the adolescent indignation', she thought to herself, smiling slightly.

David returned her glance, his briefly raised eyebrows acknowledging exactly what was going through her mind.

'Your mother and I have been discussing how you might productively spend the rest of the summer and we have come to the conclusion that you might gain something from working at GCE. We think that it'll be good for you, out in the fresh air, getting to know different types of people, seeing what life is like for those less privileged, lots of reasons', he said, his pitch lazy and perfunctory. They both waited for what they expected to be the inevitable response: astonishment, indignation and refusal. Instead, Hugh looked down at his lap and appeared deep in contemplation. After a minute or so of this unexpected silence he looked up glancing from his mother to his father.

'Funny you should mention that', he said casually, 'I've been thinking about getting a summer job, but I thought that I'd end up stacking shelves in a supermarket. I mean, you've never let me anywhere near your work before', he said directing his remark towards his father. 'And I remember grandad used to tell me all sorts of tales about his days on the shovel, made it sound fun in a rough and tumble kind of a way. Plus, I've heard that they earn a thousand pounds a week, right?' he said, his enthusiasm growing.

'No! No, they don't', interjected David hastily, 'but if you can keep up with the work there's still a very respectable wage to be made. That's if you can keep up', he reiterated. 'It's hard, physical graft, a lot of grown men can't do it.' David glanced over at his wife looking for a twinkle of recognition that he'd pulled a good argument out of the hat. They both knew that Hugh had been competitive from an early age and was ready to rise to a challenge, particularly a physical one.

Hugh was more than pleased with the proposal. This would nicely fall in with his plans for the planned gap year with Jane. He was likely to earn much more at this job than he would if he was obliged to work in a supermarket or behind a bar. He knew that there would be uproar when he told his parents of his plans, but their inevitable objections he could handle, what would be more problematic was his father's refusal to fund the trip. He had a small amount of money in his bank account, gifts from family accumulated over the years, but not enough for his purposes. A solid income, even if for only a couple of months, would get him over the bar. Once he had sufficient funds to take the trip the parental protests could be pretty much ignored. 'It's all falling into place', he thought to himself contentedly.

'OK, seems like a good idea', he said, a smile blossoming on his face. His parents looked at one another, each one's expression of surprise mirroring the other's.

'OK!', his mother exclaimed, 'good for you! Come on then', she said briskly as she stood up from the sofa, 'put your shoes on we're going out.'

'Out? Out where?', he replied, taken by surprise at this sudden command.

'Well, let's strike while the iron's hot. We'll just catch the shops if you hurry up. You're going to need a pair of work boots.'

'Yes, absolutely', said Gallon, 'proper preparation and all that. We'll aim for a Monday start, OK? Don't let me down now. I don't want to hear any backtracking come Sunday evening. You'll be working with lads whose daily bread depends on the reliability of their workmates, so take some responsibility for your decisions', he added gravely.

'No, I'm serious dad. I want to do it', replied Hugh earnestly.

'Good, I hope you'll feel the same way on Sunday night.'

Kate and Hugh walked off together through the lounge in the direction of the garage. Kate, unbeknownst to Hugh, turned around to look at David with her face configured into a comic expression of mock astonishment which he duly acknowledged with a smile. As they were about to get into her car she turned to Hugh with a conspiratorial smile on her face: 'Come on then, what's going on? What's the real reason? Don't be letting your father down now that you've committed.'

'Nothing', Hugh replied nonchalantly, 'there is no 'real' reason. I just think that it'll be a really good experience', and opened the car door.

'Hmmmm', she mused aloud. 'Let's hope so, but I'm your mother sonny Jim, so don't think that you can pull the wool over my eyes for ever', she said smiling. Despite her maternal suspicions, she nonetheless warmed to the continuity that Hugh's diversion into manual work represented given her family's history. It would give him some insight she thought, a sense of how lucky he was to possess the future that awaited him, but she was also aware that she would have to keep a close eye on him too.

She was fully seized of the fact that David had never been able to command Hugh's respect, and as a result he had been unable to mould Hugh as she had hoped a father would. It had been left to her, but she could only take him so far down the road to manhood. Hugh and David were different in too many ways. She knew why this was so and this knowledge inhabited every decision she made about Hugh, shaping every timber of the carefully crafted world she had created for her boy. She had seen a certain wildness in him as he had grown, a wildness that was wholly alien to David. Hugh had been born with a hard, grim inheritance slumbering in his bones, but she would see to it that it would not awaken.

CHAPTER TEN

Frankie and Jenny, both glowing with the effects of drink, sat laughing as Paddy approached their table, his legs unsteady, a lifetime in the trench having withered the cartilage in his knee joints to a thin film. 'Hey Frankie, that fella I was telling you about earlier has just walked in. He's over there at the bar now, the one with the eye-patch', he said nodding towards the tall, broad – shouldered man talking with one of the waitresses. 'Come on', he continued, 'I'll introduce you', and he turned his back on Frankie and started shuffling towards the bar.

Frankie had been distracted from the need to find a replacement for Mick by a combination of beer and the persistent attentions of Jenny. He quickly rose to his feet as the urgency of the situation quickly flooded back to him and, as he did so, he knocked a glass half full of beer over Jenny's lap. She shrieked in alarm and started to frantically wipe the beer from her skirt. Frankie apologised somewhat distractedly as he watched Paddy disappear into the crowd and then turned to focus his full attention on her, reminding himself that he needed her to retain her good humour if he wanted a roof over his head that night. Jenny's annoyance quickly subsided. 'Don't worry about it love, I'll get a cloth from behind the bar.' Frankie smiled at her and once again apologised.

'Maybe that's the signal to head off home, eh?', he added, seized by a recognition of practical realities.

By the time he arrived at the bar Paddy was stood next to Danny. 'Danny', he announced gravely, 'this is Frankie Conroy. Frankie, this is Danny Greene.' The two men nodded at one another in silent acknowledgement. Frankie noted the patch Danny wore over his left eye but refrained from either comment or query. Despite his years Danny retained the rangy, athletic physique of a man half his age and he wore the look of someone into whose private life one would not causally intrude upon. Plus, Frankie too had heard enough rumours of his exploits over the years to suggest a likely explanation.

'Pint?', offered Danny, immediately detecting the most direct route to Frankie's friendship.

'No. No, thanks. I can't Danny, much as I'd like to. The woman's ready for the off and I'm the bed warmer, so I'd better keep her happy.' Danny once again nodded in acknowledgement.

'I hear you're looking for a third man?', Danny continued.

'We are indeed, and any man recommended by Paddy here is good enough for me.'

'Three – ways?', enquired Danny referring to how the money yielded by their work as a gang would be split between them.

'Of course!', confirmed Frankie in a tone which indicated that any other arrangement would be inconceivable, yet as he said this he was conscious that technically this was something that he should have confirmed with Gene, as he was the ganger man. Mick had been on a day rate, but he wasn't going to insult this man by offering him the same terms. 'You're bedding down here I'm told?', he asked looking from Paddy to Danny.

'I am.'

'Well, we'll pick you up outside at six. OK with you?'

Danny nodded confirming his agreement.

Arrangements having been concluded, Frankie quickly drained his glass and cast his eyes around the bar looking for Jenny and as he did so he caught sight of Mick stumbling towards him out of the crowd obviously drunk, a sheen of grimy sweat coating his face.

'Look Frankie', he said, his breath foul with beer, 'it's not for me to tell you your business, but the missus tells me that she's arranged to meet your ex in here soon and she didn't seem in the best of moods with you this morning'.

'Fuck!', exclaimed Frankie. 'You could have let me know earlier, Jesus!'

'I've only just been told myself', replied Mick. In fact, his wife had told him hours ago, but they'd jointly decided to hold onto the information in the hope of witnessing the confrontation that he had been prevented from enjoying that morning.

Frankie eyed Mick suspiciously and he peered behind the bar with a renewed a sense of urgency eager to find Jenny and get her off the premises before Mary arrived. He caught her eye as she emerged from the other side of the bar and tipped his head towards the door recognising that she wouldn't hear him above the jukebox if he attempted to call to her. She smoothed her skirt down over her long, shapely thighs where she'd attempted to clean the beer he'd spilt and smiled at him in acknowledgement, and he noted with some relief that she was holding her coat over her arm.

Jenny lifted the bar hatch to join him and no sooner had she done so than Mary walked in through the door looking somewhat more presentable than she had that morning. Mick's wife waved at her from across the room and they reciprocated smiles of acknowledgement. As she walked towards them Mick's wife nodded discretely towards Frankie and Jenny as she raised her glass to her lips.

At first Mary glanced at the customers standing at the bar with a confused look on her face not knowing what she was expected to see. It didn't take her long, however, to spot Jenny and Frankie making their goodbyes. She stormed towards them like a charging bull pushing through the crowd of customers, a furious expression on her face. 'You didn't waste much fucking time, did you mister?', she bellowed at Frankie, her heavily made-up face now contorted in anger. 'And with this old fucking scrubber an' all', using her thumb to indicate Jenny who was now stood behind and to the side of her. Jenny, not to be outdone, grabbed Mary by the shoulder and spun her around.

'Who are you calling a scrubber, you ugly bitch', and pushed her in the chest sending her tottering backwards on her high heel shoes. After colliding yet again with the folk she had bustled through moments ago, Mary finally steadied herself and, with eyes narrowed and fixed on Jenny, she launched herself towards her. Frankie anticipated the move and inserted himself between the two women and attempted to physically restrain Mary, gripping her upper arms.

'Mick', called out Frankie, 'get your woman over here and get her to calm this one down will you'. Mick's wife hesitated for a moment, trying to work out if she could feign deafness in order to prolong the spectacle, but finally decided that she had no choice but to at least make an effort to restrain her friend.

Mary broke free of Frankie's grip and was now attempting to reach over his shoulder in an attempt to grab a handful of Jenny's hair, all the time shrieking insults at her. Jenny too was now alight with anger and was also pitching to get a grip of Mary. The group of men surrounding the altercation stepped back and were guarding their drinks as they observed the spectacle before them. Mick's wife arrived at the scene and interposed herself between Mary and Jenny in an effort to calm her friend. 'Come on now Mary love, you know he's not worth it', she said in a placatory tone. 'I know he's not, it's that bitch I want', replied Mary once again lunging at Jenny. 'Not in here Mary, you're just going to get thrown out', said Mick's wife anxiously, her involvement in the fracas now giving her an incentive to bring it to a close. 'She will 'an all', came a deep, harsh voice resounding from behind the bar. 'We'll have less, otherwise you'll be out the door on your arse, woman or no woman.' The authoritative tone caused everyone to turn to its owner, the landlord of the pub, a man well-known for his lack of patience in dealing with such incidents. His presence signalled an end to the confrontation.

'I'll bloody well have you, mark my words', said Mary jabbing an index finger to within inches of Jenny's nose. Not to be outdone, Jenny grabbed the finger and used it to push the fist to which it was attached into Mary's face, a move which threatened to re-ignite the fracas once more until the landlord once again called out to them. Both women accepted that this was the end of business, at least for today, and Mary was escorted by Mick's wife back to their table. Jenny turned to face the landlord.

'I'm sorry Jim, but she just came for me. What was I supposed to do?', Jim simply grunted his disapproval and returned to the beer cellar from where he had emerged, satisfied that he was no longer required. 'What the fuck was that all about Frankie?', she demanded turning to face him, adrenaline still whizzing through her.

'Just some off the head woman I used to knock around with', he replied, trying to make light of the situation. 'Come on, we'll talk about it at home.' It was with a mixture of embarrassment and relief that that he nodded to Paddy and Danny as he bid them farewell.

CHAPTER ELEVEN

David was making tea in the kitchen when he noticed the shoe box containing Hugh's recently purchased boots on the floor by the door. He picked it up and pulled out one of the boots and turned it in his hands to examine it. As he did so he caught the earthy odour of fresh leather and boot blacking in his nostrils. He dropped the boot to the floor and put his own foot next to it. Even in his shoes, his own foot looked child-like next to the size twelves and the difference rankled with him for reasons he couldn't fathom. He'd never had cause to put on a pair himself, but one of his earliest childhood memories was of his father's work boots, battered and torn, their deep, black lustre long since worn away, sitting by the back door of his childhood home. He recalled being disgusted by their battered appearance and the ripe smell that issued from them.

This reaction was typical of a general prissiness which had coloured his developing personality, provoking concern in his father. As a child David had been unnaturally fussy when it came to dress and would spend a noticeable amount of time carefully reviewing his apparel in front of the mirror before leaving his room, an unusual habit in a boy of his age. He had carried this fussiness with him into adulthood. Even now, he insisted on wearing a suit and tie to work which, while wholly in keeping with his job as an accountant, was completely out of place in his current occupation and was met with considerable derision and mockery by the men in the yard.

Hugh wandered into the kitchen, half noticing the new boot lying next to the open box on the floor. David turned to him, gesturing towards the opened boot box.

'I hope that those get dirty before your mother has to throw them in the bin', he said snarkily. Hugh, indifferent to his father's low-grade sniping, batted the comment away.

'I'm looking forward to it. I feel like part of it already after listening to Grandad for so long.'

'Well, we'll see if you feel the same on Monday night after your first shift. You're going out?', he asked, noting that Hugh had climbed out of his habitual jogging pants and t-shirt and was now looking as close to smart as he was prepared to get. 'Meeting Jane', I suppose?'

'Yes, we're going for a pizza', replied Hugh. A silence descended upon them which was soon broken by Kate who had sauntered into the kitchen.

'Well, we've got the big, rough navvy lad sorted with some boots', she said to David before smiling affectionately at Hugh. David didn't respond. 'What would you like for supper David?'

'Just something light for me, please. I might go out for run later.'

'I can grill you some fish, if you like. Bit of salad to accompany it?', she asked.

'Great', replied David and wandered back into the lounge.

'What time are you meeting Jane?', asked Kate. As she did so a car horn sounded outside providing an answer to her question.

'Ask her to come in', said Kate. Hugh went out to the car and moments later Jane appeared. She was tall and olive-skinned and her long blond hair cascaded over her fine, angular shoulders.'

'Hello Mrs Gallon', she said with a pleasing smile. 'How are you?'

'Very well, thanks Jane and I've told you before, my name's Kate. You look lovely Jane', she continued, 'I hope he's treating you as he should', she said looking at Hugh with faux suspicion. 'How are your mother and father? I haven't seen them at the golf club for a while', Kate enquired.

'Oh, Dad's been really busy recently, some big contract at work. I think that they plan to play a round this weekend'.

'Oh, it will be nice to see them. Anyway, I'll let you two get off, I'm sure that you're hungry', said Kate as she opened the refrigerator door in search of David's supper.

'OK, bye Mrs...., Kate', said Jane as they walked towards the back door.

'See you, Mum', said Hugh smiling. Kate watched them as they walked out the door.

'They look nice together', she mused to herself though she didn't expect Jane to be around for long, pretty as she was. They were both young and their paths would be diverging soon as they both began new chapters of their lives at their respective universities; new goals would emerge, new relationships, new everything; their lives were just beginning, a feast of opportunity lay ahead.

The array of possibilities that confronted Kate as she passed through adolescence were much less full of promise, but she had been focused and determined. She had been aware of her priorities from a tender age: marry rich. As much as she had loved her father, the financial instability he brought to the home had been dizzying for her. She had been acutely aware of the thousand deprivations that are the inevitable result of too little money, and there was never enough or never enough for long enough. She had promised herself as a child that her children would never suffer the humiliations, both large and small, that she had endured and the fact that she might have to compromise on other aspects of her romantic relationship, well that was a price she was willing to pay. This was the pact that she had made with her future, and she was not going to break it.

Kate was fully aware of the weaknesses in her marriage, of the weaknesses in her husband, but he had nonetheless fulfilled his part in their unspoken bargain. He had created an environment in which she, and more importantly, Hugh, could flourish and she was going to respect that whatever his personal shortcomings, whatever the cost to herself.

Growing up she rarely had the opportunity to associate with anyone for whom a university education was a realistic prospect. It simply didn't happen in her world. The fact that this was a part of David's plans leant him an appeal that went beyond the standard offerings of the young men who surrounded her and who yearned for her attention. He had a future. The lads she knew had only a recurring present. They were the sons of navvies who would themselves become navvies, each day, each month, each year the same as the one previous to it. That was not for her. There was more out there, and David Gallon was going to give it to her, whether he knew it or not. While her friends cooed over the appeal of the handsome young working lads in their circle, she was content to forgo the physical attractions of her various suitors and aim for a rarer prize, not that her friends would consider David any kind of prize at all, in fact they barely noticed him. The qualities that drew her girlfriends to potential partners, the qualities they giggled and speculated about, were to her mind, ephemeral, transitory and insubstantial. She was not going to allow short-term self-indulgence to condemn any of her children to the life that she had experienced as a child.

David Gallon seemed to her studious and somewhat solitary, but he had a vulnerability that she had found endearing, at least at the beginning of their relationship. He certainly didn't have the physical presence of his peers, but Kate was secure enough in her own good looks that she didn't need any man to underwrite her attractiveness.

She had been aware of the power that her looks exerted from a young age and she had treated them as an asset to be managed. It certainly hadn't proved difficult to catch David's attention. She hadn't expected it to be. Her father had worked for his father many times over the years, so Kate and David were aware of each other and, despite the fact that David's family had long since migrated from the bleak terraced houses of their shared background, he and his family remained loyal to the local parish church.

David's frequent returns home from college had surprised her as her understanding of university life, such as it was, had persuaded her that it was an uninterrupted carousel of parties and wild nights out on the town. While her confidence in her own appeal was undoubtedly robust, it did not extend to speculating that she was the sole reason for David's increasingly regular attendance at Mass as she matured into ripe adolescence. If the truth be known, she just didn't think about David's motives with that degree of forensic interest. Nonetheless, she was always careful to remain sparing in her acknowledgement of him on the occasions that their paths would cross, and she was fully aware of the effect that such encounters had on him. The almost comic panic with which he had returned her greetings had amused her, not because she was naturally callous of spirit, but because his stuttered, pink-faced responses to her simple acknowledgements of his existence confirmed to her that the future that she had imagined for herself was well within her grasp.

Even as a child, her upbringing had forged within her an iron grasp on the harsh realities of life, and she was shrewd enough not to advertise her availability to any man until it suited her. She exerted control over David, and the other men around her, and this gratified her. Her looks had granted her a kind of dominion over them.

But then had come the joyous catastrophe.

She was a young woman, the tumult of adolescence behind her. She and a couple of girlfriends had been in the centre of the city clothes shopping on an early summer's afternoon. She had started a new job at a local cafe the previous week and had spent every evening on her way home from work browsing the local clothes shops scrutinising the goods on display, carefully deciding how she was going to spend her first wage. It wasn't much, but it had been a while since she had been in possession of a lump sum of that size, and she was determined to extract the maximum value from it. Her excitement at the prospect of the shopping spree to come had increased as the weekend had approached and she had planned to be outside of the first shop on her itinerary the minute it opened, preferred garments already selected, money in hand. Unfortunately, a summer downpour had put pay to this arrangement and she and her friends had been forced to delay their trip into city until the rain had finally come to a stop.

They had taken a bus to the centre of city and had alighted into a damp and dim afternoon, every dimple on the tarmac footpaths filled with rainwater slowing the progress of their dancing feet as they skipped around and over the dark puddles as they dashed to their first destination, laughing as they went. They turned a corner onto the main thoroughfare to be met with digging works taking place on the footpath and they immediately slowed down upon noticing a thin veneer of slick mud coating the pathway, a messy biproduct of the adjacent works. The girls gripped one another's arms tightly giggling warnings to each other to exercise care as they negotiated a particularly hazardous stretch of footpath, their high - heeled shoes not designed for such treacherous terrain. Kate had little patience with this overabundance of caution and she broke free from their little chain, her eagerness to get to the shops, which were now within sight, outreaching her better judgment. She hadn't progressed three meters before she slipped on a clump of shiny brown mud and landed squarely on her buttocks, her legs extended out in front of her. Kate's friends were around her in moments, their initial shock at their friend's misfortune almost immediately eclipsed by raucous laughter as they looked down at her in her preposterous predicament.

Kate tried to push herself up from the ground, but the mud was unforgiving, and she once again slipped back down to the pavement making it impossible for her friends to control the giggles through which heartfelt apologies were trying to escape. She sat motionless for a moment, appalled at the indignity of it all, her temper rising. She raised her hand and pushed back her fringe which had fallen across her face, a gesture which left a muddy smear across her forehead. She raised her eyes to her friends, a scowl now firmly etched across her face, but the fresh daub of mud did nothing but increase the hilarity which surrounded her.

She snapped, and her temper erupted in furious indignation.

'Bloody well help me up', she yelled at her friends. Their laughter ceased immediately, and they reached down as one to help raise her to her feet. Once on her feet she took a moment to right herself and confronted each of their penitent faces with a look signalling the tirade to come.

As she opened her mouth to lambast her friends, she heard a man's voice behind her. 'Are you alright Miss. I saw you fall there. You should be a bit more careful. It's very muddy, you know.'

She spun around immediately almost losing her footing again and she had to steady herself on the barrier that separated off the work area from the rest of the pavement. She collected herself to face the speaker, the new object of her fury.

And there he was. She had to tilt her head backwards to look into the young workman's face above her.

'Am I alright? Am I alright?', she shrieked at him, abandoning the poise that she had been striving to cultivate over the past couple of years. 'No, I'm not alright. I've just landed on my bloody arse because of you. Why can't you do your job properly? Look at the state of this footpath', she continued gesturing towards the ground. 'Who's your bloody boss, eh? Tell me. Tell me now, who is he?'

'Well, that'd be Mr. Mulligan. He'd be up there in the site office', replied the workman calmly seemingly unperturbed by her outburst and turning his head and nodding in the direction of a small canvass structure erected within the enclosed area.

He looked back at her and smiled almost imperceptibly. Kate noticed the glint of amusement in his eyes. Young men were not supposed to respond to her in this way.

He was altogether too calm, too relaxed and now he was almost laughing at her, mocking her anger. She unleashed a full draught of indignation upon him.

'Well, I'm going to the police about this. I know your sort very well', she screeched. 'Your boss won't give a damn that I could've seriously hurt myself. I could've ended up in a bloody wheelchair!'

The young man continued staring at her, a subtle smile now resident upon his lips. He reached into his pocket and pulled out a handkerchief and offered it to her.

'Well, Miss', he said, 'if you are going to go to the police, you might want to clean your face up a bit first. Given the state of it at the moment it looks as if you've done half a shift yourself. Oh, and don't worry its clean', he added.

She looked down at the proffered square of white cotton held between his thick, tanned fingers and then turned to look at her friends who silently nodded in confirmation and she then returned her glare to the workman, for the first time seeing the rich arctic blue of his eyes. She couldn't extract herself from their pull. A moment passed. She reached out and snatched the handkerchief from him, her eyes still locked on his, dabbed it on her tongue and wiped away the smear of mud on her forehead. She looked down at the muddy stain on the handkerchief and toyed with the fabric for a moment before thrusting it back to him and looking away, her anger gone, replaced by something else. She returned to his eyes as if the truth of this new feeling lay with him.

'You need to be more careful in future', she said quietly and with much less self-assurance before turning her eyes sheepishly to the ground, in her voice only the slightest tone of gentle admonition, and then she turned away to join her friends and they began walking away.

'Urghhh', groaned one of the girls, 'I can't believe that you put his handkerchief in your mouth.'

'But did you see him?', said another, 'he was gorgeous', and both friends giggled.

Kate wasn't listening. She had only taken three steps before she looked back at him half expecting him to have returned to his work, but he hadn't moved. He was stood there, his hands resting against the barrier. His eyes met her's as if he was expecting her to turn around, willing her to turn around. She held his gaze for a moment and then walked on.

Something had happened to her that day with the workman, something she hadn't understood. It went beyond the failure of her usual easy influence over such men; far beyond that. It was as if the rules of that game did not apply, as if there were no rules at all, as if it wasn't a game at all. The encounter had disturbed her, but not in an unpleasing way. As she had gazed into his eyes for that briefest of moments it was as if the world had tilted, she felt as if she were seeing things differently now. There was something in his eyes, an expression which had spoken to her in a language she had barely understood, but which she knew was utterly true. The image of him standing there as she had turned to him for the last time had drifted through her mind on countless occasions over the days following their encounter. She had made discrete enquiries amongst the customers at the cafe as to who he might be but had turned up nothing and she had concluded that he must be an out-of-town worker and had begun working on ridding herself of the temptation to recall these beguiling but perplexing memories. These efforts had so far failed and whenever her thoughts were idling they inevitably found their way back to him.

She had started work in the cafe as usual at five in the morning on the Wednesday of the following week, rising reluctantly at 4am, the first light of dawn still an hour or so away. Her complexion was pale with tiredness which caused her aquamarine eyes to scintillate even more than usual, like two gemstones on a bed of ivory velvet. She had arrived at the cafe to find the owner sweltering over the stove and had immediately tied a pinafore around her waist and threw herself into her allotted tasks. The cafe opened its doors at five thirty and by six o'clock it was full of workmen, the dim morning air thick with the smell of frying bacon, raucous chatter and the din of plates, mugs and cutlery rattling against laminated tabletops.

Kate took up her place behind the counter and waited for the first customers of the day who soon ambled in, bleary eyed and in need of fuel for the labours which lay ahead of them. Her's was uncomfortable work at the best of times. The combination of the stove behind her and the steaming water geyser sat on the counter created an invisible bubble of almost tropical heat and humidity around her leaving her face covered with an ever-present film of sweat and making her usually lustrous hair limp and dull. She disliked looking so unkempt, but despite this her presence behind the counter was the reason why business in the cafe had increased so dramatically since she had started work there.

The queue of customers that morning seemed never ending. She was tired, she felt grimy and unattractive and her back ached from leaning down to scribble orders onto the pad on the low countertop. A customer approached her carrying his plate, the food untouched, ignoring the line of men waiting to place their orders. As reached the counter he barked out a complaint about his bacon. Her patience was already wearing thin, and she told him in no uncertain terms to join the queue. The man, burly, but clearly overweight, dropped his plate onto the counter with a clatter and placed his hands on either side of it and leant forward until his face was inches from Kate's.

'Nobody fucking orders me around', he roared at her thrusting his head further forward, spittle flying from his mouth. The cafe immediately went silent. He was close enough for her to smell the rankness of his body odour and she recoiled, her hand cupped over her mouth, her eyes wide in fear

Then all of a sudden, the man was wrenched back, an open-mouthed look of astonishment on his face as he was pulled onto the floor and dragged unceremoniously towards the door, his legs flapping like loose wires as he tried and failed to dig his heels into the linoleum floor in an attempt to halt his unexpected progress.

Kate tried to peer through the dim light of the cafe to identify who was dragging the man, now an object of derision amongst the patrons who hurled half-eaten slices of bread and other sundry morsels at him as they jeered at him on his brief but undignified journey, but all she could see was the back of her rescuer's head. Then he arrived at the door and pulled it open. A thin stream of grey light edged its way into the cafe as he reached down and hoisted the man from the floor and hurled him out into the street, his face remaining obscured in the flurry of activity. Then he turned silhouetted in the door frame to be greeted by cheers of approval from the customers, grateful for any diversion which would distract them even momentarily from the prospect of the cold, miserable day which lay ahead of them. There was an echo of familiarity in the shape his tall, broad-shouldered frame as she strained her tired eyes to make out his features. Then, as he walked down the aisle between the tables and passed under one of the naked light bulbs hanging from the ceiling, she saw him. Her eyes widened and she recognised in him the man who had been haunting her imagination for the past four days.

She lost sight of him as he joined the back of the queue and she leant as far forward over the counter as she could, her feet almost raised from the floor as she strained to seek him out.

'Excuse me! Excuse me, sir?', she called down the line of men that ran to her right, extending back to one of the darker corners of the cafe.

'I think she's calling you', said Bill Mulligan nudging his young labourer in the ribs. Danny strode up to the counter.

'Sir' is it now?', he said smiling amiably as he stood facing Kate who was still stretched at an angle over the counter. She let her heels drop to the floor and straightened up, sweeping away the strand of limp hair that had fallen across her eyes. She remained immobile for a moment, once again caught in his eyes, and to her astonishment and deep discomfort, she felt herself blushing.

'Sorry about that, I mean Saturday', she said flustered, looking down at the tea mugs that she was needlessly rearranging on the counter. 'I didn't mean to shout at you. I mean, it wasn't your fault that I fell', and she giggled nervously. 'What would you like to order? It's on the house, you know, for dealing with that big bully. Oh and thank you for that,' she said, regaining some of her composure. The cafe owner turned a reproachful eye on her from his station at the stove as she uttered the words 'on the house' and Kate immediately turned to him and scowled. 'Where were you when your staff we're being bullied?', she demanded of him. The cafe owner nodded his head in acknowledgement of her point and returned his attention to the eggs sizzling away in the large frying pan in front of him and recalled to himself a tale of a golden goose.

'I'll tell you what', said Danny, 'you get me my breakfast and I'll get you your supper tonight.'

Kate smiled broadly at him, an explosion of giddy pleasure detonating in her stomach and cascading through every fibre of her body.

'But I look such a mess', she said peering down at her stained pinafore and hastily wiping it with her hands before looking back at him.

71

'No, no you don't', he replied, his smile replaced by a look of benign intensity. 'You're the most beautiful girl that I've ever seen.'

CHAPTER TWELVE

Hugh had just finished giving his order to the waiter and he placed his menu on the table. 'I've been saving some news for you', he said excitedly. Jane tipped her head to one side and raised her eyebrows.

'Tell all', she replied, warming to his enthusiasm.

'I've been rather clever, if I say so myself.'

'Really, how so?'

'Well, I'm going to be a rough, tough navvy, at least for a couple of months', he explained enthusiastically.

'You're going to be a what? A navvy? What's a navvy?', she enquired, her brow furrowed.

'You don't know what a navvy is? Good God girl!', he exclaimed. 'You know the men that are currently digging up every street in England, many of whom work for my wonderful father, well *they* are navvies.'

'You're going to work for your father digging up the roads? I don't know if I like the sound of that Hugh', she replied gravely.

'What do you mean?', he asked a little deflated.

'Well, I've seen them. They all look a bit scary to me, a bit, well, rough....', she replied, slightly embarrassed at the words she felt compelled to use, conscious that they would sound condescending. 'Well, not rough exactly', she backtracked, 'but definitely scary'. Hugh noted the snobbishness in her voice not untypical of St. Ann's girls.

'Scary?', he enquired, looking for elaboration, 'scary how?'

'There sort of like beasts of the field, aren't they? Out in all weathers, muddy clothes, when they're even fully dressed that is, and they all look as if they've either just been in a fight or are getting ready to start one.'

'Naked navvies?', he enquired, exaggerating his earnestness, 'I don't think that's the kind of thing my father would encourage.'

'I'm sure that they're very nice and I hear that a few go to Mass, but......'. She trailed off, conscious that her condescension was becoming more apparent with every sentence. 'I just can't imagine that I would have anything in common with them. You know what I mean'.

The waiter arrived with their food. There was a moment or two's silence while the waiter handed them their pizzas. Jane took this as an opportunity to regain some credibility and thanked the waiter profusely before engaging him in a brief, but meaningless bout of chit chat.

' See?', she said looking pointedly at Hugh once the waiter had left their table, 'I've got no problem with working class people, but those diggers are different.'

'Well, as I said, I'm going to be one of them. You've got to remember, that's where I come from. I've got those navvy genes somewhere in me. Both of my grandfathers did that kind of work and their fathers before them. It's in the blood or coded in my DNA should I say. You did A-Level biology too, you should know that. The capacity to do that hard, physical labour its built into a man. Navvies are born, not made you know. That's why so many Irish men do it, it's in their genes.'

'Ah well then', she said, 'why isn't your father a navvy? According to your logic he should be, eh? Anyway, it's just not as simple as that. We're not complete slaves to our DNA, you know. The environment does influence how our genes express themselves, we're not just victims of what we inherit from our parents and grandparents. Plus, where do grandmothers fit into this theory of the navvy gene? And granddaughters for that matter? Why aren't women out there digging the roads, God forbid?'

'You're just being silly now', he replied. 'You know as well as I do that men are genetically built for physical labour in ways that women just aren't: they're stronger, tougher, you know. I don't have to state the obvious, do I?'

'And more aggressive,' interjected Jane, a note of smugness in her voice, 'which brings me to your conduct at Richard's party. I know that we didn't get chance to talk about it, but I wasn't at all happy with the way you behaved Hugh. All that punching and fighting, and I know it's not the first time. I was warned'.

'Warned?!' exclaimed Hugh. 'What do you mean 'warned'?'

'About your tendency to, well, you know, involve yourself in brawls.'

"Involve myself in brawls?' You make it seem like a hobby. You know that's not the case.'

'Of course *I* do. I wouldn't be here otherwise, but people do talk, and your behaviour at Richard's party will have only added fuel to the fire.'

'I saved my friend from being beaten up in his own house by three intruders', he replied flatly.

'I know', she replied, 'but couldn't you have just talked to them, explained to them that what they were doing was wrong? I mean, often people like that just need someone to listen to them. You know, they've usually been brought up in really bad environments Hugh', she said plaintively 'That's why they behave like that because no one has really cared about them, taken the time to listen to them.'

'You're being naive Jane. Did you see those guys? The big one had Richard by the throat. I think it'd gone beyond the talking stage. He picked on Richard because he thought that he could get away with it. A bully is a bully Jane, and you can't let them get away with it. They're not the victim. That's a lesson my grandfather instilled into me from when I was a kid. No kind of man will stand by and allow someone to be bullied. It's just wrong. I mean I'm not trying to be a hero or anything, but the bottom line is that sometimes you have to be prepared to use force if you want to do the right thing, or at least stop the wrong thing from happening. It's just the real world. If you're not prepared to do everything in your power to stop the bad guys from winning, what's the point in doing anything at all?'

'Perhaps', she replied reluctantly. 'I just hate to see violence. It frightens me.'

'Well, it is in the world, and it'll take some weeding out. I mean, it's in people, and men don't have the monopoly on it by the way. They're just better at it. I mean, would you have rather seen Richard beaten up by those lads? I can see that it might frighten you, but often enough its just that kind of fear that allows the bullies and thugs to get away with it.'

'I suppose so', she replied sadly. 'Poor old Richard. He looked so pathetic sat there on the stair.' She didn't like the feelings that these recollections provoked and so quickly changed the subject. 'You miss your grandfather, don't you?', She said tenderly. 'You talk about him a lot.'

'I suppose I do', he replied sheepishly before warming to his theme and smiling broadly. 'He was some man you know. Did I tell you about the time he had a prize fight with a kangaroo at the circus?'

'Yes, yes you did', she replied hastily. 'Do you think that he might have been stringing you along a bit there, you know, just for fun...?'

'Oh no', Hugh replied decisively. 'He never told lies. That's one thing he was adamant about. He really disliked liars. Now, he was a proper fighting man......'

'Yes, you've said', replied Jane, 'you've said that a few times actually'.

'Well, he could look after himself, that's all. It was a different world then, I suppose.'

'Ah yes, so he was the provider of both the tough guy gene and the navvy gene, eh? On that subject, why didn't it get passed to your dad? As I said, it kind of disrupts your theory a bit, doesn't it?', she said playfully.

'Urrrm, you're right about that', he conceded. 'I don't know what happened there. The genetic rhythm definitely missed a beat with him. I sometimes wonder if my grandma, you know, strayed from the path of moral righteousness .....', he said smiling slyly.

'How dare you Hugh Gallon!', erupted Jane in mock indignation. 'How could you even think something like that about your own grandmother?', and went to rap him gently on the knuckles with her spoon. He pulled his hand away quickly, laughing at his own mischievousness. As he did so, she looked squarely into Hugh's smiling face and a thought flew through her mind, its contents suggesting a slight tweak to Hugh's speculation. She silently upbraided herself for even considering it. She would address this squalid little thought with the priest the next time she went to confession, she thought.

'So, back to this job', she continued. 'Obviously your father knows about your plans, but have you told your mother?'

'She was in on it', he replied casually.

'Your mother? Now that's a surprise. I wouldn't have thought she'd have wanted her golden boy to move in those kind of circles.'

'There you go again. 'Those kind of circles'. I'm sure you lifted your nose slightly when you said that. Look, you're looking at this in entirely the wrong way', he is tone becoming more conciliatory. 'If the weather's good, I'll get a nice tan and from what I hear doing that job is like doing a ten-hour circuit class, so I'll have muscles popping up everywhere! Most importantly though, I could be earning five or six hundred pounds a week. A couple of months of that, plus what I've got in the bank, and I'll have enough to go travelling', he said excitedly.

'Ah, about that', said Jane with a slight sigh. 'Look, I don't know if that's going to happen for me. I dropped a few hints to my mother and she was, like, totally against it. I mean adamant.'

'Jesus, Jane! it was you who suggested the idea', replied Hugh, clattering his cutlery on to the table, surprise and disappointment replacing his previous good humour.

'I know', she replied apologetically, 'but she told me that employers just look at a gap year as an excuse to lie on beaches and go sightseeing. The days of being viewed as intrepid and independent are gone. They just think, well, that's a year squandered, and it gives everyone who doesn't take a year out a year's head start, if that makes sense'.

'Why wouldn't that make sense?' his irritation evident. 'You sound like a careers advisor. When did you decide this?'

'Look, it's not decided. I'm just keeping you posted on the signals, that's all.'

'Yeah, right', he replied indignantly. They both looked down at their plates unsure of what to say next. Hugh certainly felt deflated, but he didn't want to overplay his hand. Jane had her car with her this evening, and he'd taken it for granted that there might be some intimacy on the cards later, albeit the limited sort that passed for intimacy in Jane's well-regulated Catholic mind. Despite the fact that she'd seriously let him down he decided that guilt was the way to go, not recrimination, if he wanted to bolster his chances of some kind of sexual contact later that evening.

'I feel really let down Jane', he said, 'we could have shared so many great experiences, spent so much time together, really taken our relationship to the next level.'

'I know', replied Jane plaintively, 'I'm so sorry Hugh. I hate to let you down. I'll try to make it up to you, I really will', her earnestness palpable.

'Bingo!' he thought to himself, all thoughts of the gap year trip brushed to one side.

CHAPTER THIRTEEN

Gene peered through his bedroom curtains out into a day which gleamed with warmth beneath the soft, pellucid blue of an early morning sky. Cora had endured a difficult night and he himself had only got the benefit of a couple of hours sleep in the chair beside her bed. He felt old and weary, but he took some momentary comfort in the knowledge that the physical demands of the work would sharpen him up, would invigorate him and hopefully distract him from worry about Cora's condition. He ran through his own morning routine, attended to Cora and left the house.

He spotted Frankie waiting for him at their agreed pick-up point and pulled the waggon into the curb to allow him in. 'Any point in heading to Mick's place?', Gene enquired once Frankie was in the waggon.

'None. His missus was waiting with the cheque in the pub yesterday.'

'I knew that man was no good', spat Gene dismissively.

'We've got another fella though. You might know him, used to be around here years ago. Head off to the pub. We're meeting him there.'

'Oh, right', replied Gene, pleasantly surprised that Frankie had used his initiative in securing a replacement for the absent Mick.

'You might even know him', Frankie continued. 'Danny Greene, big fella, one eye.'

'Bloody hell, Danny Greene! Is he still alive?', said Gene, a look of surprise on his face.

'Is he any good?', enquired Frankie, 'because I had to put him on the split', expecting Gene to be irritated at his failure to consult him about a crucial bit of gang business.

'Danny Greene, eh', Gene was momentarily lost in thought before recovering himself. 'Oh, no problem, he'll be a great man to have around. Good worker, from what I remember, knows the job. Bit of a wild one though, or at least he was. I half remember that there was a bit of a fuss with the boss man years ago'.

'Oh really?', replied Frankie, his interest piqued.

'Yes. I don't know the details, just some old gossip. You know how lads talk. Something to do with his wife. Cora was friends with her mother but she never went into any detail about it, not that I was much interested anyway.'

Danny was waiting for them outside 'The Harp'. He walked round to the passenger side of the waggon and Gene's eyes followed him hoping that the sight of him might spark some dormant memories into life. Danny climbed into the cabin and nodded at them both as he settled himself into the passenger seat.

'Don't I know your face?', asked Danny glancing at Gene as he pulled his seat belt on.

'Aye, you were around here about twenty years ago, right? Worked with Tommy Jones and that Belfast lad, Eammon something or other.'

'Aye, I was. Eammon James drank himself to death a few years ago and Tommy, last I heard of Tommy was that he was living rough in Winchester, somewhere like that', he replied.

'Well, there's a lot of lads at this game who go that way, I suppose. What brings you back here?', asked Gene, not wanting to appear as if he was prying, but not quite succeeding.

'Work', came the conclusive reply. Gene decided not to pursue the question further.

They passed the remainder of the journey in silence before pulling into the yard and parking up. Danny and Frankie got out of the waggon and headed towards their tackle. The yard was starting to fill with waggons. The noise of coughing engines and the crash of heavy tools filled the air. Jones was perched in his usual place, and it didn't take him long to spot Danny as his eyes scoured the yard seeking out some pretext to bark out orders to the men scurrying around below him.

The sight of Danny Greene sent a shudder down Jones' spine and his blood seemed to heat up as it raced through his veins. His mind emptied out and he found himself staring uncomprehendingly at Danny in a fruitless attempt to grasp the implications of his presence. And then suddenly out of this numbed confusion emerged a gleaming point of focus: fear, a rare contaminant in his highly cultivated sense of himself. He immediately brought the full force of his arrogance down on this impudent emotion, so quickly in fact that he would have denied its existence, even to himself.

He hurried into the office.

'What are you fuckers still doing here', he bellowed at the agents who quickly gathered up their things and headed out the door in a flurry of activity. He waited for the last of them to scurry out of the door and turned to Gallon. 'Well, David', he said, 'it looks like he's here after all'. David looked up.

'What're you talking about? Who's here?'

'Danny Greene', Jones answered reluctantly.

'You are fucking joking', replied David, rising from his chair and quickly striding to the window. 'Where is he?', he asked, frantically scanning the yard through the dust-flecked glass. 'Where the fuck is he?', he demanded, not attempting to disguise the urgency in his question.

Jones joined him by the window and peered out. 'Down there, by the pipes' he observed calmly, inwardly gratified by his boss' momentary panic.

David's gaze flew across the yard and fixed on Danny Greene, 'Do you want me to run him off?', asked Jones. David looked at him, a sceptical expression on his face, and turned back to the window without comment.

'Which gang is he with?', he asked still staring at Danny. Before Jones could answer, Gallon muttered to no one in particular 'Ah, he's with Gene', as his eyed followed Danny walking towards Gene's waggon.

'Do you want me to run him off', repeated Jones eager to prove himself of worth to his employer.

'Run him off? Do you think you'd be up to it? He's a tough lad, and you did require some assistance last time you tried, didn't you?', said David without turning to him. Jones remained silent and looked out of the window, grinding his teeth together, barely containing his indignation.

David was too busy trying to manage his own response to the spectre in their midst to notice Jones' struggles. He simply wanted to absorb the shock as best he could and reveal to Jones as little of his consternation as possible. He quickly considered his options, of which there were few, and settled on minimisation. Rather than confronting the problem he instead chose to deny its existence. 'Fuck it', he said turning to Jones whose pride was still recovering from the recent affront, 'it's all ancient history. Who gives a fuck? Let him carry on'. David continued to peer down at Danny scrutinising him with an almost lascivious concentration, absorbed in the feline quality of Danny's movement as he walked across the yard towards the waggon.

'What happened to his eye?', he exclaimed spinning round to face Jones, 'and that patch he's wearing, it looks like the sole of an old boot!', he continued smiling gleefully. Your odds just might have changed my old friend', he said reaching up and patting him on the shoulder as he walked back to his desk and sat down, picking up a large ledger and peering into it. Jones smiled weakly at him and moved across the office and began investigating a large and intricately designed technical drawing pinned to a wall of the office, both men attempting to disguise their attempts to navigate the implications of Danny's presence amongst them. Jones struggled to master his reaction to David's insult, a reaction which he focused on to distract him from the deeper and more troubling matter of Danny's return which his bravado had been designed to mask. He stood in front of the drawing for just long enough to allow Gene's gang to exit the yard, although he would not have admitted even to himself that this was the trigger that permitted him to leave the office.

David flipped through the ledger hoping to find something within that would distract his attention away from the feeling of nausea churning away in his stomach. The ledger remained in his hands for less than thirty seconds after Jones' departure before he hurled it across the room in an explosion of anger and frustration. The old feelings of humiliation and disgrace were welling up inside him. It felt as if he were trying to hold back an oncoming tide with his bare hands. He had detested Danny Greene with a loathing piped straight from hell from that first Sunday when he had walked into the church with Kate. He was a living, breathing emblem of all the things that David would never be, an incarnate rebuke to his burgeoning manhood, a son a father might be proud of, a man respected, nay feared, by his peers.

'Well', he thought, fortifying himself, 'now I am the one who is respected, I am the one who has Kate', and he smiled to himself. He could afford to treat Greene with indifference, perhaps be cavalier with him even, now that he had Jones around. That would negate the gossip, the slights on his masculinity, and finally put the whole squalid business to rest. With this change in perspective his earlier nausea evaporated to be replaced by a warm rush of satisfaction, but before it had time to blossom another question sprung into his mind: What was he going to tell Kate about Greene's reappearance? This new dilemma didn't have time to torment him before a solution presented itself: he would tell he nothing. She never came to the yard and had little to do with the business in general, and it was hardly likely that they would bump into one another socially, so why should she know? Long distance men like him never hung around anywhere for too long anyway, they were just misfits and itinerants, so why rock the boat?

A comforting wave of relief washed over him, He had resolved a couple of potentially dangerous problems in the past five minutes, he thought to himself. He leant back in his chair, gratified by his own wisdom and decisiveness.

It did not for one sleek moment enter his mind that this gratification was based on nothing more than denial, deception and cowardice.

CHAPTER FOURTEEN

Frankie stood up in the trench and arched his back conspicuously, stretching out his arms behind him, tensing the muscles along their length until they stood out like knotted cords. 'Have you seen the curtain twitching up in the bedroom up there, Gene', he said grinning and gesturing towards the house adjacent to where they were working. Gene looked around and peered through squinting eyes at the house Frankie was nodding at.

'What are you talking about?', he asked, a puzzled expression on his face.

'There's someone spying on us from behind that bedroom curtain, I'm telling you', replied Frankie.

'They won't be doing any staring at me, that's for sure', continued Gene dismissively, 'and you might want to pay a bit more attention to your work', he continued, his tone serious, as he flicked the blade of the hammer across the floor of the trench, sweeping away the muck to reveal a buried electric cable.

'Woah, a close one!', exclaimed Frankie further clearing away the debris from around the finger-thick cable.

'Indeed it was', replied Gene gravely. Severing buried electric cables was an occupational hazard in this work and few men had been spared the jolt of electricity that came with damaging an electric cable, a shock known as 'The Great Awakener.'

Positioned behind the twitching curtains there was indeed a young woman peeking down at the workers in the street below. 'Here Mandy, come here', she called to her friend in the other room. 'Look what we've got here.' Mandy wandered into the bedroom and walked over to the window. 'No, come here, don't let them see you', giggled Amy, pulling her friend to the side of the window so that she could avail herself of the cover provided by the curtains. 'Now there's a nice bit of beef', she continued nodding down at the trench. Mandy crept up to her and took her turn peering through the crack between curtain and wall to stare down at Frankie.

'Too right', sighed Mandy and they both giggled. 'Let's make them a cup of tea', exclaimed Amy, smiling mischievously at her friend.

'I'll do it, I'll do it', replied Mandy excitedly, almost tripping on the stairs in her haste to get to the kitchen. A few minutes later she called up to Amy, 'tea up!'.

'Are you coming out?', asked Mandy as she placed three mugs on a tray.

'Too bloody right I am', replied Amy, halting briefly at the mirror to adjust her hair. 'Biscuits!', she exclaimed as she reached the bottom of the stairs. I've got to have something to offer them', she explained, 'I can't go out there empty-handed, they'll know that I'm just having an ogle'. They both giggled again and as Mandy reached out for the door handle she suddenly stopped to check with her friend that she looked presentable and, after receiving a confirming nod, they walked out onto the path and strolled up to the trench.

'Good morning lads. You've been working hard this morning, haven't you? I bet you've got a right thirst', said Amy smiling as she looked along the fifty or so meters of trench that had been dug out, raising her hand to shield her eyes from the sun as she did so. She passed a mug of tea to Frankie. 'Don't let your mate die of thirst, will you', she added looking down the track at Danny who was directing the grab driver in his delivery of sand and aggregate.

'Well thank you, ladies', said Frankie, wiping the sweat from his forehead with more than a touch of theatricality and smiling as widely as his mouth would allow.

'Danny', shouted Gene down the track, 'tea up!'. He laid the hammer down by the side of the trench and wandered down to where Danny was working, accepting with complete indifference the fact that he was quite invisible to the two women. 'Go up there and get a pot of tea, Danny. I'll sort this out'. Danny nodded and walked up to join Frankie.

'I hope that we didn't disturb you this morning,' said Frankie.

'Oh, no', replied Amy, 'we're early risers, aren't we Mandy?', She replied turning to her friend.

'How long will you be on our street?', asked Mandy as Danny joined them and collected his cup of tea.

'Don't worry', replied Danny, 'we should be out of your way by the end of today.'

'Oh, we weren't worried about it, were we Ames'. They both giggled.

'So, where do you ladies do your drinking?', enquired Frankie, a mischievous grin on his face.

'You don't mess about, do you?', replied Amy.

'Just making conversation', replied Frankie and turned to clatter the shovel on the footpath to dislodge a clump of clay which had attached itself to its face. As he did so the musculature in his back momentarily clenched and rose into an almost architectural form, which he knew it would.

'Well, we go to the 'The Albion' on a Fridays, don't we Mandy', she said looking at her friend for confirmation that she wasn't saying too much, 'and to 'The Fox' on a Saturday'.

'With your boyfriends, I suppose?', replied Frankie barely attempting to disguise his real agenda.

'We're both young free and single at the moment aren't we Mandy?', directing her attention to Danny. They chatted for five minutes or so until Gene re-joined them, his return indicating that the tea break was over.

''The Albion', eh? Who knows, we might see you up there one of these days', said Frankie, 'give us the chance to repay you for that lovely cup of tea', he said handing her back the empty mug.

They both giggled again and began walking back towards the house.

'Don't forget, Friday nights at 'The Albion', shouted Amy as they got to the door of their house. 'Shhhh. Don't look so keen', said Mandy nudging her as they walked through the door laughing.

The grab waggon eased its way out of the cul-de-sac and Gene picked up the hammer. 'So, I think I might be taking a trip up to 'The Albion' this weekend', said Frankie as he stepped into the trench.

'Why do you want another one man?', asked Gene. 'Jesus, you've only just moved in with one and now you're looking for another!'. He shook his head in genuine perplexity. 'You only need one good one, you know.'

'You never know how long these things are going to last and it's always handy to have a backup plan', said Frankie chuckling lightly.

Amy was making tea for them both as Mandy sat watching her from the kitchen table. 'What do you reckon then?', she asked.

'I liked that one in the trench – thingy, the one with the cheeky grin', replied Amy, 'he had lovely eyes'.

'And teeth', chimed in Mandy.

'Oh, you like him too?'.

'Who wouldn't', she replied giggling. 'I liked the other one too, the pirate', continued Mandy smiling and both girls broke out into peals of laughter. 'He was a bit sort of scary looking, but sexy too. His muscles….'.

CHAPTER FIFTEEN

'Oh, I forgot to mention, my lad will be starting with us on Monday', remarked David casually from behind his desk without raising his eyes from the paperwork he was working on. Jones had his back to him, looking at a technical drawing on the wall which marked the progress the gangs had been making. He had met the lad once when he had dropped something off at Gallon's house but hadn't been properly introduced to him. To the extent that he'd given Hugh any thought at all, Jones had assumed that he was just another spoilt, rich kid.

'I thought you said that he was off to university soon', asked Jones turning to David, and when no answer was forthcoming, he changed tack. 'Are you going to put him with one of the agents?', he enquired, returning his attention to the drawing.

'No, he wants to go out on site, or so he says. I don't think he knows what he's letting himself in for. Any suggestions?' Jones wandered over to his desk, obviously giving the matter some thought.

'We can't just dump him on a gang without any experience of the work, there'd be hell on. I mean, I could tell them to do what they're fucking told, but that might not be the best kind of start for the lad.'

'Good point', replied David.

'We could stick him with one of the snagging gangs. That way he gets his hands dirty without disrupting any digging gangs or creating any bad feeling,' suggested Jones. 'Snagging' was the name given to the minor remedial works undertaken to correct construction mistakes left behind by departing gangs and was usually reserved for the older men who had passed their physical prime and who were happy to accept a salaried position.

'Excellent idea', said David. 'He'd get a reliable wage coming in too'.

'I can put him with Gary and John if you want, they're unlikely to kill him with work. When did you say he's starting?'

'Monday', replied David.

'OK. I'll have a word with the two of them when they get in this evening.'

A couple of hours later waggons started rolling into the yard, the day's work complete. Jones' desk was positioned by a window so that he could monitor all comings and goings and he caught sight of the vehicle that he was looking out for. 'Gary's coming in', he said to David, 'I'll have a word with him about your lad', and he headed down into the yard. He strode over to where Gary had parked his waggon greeting some of the lads on the way as they unloaded their vehicles. It had been observed more than once that he was a much more genial man when he was down in the yard amongst the boys than he was when roaring at them from the protective height of the gantry.

'Now then Gary', said Jones in his friendliest of tones as he approached the driver's side window of the snagging gang's waggon. Gary was one of the older men at the firm and had been with GCE from its beginnings under Gallon Senior. 'I've some good news for you', Jones continued. 'You'll be getting another man come Monday. Now, he's not replacing anyone, before you start. He's just a young lad looking for a couple of month's work.'

'Why's he being dumped on us? he's not some fucking arsehole is he?', Gary asked gruffly not bothering to look at Jones.

'Look, if he's no good just let me know', said Jones.

Gary eyed him suspiciously. He didn't like Jones and he certainly didn't trust him. He'd witnessed scores of bullies like him over the years and he wasn't about to start to give this one his respect, not at his age. Jones knew that because of his length of service Gary's position in the firm made him untouchable. Gary had even been invited to Gallon family functions when the old man was alive and as a result, Jones was always a little unsure of himself when dealing with him. He was well aware that his authority within the firm meant nothing to Gary and who therefore made no effort whatsoever to disguise his dislike for him. That having been said, Gary was renowned for his irritable nature and Jones had allowed himself the conceit that attributed any resentment directed towards him personally to Gary's generally sour disposition. 'Well, we'll take him, but if he's no good, we'll leave him where we sack him'.

'Thanks', said Jones and turned to walk away, annoyed at himself for offering gratitude to a subordinate for simply complying with a reasonable management instruction.

The waggons were rolling into the yard with increasing frequency and the inevitable congestion was starting to develop. Clouds of diesel fumes hung heavy in the air like ethereal funeral garlands against the pale blue of the evening sky. Horns blared, engines revved, and gears were crashed through their motions shattering the peace of the otherwise languid early summer's evening. In the midst of this confusion Gene was trying to manoeuvre his way through the bottleneck developing at the entrance to the yard. He was conscious that Cora had been alone at the house for three or more hours since the nurse's last visit and he was eager to get the waggon unloaded and to return home to her. He disliked leaving her side at all and would have retired completely long ago if his finances would have permitted him to do so, but the cost of years of private medical health care had taken its toll on his savings.

After ten minutes of toing and froing he finally managed to identify an opening and eased the waggon slowly towards it. Just as he was about to pass into the open space of the yard another waggon flew in front of him and blocked his path. Gene wound his window down and stuck his head and shoulders through the window frame.

'What do you think you're doing, you bloody jackass', he bawled at the driver of the offending vehicle. What happened next caught Gene utterly by surprise. A rough-looking, heavy-set young man leapt out of the driver's side of the waggon skewed across their path and within moments he was screaming in Gene's face.

'Who the fuck do you think you are, you old cunt'. The man was beside himself, his face contorted with rage, 'I'll knock the fucking shite outta ya', and he reached in through the open window and grabbed Gene by the lapel of his jacket and tried to pull him through the window casement, crashing Gene's head against the door frame in the effort to do so. Gene was stunned into inactivity by this sudden turn of events. He didn't understand what was happening to him, nor for that matter did Frankie who grabbed hold of Gene's arm in what would have appeared to an observer to have been an almost comic scene of tug of war as the young thug persisted in his effort to pull Gene out of the waggon. The youth started to jab punches through the open window with his free hand, his temper showing no signs of abating, his face flushed with malice. The situation had escalated with incredible speed and seemed to have continued for minutes when in reality only thirty or forty seconds had elapsed since Gene had first remonstrated with the kid. Suddenly, the attacker appeared to leap backwards, detaching himself from Gene in the process, his facial expression shifting from one of violent outrage to one of incredulity. Gene felt separate from the events in which he was a confused participant, as if he was involved in the scene as a spectator, not as an actor. Then Frankie and Gene saw a figure bending over the stricken form of the youth and, as he raised himself to the vertical, he lifted the kid with him then once erect hurled the youth back down to the ground with bone-crushing force.

The kid, now panic stricken at the speed with which he had been undone, tried to make his escape while still in a prone position, pushing his heels into the dirt and scrambling backwards frantically looking from left to right to ensure that he avoided the wheels of the snarling waggons prowling around him. The figure knelt down once again and his hand disappeared around the curve of the kid's neck, leaving only his thumb visible as it pressed down on his Adam's Apple and he appeared to be whispering something into his ear. This entire incident had lasted seconds, and it was not until the figure turned and they both saw it to be Danny did Gene and Frankie catch up to the turn of events. The kid clambered unsteadily to his feet, his chest heaving and made a dash for his waggon, turning only once to ensure that Danny was not in pursuit.

Danny walked calmly passed the windscreen of the waggon and resumed his place in the passenger seat. 'I can't do with this road rage nonsense', he said casually. 'I thought I'd better deal with him before you had to', he said looking at Gene who nodded, silently acknowledging Danny's effort to save his face. Danny turned back to looking through the windscreen. 'There you go', he said nonchalantly pointing to a gap in the traffic created by the kid's waggon as it reversed at speed back on to the road. Frankie and Gene were still staring at him, still unable to fully process the events of the past couple of minutes before exploding into peals of laughter, giving vent to the nervous energy which had accumulated within them during the episode. Danny looked at them briefly and smiled and the waggon resumed its progress into the yard.

CHAPTER SIXTEEN

Friday came around all too quickly for men trying to make good on the meters sacrificed to Monday's rain, but with the addition of Danny's energy and experience Gene's gang had managed to compensate for the lost afternoon. Danny was a seasoned hand at the work and he engaged efficiently and without fuss, never appearing to slow down or break his rhythm. The man charged with piping-up and backfilling the trench could reasonably be considered the busiest man on the job as it was his task to lay in the pipes and their spurs to individual houses, backfill the trench with sand and aggregate, compact the same using a heavy, cumbersome mechanical tool known as a 'whacker', and then perform the same operation upon a thin course of tarmac which would then harden and seal the trench. In addition to this, he, along with occasional assistance from the grab waggon, had to remove the 20 or so tonnes of debris that that the men at the head of the trench had excavated during the course of the day.

'So, where will it be this evening gentlemen?' Gene asked as he turned to face his workmates as they sat in the waggon, a week's work behind them, ready to leave site.

'I think I try one at 'The Albion'', said Frankie, with an exaggerated wink to Gene, 'pay a little visit to Amy and Mandy, you know, the lasses from the other day.'

'You're looking for trouble there lad', said Gene with a reproving shake of his head.

'Don't be so serious man', replied Frankie, smiling. 'I'm just keeping her warm. Forward planning, that's all. Will you be accompanying me Mr. Greene', he asked looking at Danny, who answered with a slow shake of his head.

Whenever Frankie moved to a new city his first priority was to find a woman as quickly as possible, a woman who would, first and foremost, attend to his domestic needs. Digging work was time consuming and left little opportunity to arrange for the comforts, or even the necessities, of daily life and he had never understood why men would burden themselves with the discharge of these additional domestic responsibilities. In his time at the work Frankie had come to realise that most of his peers shirked these onerous domestic tasks and as a result they ate badly, dressed shabbily and were driven into the pub by the solitary nature of their living arrangements, handing their wages over to the local landlord and waking up each morning with a throbbing head. The pubs were full of them, men just a step away from the doss house or the park bench, a fate which caused Frankie to shudder.

He had discovered early on in his life that he appealed to women, and he had made the most of it. He was nonetheless certain that he could do more with his good looks and charm than simply use them to find his bed and board and he was convinced that it was only a matter of time before he found a woman wealthy enough to allow him to hang up his boots for good. Until then he would happily pass the time enjoying the comforts that his looks had made accessible to him.

'Well, I'm just going to have a couple', conceded Frankie. 'I'm meeting Jenny later on'. They dropped Frankie off at 'The Albion' and headed to 'The Harp'.'

'You don't take a drink yourself Danny?', enquired Gene.

'No, not so much these days, all the good's gone out of it for me, but I found plenty in it at one time though.'

Aye, I remember you here first time around, you certainly stirred things up a bit', he said smiling at the understatement, 'and a few other places too, I heard'.

'Well, that was then. I was a brought up pretty wild. My old fella was a fighting man and his before that and what's bred in the bone comes out in the marrow, as they say. It's knowing what to do with it. That's the trick. We both know that there's a lot of loose lads around this kind of work, a lot of *maistins*'.

'You've got some of the Irish, eh? *Mastins*? Bullies, right?', said Gene.

'I know a small bit', replied Danny. 'My father dragged me around Ireland for a few years when I was a kid. I picked up a few words, that's all.'

The waggon pulled up outside 'The Harp' and Danny climbed out of the waggon and nodded at Gene who returned the gesture and then drove off. Gene watched him enter the pub, surprised at his candour, after all, he'd barely spoken a word to anyone during the week. Not that he had been stand offish or belligerent, God knows there were enough of those men around. He just seemed reserved, self-sufficient, a man unto himself. The long-distance men were often like that, Gene thought to himself. But for all his fearsomeness, and there was plenty of that, there

93

seemed to be something wounded about the man. Maybe it was that which lent him his aura of danger. A wounded animal is a dangerous animal, after all. Lord knows, he'd seen how Danny had dealt with the young thug only a couple of days ago, and in his defence at that. Maybe that was it thought Gene. Their conversation amounted to a fair exchange of vulnerabilities. Not only had Danny saved Gene from a beating, but he had also saved his face as well. He had preserved his dignity. A man can recover from a busted nose or a broken jaw, but being deprived of his masculinity, that was a hurt that endured. Danny had spared him that humiliation, a pain that still smarted even at his age. This seemed to have given Danny an opening, a way to trust Gene, a way to show him a seldom seen side of himself perhaps, and for Gene, this took some of the sting out the events of earlier that week.

CHAPTER SEVENTEEN

Hugh drew deeply on a joint and passed it to Roger, one of his friends, who together with a couple of others would spend the first part of their Friday evening smoking weed in Roger's bedroom while his parents were out of the house attending their regular bridge parties. Roger was sat on the floor leaning against his bedroom wall and, either unable or unwilling to make the effort to rise to his feet, asked Nigel who was sprawled out on his bed to open a second window to dispel the blue fog of cannabis smoke that hung in the air.

'Are you sure?', replied Nigel languorously, 'it's pretty chilly out there, you know', hoping that Roger would concur and so spare him the need to exert himself.

'You are one lazy motherfucker', said Roger in response, giggling.

'He's one stoned motherfucker, you mean', added Hugh.

Roger passed the joint along to Richard who examined the damp roach, his face screwed up in disgust. 'Not for me', he commented passing it to Nigel. 'Can't be good for you', he said as Nigel took it from him.

'Fucking looser', said Nigel, directing his remark at Richard and the rest of the company immediately took up the cry of 'loser, loser, loser' pointing in a collective gesture at Richard. This chorus lasted less than twenty seconds before the chant dissolved into a chorus of giggles and guffaws. The laughter subsided and everyone fell into a silence broken a minute or two later as Hugh rose to his feet exclaiming.

'Look upon me in awe mere mortals for I am soon to become a digger of ditches, a quarrier of the highway, an earth mover of the highest renown. I am about to become a bronzed sex God! The object of the soon to be requited lust of every fair maiden at St. Ann's Roman Catholic Girl's School....', with which he slumped back down onto the floor smiling, resting his back against the wall to ease his descent.

'What the fucking hell are you talking about?', said Nigel giggling.

'I'm starting work with my dad's company on Monday, out with the big boys, digging down deep and throwing well back!'

'What's that all about then?', asked Roger distractedly.

'He's starting work at his Dad's firm. He's going to be a builder, right? Doesn't your father have a building company or something?', asked Nigel indifferently.

Hugh, tiring of the effort to make himself understood, tried a more direct approach.

'OK, you know those blokes that are digging up the roads, something to do with cable TV or something, well I'm going to be one of those.'

'What?', exclaimed Nigel. 'They're men, tough-looking men at that, doing tough-looking men's work. You're not a man, not yet anyway', he said dismissively.

'You can ask Jane about that', replied Hugh, winking at Richard.

'Bullshit!', they all cried out in unison. Nigel turned to him.

'You've no chance of getting into that underwear mate. None. Zero. She is and will remain in perpetuity, the blessed virgin of St. Ann's. So endeth today's lesson', and, as if to solemnise this pronouncement, his hand described an imaginary crucifix in the air in front of him.

Richard looked at Nigel gravely and said with a somewhat pained expression on his face, 'I really don't think that you should take the Lord's name in vain that way Nigel'. A dozen assorted pillows and cushions rained down upon him.

They chatted for a while longer as they waited for the more dramatic effects of the weed to wear off and headed out for a couple of subsidised beers at the golf club, a venue where the younger looking members of the company would be certain of being served. The night had turned cool, and it shocked some alertness back into their befogged minds.

'Were you serious in there?', asked Richard as he and Hugh hurried along the pathway in an effort to escape from the chill. 'I mean, and I don't want to sound awful, but those blokes all look like criminals or disbarred bouncers. They'll eat you alive man!'.

'Jesus, Richard, you too? Why is everybody I know such a bloody snob. They're just working men'.

'I'm just surprised that your parents have sanctioned this, I know mine wouldn't'.

'Well, the less said about that, the better', replied Hugh.

'Anyway, the plan was to use the wages for the trip, but it looks like Jane's getting cold feet on that idea now'.

'Did you ever really expect her to go ahead with it? That was never going to happen?', replied Richard.

'Yeah, well, I'm committed now and I'm not going to give my father another stick to beat me with by pulling out. Anyway, I think it could be good. I mean it. It'll help me to get in shape and get a tan if the weather stays decent and it sort of represents an aspect of my heritage, you know, the Irish navvy thing'.

'Your father's never been a navvy', said Richard dismissively, 'or has he? Doesn't seem the sort at all.'

'No, of course he hasn't', replied Hugh. 'He wouldn't last two minutes at that kind of work. He's a pussy.'

CHAPTER EIGHTEEN

David sauntered into the house and Kate, having heard the car pull into the garage, called down to him from upstairs. 'Is that you David?'.

'It is', he replied.

'I'll be down in a second'. He wandered over to the fridge and opened the door, peering inside and examining the contents. He didn't hear her coming down the stairs and was startled when he heard her voice behind him.

'Fancy anything in particular? I got some nice steaks from the butchers today?'

'Errrm, no thanks' he replied. 'I'll probably go out for a run later. Something light will suffice.'

'A salad?', she suggested.

'Perfect. Any plans tonight?'

'I'm going to pop round to Rachel's for an hour. Diane's supposed to be joining us', she said as she pulled various green and leafy items from the fridge. 'Tuna?'

'Yes, please'. What time are you due back?', he asked.

'11-ish, I suppose'. She quickly prepared the salad and passed it to him and then sat down at the kitchen dining table and poured herself a glass of wine.

'Do you want some bread with that?', she asked.

'No thanks, it'll be fine. Where is he? I can't hear any music blaring out or any clomping about upstairs.'

'He's out with his friends. They've gone to the golf club for a few drinks. I think.'

'Are you OK with him going to the pub at his age? I never did', asked Gallon.

'Well, it's the golf club, not the pub. There's a difference. You were a lot more reserved than Hugh at that age, weren't you? You had other interests,' she said charitably. 'They're just young lads finding their feet, I wouldn't worry about it', she added reassuringly.

'Oh, I'm not worried', he said causally, 'I was just interested in your take.'

'No', it doesn't bother me at all', she said, then added, 'within limits of course. Boys will boys and all that.'

David munched away the salad and stood up from the kitchen table and went to the dishwasher with the empty plate. Kate rose from the table and took it off him. 'I'll sort that out,' she said. He handed it to her and wandered into the lounge. She heard the TV go on. Kate refilled her wine glass and went back upstairs and refreshed the little make up she typically wore and returned downstairs. 'OK, I'm off', she said to David as she kissed him perfunctorily on the top of his head as he sat on the sofa aimlessly skipping through TV channels. She walked out through the garage, selecting a bottle of wine from the rack which was located on the rear wall and wandered down the driveway onto the avenue and took in a deep, invigorating breath of the lightly perfumed summer air.

The walk to Rachel's house took around five minutes. Kate entered the house through the front door announcing her arrival with a loud greeting.

'I'm in the conservatory', came the reply and Kate wandered through the expensively decorated lounge and greeted her friend with a broad smile.

'I come bearing gifts', she said as she sat down on the sofa holding out the bottle of wine. 'Where's Diane? She's not one to miss a girly night in.'

'She'll be along in while, it's still early yet', replied Rachel pouring wine from an already opened bottle into a glass sat sparkling on the low table between them.

'How's your week been?', she continued.

'Oh OK, the usual, other than Hugh starting work for his father on Monday. As I said on the phone the other day, there's something going on with that lad. If he thinks that he can pull the wool over his mother's eyes, he's got another thing coming', she said, her eyes twinkling.

'Oh, I don't know', replied Rachel thoughtfully, 'I think that it'll be good for him, don't you, out in the fresh air, meeting different kinds of people. I mean, it's a family tradition, isn't it, nothing wrong with honouring that, surely?'

'You're just romanticising it', said Kate flatly. 'And so's he, but that's not such a bad thing, I suppose. So few young people today have any idea of what real work is. I mean, office work can be demanding in its own way, but hard, physical graft, that's different.'

'Have you seen some of them? Shirts off, all muscle and brawn?', replied Rachel smiling mischievously, 'I wouldn't mind a bit of that kind of physical graft', her smile breaking into a laugh which lasted a fraction too long and was a fraction too loud, an indiscretion suggesting to Kate that the glass of wine in front of Rachel was not her first of the evening.

'I mean obviously, one wouldn't, but there's no harm in a sneaky glance', she continued. Kate smiled indulgently and took a drink from her own glass.

'Obviously, that kind of man doesn't appeal to you?', Rachel asked.

'Oh, why would you say that?', replied Kate.

'Well, I mean, look at David. He's undoubtedly got many good qualities, but you wouldn't call him rugged, or would you?', she added almost immediately, not wanting to be seen as being critical of her friend's husband.

'No, rugged he most certainly isn't', laughed Kate, 'but he's no worse for that.'

'No, of course not', replied Rachel hurriedly. 'I suppose if Trevor was a bit more manly I wouldn't be noticing random workmen who just happen to be showing a bit of muscle on the street', she replied. Rachel toyed with her glass. 'I think men just lose interest after a while, you know, in the physical side of things', she opined, catching Kate off guard with her candour. Kate smiled and looked at her quizzically.

'Maybe it's just age?', offered Kate.

'My interest certainly hasn't faded and I'm no spring chicken', said Rachel ruefully.

'Nor mine', added Kate and they both laughed. 'Is David the same?', asked Rachel.

'Hmmmmm', mused Kate. 'It still happens now and again, but more I think to remind ourselves that we're man and wife rather than brother and sister', they both laughed again. 'He does his best, I suppose. He's worked hard to give us all a good life and that's important. I mean, I've done the mad, passionate thing and it was incredible, but you can't allow your head to rule your heart.'

'Ooooo, tell me more', said Rachel excitedly, eager to explore this revelation further. 'I wouldn't have thought that was your thing. You always seem so in control, on an even keel', continued Rachel throwing down more bait as she rose to her feet. Kate smiled but said nothing. 'More wine', Rachel asked without turning to look at Kate.

'Oh, yes please', she replied.

'It wasn't a question', said Rachel turning her head and smiling at Kate as she walked towards the kitchen.

Kate sat back and allowed the effects of the wine to wash over her. Her thoughts drifted, uncaptained.

They had met a six o'clock under the city hall clock. Kate had twice tried on each of the three new dresses she had purchased on the previous Saturday before finally settling on a light cotton summer frock whose emerald floral design she thought best emphasised her eyes. She had to fight hard to resist the temptation to apply more make-up than she would usually wear and, as she looked at herself in the mirror, she was confronted only by what she saw as her flaws, utterly invisible to anyone else though they were. Her hair, freshly washed to banish the lingering odour of the cafe, hung down her back as if laced with black diamonds, its shimmering length tied at the nape of her neck with an emerald ribbon. She was fully aware that she had never fussed over her appearance to this extent, ever; she had never felt the need to work this hard to impress a man, but at that moment perfecting her appearance was the most important thing to her in the entire world. Eventually, reconciled to her dissatisfaction with what she saw in the mirror before her, she grabbed her handbag and raced down the stairs of the tiny terraced house.

The clattering of her feet on the uncarpeted staircase had alerted her father in the adjacent living room and before she could exit the house he called out.

'Jesus, Kate! What's all the smashing and banging about? A little more feminine grace might slow you down a bit, but it'll reduce the odds of you breaking your neck.' She entered the living room. Her father's attention was focused on pouring beer from an opaque brown bottle into a chipped ceramic mug. The cup filled, he turned his attention to her, and she performed a mock curtsey.

'Mea culpa, mea culpa, mea maxima culpa, father dearest', she said smiling, a mischievous expression on her face.

'My God!', he exclaimed in a thick Kerry accent. 'Now isn't that a beauty!' a huge smile on his face. 'How is a rough, old Paddy like me responsible for this vision before me?', he said shaking his head in quiet wonder.

'You're not. I look like Mum, remember', she said smiling back at him, warmed by his compliments, and she turned to leave. As she opened the front door, he called out to her.

'I hope it's that young David Gallon your out and about with. Remember, he's your future, lady. I've told you often enough, don't be wasting your time on trench monkeys like me.'

She let his words go unanswered and dashed to the bus stop.

He was waiting for her below the clock tower, a small bunch of flowers in his hand.

'Mr. Mulligan, my boss that is, told me I should get you these', he said thrusting the flowers at her with clumsy enthusiasm.

'Mr. Mulligan told you, eh? Didn't think of it yourself?', she said smiling, nonetheless touched at the gesture.

'Well, I'm not much of a ladies man really', he replied, slightly abashed. 'He gave me a few pointers about, you know, how to go on. I don't want to be making a fool out of myself.'

She watched him carefully him as spoke, his glistening eyes shifting nervously. It put her at her ease to see that she was not the only one unsure of themselves.

He had invited her out for supper and 'supper' consisted of fish and chips eaten out of a newspaper wrapper as they sat facing one another on a bench in a small garden area on the outskirts of the city centre, the evening bees buzzing lazily in the air around them as the blue of the sky above deepened from cyan to azure and the sun began its languid journey to the horizon.

'What would you like to do the rest of the evening?', he asked.

'Isn't that for you to tell me?', She replied, 'or should we ask Mr. Mulligan?'

They both laughed.

'Oh no need for that. I'm getting the hang of this courting thing a bit now. I might even be a natural, you know', he replied with a wink and a smile. His face opened up like a morning blossom when he smiled, she thought to herself.

'You know there's a fair in the park. How about we go there?', he offered.

'Oh, yes! Let's', she cried excitedly.

'I know some of the lads that work on it', he added.

'You do? How? Those fairs are normally from out of the city.'

'This one too', he replied. 'I worked on it for a year or so a while back.'

She looked at him, a puzzled expression on her face.

'How old are you?', she asked.

'Nineteen', he replied.

'So when did you work on the fair?'

'Oh, I was around fourteen, I suppose.'

'You were working at the fair when you were fourteen? What about school?'

'Oh, I didn't bother much with that', he replied, his face reddening slightly as he shuffled uncomfortably in his seat, the admission clearly a source of embarrassment to him. He averted his eyes. 'I wanted to go to school, but my father didn't see the point. Had me out working with him up and down the country, digging, tarmacking, that kind of thing. He never lasted long in one spot, always one for trouble that fella', he said shaking his head. 'I was a big, strong lad for my age, you know, and he saw he could make a few quid out of me. Anyway, we had a big bust up when I was about thirteen or fourteen. He used to knock me around a bit and like most of those *maistins*, I mean bullies, and he didn't like it when he got a bit in return. I ended up working on the fair after that. They're good people, fairground people. Don't get me wrong, I can read and write. I taught myself to do it as much as anything. I just didn't have much schooling that's all. I read books all the time now', he said turning to her, in his eyes an expression of gentle defiance embedded within a deep yearning for approval. For the briefest of instants, she saw the face of a vulnerable young boy in the rugged, even forbidding, countenance of the young man before her. She couldn't help herself.

'Oh, you poor man', she said sighing and reached out and placed her hand on his knee in an instinctive desire to reassure him.

'They're a funny lot fathers, aren't they', she said and smiled affectionately at him.

'There weren't many laughs with mine, I can tell you', he said, 'but there's plenty of fun to be had where we're going', he continued rising from the bench in a burst of energy, 'so let's not keep it waiting.'

Danny was greeted like a prodigal son by the fairground workers and he and Kate skipped their way from one exhilarating ride to another without a penny being spent. She shrieked on one ride, squealed on another and screamed like a banshee on the next, but all were mere punctuations in the unceasing flow of laughter that they sent reeling through the sweet air of that summer night. The brashly flashing lights, the whirling music of the rides, the smells, the bustle of giddy fair goers, all came together to make an evening filled with excitement and delight. Then out of nowhere the sky cracked out overhead and a summer shower fell down upon them like an ocean unleashed, sending them racing towards the shelter of the trees clustered deep within the hinterland of the park.

They found themselves alone beneath the canopy of an ancient Oak tree, the raindrops drumming madly on the broad green leaves overhead, immersed in the newly revealed twilight, laughing, laughing like they'd never laughed before as they tried to catch their breath, the refreshing coolness of the new - born rain on their skin heightening their awareness of the small world they made, intensifying their awareness of each other. He removed his jacket and raised it above them, another layer of protection, and she moved closer to him, raising her eyes to his, stray droplets of rainwater rolling slowly down her cheeks like tiny pale jewels on alabaster and he gazed down at her. No laughter now, just the distant melody of the fairground, the slow tapping of raindrops as the shower faltered and the quiet intensity of their breathing. He threw his jacket to the ground and pulled her to him, their lips meeting with the force of inevitability and as they kissed it was as if new stars were being born within her.

Kate's reverie was shattered as Diane sat down heavily on the sofa beside, her. 'Sorry Kate. I wasn't being rude, but I had some work stuff to talk about with Rachel in the kitchen. Didn't want to bore you with it. And double sorry that I'm late.'

'Oh, I didn't hear you arrive', replied Kate distractedly, 'I was miles away.' Diane began regaling her with tedious details concerning the reason for her late arrival, but Kate paid her scant attention, astonished and confused that she'd so casually tampered with memories so richly seeded with the potential for guilt and pain.

CHAPTER NINETEEN

Gene pulled the waggon into the almost deserted yard. Saturday mornings were reserved for remedial tasks on the previous week's work and so there was little pressure on gangs to get in early.

'I'll head up to the office and get the snagging list off the agent', Gene said to Frankie and Danny as he slowed the waggon to a stop next to a mountain of concrete flags and climbed out of the waggon and strolled stiffly in the direction of the timber staircase.

Frankie and Danny exited the van and began heaving the stone flags from the stockpile onto the back of the waggon when another GCE waggon sped into the yard and came skidding to a stop thirty meters from them, shrouding the vehicle in a yellow haze of dust. Danny and Frankie shot glances at one another questioning the unnecessary drama of the van's arrival before turning their attentions back to the vehicle.

A figure emerged from the rapidly dispersing dust cloud, his face twisted into a mask of grim aggression.

'I'm here for you, you one-eyed bastard', bawled the figure as he marched towards the pair. Frankie immediately turned his head to gauge Danny's reaction to the outburst, unsure himself as to how to respond to the barking monstrosity heading their way.

He was a shortish fellow, but wide and thick across the shoulders and deep through the chest, his boulder head rocking with each bellowed threat. Danny turned to face him unsure of the origin of his anger but braced to deal with it. Two other lads scrambled out of the cab and leant casually against the side of the waggon, all the better to spectate on the thrashing they were expecting to see delivered by their friend.

'That's the kid from the other day', said Frankie and nodded towards one of the men loitering at the waggon, 'the one you gave a rattle to'.

'Aye, I know', said Danny calmly.

The man was almost upon them, his threats becoming lost in a blather of barely intelligible grunts and snorts, catapulting tiny gobbets of saliva into the air before him. Frankie again looked at Danny. He certainly didn't want to pre-empt his mate, but he took little reassurance from Danny's relaxed pose as he leant against the tailboard of the waggon seemingly indifferent to the rapidly approaching threat. Then, just as the belligerent appeared to be tightening his right side to strike, Danny drew the back of his hand across his body and then sent it crashing into face of the would be attacker who spun one hundred and eighty degrees on his heels in a grotesque pirouette before falling to the ground, arms dangling redundantly by his sides incapable of cushioning his fall, and there he lay, crumpled, unmanned and silent.

Danny stood tall, his fists clenched by his sides, and directed his gaze at the aggressor's two associates, inviting their response. Neither made eye contact with him. Instead, they looked with slack-jawed astonishment at their mate's motionless frame laying face down on the dirt floor of the yard.

'Well?', growled Danny as he strode towards the two men, his face a study in calculating menace. The younger of the two, having already tasted the bitter fruits of Danny's anger a few days earlier, made for the door of the waggon and locked himself inside the cab. His companion watched him retreat and spat on the ground in disgust and leant over the side of the waggon and retrieved a pickaxe shaft from amongst the clutter of tools in the back of the vehicle. He turned to face Danny, slapping the shaft in the open palm of his left hand and grinning malevolently at the oncoming threat.

'Danny!', Frankie cried out and Danny turned to see Frankie holding a pickaxe by either end of its mottled steel head which he proceeded to drive down into the ground separating it from the shaft which, for a moment, stood there erect unsure of which way to fall. In one sweeping motion, Frankie half gripped, half palmed the shaft in Danny's direction. Danny plucked it from the air and turned to once again face his opponent who came to a stop as if restrained by a tether, the sudden introduction of this equality of arms diluting his courage to naught. He stared anxiously at Danny, his previous composure vanishing in the face of Danny's grim countenance. His mate started the waggon and pulled it up behind him. Just at this moment, the original would-be attacker rose unsteadily to one knee.

'Where is he? Where is the bastard?', he groaned, casting his unfocused eyes around the yard unable to properly orientate himself. He lumbered upwards, unsteady as a foal. Danny walked slowly towards him and backhanded him across the face sending him crashing once again back to the ground and then turned and walked back to Frankie and the waggon. The driver leapt out of his vehicle and together with his mate dragged their stricken champion back to their waggon and manhandled him unceremoniously into the cab.

'If I see any one of you men again, there'll be no get out for ye', yelled Danny at the retreating trio. The waggon crashed through its gears and burst for the exit. 'Quick thinking with the pick', said Danny turning to Frankie as the waggon disappeared out of the gate without so much as pausing to check for oncoming traffic.

Unbeknownst to Danny and Frankie, the entire episode had been witnessed by the occupants of the office: Gene, a couple of the agents and Jones. The younger of the two agents, Spencer, a cousin of Jones' in his early twenties, could barely contain his excitement at the series of events which had unfolded before them.

'Did you see that from the big fella?', he said turning to Jones, his eyes wide with incredulity. 'He didn't even punch him, he just gave him a back hander, fucking hell!' Spencer let out a low whistle of admiration. Jones ignored him and turned away, returning silently to his desk.

Spencer then directed his enthusiasm to Jimmy Fletcher, a long – standing site agent, who, disregarding Spencer, turned to Gene.

'You know yourself Gene, we can't have that kind of thing on company premises. What if Gallon had been here, he'd have run him off the job.' Gene looked at him sceptically. Fletcher rephrased his last remark. 'OK, he'd have sacked him.'

'You saw the same as I did, Jimmy', said Gene tersely, 'that man was going about his work when those three thugs put fight on him. Three of them. What was he supposed to do? It should be them that are getting ran', and with that he turned his back on Fletcher as if matters were concluded and left the office.

The young agent interjected excitedly. 'I don't think we'll be seeing those lads again judging by how quick they got out of the yard. Word'll be all round the other gangs too.' Fletcher looked at him silently acknowledging the accuracy of his observation. News of this would indeed spread quickly through the men.

'It was the Mulligans. They aren't that good a gang to be honest', said Fletcher, directing his observation at Jones who looked up at him blankly. 'I'll go down and have a word with Danny Greene', he continued. Jones merely nodded in acknowledgement and returned to his work. Fletcher descended the staircase more quickly than he would have preferred given the state of his knees, but he wanted to catch Gene before he reached the other two and he did not want to call out to him and alert Jones to the fact of their conversation. Gene heard Fletcher's hurried descent and stopped and turned towards him. The two men had known one another for many years. 'Look Gene, we both know that tempers can flare in this game, but your mate is running out of firms that'll have him. We all know his history. No one is saying that he was at fault, but there's something going on with that wanker Jones and him and I don't know what. If you ask me, it's only that they're short of gangs that he's not been sacked.'

'Do you think Jones would have the balls to come down and sack a man like that to his face?', responded Gene, not doubting the answer.

'Look, I get what you're saying, but Jones is no pushover either. He's a full-weight wanker alright, but I wouldn't underestimate him. I mean, look at the size of him', replied Fletcher. Jones was watching this exchange from the office window and although he couldn't make what was being said he wanted to observe Danny's response when Fletcher spoke to him. Fletcher and Gene walked towards the waggon and Gene peeled off to get into the cab as Fletcher approached Danny. 'Look Danny, I saw what just happened from yonder', he said nodding his head in the direction of the office, 'so nobody's blaming you, but I've seen men sacked before for fighting no matter who was at fault and you know as I well as I do that the boss man here's an office man, an educated type and that kind of fella'll shit himself with any sign of this rough stuff. I'm not telling you how to go on, just a word to the wise.' Danny nodded his head in silent acknowledgement as he climbed into the waggon.

Jones returned to his desk and sat down. 'What're you going to do? Are you going to tell David? Will he be sacked?', asked Spencer excitedly, but Jones once again ignored him, and Spencer took this as Jones being no more than his usual irascible self and returned to his desk. Jones knew that there must be a way to take advantage of this situation, but he couldn't settle on what this advantage could be. He mulled over his options. David had to be told, that was indisputable. It would be common knowledge soon enough anyway and with this would come a consensus that Greene was acting in self-defence and if one thing was certain it was that Gallon was wary of attracting the disapproval of the men, so it was unlikely that he would use this as a pretext for sacking Greene. Fighting men were respected, there was no doubt about that, and it was inevitable that Greene's stock would rise even further once recent events became public knowledge.

It was clear that the Mulligan's gang were finished at GCE. Their reputation as tough guys was in tatters and they would disappear to lick their wounds and exchange recriminations. Then it occurred to him. These Mulligan's were part of a larger, well-known family who had a reputation to preserve. Many of its members were active on the periphery of semi-organised criminal activity in the city and the use of violence was an everyday practise for them. The unexpected and decisive humbling of two of their members could not be ignored and they would be obliged to deal with the perpetrator lest it be thought their grip on the city was weakening. Perhaps there was something to exploit here, he thought. He didn't know the Mulligans well, but he would have their ear when they brought the waggon back into the yard. If he could escalate the situation, perhaps point them in the right direction, then maybe they could do the job of getting rid of Danny Greene for him. After all, Danny Greene was new to city and, as such, he was stranger the Mulligans. He had to admit that very few men who knew Danny Greene would take the risk of confronting him as they had tried to do. There was a better than good chance that the Mulligans might need some assistance in locating Danny. He smiled and congratulated himself on his tactical nous and returned to his work.

CHAPTER TWENTY

Kate and David were sat the breakfast table in the kitchen. Kate was freshly showered and sipping on a cup of coffee while David was working his way through a brunch of jacket potatoes.

'What time did you get back last night? I didn't hear you come in', he asked.

'It wasn't too late. Rachel was already half-pissed when I arrived, and Diane didn't get here until almost nine thirty which meant that we had to spend half an hour listening to the reasons as to why she was late. Oh', she continued, 'Rachel was admiring the physical virtues of your workers, or at least she began the evening admiring them. She finished it rather weepily, as usual.'

'I don't know why you bother with her', replied David dismissively, 'she seems to finish every evening in tears and it's not that she has a great deal to cry about. Both her and Trevor have great jobs, lovely house, nice kids….Some people seem to enjoy finding something to feel miserable about.'

Kate was pretty much certain that Rachel's marriage was in trouble, but she had resisted the temptation to enquire into this once Diane had arrived.

'She's alright really', replied Kate, feeling a twinge of disloyalty. 'She's under a lot of pressure at work', she continued as she rose from the table and walked to the bottom of the stairs to call Hugh.

Hugh ambled down the stairs wearing only a pair of shorts, hastily pulled on after he had rolled out of bed; his hair, too long at the best of times according to his father, was dishevelled and his eyes were bleary as he sauntered into the kitchen. His mother was standing over the hob. 'Pretty as a picture', she said smiling as he passed her and collapsed onto a chair at the table.

'You're going to have to get used to rolling out of your pit a bit earlier than eleven o'clock', said David, checking his watch. 'I've already done a morning's work and your mother's been out for a run. I don't even think he'll get to the yard on Monday, to be honest', he said looking at Kate.

'He will, won't you lad', she said walking up behind Hugh and tousling his hair affectionately.

'He's a mummy's boy, that's his problem', said David dismissively as he glanced over at them, a twinge of jealousy creeping through his bones as he observed the authenticity of feeling evident in Kate's eyes. He got up and passed his dish to her and walked into the lounge.

'So, what did you get up to last night?'

'Oh, we went to Roger's, then to the Club house, then a few of us went back to Richard's house. We were up pretty late listening to music.'

'Did you meet Jane?'

'No, she had some relatives visiting so she couldn't come out. I'm seeing her this afternoon though.'

'Oh, what're you doing?'

'We're just going down to town. She's got a few things she wants to buy. We'll probably meet up with a few friends later for coffee.'

'Plans for tonight?'

'Nothing, I'll probably just hang around here.'

'Look', she said turning from the hob and sitting down next to him, 'you don't have to do this silly job if you don't want to, you know', she said quietly. 'Don't take any notice of your father. It's not as if he ever got his hands dirty.'

'I know', replied Hugh. 'The fact is, the more I think about it, the more I want to do it. That it's beyond him is one of the reasons why, frankly. 'Mummy's boy', did you hear him?', he said shaking his head in disgust. 'I mean, I know the practical reasons: the money, the fresh air, the physicality of the work, in themselves all good stuff, but it also brings me a bit closer to Grandad, you know, doing what he did, going through what he went through. I know it's not exactly the same, but.....I don't know, he told me so many stories about it and I'm probably never going to get the chance again, what with university and all of that stuff.' Kate looked at him intently and she sighed in witness to the bond that remained between her son and her father. Then she smiled tightly and to his surprise she hugged him, not wanting him to witness the tears that glistened in her eyes.

CHAPTER TWENTY-ONE

'Oh its lovely to be outside', said Cora excitedly as she looked up at Gene who was struggling to negotiate the uneven ground as he pushed her wheelchair through the gate of his allotment garden. 'I wish we could do it more often', she continued, her sallow-skinned face swamped by the thick woollen bobble hat covering her head and the even thicker woollen scarf coiled around her neck.

'Are you sure you're warm enough, love?', he asked walking around the chair and leaning over her to ensure that the blanket covering her legs was properly tucked in despite the fact that, by any measure, it was not a cool day.

'I am, thanks. It was nice of the doctor to agree to my coming out today, wasn't it?'

'Aye, it was', replied Gene flatly. He had resisted the temptation to read too much into the doctor's agreement to today's little excursion. He'd made the request at her bidding, though he didn't expect it to be granted given how weak she had become. The doctor had simply stated that at this stage he couldn't see what harm it would do, providing that she was kept well wrapped up and didn't stay out for too long. She was certainly well enough cocooned as she sat in the wheelchair smiling, peering out from the nest of insulating fabric like a young bird eyeing its surroundings for the first time.

Gene wandered around his small allotment periodically squatting down to more closely inspect the various vegetables growing in the neatly ordered rows of tilled soil and carefully shaped flower beds. He plucked a small bunch of mint and washed it under the free - standing tap located in the corner of the allotment and then offered a small portion of it to Cora. 'I won't love, thanks, but let me smell it'. She reached out and attempted to take the small posy from him. He feared that it would become lost in the thick upholstery of her padded gloves, but she managed to clasp the tiny stems between the thumb and the base of the index finger of her right hand, enough of the leaves emerging to form a small nosegay. She raised the sprigs and inhaled weakly, not taking her eyes away from his. 'Oooh, lovely', she said smiling up at him. 'So fresh! You know my father used to put this down to keep mice out when we were kids'. She sniffed it again as if to underscore the memory. He smiled back at her then turned to the toolbox behind him, fashioned years ago from scrap timber, and pulled out a key from his trouser pocket and unlocked it, retrieving a shovel from within.

Gene took off it his jacket and rolled up the sleeves of his shirt and walked half - way down the length of allotment and started turning the soil over in unhurried sweeps of the shovel. The day was warming up he thought to himself and undid the top few buttons on his shirt revealing tussocks of white chest hair before turning to Cora who was staring at him, a curious expression on her face.

'You alright love?', he asked.

'Here a minute', she said smiling mischievously. He drove the shovel into the soil and turned towards her, asking her if she was too warm as he approached. He stood in front of the wheelchair, hands on hips, waiting for her to speak and she gestured with a slight flick of her head for him to come closer.

'You're still a fine figure of a man you know, Gene', she said in a hushed voice, almost conspiratorial in tone. 'You used to drive me wild, you know', an impish expression illuminating her face as she looked up at him. Gene sent a huge crack of surprised laughter exploding through the warm silence of the summer's morning.

'I know, and you me', he said, still chuckling, then more quietly, 'we were always blessed that way.' They smiled at one another each silently acknowledging the golden secret long nourished within the private enclosures of their matrimony.

CHAPTER TWENTY -TWO

Jane parked her car outside the garage of the Gallon household, got out and rang the doorbell. She was greeted by a smiling Kate.

'Good afternoon Jane. How many times have I told you that you don't need to ring the bell, just come in', she said ushering Jane into the house. 'I'm just getting ready. Sit yourself down, I'll give him a call', and she proceeded up the stairs. Jane walked through into the lounge where David was sat reading a newspaper.

'Hello Jane', he said, managing to infuse a fleeting tone of friendliness into the greeting, despite his irritation at having to struggle to make polite conversation with a barely known adolescent rather than enjoy an uninterrupted moment of peace and quiet.

'What are your plans for today?', he said, turning to face her from his armchair, conspicuously allotting her his attention. His eyes were immediately drawn to her long, tanned legs exposed below her summer shorts before immediately shifting his gaze in a moment of flustered panic, hoping that she hadn't noticed. He coughed lightly.

'Oh, we're just going into town to pick up a few things', she said sensitive to the awkwardness of the of the situation, hoping that Hugh would arrive soon. David didn't immediately follow up.

'What are you and Mrs Gallon got planned, anything interesting?', she asked breaking the heavy silence.

'Oh, nothing too exciting just a round of golf up at the Club and probably a few drinks afterwards', replied David.

'Sounds like fun', she added dutifully. 'Do you play often?' Just as she articulated the final syllable of her question Hugh entered the room and she hurriedly rose to her feet. 'Lovely to see you Mr. Gallon', she said perfunctorily and turned to Hugh. 'Ready?'

'Ready', he replied. Hugh turned to David as he left the lounge, 'see you', he said tersely and walked to the foot of the stairs and with considerably more ebullience shouted up the stairs, 'we're going mum, I'll see you later.'

'You'll have to fend for yourself for supper', came the reply.

'OK, we'll get a pizza.'

'Bye Jane', Kate called down.

'Bye, Mrs Gallon.'

'I hope that I'm not being impolite, but your father isn't the easiest person to talk to, is he? And I'm sure I caught him ogling my legs', said Jane as she pulled out from the Gallon driveway. Hugh looked at her.

'You couldn't be impolite if you tried, Miss Goody Two-Shoes', he said smiling. She raised her arm and slapped him playfully on his thigh, biting on her bottom lip as if to exaggerate the intent. 'I am not a Miss Goody-Two Shoes, and anyway, there's nothing wrong with being polite'. Hugh smiled affectionately.

'You're right about him though. I can't remember the last time I had a conversation with him. I can't remember the last time I *wanted* to have a conversation with him. He's just a blank space around the house, an outline of a man. He *is* annoying though, I'll give him that.'

'But aren't all fathers like that?', said Jane.

'I don't know, but he's got a problem with me, always has had. Even my mum's noticed it. In fact, it became a bit of a problem a few years ago, you know.'

Jane looked at him, a concerned expression on her face. 'What do you mean?', she asked.

'He was just really nasty to me all the time. Finally, one day he said something awful about my grandfather, I can't remember what it was now, and I just snapped and gave him a great wallop on the chin. I mean, I was only a kid, so it didn't do much damage, but I'd wanted to do it for so long. I'll never forget the expression on his face. It was mixture of astonishment and horror. It was quite funny really, when I look back. That brought things to a head. My mum had a long talk with him. I think she threatened to leave him if he didn't stop treating me the way he was.'

'And did things improve after that, I mean with you and him?'

'I suppose so. He wasn't as obvious anyway. I can't say I cared much. Even though I was only kid, he knew that I wasn't scared of him after that and no bully likes to find that out.'

'Oh poor you', she said, rubbing his knee affectionately

'Oh, it's not like that', replied Hugh smiling. 'It's just me, it's in my genes. I just won't sit back and let these bullies hold sway. I can't. I like to think of it as a gift from my grandfather. He was the same.'

'So, we're back to genes again, eh?' she said, a note of exasperation in her voice.

'Not today', he replied smiling. 'I think I've made my point already.'

Jane parked the car on the top tier of the multi - story car park in the centre of town and they got out and walked towards the stairway which would take them down to the mall. As they were approaching the stairway three lads of around Hugh's age were emerging from the top of the stairs laughing boisterously and rough housing amongst themselves. He glanced at them briefly but didn't pay them much attention. Jane didn't appear to notice them at all. She was preoccupied with her prospective purchases and was busy discussing these with Hugh as the rowdy little crew passed them, a little too closely sensed Hugh given the size of the car park. As they got behind them one of group barked out, 'look at the arse on that!', their proximity clearly indicating that they were referring to Jane. Hugh spun around instinctively.

'What did you say?', he asked angrily, his eyes scanning the group, unsure of exactly who had made the remark. They turned to face him as one. The tallest of three glanced briefly at his companion to his left and turned back to Hugh.

'Fuck off wanker', he snarled before spitting on the ground and turning once again to his friends, grinning inanely.

Hugh bristled and made to take a step towards the lout, but Jane reached out and grabbed him by the arm. 'Come on Hugh, don't get involved with these people', she said anxiously. 'Let's go.'

'These people? These people? Who the fuck do you think you are?', said the tall kid, feigning indignation before once again turning to his friends for confirmation of the righteousness of his protest.

'Come on Hugh', said Jane, tugging on his arm, growing increasingly concerned at the turn of events.

'Do what the bitch says wanker, fuck off', his tone now carrying a hard snap of aggression. His companions too had braced themselves and stared directly at Hugh buoyed up by the aggression of their leader.

Behind his impassive expression Hugh was silently weighing up the opposition. The kid doing the talking was around Hugh's height, but he had arms like strands of spaghetti and his ears were wider apart than his shoulders. One of the wing men had a sturdy build, but he wouldn't return Hugh's glare, immediately signalling to Hugh that his heart was not in the confrontation. The third member of the group had barely taken his eyes of the tall kid. He was the target audience for the performance, a sycophant just along for the ride who didn't present a real threat. Hugh turned to face Jane and put his arm on her shoulder and turning her gently in the direction of the stairwell, they both walked away.

'Oh my God', said Jane in a hushed voice, 'what morons!'

'Yeah, go on ladies. See you later', shouted the tall kid by way of farewell. Hugh could hear them guffawing loudly as they continued on their way.

'I'm really proud of you Hugh, not rising to the bait', she said, smiling and wrapped her arm around his waist and gently squeezing it by way of reiteration.

'I'm so glad you took on board what I said the other day.' She looked up at him expecting him to acknowledge the compliment. His expression hadn't changed; his hard, fixed countenance breaking into a weak smile only when he became aware that she was looking at him. They got to the head of the stairs and started their descent.

'Look', he said, 'I think I've left the car window open on my side. Pass me the keys, I'd better go close it with those idiots in the vicinity.'

She looked at him, an alarmed expression on her face. 'Don't go back up there Hugh, they'll only start again.'

'They've had their fun', he replied smiling. 'They were only doing it to impress you anyway. Look, I'll meet you at the bottom of the stairs. If I'm not there in twenty-four hours, call out a posse', he said. 'They'll be gone by now anyway', he added by way of further reassurance.

'OK', she said not entirely convinced, 'but don't do anything silly.' She passed him the car keys and he tucked them into his pocket and turned towards the way he had come. 'I'll wait here', she said, 'in case you need me.'

'What? You're going to wait in this urine stinking stairwell? People will think that you're up to no good', he replied. She smiled in acknowledgement of his point and turned to walk down the stairs.

As soon as she was out of sight he sprinted up to the top of the staircase, his eyes scouring the car park for the three miscreants. Almost immediately he spotted them: two were leant against a dilapidated, rust-bitten car which Hugh judged to belong to the oldest and tallest of the group now standing in front of his friends going through the specifics of his recent triumph. Hugh strode towards them. 'Well, well, here he is again', said the tall kid. His companions turned to look in Hugh's direction. Hugh increased his pace imperceptibly, but he didn't rush. As he approached, the standing figure stiffened and turned his body square on to Hugh, his face twisting into a noiseless snarl. 'So you want more, do.......'

He didn't finish his question. Hugh brought a right hook to bear on the side of his face, a sharp crack like a slab of meat hitting a butcher's block reverberated around the car park. His head twisted unnaturally, and he fell to the ground, unconscious before he hit the tarmac. Hugh turned to the other two, still reclining against the side of the vehicle, their eyes wide, their mouths agape. He landed an uppercut on the sturdy-looking kid which sent him sprawling backwards across the bonnet of the car before sliding onto the ground whimpering like a lonely dog. Hugh glared silently at the third member of this disappointed party. 'Look mate, I didn't say anything. I wasn't involved. I told them......' he pleaded.

'Fuck. off. Now', said Hugh and the third young man edged his way along the side of the car not wanting to cross Hugh's path.

'No wait', demanded Hugh, 'get me his car keys'.

The kid fumbled frantically in his prone friend's pocket. 'I think you've hurt him, you know. He's not moving', he said looking up at Hugh, his voice quivering with fear.

'Give me the fucking keys', barked Hugh ignoring his concerns. He handed them to Hugh, trying to stay out of striking range, an anxious expression painted onto his face. Hugh took the keys from him and hurled them over the kid's head and turned back towards the stairwell. As he walked, he felt a burgeoning euphoria, his entire body fizzed with a strange elation and he had to stifle a nervous laugh. He composed himself within three strides and descended the stairwell to meet Jane.

CHAPTER TWENTY-THREE

Frankie and Jenny entered 'The Harp' hand-in-hand. The ranks of daytime drinkers were beginning to thin-out and were being replaced by the more smartly dressed evening crowd, the men freshly shaven and trailing odours of high street cologne, the women coloured with bright shades of cosmetics on faces framed by carefully coiffured hair. The music spilling from the juke box filled the room with a lively, brash mood, nicely setting the tone of the evening ahead. Jenny was working this evening and she took her place behind the bar and served Frankie with a drink. 'I'll be keeping my eye on you mister, so you'd better behave', she said playfully, but both silently recognised the grain of truth embedded in her light-hearted caution. 'You've got me all wrong, you know Jenny', he said in mock indignation and turned to survey the room as she continued with her work. He was gratified that she recognised his appeal to other women, that she would not be tempted to take him for granted.

He spotted a customer known to all as 'The Professor' sat alone against the backrest reading his newspaper. 'The Professor' had been a regular patron of the pub for as long as anyone could remember and, all things being equal, he had occupied the same seat in the tap room every day for the past thirty years largely by virtue of the fact that he was usually the first customer of the day. He had been tall as a young man but had now become somewhat stooped as the passing years weighed down upon him. He had a high forehead beneath which sat a pair of rheumy eyes which would nonetheless still sparkle with enthusiasm when he set about declaiming on a subject close to his heart. On his sharply hooked nose sat the wreckage of a pair of National Health spectacles, the left arm of which was attached to the frame by means of a pink sticking plaster. He was carefully dressed, but his clothes were threadbare and in need of replacement.

The Professor had made his peace with his alcoholism many years previously and had learned to satisfy the demands of his dependency by way of an occupational pension which was supplemented by an annuity from a sister he rarely saw. He had acquired the nickname by virtue of his former employment as a teacher at the local grammar school. It was rumoured that he had been forced into early retirement decades earlier for reasons not unrelated to his fondness for the drink, but this did not affect his standing in the pub where he was held in high regard as a result of the breadth of his knowledge, despite the fact that the taproom of 'The Harp' public house was not a venue generally noted for its appreciation of learning and scholarship.

He was a kind - hearted and friendly man who, despite a once formidable intelligence now somewhat frayed around the edges, never spoke down to the less educated among his friends and acquaintances in the pub. So, in addition to the respect of his fellow patrons, he could also rely on their affection.

Frankie walked over and sat down next to him.

'Jesus Christ, it's a bit late later to be reading the paper now, no? That's as a good as yesterday's news.'

'And hello to you too', said The Professor smiling as he peered over the rim of his spectacles. 'As a matter of fact, I am completing the crossword and the newspaper I think is two weeks old', he said lowering his glasses and bringing the newspaper up to his eyes to more thoroughly inspect the date.

'How are you Mr. The Professor?', said Frankie archly, rising to his feet and bowing slightly correcting his previous lack of manners.

'Oh, I'm nearly as good as I was before I got worse', replied The Professor with his stock response. How was your week?'.

'That gobshite Mick jacked on Monday', replied Frankie resuming his seat, 'but we've got a new lad with us, a better man all together.'

'So I've heard. Danny Greene, isn't it?'

'You know him?'

'Yes, I do, somewhat. I haven't seen him around for a long, long time though. I hear he took a bit of a dislike to a couple of the Mulligans today.'

'He didn't have much choice in the matter.'

'Chaps like him seldom do. He saved my bacon many years ago, actually. He was only a lad then, but he was a big, strapping thing even in his youth. I knew his father a bit too. He was a mean piece of work that one, but obviously the lad survived him. He left city over some woman, or so I was told. I don't take much notice of gossip myself', he said raising his nose slightly as if to avoid an unpleasant smell, allowing himself this small gesture of haughtiness.

Frankie smiled indulgently. The Professor was well-known as a font of news and rumour in the taproom of 'The Harp'.

'He seems like a sound enough bloke to me despite the tales you hear. I'm surprised you haven't seen him. He's got digs upstairs you know.'

'The tales? Oh, his fighting exploits, you mean. I would imagine that now he has matured into a perfect specimen of the *viri pugnator*.'

'The very what?', asked Frankie, a confused expression of his face.

'Its Latin for 'fighting man', replied The Professor, 'the epitome, the quintessence, the exemplar of the male of the species. The warrior, the gladiator, the brave, you know. The man whose reason for being is to fight. The man who won't be cowed or mastered.'

'Oh', replied Frankie. 'You mean a tough guy? There's plenty of those around or plenty that think they are anyway. I suppose that there's no harm in being able to look after yourself.'

'There's always harm in it, otherwise what'd be the point? It's about the distribution of harm, is it not?', asked The Professor.

Frankie peered at him, not quite getting his point. 'I judge a man by what I see and hear. He saved Gene from getting a hiding the other day and that's good enough for me. I've no interest in that fighting nonsense anyway, unless I've no choice in the matter.'

'Ah, and that's the rub', replied The Professor, folding his newspaper and placing it on the table before him, clearly warming to his theme.'

'We all have the choice.'

'What the fuck are you talking about?', replied Frankie smiling sceptically as he raised his pint to his lips.

'Of course, we all find ourselves in disagreeable situations from time to time where we have the option of using violence to defend ourselves and yet decline to do so, either because we don't have the skills or we're just too afraid or we disagree in principle with the use of force......there are a hundred reasons why we might not fight when we're given a choice in the matter, but the thing is, we are always given the choice to bring into play something that's already within us, something that's part and parcel of what we are as human beings. The option is available.'

'We all have what in us? An appetite for fighting? I know plenty of men who have none of it', replied Frankie dismissively 'and as I said, I haven't much of it myself.'

'Not the appetite so much as the capacity. Oh, it's more easily tapped into by some than by others, I'll grant you that, but it's never so deeply buried that its lost in anyone. We all have it to a greater or lesser degree is what I'm saying. And I don't just mean men either.'

'Now you're talking shite', said Frankie. 'How often do you see women fighting?'

The Professor looked at him askance.

'OK, it depends what pub you go in to,' replied Frankie laughing, recalling the recent fracas between Mary and Jenny. 'But you can't be saying that women have an appetite for the rough stuff like men have.'

'I'm not saying that. I'm saying that they have an instinct towards it just as men have, perhaps not as pronounced, but it's still there. You can find the sweetest, most placid girl in the world, but if she turns around to see some lunatic with hands around her child's throat, she'd be on him like a savage beast, just like that', he said clicking his fingers. 'It's just under the surface, you see.'

'But how often will that happen?', countered Frankie.

'More often than we'd probably like to know', replied The Professor, 'but that's not the point. Don't get me wrong, I'm not trying to say that all men and all women are prone to violence, of course not. I'm just saying that its always an option for all of us, an option that thankfully, for all sorts of reasons, is not generally taken. Society civilises us, well, most of us anyway. We've developed other ways of dealing with conflict. Or we think we have. How many wars are going on at the moment? How many people are engaged in acts of violence as we speak? All I'm saying is that capacity for violence is lurking in us all just waiting for the right circumstances to express itself. And just as its more pronounced in men than it is in women, its more pronounced in some men than in others, and sometimes we should be grateful for it, I mean, look at the situation with Gene.

It's what we are as men. Our hormones dictate it. It's written into every cell in our bodies. But as I said, we do have the element of choice, in most cases anyway. The way that we're brought up can make a big difference in how we make those choices. Look at Danny. From what I remember of his father, Danny Greene will have been dragged up and no doubt the father's example would've steered him in a direction of the father's making, but there's more to it. He is his father's son and he no doubt inherited his father's appetite and ability for the fight. Always just beneath the surface, you see. With you, with me, with most, men, it's buried a little deeper, but it's always there.

Today Danny had a choice. He could have run for cover, he could have begged and pleaded. Enough men do, but for them the *viri pugnator* is buried deep. You should bear in mind that for most of human history this is something that has been admired in a man, but not so much today, well, not so much outside of the world of the working man.'

'Jesus Christ, you do have some theories, don't you? So, at the back of it all, what you're saying is that some people like to fight and some don't. You've gone a long way around the houses to say that.'

'What I'm saying is that some people *have* to fight, and sometimes that's not a bad thing. Frankie looked at him, nonplussed.

The Professor smiled indulgently sensing that he had taken his theorising as far as he could. He was about to return to his glass when he saw Mick staggering towards their table, perspiring and bedraggled, clearly drunk.

The Professor nodded towards him to indicate his approach and Frankie turned.

'Fucking hell, look at the state of this', Frankie muttered under his breath.

'How are you now lads?', garbled Mick. 'I hear the Mulligans are going to knock the fuck out of your new man', he advised before belching loudly, 'so you might need me back after all.'

'Spent up Mick?', asked Frankie, ignoring his reference to Danny.

'It's not me, its them fucking horses, them bookies', he replied, shaking his head in disgust.

'Well, we're OK for the time being, thank you', replied Frankie, his tone perfunctory. 'Anyway, what've the Mulligans got to do with anything? It's not like you to go telling tales', he said, winking at The Professor. 'Do you want me to give Danny a shout so you can tell him personally like?'

123

'Look, don't be involving me. It's nothing to do with me', Mick replied hastily, raising his palms to them both and backing away from the table, 'I'm only passing on what I've heard', and turned to stagger off back to where he had come from.

'He's a fucking weasel, that man', said Frankie. 'We only had him in the gang because there was no one else around.'

'That wife of his isn't much better. I could tell you some tales about her, if I was that kind of man, I mean', replied The Professor.

'Pint?', offered Frankie, holding up his empty glass.

'Have you ever known me to refuse?', replied The Professor smiling.

The thrum of conversation was growing, punctuated by outbursts of laughter that ricocheted around the room and then dissolved back into the thick edgeless clatter from which they came. Frankie made his way to the bar, nudging his way through the densely packed crowd of customers toing and froing around the service area, acknowledging acquaintances as he went. Finally, he attracted Jenny's attention and placed his order. As he leant against the bar he glanced around the room and was taken aback to see Jones walking through the door accompanied by two surly looking companions, neither of whom Frankie recognised. He had never seen Jones in 'The Harp' before and his presence there tonight did not bode well for someone. He had heard mention of where the man usually did his drinking but this was in a pub at the other side of city, a more upscale area which Frankie did not frequent. His train of thought was suddenly interrupted by Mick who arrived next to him at the bar and once again tried to engage Frankie in conversation, rambling incoherently, but Frankie ignored him, his attentions focused on the unwelcome presence in their midst.

He averted his eyes and turned his back to the door hoping that Jones wouldn't spot him, all the while monitoring his lumbering progress through the reflection in the mirror behind the bar. Jones pushed his way through the crowd, his companions following in his wake. Occasionally, a disgruntled customer would turn angrily to confront him as he barged past but would quickly lower their eyes or smile uncomfortably when confronted by Jones' stern expression and awful bulk. Jenny returned with his drinks and Frankie took them from her and quickly returned to his table not wishing to get involved in conversation with the man, leaving Mick muttering to himself as he counted change, his palm raised inches from his eyes to compensate for his impaired vision, a usual by-product of his drunkenness.

Jones caught sight of Mick as he approached the bar. 'How are you Michael?', he said joylessly, crashing his hand down onto his shoulder, causing him to wince in pain. As his palm landed, he slid Mick to one side creating space for him to install himself at the bar. The coins splashed out of Mick's hand and fell to the floor as he was manhandled out of Jones' way. Mick lowered himself onto one knee and began trying to corral the escaping coinage as if his life depended on it. Despite his drunkenness, it didn't take him long to retrieve his errant coins and he clambered back to his feet.

'I'm well Colm how are you? Can I get you a pint?', he asked, smiling uncomfortably. Jones ordered his drink, disregarding Mick's offer, and scanned the room. 'Have you seen Frankie', he asked glancing down at Mick as if he were a recently deposited puddle of animal waste.

'Yes, yes. He's over there with The Professor', replied Mick, nodding in the direction of the men.

Jones' drinks arrived and he passed them to his companions and used his thumb to indicate where he was going. He trundled over to the table, colliding with other patrons with complete indifference, causing drinks to slosh over the rims of glasses and to splash onto carefully ironed clothing. He presented himself in front of Frankie and The Professor silently waiting for them to acknowledge his presence amongst them.

'How are you?', said Frankie after a moment or two, smiling unenthusiastically, and Jones took this greeting as an invitation to insert his bulk into the narrow gap between the two men, almost swamping The Professor as he lowered himself down onto the seat in his lumpen, ungainly way. His took a moment to arrange his frame, his back turned to The Professor, completely disregarding him. The Professor, his conversation with Frankie now brought to a premature close, had to edge his way further down the seat to accommodate this unwelcome mass and having done so he glared indignantly at the expanse of Jones' back and then mouthed the words 'wanker' to Frankie over Jones' shoulder. Frankie struggled to disguise a smirk in response to The Professor's uncharacteristic use of profanity.

'Now then Frankie, as we both know, we had a bit of bother in the yard today, did we not?', asked Jones in an oily, patronising tone.

'Aye, we did indeed. You're getting some awful thugs in that yard these days, you should be more careful about who you set on', replied Frankie unperturbed by Jones' looming presence. 'Lucky the man was able to defend himself.'

'Lucky?', replied Jones, a surprised tone in his voice. 'Yes, I suppose it was.....', he replied thoughtfully. 'Now, as you said, the man was only defending himself and of course every man has a right to do that, but a word to the wise. You know I like to keep a happy ship down there', he said smiling thinly and attempting to adopt the tone of the caring, benevolent employer, and failing. 'Now I've heard that some of them Mulligans might be looking for some kind of payback against your mate and I'd hate them rolling up at the yard looking for him, could make us look very bad if the wrong people were there, you know, council officials, other contractors, that kind of thing.' Any pretence at benevolence was quickly jettisoned and a sinister look came over the vast expanse of Jones' face. He looked down at the table as he spun the ash tray giving Frankie a few moments to absorb the gravity of his concerns, 'Look', he said holding up his hands, 'it makes no difference to me if a man wants to fight, I mean, I've done my fair share of it', he said, an indulgent smile now warming his face, 'but if they were going looking for him, the yard is where they'd come and it becomes a problem for GCE. And from what I hear, they *are* looking for him', he said with emphasis.

'What are you saying, that he ought to stay out of the yard? Jack his job? Get out of city?', said Frankie feigning indignation.

'Not at all!', replied Jones indignantly, 'perish the thought! Who am I to tell a man what to do or where to go? I mean, all things considered it would probably be the best thing to do, considering the alternative, but that's none of my affair. I mean, he hasn't had much luck in this city historically speaking, now has he?', he said tapping his eyelid, 'and he is a long distance man after all, what would moving to another city mean to him when there's a bunch of animals like the Mulligans on the prowl. But, you know, it's up to him. Just a word to the wise, that's all. In the interests of a happy ship.'

'Why are you telling me this?', asked Frankie, 'why don't you tell him yourself?'

126

'Oh, its no big deal you know, we were in here for a pint and I saw you. Just thought you might want to know. You know I like to help out the good gangs if I can. Just doing my bit, that's all. Just trying to help out. I mean, I'd want to know if those thugs were looking for me. Dangerous men you know those Mulligans. They wouldn't be satisfied with just a punch or two and with him only having just the one bulb already…....'

With that Jones rose to his feet, his pint glass disappearing into the pink fleshy mass of his hand, and he made his way back to the bar where his associates were waiting for him. He chatted briefly with them, nodding at Frankie as if to identify him, and they then drained their glasses and made for the door.

'Now he's a bad lot', said The Professor turning to Frankie with a look of disdain, 'always has been. He gave me a right thumping years ago for no discernible reason other than he knew he could. Obviously, he believes that you're going to go running with this news to Danny Greene, but if he wants rid of him, which clearly he does, why doesn't he just sack him? You don't need to be involved.'

'I know', replied Frankie starting to feel a little unnerved at Jones' choice of messenger boy.

'Look', continued The Professor sensing Frankie's unease, 'one thing is for certain: if Jones is up to something then he will inevitably make a balls of it. The man made a fundamental commitment to stupidity many years ago, and it's a deal he can't get out of. He'll show his hand soon enough, don't worry about that.'

'Aye, that's what's got me thinking. Somethings not right', replied Frankie and sat back in his seat while The Professor got up and went to the bar. He'd known Jones since he arrived in city, but this was the first time that they'd ever spoken outside of work. He couldn't get to the bottom of it. If Jones wanted a man gone then he'd just sack him, there'd be no compunction or hesitation. Jones enjoyed sacking men. There was something else going on, he thought, but whatever it was Jones was clearly keeping it to himself, but it spelt trouble for whomever was involved in his plans, and that now included him.

CHAPTER TWENTY- FOUR

Kate and David were sat in the lounge of the local golf Club, the centre of their social life, a comfortable and well - appointed room richly decorated in a slightly outdated suburban style which nonetheless satisfied the suburban expectations of its affluent members. They were accompanied by Kate's friend, Rachel, and her husband, Trevor, and another couple, Clive and Ruth, and had recently returned to the club after dining at one of the more expensive restaurants in the city. Clive was a senior official at the local highways authority, a man whose favour David was keen to secure. Indeed, this was the latest in a series of lavish dinners that Clive and his wife had enjoyed at David's expense. All six had consumed a large amount of wine at dinner which had camouflaged Clive's almost total lack of social skills with a general mood of artificial conviviality and bonhomie. He had proven himself to be a pompous and self-regarding man and had dominated the conversation for most of the evening sharing tedious anecdotes of his and Ruth's recent holiday in America, a trip for which David had provided the airline tickets.

As the evening wore on Clive was working his way through his store of risqué jokes, a gambit he would not have considered less than two hours ago before the wine had dissolved the usual rules of decorum, and he was veering awkwardly into the vulgar and juvenile. He was in the midst of one such story when Trevor protested, taking exception of the coarseness of his language. David rose to the defence of his newly acquired friend despite the fact that Kate, Rachel and Ruth had all expressed similar disapproval at different points over the course of the evening. In the face of these slurred protests Clive bowed to the collective will and retreated into what he believed, in his wine drenched state, to be a less controversial tale told with the enthusiasm of a man now fully believing himself to be the star of the group. 'An Englishman, an Irishman and a Scotsman......', he began with gusto. A collective groan went up from the assembled company.

'You can't be serious', protested Kate, 'in this day and age you're making jokes about thick Irishmen and stingy Scotsmen? Notice how the Englishman always turns out to be the hero, eh?', she observed glancing round the table and nodding in agreement with her own insight.

'You know, the Irish only got that reputation because the English closed all their schools, Catholic schools. Deprived them of an education', continued Kate authoritatively.

'Don't talk rubbish. We closed all their schools because they were too thick to make use of them', Clive retorted, guffawing and looking to Trevor and Rachel for confirmation. Trevor grinned uncomfortably and made a stab at changing the subject, but Clive was now fixed on mining the theme, indignant at Kate's combative response, and wanting to antagonise her further.

'Ok, there might be an odd one or two with brains but look at the bulk of them, a spade in one hand and a pint of Guinness in the other; that's all they're interested in. What else do they need to know? I mean, you only need to look at the navvies digging around our city, they all look like escaped convicts', he continued, as if that settled the matter. Kate glared at David, her brow furrowed, urging him to respond.

'It's actually called a shovel; a spade is used for gardening', David pointed out weakly, failing to satisfy Kate's unspoken demand for solidarity.

'Spade, shovel, who cares?', said Clive dismissively, 'they're all as thick as pig shit anyway.' Kate was having no more of this, her indignation peaked.

'You should know that more Irish writers have won the Nobel prize for literature than any other country, apart from the US anyway. Since the English stopped interfering, they have one of the best education systems in the world', she said in deep earnest. 'Perhaps you should learn your facts before you start spouting your ignorant nonsense', she said angrily.

'Steady on love', replied Clive patronisingly, 'nobody likes a mouthy woman. Tell her to be quiet David, men are talking', and once again he rocked with laughter.

'You, Clive, are an ass', said Kate baldly, looking directly at him, 'an uneducated ass at that.' Clive fell silent and his eyes narrowed into a malevolent glare.

'And you're a gobby mare', he replied, his voice hissing with bitterness. Trevor quickly rose to his feet seeing that matters were quickly getting out of control and held out his hands.

'Look we've all had a bit too much to drink', he said in attempt to draw the poison from the conversation, 'let's just all calm down, eh?' David muttered in agreement. Then he turned to Kate. 'I can't believe your attitude', he hissed under this breath. 'This man can put a lot of money GCE's way'. He then turned back to face Clive. 'Look, I'm sorry about her behaviour. It's the wine. Affects her that way.'

Kate glared at David and rose to her feet, her face flushed with indignation and red wine. 'This man calls your wife a 'gobby mare' and you *apologise* to him?', she said, deeply affronted. 'If it'd been your father sat there, he'd be nursing a bloody nose by now', she said angrily and grabbed her coat, turned and strode towards the exit. As she reached the door, she turned as if to return, but as if in a moment of self-restraint instead turned back to the door.

'Well, I don't know what I said wrong', said Clive, 'I was just trying to cheer everyone up with a few jokes. She hasn't got much of a sense of humour your wife, has she?', he asked, looking at David. 'Is she that touchy all the time?'.

'Her parents were Irish', said Rachel tersely. 'Mine aren't and I still think that she was right. You are an ass Clive', and she got up from her chair and followed Kate out of the door, catching up to her in the car park.

'Are you alright?', she asked when she reached Kate.

'Yes, I'm fine. It's him. He's just so weak, such a bloody coward', she said angrily and shook her head in frustration. If that ignoramus would've said any of that in front of my father......'

'Clive's an oaf, but really Kate, is that the way you want your husband to resolve disagreements with ill-informed bigots, by punching them?', replied Rachel earnestly, her middle-class sensibilities coming to the fore.

'You're right. I know', Kate replied resignedly, 'but sometimes I just want to see him be a man. All my father would've had to do was just look at him in that way that he had, and Clive would have shrivelled up. It's not about winning an argument, or persuading someone that they've said something inappropriate, well maybe sometimes it is, but do you think that an ass like Clive would've cared about being disapproved of? He certainly didn't bother him earlier on in the evening. I saw it with my father, the way other men responded to him. He could charm the birds out of the trees if he wanted to, but they knew he was not going to tolerate any bullshit.

No, it's about respect and with men, and a lot of that, not all, I'm not saying all, but a lot of it has to do with fear, the fear of aggression. They're just different to us. Clive would not have dared to tell that stupid joke if an Irish man had been there. He wouldn't have dared tell that joke if any of the men it was directed at were there because he knows that they would've punched him between the two eyes. He said it because he knew he could get away with it. He knew he was offending me, and he was trying to wind me up. He's a bully, simple as that. I feel sorry for his wife. And David just sat wittering on about spades! If a man can't stick up for himself, what good is he to himself? What good is he to a wife?'.

'Well, what did I say, very thin-skinned these Irish. The half-Irish are even worse, don't know whether they're coming or going, eh David? Must make married life fun, eh?', continued Clive guffawing loudly and roughly grabbing David's shoulder and shaking it as if to emphasise his good humour and bonhomie. David smiled weakly and shifted in his seat uncomfortably, 'As I said, it's just the wine. She gets a bit cantankerous after a few glasses of the stuff.'

CHAPTER TWENTY-FIVE

Monday morning arrived and Hugh was waiting for his father in the kitchen as he sat down for breakfast. They ate their food in a silence which continued as they pulled into the yard and Hugh jumped out of the car and waited for his father to alight before accompanying up the stairs and into the office. David sat down behind his desk and nodded in Jones' direction.

'This'll be the man who's looking after you', he said and proceed to unlock a drawer in his desk and pull out a ledger.

Jones immediately dropped what he was doing and rose to greet Hugh, his hand held out and a huge smile emblazoned across his face. Hugh was taken aback by Jones' mountainous size and by the enthusiasm of his greeting.

'Hello Hugh', he bellowed, 'I've heard a lot about you. A very clever young man, this one here', he continued, directing his compliment to the site agents sat in the office. He turned his attention back to Hugh. 'First things first, would you like a cup of coffee?', he asked solicitously. Hugh accepted the offer and Jones turned to the kettle sat on a small table below the widow. Out of the corner of his eye, Hugh noted the surprised looks on the faces of the agents at Jones' offer. Clearly, he wasn't in the habit of running around after his subordinates. Jones passed a cup of steaming coffee to Hugh.

'Your father has probably told you already, but you'll be going out with a snagging gang today. It's a steady introduction to the work. You'll be with a couple of experienced men, and they'll give you an idea as to what goes on here. You just sit down and finish your coffee and I'll let you know when they get in.'

Jones turned and went out onto the gantry. Spencer, the young site agent, waited until he was out of the door and dashed across the office to sit in Jones' chair rocking back and forth proprietorially, as if testing out its comfort for the day it would be his. Spencer was Jones' nephew and Jones had recruited him as a favour to his sister who knew enough of her son to recognise that, in the absence of his long-since absconded father, Spencer was disaster - bound without the presence of a controlling male influence. Fortunately for Spencer though, Jones had done little more for him than provide him with a paying job and had completely lost any interest he may have entertained in the idea of attempting to shape his nephew's character. As Spencer languished in Jones' chair Fletcher glanced up at him from the paperwork he was occupied with.

'I wouldn't let him catch you in that seat, uncle or no uncle', he remarked dismissively and turned his attention back to his work. Spencer leapt from the chair immediately, evidencing his anxiety at the prospect of Jones' wrath and flushing slightly at the abruptness of his response to Fletcher's warning.

'How come you're doing this then? Is your Dad making you do it?', he asked quickly turning his attention to Hugh in an attempt to disguise his embarrassment.

'No', replied Hugh, 'I want to do it.'

'Bloody hell', replied Spencer, 'you might change your mind by the end of the shift', then after a moments pause, 'you might change your mind by dinner time', he said laughing. 'But you're only out with the snagging gang. That's not too bad'. Hugh bridled at his use of the word 'only'. While he accepted that his inexperience imposed limits on what he was able to do, he was slightly embarrassed to find himself at the nursery end of the work.

'Have you been on the tools?', asked Hugh.

'No fucking way', replied Spencer without hesitation, 'and I've no plans of doing it either. They work like bloody animals those lads, out in all weathers. No chance. I'm training as a site agent, me. At the moment, I just go out marking up the underground utilities for the lads. It's alright. Steady enough.'

Jones reappeared at the door of the office and Spencer scurried back to his desk.

'They're down in the yard', he said smiling warmly at Hugh. 'Come on down with me, I'll introduce you.' The yard was in its usual state of barely restrained chaos and Jones and Hugh threaded their way to where Gary had pulled up his waggon to load materials for the day's work.

'Gary, this is Hugh, the lad I mentioned last week. He'll be going out with you today. He hasn't done much of this before, so you might have to show him the ropes, but he's a strong young fella so he won't be a dead weight, isn't that right Hugh?'.

Gary looked at Hugh silently as if weighing him up and then went on with his work not looking directly at either Jones or Hugh.

133

'You can load a dozen or so of them onto the back of the waggon', he said flatly, gesturing towards some fittings with a nod of his head. As Hugh walked off to retrieve the required items Gary turned to Jones.

'What if he's a waste of time, how long do we have to carry him?'.

'If you want my opinion, I don't think that he'll last the week out. I don't even know why he's here', replied Jones in hushed tones.

'Well, we'll see soon enough. If he slows us down then you'll have to find him another gang', said Gary curtly.

'Sure', said Jones, recognising that if Hugh couldn't keep up with a snagging gang then he certainly couldn't keep up with any of the others. He turned and headed off in the direction of the office.

Hugh threw the fittings into the back of the waggon and stood by the door not entirely sure of what to do next.

'Do you need me to get anything else?', he asked, trying to convey his enthusiasm without coming across like an over eager kid.

'Hop in the van', said Gary gruffly, which he did. Steve, the third man in the gang, clambered in next to him. They negotiated an exit from the yard to the sound of Gary mumbling complaints as to the lack of organisation and system. Hugh was to discover that his grumbling was a regular feature of their departure protocol over the forthcoming days.

Once clear of the yard Gary fell silent which Hugh found disconcerting. It occurred to him that the lack of conversation might be a result of Gary's ill-humour at his forced inclusion into the gang. This observation further increased Hugh's discomfort. After twenty minutes or so of this silence Gary suddenly began talking as if he were resuming an earlier conversation. 'I used to work with your grandfather you know, long before all this cable TV carry on, oh, thirty – odd years ago when I was young and fit. He was a man out on his own, that lad. Some boyo altogether', he said chuckling to himself. 'We worked for a bloke called Jack Bundy, he's long gone now of course', he paused for a moment as if in respect for the memory of the long dead Bundy.

'Aye, they were the good times alright', he concluded wistfully, the memories of his youth now having all the characteristics of a dream to him. He had conducted the entire monologue without once looking at Hugh.

'Really? I'd be interested to know more about that, you know, those days. I got on really well with my grandfather. He was never short of a tale or two', replied Hugh eagerly. For the first time that morning Gary looked directly at Hugh and smiled.

'You can say that again. More tales than the Brothers Grim and some of them almost true as well', he said smiling. 'We sank a few pints together me and Joe. Oh I could tell you plenty of tales about Joe alright. He was some boyo', repeated Gary as he silently berated himself for his lack of goodwill towards his old friend's kin. 'Over a pint one day, eh?'

'Sounds good to me', replied Hugh. They travelled for another couple of miles without further conversation, the frigid silence of earlier now replaced by one less chilled.

'OK, this is it', said Gary pulling the waggon into the side of the road. 'Right lad, you can start unloading the pedestrian barriers from the back of the waggon.'

Hugh opened the door and leapt out. Steve pulled the door closed behind him and turned to Gary.

'What was all that about Joe Hanlon? I didn't know that you were mates with him', he said, his surprise evident. 'The guy was an absolute gobshite', he continued, 'you wouldn't trust him as far as you could throw him. I even heard The Heifer was a half-decent kid before he started working with him.'

'I know that he pulled a few strokes', replied Gary mounting a defence.

'A few dirty strokes', interrupted Steve.

'He wasn't everybody's cup of tea, fair enough, but he never did me any wrong and even at his worst you can't go blaming him for Jones. That man was a bollocks the day he was born. Hanlon was a tricky fellow alright, but he was great craic in the pub.'

'All I'm saying is that I heard some bad things about the man', continued Steve, indicating a settled opinion reconfirmed upon review.

'Well, you might want to keep what you heard to yourself. Remember his grandson, that young lad out there, is the gaffer's lad.'

'I'm no gossip', said Steve in conclusion, opened the door and exited the waggon.

'What are we going to be doing?', Hugh asked Steve as he stacked the barriers on the footpath.

'Oh, we haven't much to do here. There's a blockage in one of the pipes under the grass verge there so we'll find out where it is and dig down to it. We might have to replace a length of it yet, we'll see. You can make a start by putting out the road signs there, the man at work and the road narrow, oh, and put a couple of cones around the waggon. Gary took the top layer of grass off the verge and stacked the sods by the side of the excavation.

'We'll put these back on top when we're done', he said to Hugh. 'You can start digging down until you hit the duct.' Hugh pushed the shovel into the soil and jabbed the underside of his boot onto the shoulder of the blade to drive it into the ground and then tried to lever it up in an attempt to scoop out the soil. Gary took the shovel off him, chortling.

'You are green, aren't you? Watch me', he said. He sat the edge of the blade on the surface of the soil and pushed down onto the shoulder with his foot. 'You don't need to jab at it, just put your weight down and push through', and he passed the shovel to Hugh and returned to the waggon.

'Fucking hell, he's taken a shine to you boy', said Steve chortling as he joined Hugh, 'he'd normally run a fella off the job for that kind of performance.'

'We've all got to start somewhere I suppose, haven't we?', replied Hugh in mitigation.

'Aye, my father had me out when I was twelve years old, could hardly pick the shovel up never mind use it!'

'You were only twelve? Bloody hell!'

'Aye, had me fetching and carrying until I was strong enough to do a bit of proper labouring.'

'What about school? Surely it was against the law to have someone of that age out working?', Steve started laughing.

'School? Nah. I was never much good at that. I was going to be on the end of a shovel sooner or later, so why not sooner. Family needed the money. But that was a long time ago. Anyway, you carry on. My old knee's playing up again. I've got some spray stuff for it in the van', and with that he headed in the direction of the waggon.

Hugh watched him as he trundled off, limping slightly. It occurred to him that perhaps he was just playing a silly game by being out here. As he'd been repeatedly told, these men were doing it for real and he was just out here making a fool out of himself, unable to use the simplest tool available to man, there only by virtue of the fact that he was the boss' son. He felt an ache of embarrassment in his soul.

Steve returned from the waggon. 'Now lad, as you say, we all have to start somewhere. Don't worry about it. Just don't have him needing to show you again. OK, so what you're trying to do is to dig down until you feel the pipe, then dig around it so that it's exposed. Then we'll cut out the blocked section and put a sleeve over it, OK?'. Hugh nodded to confirm his understanding and attacked the exposed earth furiously, tearing at the ground with the shovel. 'Steady on, steady on', said Steve, 'there's no mad rush here. We're not on price. We've got until dinner time to get this done.' He took Hugh's shovel from him and proceeded to dig the hole with a conspicuous economy of effort, the shovel blade sliding through the soil leaving neatly delineated channels within the excavation.

'You can finish that off', he said returning the shovel to Hugh and then turning to Gary who was reviewing a technical drawing as he leant against the waggon. Hugh had watched Steve carefully, noting every element of his posture and the dynamics of the operation. He proceeded to dig as he had been shown and immediately felt more in harmony with the tool. Gary approached him.

'Change of plan. We're going to have to put a concrete box in there, so the hole'll have to be wider and deeper: aim for a meter and a half square. We're going back to the yard to pick up some stuff'. Hugh set himself the task of emptying a cubic meter and a half of soil from the verge before their return, not reckoning with the resistance of the dense, hard loam, well over a ton of which would have to be excavated. He set about the task methodically, as he had been instructed to do.

He took a break after fifteen minutes or so and wiped the sweat from his face. He removed his pullover, stripping down to the T-shirt underneath. He peered into the pit he'd dug and then looked at the mound of excavated material heaped

137

next to it and could not reconcile the respective volumes of the two. The mound of rock and soil had been growing steadily, but there appeared to be no appreciable increase in the depth of the hole. His hands were beginning to burn, the friction between the wooden handle of the shovel and his palms rubbing away at the soft, untutored skin. He continued digging. After a further ten minutes the pain in his hands became more acute and he looked at his right palm and saw three blisters bubbling up at the top of his palm, flour white and minutely corrugated like the soft shell of a deep-sea crustacean. His lower back began to stiffen and every movement felt as if he were tearing muscles out of their moorings.

After thirty minutes his T-Shirt was drenched, and his face was painted with streaks of dirt where he had tried to wipe away the sweat seeping from him in the rising heat of the morning. His hands rang a pained alarm every time he gripped the shovel and he had grazed his knuckles once or twice on rocks protruding from the side of the hole leaving small rags of skin smeared over their jutting edges. Nonetheless, he continued, the mound of debris growing ever higher and the excavation sinking at a disappointingly slow rate. After an hour of consistent effort, he felt the energy draining from his body and he struggled to ignore the aches, cuts and abrasions that tormented him. He started to wonder where Gary and Steve were; at least their return would provide him with a reason to stop and take a rest.

His work rate slowed as his body urged him to stop, but he resisted the temptation to break his rhythm as the last thing he wanted was for Gary and Steve to return to find him slacking. The morning wore on sapping his energy and strength until finally the waggon pulled up. 'The agent needed to get permission for us to go ahead', said Steve by way of explanation for their late return, and he and Gary proceeded to unload segments of the concrete box from the back of the waggon. Grateful for the opportunity to stop, Hugh speared the shovel into the ground and walked to the waggon to retrieve the flask of hot tea that he had prepared that morning.

'Have you been rolling in the muck?', asked Steve smiling as looked at Hugh. 'You're wearing more of it than you dug out.'

'My bloody hands are killing me', Hugh replied peering at pink, raw circles of flesh at the base of his fingers, the blistered skin having long since rubbed away.

'Aye, that'll happen', observed Steve casually. 'Watch this', he said and pulled a cigarette lighter from his pocket, flicked it into life and held the flame under his raised palm, grinning and looking at Hugh who, astonished at the feet, cricked his neck to peer at the palm to confirm that all was what it seemed. 'Don't worry you'll get all the callouses you want soon enough.' He reached into the cab and rummaged under the seat and pulled out a pair of heavy fabric gloves caked in dried mud and smelling of diesel. They had clearly been there for a long time.

'Here', said Steve throwing them to Hugh. He examined them trying hard not to show his disgust at the fetid rags, not entirely successfully. 'Up to you', said Steve, 'but that hole is only half - dug and we'll be needing it soon.' His hands felt as if he was holding onto burning coals and two of his knuckles bore livid striations marking their clash with the inner wall of the pit. He pulled the right - hand glove on satisfying himself with protecting the most painful and vulnerable hand. The interior of the glove was disconcertingly damp.

He returned to the pit and began digging. Whether the gloves actually helped in protecting his hands or the nerve endings under the raw skin had been worn into docility he didn't know, but the pain gradually subsided as he proceeded deliberately and methodically to empty the pit. After twenty minutes he was joined by Steve who stood on the bank of the hole and drove his shovel into the bench of loam Hugh had created and levered it loose down to Hugh. This speeded up progress as Hugh then only had to throw the muck and rock out of the trench rather than loosen it first. The problem then was that Hugh had to get the debris out of the trench as quickly as Steve was dislodging it. This involved a different technique which placed an immense strain on his calf muscles, but he was determined not to let the loosened debris accumulate and he worked frantically to clear it from the bottom of the pit. Looking up at Steve, he could not help but feel that he had the easier job as he causally worked his shovel. With two men digging it didn't take long to complete the job.

Eventually Steve nodded down at Hugh to confirm that the desired dimensions had been achieved they unloaded the concrete segments from the back of the waggon and stacked them by the side of the hole. Gary had been working further down the track and wandered up and sat in the cab of the waggon. Steve looked at Hugh.

'Dinner', he said and wandered off to join Gary.

The call came as a welcome relief to Hugh. He pulled off the glove. His hands were pink and surprisingly clean, wrinkled with sweat except for the pools of scarlet where the blisters had burst. He had never experienced hunger like this before. He had torn through his energy reserves over the course of the morning, his metabolism racing to satisfy the demands placed upon it by his starving muscles and he was in dire need of calories. The sandwiches and snacks which his mother had prepared or him were wolfed down in minutes, but they hardly scratched the surface of his hunger. He would ensure that he brought enough food tomorrow, he thought to himself.

'I'll stay here and sort that box out', said Gary, 'you two can head on to dig out the next one'.

'Sound', replied Steve and he exited the cab and began rooting around in the back of the waggon. Gary picked up his newspaper and browsed through it. Hugh's musculature, released from the morning's shocks, began to wilt and he started to feel drowsy, his eyelids growing heavy. Although he'd gone to bed at what he thought was a reasonable time the previous night he was just not used to such an early start to the day and his body was trying to recapture the sleep that it had been denied. He caught himself drifting and immediately braced himself. As urgent as the need for sleep was, he would not embarrass himself by dozing in the cab. That would surely be unforgivable and would test the patience of the two men who had showed such forbearance towards him. Instead, he focused on his blisters, turning his palm to scrutinise them.

'I haven't had any of those for over fifty years', remarked Gary smiling as he looked up from his newspaper. They'll be gone in a week or so and the skin'll toughen up. Your girlfriend might not be too impressed with the result though.' Hugh smiled at him, reassured by his change in attitude, and exited the cab, wanting to be rid of the drowsiness that was beginning to torment him. As he closed the door behind him, Gary exited from the other side. Steve had thrown the tools that Gary would need from the waggon onto the verge and jumped into the driver's seat. Gary looked over the back of the waggon and gestured for Hugh to join Steve.

'Where next?', asked Hugh once the vehicle had set off.

'Ten minutes down the road. We'll be doing the same thing we did this morning, digging out for a box.'

'How long have you worked for GCE then?', asked Hugh hoping to stimulate a conversation that would distract him from his drowsiness.

'Oh, a few years now. They're a steady enough outfit, regular payers. I've worked for them a few times over the years, been ran off a few times too', he said smiling as he glanced mischievously at Hugh, 'Gary's been with them the longest though. He goes back to when they started. He's taken a bit of shine to you, which is a novelty. He's not the friendliest of men at the best of times. Mind you, as he said, he was big pals with your grandad in the old days. Bit before my time though'.

'Have you worked with Gary for long?', asked Hugh eager to learn more. 'Five years on and off', he replied.

'How come you do this snagging work then, why not do the price work, more money isn't it?'

'It can be, but it's usually one week good, one week bad and as often as not you're working harder in the bad week than you were in the good one. Plus, its busy work, young man's work, and I've done my fair share of that. This is nice and steady, reliable money.' He pulled the waggon up and got out. Hugh followed.

'Should I put the road signs up again?', he asked.

'You're learning', replied Steve.

Frankie looked up at Gene from the trench and gestured for him to quieten the jackhammer, but before speaking he turned around and glanced down the length of the trench to ensure that Danny was out of earshot. 'Jones come into the pub on Saturday night', he said conspiratorially.

'Oh yes, and what did that bollocks want?', replied Gene, intrigued.

'He was in stirring up bother, telling me that the Mulligan's were on the lookout for Danny and how Danny might be better off getting out of city before they found him.'

'Why would Jones be interested in that kind of gossip?', replied Gene taking off his woollen cap and scratching his head. 'It's nothing to do with him.'

'Don't I know that. The trouble is, do I tell Danny and make myself as bad as Jones?'.

'Oh, you've got to tell him', said Gene gravely, 'at least to put him in the picture. You never know what that bollocks Jones might be up to and it's better that Danny has a notion as to what's going on. He's long enough in the tooth to figure it out.' Frankie knotted his brows.

'Maybe you're right. I'll grab him now.' He walked down the seventy or so meters that they had dug out that morning. Danny had backfilled the stretch and was about to lay down a base coat of tarmac as Frankie approached him.

'Look, I'm not one for stirring up trouble Danny, but I thought I should tell you that Jones came into the pub on Saturday night spouting off. Now, he dressed it up as trying to be helpful, but you know that wanker, there was something more to it than that. He reckoned that the brothers and cousins of those lads you had the carry on with in the yard the other day are on the hunt for you. Now, it's not my business, I'm not trying to whip up any trouble, but I thought you ought to know, you can do what you want with that information.'

'Is that right?', replied Danny, resting his foot on the shoulder of the shovel and leaning on the handle.

'And these Mulligans, I suppose there a dodgy crowd?'

'They are.'

'And what was Mr. Jones' solution to this problem of mine?'

'He said you should get out of city.'

'Did he now', replied Danny, smiling wryly. 'A man might wonder why he'd be so interested in seeing the back of me, but I might know the answer to that', he replied glancing up at the sky. 'Looks like the weather'll stay clear for today, eh?'

'Aye, it does' replied Frankie. Danny straightened his back and resumed his work.

The route Gary took back to the yard from the job passed close to Hugh's house and they dropped him off in the vicinity of his home. 'How was your first day then?', asked Gary as they pulled up.

'Well, I'm sore in a few places, but I'll get used to it', replied Hugh.

'Aye, you will. It only hurts for the first thirty years or so', added Steve grinning.

'We'll see you in the yard in the morning', advised Gary as Hugh eased himself out of the vehicle trying to disguise the effects of the cramps that were gripping his calf muscles like hot pincers. He remained on the footpath watching the waggon as it pulled away not wanting his workmates to see him hobble the hundred or so meters to his home.

He walked stiffly around to the back door of his parent's house and sat down on the step and eased off his boots and left them by the side of the door. They had lost their glossy sheen within the first hour of the day and were now caked in mud, the leather scuffed and creased. He limped in through the door to find his mother in the kitchen. 'Hello mum', he said weakly as he collapsed down into a chair.

'You look exhausted', she said smiling. 'Let me have a look at your hands.' She walked over to him and held his wrists in order to properly inspect his palms.

'Ouch!', she said and winced. 'You look like you've been down the mine. Were you rolling around in the muck or shovelling it?', she said smiling.

'I am exhausted', he said emphasising each word. 'I need to bring more food. I've been starving all day.'

'Had enough?', she enquired.

'Every bit of my body is hurting', he replied. 'My hands, my back, my legs. My muscles are cramping, I could eat a horse and sleep for a week. Other than that, I'm fine'. His mother smiled at him.

'Well good for you, your first day as a navvy done. Take yourself up for a shower and there'll be a big dinner ready for you in the next half an hour.' He reluctantly rose from the chair, his body having entered into a state of relaxation which it was reluctant to relinquish and walked like a man on stilts to the foot of the stairs.

'One of the blokes I'm working with used to know Grandad', he said without making the effort to turn around, his energy levels having crashed with the effort of raising himself from the chair. His mother watched his bedraggled figure slowly climbing the stairs and she smiled wistfully as she recalled memories of her late father, his head bowed between his broad, heavy shoulders, lumbering up the stairs

143

of a far less comfortable home, condemned to a far less comfortable life. She took pleasure in the recognition that Hugh's involvement with this work was voluntary and temporary, that he was free to leave this hardship and grind, this savage amusement, as her father used to call it, any time he chose to do so. And she felt pride in him too, pride that he had the determination and the strength of character to put himself through this challenge in order to understand the hardships that his forebears had endured.

Hugh stood under the shower and watched the grey-brown water fall off his body and swirl down the plug hole. His blisters had redoubled their complaints since coming into contact with the soap and hot water, but at this point he was used to the sharp nips of pain radiating from his hands and any discomfort he was feeling was easily smothered by the prospect of the food, relaxation and comfort that awaited him. He dried himself off and pulled on jogging pants and a T-shirt. He felt fresh and clean and invigorated, and he wandered into his room and threw himself onto his bed and picked up the phone to call Jane.

'How was it?', she asked excitedly, 'did you stay all day?'

'Of course I stayed all day', he replied indignantly then caught himself. 'Sorry Jane, I'm just a bit tired. It was fine, hard, but OK. My hands are covered in blisters and my back is sore, but otherwise it was good.' They chatted a little while longer and once again Hugh felt himself becoming drowsy as he reclined on the bed.

'Look, I'm going to have to go. Supper's ready', he said, not wanting to tell her that he had almost drifted off to sleep during their conversation. He trundled down the stairs just as his father walked in through the door.

'Hello Murphy, how are ya?', said his father in a caricature of an Irish accent. Hugh smiled at him weakly and sat down in the kitchen.

'Supper will be ready shortly', called his mother and Hugh and David made their way into the dining room.

'How was it?', asked David.

'It was good. They're decent lads, Gary and Steve', Hugh replied earnestly. 'We dug a couple of boxes. Here, look at my hands', he said displaying his blisters.

'Ouch! They look sore', said his father wincing. Kate entered the dining room and set down a plate in front of Hugh on which sat a mountain of pasta. Hugh immediately began wolfing it down. She returned moments later with a plate which contained a third of the amount of food and placed it down in front of David who silently contemplated the difference in portion sizes, unable to remember the last time his appetite had been so robust as Hugh's was tonight. Then Kate joined them with her own small portion which she had barely finished before Hugh was asking for more. She took his plate and rose from the table.

'You *are* hungry', she remarked as she returned from the kitchen and passed him the plate replenished with the remainder of the spaghetti. 'I don't think I've ever seen you eat as much. They must've been keeping you busy.'

'It's the kind of job where you burn up a lot of calories', he said, the contents of second plate surviving only fractionally longer than the first. He thanked his mother and rose from the table and waked into the living room. David was shifting what remained of his food around on his plate.

'Well, he did it, one day at least', observed David.

'I never doubted that he would', replied Kate decisively. 'He's made of tough stuff that lad', she continued. 'Would you like a cup of tea?', she asked and without waiting for a reply wandered through to the living room to make the same offer to Hugh. He lay fast asleep on the sofa, snoring quietly.

CHAPTER TWENTY- SIX

Gene pulled into the yard later than usual and so avoided the usual melee of returning vehicles dropping off their compressors, the final job of the day. Frankie and Danny hopped out of the waggon to unhook their compressor and, although they were chatting as they worked, Frankie had a sense that Danny's mind was elsewhere. He saw that Danny was scanning the yard and his eyes had obviously found their target when he saw them fix on Jones lumbering down the staircase from the office.

Danny immediately stopped what he was doing and turned smiling to Frankie. 'Time for a bit of fun', he said and marched off towards the staircase. As Jones reached the bottom of the stairway, he spotted Danny striding towards him across the open expanse of the yard and, as there was no doubt about where he was heading, Jones stood his ground unsure of what to expect. His body buzzed with the unfamiliar discomfort of adrenaline coursing through his veins, and he braced himself, not anticipating fisticuffs, but mustering himself for the possibility. His complexion grew slightly wan, and a slight tremor trickled through his pink, tubular fingers.

Danny started speaking several meters from Jones as if his words were in a hurry to escape. 'What's up with you, you big stack of shite, passing on messages like a fucking schoolgirl. My affairs have got fuck all to do with you.' He barked, planting himself squarely in front of Jones, his very demeanour asking a question of him

Jones wasn't used to being spoken to like this. His eyes quickly flicked around the yard to see who might have heard Danny's outburst. Fortunately for him there was no one within earshot, but Danny's body language, bold and confrontational, spoke loud and clear to anyone to anyone taking notice of the scene. The initial shock of Danny's aggression blew through Jones like a gust of wind, but he quickly collected himself.

'It's my affair when you're bringing your troubles into this yard. I'd remind you that this is a place of business not a place for your playground squabbles', he replied propping himself up with the disguise of professionalism. 'What I told your mate was a warning for you. We won't have that shite going on in this yard, alright? If you were any kind of a fucking man you'd be up in 'The Royal' sorting them Mulligans out yourself instead of leaving it for us to deal with when they next decide to come down here looking for you.' That's more like it, Jones thought to himself.

Danny glared fiercely at Jones, a menacing half-smile lurking around his lips, silently savouring the tension between them, noting the subtle tells of fear on Jones' face, signs which even Jones himself was unaware of.

'Me and you aren't done. Not by a long fucking way', said Danny with a calm malevolence and raised his hand to adjust his eye patch, his bulbous knuckles big as rivet heads. He turned and walked back to the waggon. Jones watched him as he moved away, unease growing in the pit of his stomach. He suddenly felt vulnerable, exposed, and he quickly glanced around the yard again to confirm that there had been no spectators to the encounter.

Danny got into the waggon and turned to Frankie and Gene. 'Who's the head kiddy of these Mulligans, then?', he asked.

'He's called Tony Mulligan', answered Gene gravely.

'And he drinks at 'The Royal' pub, right?'

'Yes, he does', said Gene. 'It's up near where I live. He's a dangerous man, but you probably worked that out for yourself already.'

'Drop me off on your way home will you Gene?', asked Danny.

'Sure', he replied.

As Jones ascended the office staircase, the unwelcome physical discomfort he'd experienced throughout the confrontation with Danny began to leave him. It was just his body preparing itself in case Greene turned nasty, he said to himself. It wasn't fear, it was just nature putting him at the ready. Greene didn't worry him. Not at all. He was too big and too strong, he reminded himself. As he clambered to the top of the staircase, he raised himself to his full height and thrust his shoulders back as if to confirm to himself the enormity of his physical stature, to reassure himself of the strength within.

He entered the office. David was out at a meeting, but Fletcher and Spencer were at their respective desks busying themselves with paperwork. Spencer glanced up and seeing it was Jones quickly returned to his work not wanting to give him the opportunity to chastise him for daydreaming. Jones ambled causally over to Spencer's desk.

'How are you lad?', he asked with uncharacteristic good humour. Spencer looked up at him suspiciously. He was not used to this kind of amiability from Jones, despite the fact that he was his nephew. Although Spencer was in awe of Jones he was all too often on the receiving end of his bullying and his rudeness, yet not disproportionately so as Jones was fairly even-handed when it came to giving vent to his arrogance and ill-temper. Nonetheless, Spencer had convinced himself that this was just how alpha males behaved and such displays should not be taken personally. In fact, he was more than happy to try to emulate Jones' behaviour, when he could get away with it that is.

Jones sat his bulk down on the corner of Spencer's desk causing it to creak ominously and Spencer reached out instinctively to catch the various items arrayed on the desk in case it tipped over under his enormous weight. Jones looked at him disapprovingly, not appearing to notice the strain he was placing upon the wooden frame now supporting him.

'Well, you just missed a bit of fun down there lad', he said looking towards the yard and smiling.

'Oh?', replied Spencer enthusiastically, flattered that Jones was paying him some positive attention for a change.

'Yeah, I just had to fire a few fucks into that Danny Greene fella, let him know who's boss around here.'

Upon hearing this Fletcher looked up and glanced sceptically at Jones before returning to his work.

' I didn't crack him though. Didn't need to. I could see in his face that he was shitting himself and him with only one eye. I mean, it wouldn't be fair, would it?' he continued as he peered nonchalantly out of the window.

'How come?', asked Spencer rising to the bait.

'Oh, you know, that trouble in the yard the other day. I told him that if there was any more of that nonsense, he'd have me to deal with. You should've seen the look on his face. He went as white as a sheet! Shaking like a shiteing dog he was.'

'Fucking hell', exclaimed Spencer, his admiration evident. 'I've heard he's a right hard bastard, but, I mean, obviously not in your league.'

Jones nodded in approval. Spencer had said the correct thing. He stood up from the desk.

'You know, now I think about it, it's been a long time since me and you went out for a pint, eh kid?'

'It has', replied Spencer, silently noting that they had never gone out for a pint together, despite the fact that he would have relished the opportunity to do so. It would have been a definite feather in his cap for his mates to see him out and about with such well-known tough guy. 'Whenever your free Uncle Colm', he continued enthusiastically. Jones nodded at him and smiled before crossing the room to his own desk. He had abandoned the notion before he reached his seat. He wasn't going to waste a night listening to the kid's shite talk, he thought to himself.

Gene pulled up outside 'The Harp' and Frankie exited bidding his farewells and Gene resumed their journey onward. After five minutes or so he turned to Danny.

'I don't feel right about you having to deal with all this trouble over a situation I caused'.

'Look, it was my decision to get involved in the first place', replied Danny. 'I could've left it alone, but I can't do with that kind of ass. He was a bully and that's all there is to it. He thought that he'd get away with it because you're a bit older than him. As to other developments, well, that's up to me. With a bit of luck, it'll come to an end this evening.'

'I'd feel a lot better if you let me come in with you, watch your back', replied Gene tentatively, not entirely behind the idea of getting involved with a dangerous mob like the Mulligans at his age. Maybe a few years ago when he was in his prime he thought, but he had Cora to think about.

Danny recognised that Gene would be more of a hindrance than a help if things did take a turn for the worst, which they just might do, but he respected the old man's willingness to play a part, nonetheless.

'Thanks, but I'd feel a lot better if I'm on my own. No offence to you, but it's just my way.' Gene nodded in acknowledgement, quietly relieved, and pulled up outside a run-down pub situated at the edge of the housing estate where Gene lived.

'It's a rough old joint in there you know', he said by way of warning.

'I can imagine', replied Danny glancing at the front of the pub as he exited the waggon.

'Do you want me to wait for you?'

'You're alright. There's no knowing how long I'm going to be', he replied and with that he slammed the door closed and Gene drove away, peering at Danny through the rear view mirror as he made his way towards the pub. 'Rather him than me at any age', he murmured to himself revising his earlier estimation.

Danny pushed through the doors of the pub and strode towards the bar noting the tackiness of the décor and furnishings, the grubbiness of the place emphasised by the raw glare of the strip lighting overhead. A damp, musty smell thickened the air and the carpet, stained with ancient spillages, clung the soles of his boots. He ordered a drink. The waiter was sat on a buffet, his head buried in a newspaper. He rose with a sigh and, without acknowledging Danny, pulled a pint and then put the glass of thin, lifeless beer on the bar top.

'I'm looking for Tony Mulligan', said Danny as he pushed a note across the sticky wooden counter. The barman nodded towards a group of men sat in the corner of the room.

'Tony is the one wearing all the gold', he replied morosely and returned to his buffet and newspaper. Danny surveyed the crowd from a distance. They were a rough looking bunch, all talking at once, their voices loud in competition, but he didn't recognise any of the faces amongst the company which made matters a little more straightforward. After a brief survey of the group, he identified the man he was looking for.

Tony Mulligan was sat within the recesses of a dim alcove, his tree-trunk arms, decorated with a web of indecipherable tattoos, were stretched out along the backrest to either side of him. Thick gold-plated chains hung from his neck and wrists and his bulbous fingers were hooped with industrial-looking sovereign rings. He leant out of the semi-darkness of the booth to emphasise a point, stabbing the air with his index finger, the enormous white dome of his bald head laced with a livid seam of scar tissue, as if a sleeping millipede was resting under his scalp.

Danny raised his glass to take a sip from his drink and his nostrils were assailed by the sour odour rising from it and he immediately returned the drink to the counter with a thud. 'Your beer's shite', he said dismissively to the bartender without looking at him and walked across the room towards the Mulligans.

'Get of my fucking way', he snarled at one of the younger members of the crew sat on the periphery of the semi-circle of men arrayed around Tony Mulligan's table. The kid looked up at him and instinctively shifted his body to allow Danny through. Silence descended on the table. 'I want to talk to you', he said looking down into the semi-darkness of the alcove, his tone hard and authoritative, a statement of fact, not a request. Another of the younger members of the company jumped to his feet.

'Who the fuck do you think you are?', he barked.

'Sit down before I tear you fucking head off', Danny replied causally and turned to look at the speaker, his expression stern and implacable. The kid gibbered an attempt at a response and looked into the shadows enveloping Tony Mulligan for guidance. A moment or two passed in silence and then the naked crown of Mulligan's head emerged from the shadows and nodded for him to return to his seat and turned to scrutinise Danny.

'What do you want to talk to me about?', he asked calmly as he reached out for his pint. The glass was three-quarters full, and he drained the contents in one draught before belching and wiping his mouth with the back of his hand. Danny ignored Mulligan's question. 'I'm going to go back to the bar and order you a pint. If you want to talk, I'll see you there', and with that Danny turned and walked back to the counter. Mulligan looked at his mates, a perplexed expression on his face.

'Who's that cunt?', said another of the junior members of the company. Tony Mulligan looked from face to face awaiting a response. None came forth.

'Tell him to go fuck himself', said a burly youth rising to his feet, eager to burnish his tough guy credentials. Mulligan looked at him with some disdain and turned his

151

attention to the bar. Danny was standing with his back to them. He appeared disconcertingly relaxed.

Mulligan didn't want to appear as if he was ready to jump at this man's request, but he was intrigued. He was both known and feared around this city, and it was a bold move indeed for anyone to confront him at the centre of his domain; bold or stupid, his reputation for violence being what it was. Mulligan let Danny wait for longer than polite company might think necessary, but this was nothing that Danny had not anticipated. In situations in which one was walking into the lion's den, Daniels require a degree of patience.

Tony Mulligan rose from his chair and, waiving away the offers of assistance coming from his associates, walked up to the bar. He picked up the pint that Danny had bought and proceeded to drink two thirds of it in one draught. 'So?', he said brusquely without looking at Danny.

'My name is Danny Greene and I work for GCE. I had a run in with a couple of your mates last week and it didn't work out too well for them. I've been told that you're looking for me. Well, as you can see, here I am.'

He turned to look directly at Mulligan and adjusted his eye patch.

'Now, I used to live in this city a lot of years ago', he continued, 'and I used to labour on a bloke, good bit older than me, took me under his wing you could say. He was a good man. His name was Danny Mulligan. We were digging for O'Malleys at the time.'

'My father was called Danny Mulligan', replied Tony, his interest sparked.

'He was a tough old customer, frightened of nobody. He'd be dead now, I imagine?', asked Danny.

'Aye, dead ten years', replied Mulligan, 'I remember him working for O'Malley. I was in the Borstal at the time. Danny Greene', he mused, 'Wait a minute, I remember that name. Danny Greene, eh? I remember my dad talked about a bloke called that. Did you work on the fair when you were a kid?'

'Aye, I did. I ended up doing a bit a prize fighting when I was a young lad, and your dad schooled me a bit. He was like a father to me was Mr. Mulligan, and that's why I'm here. I don't like the idea of shaping up with any of Danny's family. It wouldn't seem right, but I'm not a man to hide either, so if your anything like the man your father was then I'd expect that we could step outside man-to-man, one at a time and see how we get on.'

'Wait a minute', said Tony. 'I know fuck all about this. Who were the lads you leathered?', he asked.

'No idea', replied Danny. 'They were both heavy-set, bald heads.'

'That could be anyone in the family', he replied, 'could even be some of the women. Jimmy!', he shouted in the direction of the group, each one of them monitoring developments at the bar. One of the lads jumped up and walked briskly towards them.

'What the fucks going on? This fella tells me that he was in a scrap with a couple of us last week. Why don't I know about this?'.

'It was Jake and Paddy, Tony', he replied sheepishly. 'They didn't want you to know 'cause they got a hammering.'

'What both of them?', he asked, his voice rising in surprise.

'Aye', replied his mate reluctantly.

'Against one bloke?'

'Aye', replied his mate even more meekly, appearing to shrink under the questioning. Tony shook his head in disgust.

'Well', he said, turning to Danny, 'you've got some balls, I'll give you that. There's not many who'd walk in here on their own looking for that kind of business with us. I know who those two lads are; they're cousins of the wife. Not really proper Mulligans. Hangers on really. If you did 'em both fair and square, well, there's no more to be said. They've embarrassed us, but I'll deal with that myself. I'll be having words with you lot as well', he barked, looking menacingly at the team congregated around the table.

Tony looked away and appeared to gather his thoughts and then turned to Danny. 'He was some boyo my old fella, eh?' a broad smile spreading across his face, the great boulder of his head rocking with mirth.

'He was indeed', replied Danny with genuine affection, 'he was a good friend to me.' With this change of subject, the tension between them dissolved and Danny knew that he was out of danger,

'You'd have been the lad that got the lashing on Donovan Street then all them years ago, eh?', continued Joe as his laughter subsided.

'My dad went to the hospital when he was told, but you'd signed yourself out by the time he found out you were there.'

Then he turned to Danny, his former seriousness returning.

'Who said we was looking for you', he asked, 'I'd like to know who's been making threats in my name.'

'If I told you that I'd be as bad as him for telling tales, wouldn't I?', replied Danny.

CHAPTER TWENTY-SEVEN

Hugh's first week passed without notable incident, and he quickly recognised that the jobs allocated to Gary and Steve largely consisted of remedying small errors or omissions found in the work of departed price work gangs. The pains his body had endured on his first day on the shovel were more a consequence of the softness of his flesh than they were a result of the intensity of the work itself. For much of the time he felt underused, spending a significant amount of time watching Gary and Steve undertake time - consuming technical tasks, but he was nonetheless gaining an understanding of the broader processes involved in the work and slowly easing himself into its more physically demanding aspects. Yet, despite the amount of time he spent peering over his workmates shoulder, by the time Friday came around he knew that he'd done a week's work. Where there had formerly been blisters there were now callouses emerging, and the vicious aches and cramps which had plagued his first few days were beginning to subside.

During the course of the week, he had learned from Steve that on Friday evenings after work a large number of the men congregated in 'The Harp' pub and he relished the prospect of enjoying a pint or two with them on equal terms, now that he had sufficient dirt under his finger nails to justify his presence amongst them.

'The Harp' had been host to the navvy community for as long as anyone could remember and Hugh was well aware of its existence, featuring as it did in many of the tales told to him by his grandfather. For this reason, it had always held a certain rugged mystique which he was eager to explore. His mother had mentioned the place a couple of times over the years, but only to disparage it and his father had often remarked that it would save everyone a lot of trouble if he just handed the men's weekly packets to the landlord on a Friday evening. Hugh had even tried to talk his friends into visiting the place, but they had dismissed the proposal out of hand astonished that he would even consider visiting a place with such a notorious reputation.

It had been a warm summer's day and the sultry evening light reflected a soft golden hue from the stone exterior of 'The Harp' as Gary manoeuvred the waggon into the pub's car park. Though Hugh was bristling with excitement at the prospect of finally entering the much-storied premises he was also mindful that he could only stay for an hour as he had made plans with Jane for later that evening and these certainly did not include 'The Harp', a venue whose reputation both appalled and frightened her in equal measure. Steve was out of the waggon before it came to a complete stop. Hugh had been silently anticipating an hour of Gary's reminisce about his grandfather and was disappointed to learn that that he wouldn't be coming in with them, but this was soon forgotten about in his eagerness to get inside.

He made his farewells to Gary and tumbled out of the waggon and sped across the car park to catch up with Steve. He caught him just as he was pushing through the swing doors leading into the tap room. Hugh followed behind him and was immediately immersed in the heavy thrum of conversation and the raucous strains of fiddle music that infused the room. It seemed to him as if he were entering another world, a world pulsing with vigour and commotion. As he followed Steve to the bar his excitement grew and he was reassured by the nods of acknowledgement that he received from men he had seen in the yard who in these simple gestures included him as one of their own.

Steve reached the crowded bar and ordered the drinks as Hugh stood waiting behind him, feeling a little self-conscious in the dizzying novelty of the environment. He looked around nervously. His experience of local pubs had taken him no further than those bars that his parents had sanctioned, and these were sedate, well-furnished environments in which any music was of the background variety and conversation was conducted in a civilised manner and at a civilised volume. This was another world altogether. He was struck by the age range of the patrons, from chortling old men and women with their flat caps and headscarves to the athletic young men and desirable young women clustered in small groups around the room, their conversation animated, their laughter uproarious and unrestrained. As his eyes drifted over the scene before him, he tried to reimagine the space as his grandfather had experienced it those many years ago, picturing him in the vigour of his youth, carousing much as the young men before him were doing, much as he was doing. He heard ghostly echoes of his grandfather's laughter ricocheting off the walls and felt his presence amongst them in a way that he had never experienced it before. His initial discomfort vanished. He felt at home.

Then from the hidden recesses of his memory emerged unbidden an image of him sat with his grandfather in this very room. He greeted the recollection with quiet astonishment. He could picture the scene with pristine clarity, a memory undiminished in precision by repeated scrutiny. They were seated at a table at the far end of the room, a spot currently obscured by the mass of people milling around the jukebox. He had only been seven or eight years old at the time and he distinctly recalled that his grandfather's breath smelled strongly of beer and cigarettes and that he was sporting a multi-coloured swelling around his left eye. One image followed the next with increasing speed until he was able to piece together passages of conversation.

'What's wrong with your eye Grandad?', he had asked as he reached out with two hands to grasp the pint of orange juice on the table before him raising the glass to his lips and peering over the rim.

'Don't worry about that boyo', he replied in his deep, almost musical voice. 'The fella that gave it me is in a much worse state than me, I can tell you that much!', and with that he let out a jolt of laughter and reached down for his own glass.

'You see', he said portentously, as if preparing for a public lecture, 'I keep telling you Hugh that it doesn't matter what a man comes out looking like from a fight just as long as the other feller looks worse!', and with that another burst of laughter erupted from him.

'In this life', he continued in more contemplative form, 'a man has to learn to take a few shots. It's just part of the game; nothing to get het up about. The main thing is that you give it back at twice the rate of exchange that you received it. You've got to teach them a lesson or else you'll be back and forth for ever. Get stuck into them hard and get stuck into them fast. That's a man's way. What did I just say?', he asked turning to Hugh expectantly.

'Get stuck in hard and get stuck in fast Granddad', replied Hugh and then buried his head between his shoulders and launched a volley of little punches into his grandfather's ribcage. At first Joe feigned pain and then started guffawing as he lifted Hugh by the waist from his seat by which time Hugh was giggling uncontrollably. Joe held him in front of him so that Hugh was stood on his thighs and their faces were only a few inches apart and he searched Hugh's features before looking directly into his eyes.

'Stop your laughing now a minute', he said gravely, 'this is serious. If you remember anything at all from your old granddaddy remember this: a man that can't fight is no man at all. He'll spend his whole entire life getting pushed around like the old village idiot, no good to nobody and surely of no use to himself. Do you understand me now Hugh?'

'I do Granddad', he replied silently mouthing the words to himself: 'a man who can't fight is no man at all.'

'Oh, you'll do for me young Hugh,' he said smiling, 'there's no better man in here than yourself and that's for sure, except maybe myself of course', and with that they both broke out into cascades of laughter, although Hugh wasn't sure of exactly what he was laughing at.

Hugh was startled out of his daydream by the questioning gaze of a young women sat across the room from him, a look which caused him to acknowledge the uncomfortable fact that his uncomprehending eyes had been settled upon her for the several minutes during which he had been lost in his memories. She glared directly at him, her expression open and bold, her eyebrows raised as if waiting for an explanation for his prolonged scrutiny. He felt a flush of embarrassment running through him and wanted to look away from her, but he couldn't. He was captivated, transfixed by the uncompromising beauty of her face. He felt like a thief caught in the act and although there was an obvious and immediate escape route, he just couldn't bring himself to make use of it.

Even this early into his manhood Hugh was used to the admiring looks of girls and even to those of older women who would eye him with brief, predatory glances. He had his pick of prettiest girls amongst his peers, but this felt different. He had been drawn to her by something below the threshold of his consciousness; she had touched something elemental within him. And she wasn't admiring him. She was putting him to the test with her eyes of shimmering blue. His usual easy confidence around girls had vanished. He looked down to his feet, but his eyes quickly returned to her's and she smiled at him with a frankness that unnerved him even further.

He was saved by Steve who had turned from the bar and was nudging him in the ribs, directing Hugh's attention to the pint of beer that he was offering to him. Hugh murmured distractedly that he would buy the next round, assuming that this was the appropriate thing to say and, following Steve's lead, headed away from the bar his face reddening as if still under the girl's gaze. As he wove his way through the densely packed crowd, he could not resist the temptation to steal a glance behind him half afraid his eyes might find her, but she was lost in the crowd.

'Why didn't Gary come in with us?', asked Hugh looking to distract himself.

'He can't drink any more', shouted Steve above the music, 'health reasons.'

'But he said the other day that.....', replied Hugh, struggling to make himself heard.

'Yeah, I was there. He was going to tell you some tales over a pint. He does that sometimes. He forgets, or he doesn't want to remember. One or the other. It's a damn curse for a single man of his age, not being able to take a pint or two after a week's work.'

They joined a number of men seated at a large table all seemingly talking at once, bolts of laughter flashing across the space between them. Hugh immediately recognised Spencer, the trainee agent.

'How's it going?', he shouted at Hugh over the swirling din of the music. Hugh smiled and tried to answer but his voice was swallowed up by the intervening distance. Spencer stood up and changed places with one of the older men to sit next to Hugh, the better to make himself heard.

'I haven't seen you in here before', he said, his squinting eyes darting around the room and his palm slapping his thigh in time with the music. 'It's going to be a good night tonight. They've got live music on', he continued.

'Is it normally this busy?', bellowed Hugh.

'At weekends, yes', replied Spencer. 'How was your first week then? Pretty easy with a snagging gang, eh?'

'Yeah', he shouted in reply, 'it wasn't bad, a bit hard at first getting used to it. Anyway, you're the one with the easy job, driving around all day getting out of the car now and again to run your little machine up and down the footpath.'

'Yeah, it's easy enough, but I do have Jones to put up with every day remember. That's hardly a barrel of laughs', he replied and picked up his pint and drained the glass. 'Pint?', he asked Hugh.

'No, I'm OK', he said looking down at his drink before noting with some surprise that he'd already drained the glass of half of its contents. He's been so busy taking in the novelty of his environment that he'd barely noticed the deep draughts that he'd been taking from his glass.

'Guinness?', asked Spencer.

'Yes, thanks', he replied.

'So how was your first week then?', asked Steve significantly more talkative with a pint in his hand than he had been during the week. 'Have you found your calling in life?', he asked, smirking. Hugh smiled.

'It's been good. It's been a bit more technical work than I thought it would be though, not as busy. Do you think three men in the gang is really necessary? I've felt like a bit of a spare part sometimes.'

'I wouldn't say its technical, but there's probably more brains than brawn involved', replied Steve, 'You need to know what you're doing. Most of the lads on price just go hell for leather chasing meters and a lot of them don't pay attention to the details.'

'I wouldn't mind having a go at that one day. You know, price work', Hugh replied, trying to mask his enthusiasm.

'Be careful what you wish for. It's bloody hard graft, if you want to make it pay that is', replied Steve, 'but there are some young lads doing it and some of them are alright. You're a big, strong lad. One day maybe.'

Spencer returned with the beer. 'Come over here', he said, gesturing with a nod of his head. 'I'll introduce you to some of the lads'. Hugh stood up and looked down at Steve.

'I'll be back in five minutes', he said.

'Is that what you think?', replied Steve smiling.

Spencer led the way to a group of young lads gathered in the centre of the room, all dressed in their work clothes, and proceeded to introduce them to Hugh. Much to his disappointment, he introduced Hugh as the son of the boss of GCE. Further discomfort was to come when Spencer informed them that he was currently working with the snagging gang.

'What? You're helping them in and out of the waggon?', asked one, guffawing.

'Holding them around the waist so the jack hammer doesn't carry them off?', asked another to general laughter. Hugh squirmed.

They chatted causally for the next ten or fifteen minutes trying to make one another heard above the sound of the jukebox. Spencer indicated that it was Hugh's turn to go to the bar and he duly complied and made a detour to Steve's table to collect his order too. While doing so he attempted to catch a glimpse of the girl he had seen earlier, but he was unable to secure a decent angle of sight with so many customers in the way and he didn't want to appear that he was seeking her out in case she'd catch him staring at her again.

He got to the bar and ordered the round of drinks and once again glanced around the room trying to appear as casual as possible, all the while searching for girl, but to no avail. She seemed to have disappeared. The bar maid set three pints down on the bar and he pushed the glasses together and encircled them with both hands, his concentration focused on not dropping them as he turned around to re-join his newly acquired mates. 'You know what they say about men with big hands', came a voice from directly in front of him, startling him as he peered down with concentrated attention at his slippery cargo. He looked up and there she was, smiling at him. She didn't wait for him to reply but instead squeezed past him to occupy the position at the bar which he had left vacant. He stood there for a moment scouring his mind for a witty reply but none came, and he quickly realised that his moment had passed and he cursed himself. He headed off to give Steve his pint hoping that he wouldn't notice the red flush that had once again swept over his face.

Hugh stood amongst Spencer's crowd silently berating himself for his failure to ad lib an appropriate response to the girl's quip. Then it occurred to him that it was simply wrong for him to be thinking in this way given that he was in a relationship with Jane. He felt a momentary twinge of guilt at his disloyalty, but this passed quickly; he had done nothing wrong; he hadn't even spoken to the girl. She had provoked something in him of course, but this was probably something to do with his general excitement about being in the pub. She was a very good-looking

161

girl, but then so was Jane. As if to confirm his commitment to her he checked his watch and noted that it was still early, that he had time for another drink before he needed to meet her. He would put thoughts of the girl behind him and continue with his evening as planned.

The beer was starting to have an effect upon him, and it gave an upswing to his already elevated mood. He had barely finished half of his pint when another appeared in front of him courtesy of one of Spencer's friends who had bought a round of drinks for the entire group. Tales were told and the laughter was ever present and before long a band took to the floor and fiddle music infused the room with a fresh energy. The small floor area in front of the makeshift stage was soon filled with people dancing and his heart started racing when he saw that the girl was amongst them. She moved with a wild energy and a complete absence of self-consciousness, utterly absorbed in the music. He and the other young lads joined the crowd at the edge of the dance floor and began whooping and clapping in time with the rhythm of the music.

All eyes were soon trained upon the girl as she gave herself up to the music, dancing with great skill and athleticism, clearly trained in Irish dance. She revelled in her performance, her smile wide and bright, her eyes sparkling, her head thrown back in surrender to the wild rhythms infusing the room. Soon her friends withdrew, and she was left alone on the dance floor. Her movements became increasingly elaborate and audacious, and the crowd grew even more appreciative, clapping, hooting and stamping their feet in a collective reinforcement of the guiding rhythm as it increased in intensity, galloping towards its crescendo. The music came to its inevitable conclusion and the audience broke out into raucous cheers of approval. The girl made a flamboyant courtesy, smiling graciously to the crowd, and turned to Hugh winking directly at him before she exited the dance floor. This gesture did not go unnoticed, particularly by the lads in his group.

'Bloody hell, that was for you. Get over there', exclaimed Spencer nodding towards the girl as she skipped back to her friends. 'Go on man, what's up with you?'.

The rest of the group joined in and soon he was drowning in encouragement, his only life raft being his own mettle. He picked up his drink and squeezed his way through the crowd towards her table. As he struggled onwards it suddenly occurred to him that he had no idea what he was going to say to her; he couldn't simply present himself to her in the hope that she would disengage from her friends and initiate conversation. Panic flooded through him, yet it was simply inconceivable that he could turn back now that he was in the middle of no man's land.

He arrived at her table and, as if in anticipation of his arrival, she turned to face him. His heart seemed as if it were doing somersaults and he felt sure that he was blushing again. He offered her a nervous smile and complimented her on her dancing.

'And all it cost you was the price of a half of lager', as she handed him her empty glass. He took the glass from her, unsure of what she intended for him to do with it and stood there feeling more confused than ever.

'She's asking you to buy her a drink, donkey', her friend interjected. Hugh blushed again.

'Of course, sorry', he replied and immediately turned and headed off towards the bar, the horrendous tension that had accompanied his approach to her was now replaced by a sense of exhilaration. She hadn't rebuffed him which was a start at least. He noticed Spencer further down the bar and shuffled through the crowd to join him.

'Who's the half for?', asked Spencer as Hugh presented her glass to the barmaid.

'That lass', he replied grinning, nodding towards the girl's table.

'Good on you', Spencer said laughing and clapping him on the back. 'I thought that you were only staying for a couple anyway?', he asked. The reality of his schedule flooded back to him, and he frantically checked his watch. He was now over half an hour late for his date with Jane.

'Oh fuck!', he exclaimed to no one in particular. In the normal course of events, he would have immediately exited the place and dashed off to meet Jane, but this was far from the normal course of events. The music, the company, the beer and, most of all, the girl had undone any sense of normalcy. He stood at the bar contemplating his options which meant little more than searching for a rationale to justify remaining where he was: we were meeting mutual friends, so it's not as if she would be left waiting on her own somewhere; I had mentioned that I would be going to the pub after work so she knows where I am if she wanted to join me; she doesn't like to see me under the influence of alcohol, and I am definitely under the influence of alcohol at the moment, so if I did leave now she'd be annoyed and I'd have to endure her disapproval all evening. The hastily compiled list of justifications confirmed the decision that he had already unconsciously made. He collected the drink and made his way back to the girl's table, leaving his vague suspicions of guilt at the bar.

He arrived at her table and she looked up at him smiling before creating some room for him to sit down next to her. He was soon immersed in her joyful high – spiritedness; she laughed often, and he was soon entranced by her vivacity. Her stories were vivid and entertaining, and her steady flow of talk came as a relief to Hugh who was anxious that the beer he'd consumed might cause him to say something juvenile. He quickly learnt that her name was Clare and that she had worked as a nursery assistant since leaving school. He had made an immediate decision not to divulge anything about his background. As far as she was concerned, he thought, he was just another young navvy and he saw no reason to cause her to alter that view, after all, he already had a girlfriend, and all he was doing was simply enjoying this girl's company.

By the end of the evening, they were completely at ease with one another. Hugh's confidence had grown and with it his contribution to the flow of conversation. He enjoyed presenting himself as a manual worker and being appreciated as such. It enhanced his sense of his own maturity that he was being treated as a fully formed adult despite Clare being only two or three years older than him. He relished the fact that he could amuse her, this person who was so spontaneous, so alive and vital, who was interested in him as a man and not as a boy.

He was also acutely aware of her body. Her hair was a rich chestnut brown and fell down her back in a tumble of lavish curls which glistened with a golden light when she moved; her eyes were a brilliant blue and her full, cherry - red lips seemed permanently open in a wide, exuberant smile revealing two rows of small, perfectly white teeth. She was small in stature, but amply proportioned and she moved with a strange ethereal grace that he had never before seen in a woman.

As the evening drew to a close, he felt bold enough to compliment her on her figure and was taken aback by her candidness when she did the same to him, playfully squeezing his upper arms and complimenting him on his muscles as she giggled at her own boldness. Then, as her laughter subsided, she looked directly into his eyes and her expression changed to one of extreme seriousness as she raised her hand and cupped the side of his face with her palm and then stroked his cheek with her thumb, her eyes following his. 'You're the most handsome man I've ever seen', she said tenderly, as if entranced. A moment passed as she searched his eyes, then suddenly she drew back her hand and looked away. He could see that it was her turn to blush. He had never been complimented so richly or so directly by a girl before, nor had he ever felt so alive.

The bell for closing time rang out notifying the customers that the evening was drawing to a close and one of Clare's friends leant over to talk to her about calling a taxi, bringing them both back to the noisy confines of the pub. Clare smiled affectionately at Hugh and turned to her friends, conscious that she had been missing for them for most of the night. Spencer arrived at the table flushed with the effects of the gallon of beer he had drunk that night and invited Hugh to join him and his friends at the pub the following day. The prospect of going to the pub on a Saturday afternoon was one that Hugh had never considered before and, before he could tease out the implications of taking up the offer, Clare had turned from her conversation and looked at him, waiting for his answer, making it clear to Hugh that it would be her he was meeting rather than Spencer and his friends. Hugh took the prompt and she immediately let out a squeal of excitement before leaning over and kissing him lightly on the lips and returned her attention to her friends. Her unexpected kiss left him feeling slightly dazed unable to properly focus his attention on Spencer's ramblings.

The girls then stood up and put on their overcoats and Clare looked down at Hugh. 'Are you going to escort a girl to the door then?', she asked.

He leapt up to his feet, abandoning his conversation with Spencer, and she linked her arm through his as they headed outside. The night air was warm and balmy and small clusters of people waited for taxis, chatting and laughing. No sooner were they on the footpath outside of the pub Clare pulled Hugh to one side and began kissing him madly, running her hands underneath his T-Shirt and grasping at the taut muscles of his back. Hugh's heart was racing as she thrust herself against him. The pace of her breathing increased, and Hugh lost all sense of time and place, kissing her with increasing abandon. He was not thinking now, simply following the silent injunctions of his body.

One of Clare's friends stationed herself with her back to them and coughed discretely before announcing that their taxi had arrived. Clare reluctantly disengaged from Hugh, momentarily averting her eyes from him, embarrassed at where her passion had taken her. She returned her eyes to his wearing a look that he had not seen that evening: her eyes were locked on his, glazed with a sultry seriousness, her lips parted, and her breathing still not evened out. She squeezed his hand. 'I'll see you here tomorrow', she whispered and turned to go, glancing back at him one more time before she entered the cab, that same look of desire shaping her expression.

His newly found mates came tumbling out of the door, laughing and jostling one another good heartedly.

'Looks like you hit the jackpot there mate', said Spencer fighting off a mock attack from one of his friends who were now whooping and bouncing around like drunken chimps. Hugh didn't reply, preoccupied with his vain attempt to process the events of the past five minutes, his thoughts in a chaotic whirl of new emotions each one promising more than the last.

'We can drop you off if you want', said Spencer as another taxi pulled up.

'Great', replied Hugh distractedly as he tried to marshal the swirl of thoughts running amok through his mind and failing, failing completely.

CHAPTER TWENTY-EIGHT

Hugh awoke the following morning at 5:30am with a maddening thirst, but his body wouldn't respond to his half-formed efforts to raise himself from his bed and make the short trip to his en-suite bathroom to banish the rough dryness from his mouth. His head felt heavy, and the insistent ringing of his alarm clock seemed to vibrate the very fibres of his being. He reached out blindly to put a stop to the hectoring sound of the alarm and then opened his eyes to check the time. He needed to get moving. He couldn't be late in his first week and he clambered out of bed and staggered towards the bathroom. He had not crossed the full distance to his bathroom when the memory of his kiss with Clare burst into his consciousness. It was greeted by panic. What the hell had he done, he thought, and he trawled his memory for further specifics, trying to arrange the staggered emergence of images and emotions into a coherent story of the previous night's events.

He went into the bathroom, the effects of his hangover casually pushed aside as he concentrated his mind on trying to recall the hazy events of the previous night. Then it hit him: he had forgotten to meet Jane and moreover, he hadn't even attempted to contact her. This was going to be a big problem. He would just have to tell her that he went for a drink with his work mates after work and just lost track of time. It was a poor excuse, he recognised that, but it would have to do. He stepped into the shower and shuddered under the cold spray that fell upon him.

He quickly made his way down to the garage, mounted his bicycle and sped out into the crisp coolness of the morning in the direction of the yard. The air gushed into his face as raced through the city blowing away the heavy fog that clouded his thinking and allowing memories of Clare to flood into his mind: the smiling, questioning look on her face when he had first seen her, her wild, compelling dance, the brief kiss as the night was coming to a close and then the white heat of their final embrace. It all became clear to him in an instant and with an absolute mathematical certainty: his relationship with Jane was over. She was as remote from him now as any stranger might be. As he cycled through the morning he felt himself dizzy with elation, overwhelmed by a surge of excitement as he contemplated his date with Clare later that day.

Frankie was waiting for Gene at their usual meeting spot, and it was not until he'd clambered into the van did Gene notice that he was sporting a black eye. Frankie's breath carried a heavy odour of drink which quickly filled the cab and Gene was forced to wind down his window to clear the air of the noxious reek. Frankie looked over to him, the eye swollen and purple, and stuttered an apology. He explained that he and Jenny had been drinking until the early hours of the morning and for reasons that Frankie could only vaguely recall, Jenny had attacked him in a moment of drunken aggression. 'She's out of her fucking mind', he concluded. 'I need to get the fuck out of there', he added.

'Jesus Christ man, you've only been with her a couple of weeks', said Gene in a tone of exasperated disapproval. 'Why can't you just find one good one and stick with her?'

'That'd be the way to do it alright', replied Frankie without much commitment. 'Just pull up here a minute', he continued as they approached a row of shops. Frankie disappeared into the inside of one of the stores and emerged a couple of minutes later carrying a white plastic bag that clinked as he shoved it under the passenger seat of the waggon.

'Cider?', quizzed Gene.

'fourth man in the gang on days like today', Frankie replied with a smile, his complexion coarse and greasy for want of a wash. Gene shook his head disapprovingly.

'I dropped Danny off at 'The Royal' last night', said Gene as he pulled away from the kerb. 'I think that he might have had stiffer competition to face than you did.'

'He went looking for the Mulligans?', replied Frankie with some excitement.

'Aye, he did. I hope he didn't find them', continued Gene still mindful of his part in the events leading up to the confrontation.

'I wouldn't waste too much time worrying about that man. I'd think he probably knows what he's doing.'

'Well, we'll find out soon enough. There he is.' They picked up Danny from outside 'The Harp'. Frankie moved across the seat allowing Danny to get in.

'Talking when you should've been listening?', asked Danny looking at Frankie.

'That bloody Jenny from behind the bar. Mad as a fucking hatter. She'd got it into her head that I'd been seen with that girl Mandy, you know, from the other week.'

'She wasn't far wrong then. You did go meet her didn't you, that girl from the site?', replied Gene.

'Sure I did, but nothing happened.'

'Oh', replied Gene. 'That makes it alright then, I suppose', he said making no attempt to disguise the sarcasm in his tone.

Realising that he was going to receive neither sympathy nor support from Gene Frankie turned to Danny.

'How'd you go on last night?', he asked tentatively.

'Sound enough', he replied 'sorted a few things out.'

Frankie recognised that this was about as much information as he was likely to get from Danny and so he bent down to reach under the seat. As he did so Danny winked gravely at Gene over Frankie's back to confirm that matters with the Mulligans had reached a satisfactory conclusion. Gene nodded in acknowledgement, a small gesture masking the wave of relief that washed over him. Frankie sat back into the seat clutching a bottle of sweet cider which he proceeded to open and put to his lips taking a long, deep draught of the restorative liquid within. Before he screwed the lid back on, he offered the bottle to Danny who shook his head.

'You don't want Jones smelling that on your breath', said Gene, a concerned expression on his face. Frankie didn't look at him but just tipped his head by way of acknowledgement. They pulled into the yard. Danny went off to collect some flag stones and Frankie headed off in the direction of a water - filled ten - gallon drum kept in the corner of the yard. He peered into the drum and, despite the thin film of diesel shimmering on the surface of the water, he pulled off his shirt and plunged his head and shoulders deep into the foul-smelling liquid. After wiping the excess water from his face and hair he put on his shirt and returned to the waggon to help Danny.

'Jesus, I feel better for that', he said smiling as he picked up a slab.

'The wet down or the cider?', asked Danny.

'What does this kid want?', said Frankie to no one in particular as he looked over the side of the waggon and noticed Hugh approaching them from across the empty yard. Danny didn't reply and carried on with his work.

'Morning lads', said Hugh as he approached them. 'Do you need a hand?',

Frankie looked at Danny in astonishment. Each gang worked independently of every other and each had enough work of their own without volunteering to help other gangs with their's, but Gene, recognising Hugh as David Gallon's son, and always welcoming of gift horses, responded amiably.

'Sure', he replied, 'throw a few of these slabs onto the waggon if you want. Who are you supposed to be out with today anyway?'

'I've been with the snagging gang this week, but they're nowhere to be seen this morning.'

'They don't work on Saturdays', replied Gene. 'They didn't tell you that?'

'No', replied Hugh, feeling somewhat uncomfortable at the admission, as if his contribution to the gang over the week had been so negligible that they hadn't been bothered even to inform him of their working hours.

'I wouldn't worry too much about it', said Gene, noting the lad's discomfort. 'They probably just forgot to tell you. If you're looking for a half a shift you can come out with us for a couple of hours. It'll cover your beer this afternoon.'

'Sure, yes', replied Hugh struggling to contain his excitement, flattered that they were taking him seriously. Gene wandered around to the other side of the waggon where Danny and Frankie were loading the waggon. 'I'm going bring this lad out with us for the half shift. He can move all that muck we left out last night and give the site a good clean up, eh? We'll give him thirty quid, eh? Tenner a man?'.

The two men nodded in agreement and Gene called Hugh around to join them and they proceeded to load the waggon. Frankie was sweating profusely, a consequence of the previous night's drinking, and his mouth tasted like the inside of an old boot. He wandered off to the cab and returned with a bottle of cider hidden inside the plastic bag and took a long swig and offered it around. Danny once again declined, but Hugh, thinking that it was lemonade, took the bottle gratefully before gulping down the contents.

He was coughing and spluttering before he realised his mistake. Gene spun around to see what the fuss was about.

'Jesus Christ!', he exclaimed, 'do you want us to be run off the job! Drinking cider in the yard? Bloody hell', he continued utterly exasperated and wandered off shaking his head.

'His car's not here yet Gene, don't worry yourself', replied Frankie and turned to Hugh who was stood holding the bottle, a guilty expression on his face. He hadn't yet picked up a shovel and already he was on the receiving end of a bollocking from the ganger man.

'Don't worry about him', said Frankie smiling, 'if he shakes that big old head of his anymore today it's just going to roll clean off his shoulders. Go on, get it down your neck. I've another one in the waggon.' Hugh raised the bottle to his lips and tipped its contents down his throat. Now that he was prepared for the contents, he could savour the warm sweetness washing away the dryness from his mouth.

'Swigging cider at seven o'clock in the morning! Dad wouldn't be too pleased with me', he thought to himself, the beginnings of a smile drifting across his face. He took another mouthful and passed it back to Frankie who looked from Hugh to Danny.

'Jesus, you two look like two peas in a pod. Hey Gene, wouldn't you say these two lads look alike?'.

'Talking shite again Frankie, eh?', replied Gene approaching the group, 'come on, enough of this bollocks. We'd better get moving if we want to be done for a decent time.'

The morning's work proceeded smoothly enough, although Hugh was slightly disappointed to learn that he would be working alone for the duration of the half shift. He was dropped off at site adjacent to where the rest of the gang were going to be and was given instructions to tidy up the site and to tarmac a length of track which they hadn't been able to get to the day before because of a delay with the tarmac delivery. They were straightforward enough tasks, but he was nonetheless relieved that no one was monitoring his performance as he was anxious in case his inexperience would reveal itself. Soon enough however, his thoughts drifted back to Clare and their meeting that afternoon and he was grateful for the solitude that the job offered providing him with an opportunity to savour the prospect without interruption.

Yet as the morning progressed thoughts of Clare were becoming increasingly interrupted by the looming inevitability of bringing his relationship with Jane to a close. Feelings of guilt began to dog him, and he realised he would have to speak to her sooner rather than later, so when Gene arrived at eleven o'clock to ask if he wanted food from a nearby bakery Hugh asked to accompany him in the hope of finding a phone box nearby from which to break the news to Jane. They drove the short distance soon arriving at a row of shops and Hugh was both relieved and anxious to note the presence of a telephone box.

He asked Gene by buy him a sandwich and fumbled in his pocket and offered some money to Gene.

'Put your money away', came the response as Gene ambled his way towards the shop entrance.

Hugh noted with some relief that there were only a few people ahead of Gene in the queue so he would be attended to quickly and Hugh did not intend to leave him waiting in the waggon for his call to come to a close, especially not after his earlier irritation over the cider. The lethargy of the baker's trade gave him a welcome justification for making the telephone conversation as brief as possible. He was eager to avoid having to provide a prolonged explanation as to the reasons for his decision – this could easily lead to a negotiation, a prospect which he wanted to steer clear of. He approached the phone box nervously not entirely sure how Jane would respond.

They had been a couple for six months or so and the relationship had meandered along quite comfortably, but he had no illusions as to its long-term prospects. She was an intelligent and an attractive girl, but her Catholic upbringing had leant her a prudishness which Hugh would not miss. Plus, she had made it perfectly clear on more than one occasion that she intended to remain a virgin until her wedding night, a frustrating declaration for young man of eighteen years and now that their gap year had been cancelled, he had fully expected their relationship to simply peter out within the first term of their respective university courses. He reminded himself that he was merely anticipating an inevitable conversation by a few months.

He dialled her number.

'Oh, hello Mrs. Price. Is Jane there? Its Hugh.'

'Oh Hello Hugh. I'll go get her for you', replied Jane's mother. He heard Jane's voice in the background and waited a few moments, sure he was doing the right thing but trepidatious about her possible response.

'Hello?', she said, her tone cold and hard.

'Hi Jane. Look, I'm really sorry about last night. I just got caught up with a few workmates in the pub and before I knew it was ten o'clock. I know that it was very inconsiderate of me.'

'Well, I have to tell you that I'm very disappointed with your behaviour Hugh. It was fortunate that everyone else was there or else I'd have been left waiting on my own. Everybody was worried about you, you know. It *was* very inconsiderate of you', she replied.

'I know. I'm sorry.'

'So now you prefer to spend your time with a group of ill-educated workmen drinking beer in some squalid little pub rather than honouring a date that you made with your girlfriend? Should I expect this behaviour to continue, and should I just make allowances because such choices are of course simply a product of some convenient genetic imperative?', she continued her annoyance descending seamlessly into sarcasm.

'Look, I've apologised. I'm not sure what else I can say', Hugh replied, absorbing her irritation.

'You can reassure me that it's not going to happen again', she continued, 'and frankly Hugh I should tell you that if it does I'm not sure how I'm going to react.' She was entering into full scold mode now, he thought to himself, and while in the normal course of events he could acknowledge that he was at fault, Jane was definitely overplaying her hand in issuing threats.

'Look, if that's the way you feel about it, maybe it would be better for both of us if we cooled things down for a while. You know, take a break from each other?', he replied pouncing on the opportunity she had unwittingly provided to him.

'You think that we should what?', she replied indignantly.

'Just take a break from each other for a while, that's all.'

'I know what this is about', she replied, clearly losing her patience with him. 'It's because I don't want to go on your stupid gap year, isn't it?'. He hadn't considered this as an escape route, but now that it had presented itself he fell upon it with gusto. 'I just think that it shows that we have different priorities that's all, don't you?', he said shifting the onus onto Jane.

'Why didn't you mention anything earlier?', she replied, her tone softening as the moral high-ground upon which she was perched crumbled beneath her. 'I didn't realise that it was such a big deal for you. We can talk about this, you know.'

'I think we've probably discussed it enough Jane', he replied sensing that the conversation was heading into negotiation territory, a trajectory he didn't want to follow. He felt that had done the difficult job: technically, he had ended their relationship and, with the callousness typical of such situations, he now wanted to exit the scene as briskly as possible. It was at that moment that he noticed Gene leaving the shop. 'Look, I've got to go. I'm at work and I'm being called back. I'm sorry that it had to end this way Jane.'

'I'm not finished Hugh. I really think that we should talk about this.'

'Look, I've got to go. I don't think that there's anything more to be said really.'

'We've been going out together for six months and you just drop this bombshell! It's not very mature of you Hugh', she continued, climbing her way back up to the peak of the moral high ground.

'Look, I've got to go,' he said before returning the phone to its housing and rushing out of the phone box to meet Gene.

'Sorry about that', he said as he jumped into the cab.

'No problem. I'd have waited', replied Gene.

'It was the girlfriend and not a conversation I wanted to keep going to be honest.'

'You as well, eh?', he said shaking his head in disapproval once again as he turned the ignition. Hugh had to restrain a smile as he recalled Frankie's quip earlier that morning.

Danny and Frankie downed tools when they saw the waggon pulling up. Frankie was the first to the door and he collected his food and reached under the seat for the second bottle of cider. He held it up to inspect the contents through the brown glass and sighed noting that it was now half empty. He offered the bottle to Hugh, who declined. Frankie shrugged his shoulders and took a deep gulp.

'Urrrgghh. It doesn't taste good warm this stuff', he said with a shudder and took another draught, emptying the bottle completely. Hugh, feeling considerably more relaxed now that the telephone conversation was out of the way, waited for Frankie's grimace to subside before enquiring into the cause of the black eye. He wouldn't usually be so forthright, but Frankie had an easy way with him to which people readily responded and Hugh was no exception. He felt comfortable enquiring into Frankie's life outside of the job, particularly given the evidence of its complexities so abundantly marked on his face for all to see.

Danny was a different man altogether. There was something unknowable about him, something distant, Hugh concluded. He had been friendly enough during the course of the morning, but a definite and pronounced air of menace seemed to surround him and it was more than just the man's size and obvious physical strength. Hugh had antennae for this kind of danger, and they were unusually sensitive for a lad of his age and he had known with absolute certainty from the moment that he had been introduced to Danny that this was a man who was to be treated with respect.

'What happened to the eye then Frankie. Forgot how to duck?', asked Hugh smiling. 'The woman', he said sighing, 'mad fucking woman.' He raised his palms in exasperation. 'What can you do, eh?' That's the last of it anyway. She'll see no more of me, that's for sure.'

'And how're you going to manage that then?', said Gene, 'Your clothes are at her house, and she works in your local pub, not the easiest of women to avoid, eh?'

'I bagged my few rags up this morning before you fellas came. They're in her back yard. She won't see them there, and she won't see me in 'The Harp' either. I'll be paying a visit to Mandy at 'The Prince'. She'll give me the lie down, no problem.'

'Jesus Christ!', exclaimed Gene. You're some boyo, you! How long have you been in this city? A year? Ten months? You must've gone through just as many women in that time.'

'Well, when you're at this kind of work a man needs looking after and I'll be fucked if I'm going to get home from a day's work and start cooking and cleaning and washing clothes and all that bollocks. Every city I land in the first job is always to find myself a nice young woman in need of a man. That's rule number one in The Long Distance Man's Handbook, that is. I give 'em a few quid at the end of the week and they're as happy as Larry. Why wouldn't they be? I get looked after and they get a bit of Frankie and a lump of extra housekeeping money thrown in. Everyone's a winner!', he turned laughing to Hugh.

'You could always find one good one and settle yourself down', observed Gene tartly, 'or maybe just hold onto one for long enough to learn her second name.'

'There's a lot of temptation out there', Frankie replied, 'but I will. In time. When the right one comes along.'

'And who's the right one?', asked Gene sceptically.

'That'd be the one with the money, of course. I've no intention at sticking at this work until I'm an old man, that's a fool's game.'

'Is that right?', replied Gene huffing indignantly.

'No, I didn't mean you Gene, of course I didn't. I mean, times were different when you were a young', he said in mitigation.

'There's no shame in this work', replied Gene testily, 'and nor should there be. It's tough enough to be sure, but its man's work and you can get a decent living out of it. I'd rather be out in the fresh air than stuck behind a desk all day. What kind of woman would want a man who couldn't support himself anyway? You've got your head up your arse with all that nonsense, if you ask me.'

'Look, I said I didn't mean you. All I'm saying is why not go for an easy life, eh? And there's plenty of those posh women out there who'd be grateful for a man like me to keep 'em warm during those long winter nights, and why wouldn't they, eh? The lasses have always had a bit of a soft spot for old Frankie Conroy, and I'd be a fool not to make use of that', he said before laying the palms of his hands across his chest and breaking out into song: 'And when that blessed day comes no more a long distance man I', he wailed with a distinct lack of musicality.

Hugh broke out into a fit of laughter, followed by the singer himself; even Danny smiled dryly. Gene frowned and once again shook his head disapprovingly provoking Frankie and Hugh into even louder bursts of laughter. He looked at them both uncomprehendingly.

The hilarity eventually subsided, and Hugh turned to Frankie.

'So, what's a long distance Man?', he asked.

'Its just a fella that goes from place to place, working on one job 'till it's done, or until he's ran, then moving on to the next, city after city, not settling anywhere for long or putting any roots down, just going where the work takes him. Going where he fancies. A free man, just the open road before him', replied Frankie solemnly.

'A free man with occasional bouts of homelessness thrown in, eh Frankie?', interjected Gene waspishly.

'I'll be alright, don't worry about me', replied Frankie. 'I've already been on the phone to her and I'm meeting her this afternoon. She may not know it yet, but young Mandy'll be waking up tomorrow morning with a smile on her face and a Frankie in her bed.'

'And will we expect another fight between Jenny and this new one like there was between Jenny and the one before her? I mean, there are only so many pubs you can go into and that kind of trouble does seem to follow you about a bit, doesn't it? Maybe if you just took a bit of time to draw breath between them or, God forbid, try telling them the truth now and again', said Gene caustically, his irritation growing at Frankie's obvious self-regard.

Frankie turned to Hugh. 'Now our friend here is annoyed at me', he said gesturing towards Gene with his thumb, 'and after I apologised for talking out of turn and all. Learn a lesson from me lad, when it comes to women you should tell them the truth, you should tell them nothing but the truth, but you should never tell them the whole truth. The 'whole truth' is a never-ending story that gets everyone in a mix-up. The 'whole truth' never did anyone any good at all.' Hugh reflected on his earlier conversation with Jane and was forced to admit to himself that there was some validity to Frankie's claim, although he could not dispel a lingering sense of doubt that the claim in itself was not the whole truth of the matter.

They spent the next couple of hours working and it was with some relief that Hugh heard the call to start packing up at one o'clock. He was conscious of the fact that he had agreed to meet Clare at two, but he was acutely aware that he didn't have any authority within the gang dictate the finishing time. All things being equal he thought, he would have enough time to get home, take a shower and change clothes before heading off to meet her.

Gene paid him in cash in the yard and he mounted his bike and dashed home. He was grateful that neither of his parents were around as this would have obliged him to give an account of his movements last night which would only further delay him. He rang a taxi, a luxury in the normal course of events, then called Richard to tell him about recent events regarding Clare and Jane while he waited for the cab to arrive.

Hugh rushed through his narrative, conscious of the fact that the taxi might arrive at any moment, but he needed to share recent developments with someone. Richard tried to press him for details and suggested that they meet later, but when Hugh told him where he was likely to be that afternoon the line went silent. Hugh thought that they had been cut off. He was about to end the call when he heard Richard speak.

'What the hell are you going to a place like that for?', the disapproval heavy in his tone of voice. 'Look', he continued, 'I think that we might need to have a talk you and I. How about meeting tomorrow?'

'OK, Uncle Richard', Hugh replied sarcastically, 'I'll give you a call tomorrow morning. Look I've got to dash, there's a taxi waiting for me.'

His mother pulled through the entrance to the driveway as he was getting into the taxi and she waved at him to wait and he pointed to his watch indicating that he was in a hurry. He understood that he would have to let his mother know the situation with Jane, but he was equally clear that now was not the time.

CHAPTER TWENTY-NINE

Gene dropped Frankie off at the 'The Prince' pub and he dashed straight through the tap room and into the toilets to clean himself up. He looked rough, his face unshaven and greasy with sweat, a faint odour of diesel clinging to his hair. He pulled off his shirt and doused his head and neck with water and picked up the small bar of dried, cracked soap sat on the sink and attempted to scrub some colour back into his wan cheeks. Then he gave his hair a cursory wash, the bar of soap disintegrating in his hands as he did so. He dragged a disposable razor across his face. Finally, he doused himself with aftershave and pulled a comb through his hair before going into the WC and climbing into clean, if crumpled, jeans and T-Shirt that he had retrieved from the bin liner that now constituted his wardrobe. He checked himself in the mirror and smiled in satisfaction at the result of his labours. He walked out into the bar feeling like a new man, ordered a pint and waited for Mandy to arrive, his hair glistening and his mood high.

Jones was sat his desk working through some additional paperwork that David had left for him to complete. He enjoyed undertaking this kind of administrative work, menial as it was, for as far as he was concerned, they put him one step further away from the trench and confirmed him in his view of himself as a manager of men, superintending the efforts of lesser mortals. It was when undertaking these solitary tasks that he would allow himself the indulgence of wearing his spectacles at work. Though the glasses were prescribed, he avoided wearing them around the men believing that they made him appear weak, but when left alone in the office he relished the air of gravitas they leant him; he was a serious man with serious tasks to perform.

His concentration on the task at hand was disturbed by the screech of wheels outside skidding to a stop on the dry, earthy surface of the yard. He looked up startled and removed his glasses. Nobody should be coming into the yard at this time on a Saturday afternoon he thought and certainly nobody should be abusing company vehicles in the manner that the screeching from below indicated. He leapt

179

to his feet energised at the prospect of bawling a well-deserved reprimand at the culprit.

His instinctive caution, however, caused him to glance out of the window before presenting himself on the gantry to deliver the intended expletive-studded rebuke. He was surprised to see that it wasn't a waggon at all, but instead the source of the commotion was a black saloon, a BMW. He didn't have time to properly consider the meaning of this before all four car doors opened more or less simultaneously and four rough-looking individuals exited from the car: two of the Mulligans and a couple of their cronies. This did not bode well he thought, but then it occurred to him that they were obviously here looking for Danny and the flamboyancy of their arrival suggested that they meant business. He smiled to himself, gratified that his plan was bearing fruit.

He strode through the door of the office and placed his hands on the guard rail of the gantry.

'How are you lads?', he shouted down at them, a welcoming smile on his face. The group immediately turned as one and looked up at him, conferred for a moment and began striding towards the staircase. He waited for them to begin their ascent before turning to face the head of the staircase, hands on hips.

'Am I right in thinking that you're looking for Danny Greene?', he called out to them. Two birds with stone he thought: Greene driven away by a bunch of thugs who had no connection to GCE and a bit of personal credit with the Family Mulligan too which just might come in handy someday, who knows?

'No, we're looking for you, you cunt', snarled the lead member of the group as they broached the steps, each one of the men in his wake glowering like junk yard dogs. 'You think you can go around using our fucking name as you please, do you?', he bellowed as he began his ascent up the staircase.

Jones' felt his innards momentarily clench and twist as this change of circumstances registered with him, but he immediately recovered himself. Now Jones was a bully, but he was also a seasoned fighting man, well capable of reducing most other men of his ilk to bloody unconsciousness. His sense of self-worth was underwritten by his immense size and by his willingness to exercise the brute physical power that this implied and so it wasn't fear that washed over him as he stood at the head of the staircase waiting for this squad of impertinents, but instead a wave of furious indignation that they would have the gall to confront him on his own turf.

The survival instinct was strong in him, and he was well aware that should he be compromised in this situation then news of his humiliation would spread across the city like the plague. It would make no difference that he was outnumbered, only that he was outfought. He would be a laughingstock, an object of derision for the lowest of men in the lowest of pubs, a freshly polished target for every young hard man once kept at bay by his patina of invincibility. His credibility would be shattered and without his credibility his time at GCE would be over, perhaps even his stay in this city. There was no nobility in Jones' courage. The bravery on display as he confronted this vicious group was more the brother of his vanity than his virtue.

'Come one, come all then', he bellowed down at them, laughing, open mouthed and laughing. His tactical advantage was obvious to him, if not to them: the idiots were approaching him in series as they moved up the narrow stairway, one behind the other. All he had to do was deal with the first of them who would then fall back into the small column of those behind him allowing him to pounce on the jumbled mess of men left sprawling on the landing below. He reminded himself to make use of the notion of them queueing for a beating when he came to tell the tale to the boys, and he smiled at the prospect of the telling to come, but first back to business: he waited for them patiently, savouring their ignorance of the pain that was about to descend upon them.

'Come on then boys, I haven't got all day!', he bellowed at them, rubbing the palms of his enormous hands together in an exaggerated gesture of anticipation, 'The bull's waiting!', he hooted.

The lead Mulligan, heavy set and with a barrel gut, was beginning to pant heavily as he approached the top of the steps, his legs weakening under the burden of his lumpen torso. He was used to seeing fear drenching the facial expressions of the opposition, but not today; this bloke was laughing at them, an insult which sent him into a delirium of anger. His infuriation injected a fresh stream of adrenaline into him, and he increased his pace which in turn made him gasp for breath with even greater urgency, diluting his concentration on the task at hand.

Jones waited calmly for the first of them to get within range. The lead Mulligan was three or four steps away from him. His fatigue had slowed him down and he was pulling himself up the final steps using the handrail, panting like a dog in the heat, but was still moving with purpose, staring up at Jones with a fierce malevolence. Jones waited until precisely the right moment and swung his right leg back before whipping it forward and rolling his hip through the motion, his booted instep catching the man cleanly under the jawbone shattering it as if it were fine porcelain. He watched the Mulligan's eyes roll in their sockets as he was launched backwards, out cold, crashing into the man behind him. Both slid backwards down the wooden steps up - ending the two men behind them. This ludicrous bundle of yelping flesh came to a stop on the first landing: the second Mulligan trapped under the dead weight of the first, the two men behind them similarly entangled in a corrupted intimacy of confusion and pain.

Jones slowly descended the steps carefully surveying the writhing mass before him and brought his heel down smartly on the arm of the second Mulligan who yelped under the immensity of his pain as the bone in his arm snapped like a bread stick, sending bolts of agony ricocheting through his frame. He tried to splutter out an obscenity but instead he coughed up a slurry of vomit which pooled on the timber floor beside him. Jones crashed the iron clad toe of his boot into the rib cage of the third man as he passed him on the landing, puncturing his lung, not even deigning to look at the writhing mess as he descended to the yard.

On reaching ground level, he disappeared around the side of the portacabin and emerged holding a pickaxe shaft and slowly walked to the BMW. He strolled around the car, nodding in appreciation at the sleekness of its design and then raised the shaft above his head and proceeded to shatter every pane of glass in the vehicle. The second Mulligan, sprung from his misery by the sounds of the destruction being meted out to his beloved vehicle, groaned weakly as he dislodged himself from beneath his brother and with the grunting assistance of the least damaged of his associates pulled him to his feet, his brother's lower jaw hanging loose and swinging from side to side, the man drooling insensibly as they manhandled him down the steps.

Jones waited at the foot of the staircase slowly slapping the shaft against his left palm. He didn't look at them as they scrambled past him groaning, dishevelled and beaten before crawling into what remained of the car.

'Oh, by the way', he shouted after them, 'if you're thinking of going to the police, I'm just going to tell 'em that I didn't lay a hand on you, right?', and with that he threw his head back and filled the yard with his hard, mirthless laughter.

The car sped out through the gates and then all was silent. He stared after them, his euphoria quickly subsiding into confusion.

'What the fuck was that all about? 'Using our name'?', he murmured to himself as he stood alone in the yard, his brain clunking through possible explanations for what had just happened.

'Frankie fucking Conroy!', he exclaimed finally. A conclusive explanation now obtained, he raised the pickaxe shaft above his head and hurled it to the ground with the full force of his fury.

Kate and Rachel were sat in the lounge of the golf Club having just completed nine holes and both were ready for a glass of wine or two. Rachel had been out of sorts during the game, quiet and distracted, but Kate had decided that she wouldn't make any enquiries as to the reasons for this until they were off the course with their game behind them. She knew Rachel well enough to recognise that she would find this conversation far more therapeutic with a glass of wine to hand.

They nestled into their seats and Rachel began recounting the most recent instalment of an ongoing work issue involving people that Kate didn't know embroiled in circumstances that she had never encountered, but she reconciled herself to the tedium of the narrative recognising it for the preamble that it was. Besides, Rachel could tell a tale. She could deploy both sophisticated wit or vulgar humour and it was this vulgarity that particularly amused Kate, delivered as it was in the honeyed tones of well-modulated, privately educated voice. Yet today there was little verve in her tale and her pokes at colleagues were a little less barbed than usual. Nonetheless, Kate listened patiently waiting for Rachel to reveal the substance of her thinly disguised unease.

She didn't have to wait too long. After ten minutes of Rachel spinning her story, and Kate dutifully nodding in agreement and tutting in disapproval as required, Rachel suddenly broke down in tears in mid-sentence.

'My God, what's up?', asked Kate putting her arm around Rachel's shoulder. 'Surely there's nothing that can't be sorted out. Its only bloody work', she offered.

'No, no, it's not that. It's not work. It's me and Trevor', she said as she reached into her handbag for tissue paper. 'He's been having an affair.'

'Oh', replied Kate solemnly.

'He's been fucking his bloody secretary. I mean, how utterly cliched.'

'I'm so sorry to hear that, Rachel. What are you going to do?'

'Oh, I don't know', she replied as if exhausted by thoughts of her options before wiping the tears from her eyes.

'When did he tell you? How long has it been going on?'

'He told me a couple of days ago. He's only been seeing her for around a month and of course he's full of remorse. Said he needed to get it off his chest so that he could find a way back to our relationship. 'Find a way back'. I never knew he'd wandered off', she said bitterly.

'Are you going to divorce him?'.

'I don't know. He tells me that it's over, the girl has gone and that he needed my forgiveness.'

'The selfish bastard!', exclaimed Kate.

'I know. If it was finished, why didn't he just keep quiet about it? Why do I have to pay in grief for what he has done in pleasure?' She began to compose herself. 'I suppose I should divorce him; that's the advice I'd give anyone else, but I still love him, even though he's a complete wanker.' She looked at Kate and smiled weakly. 'He's been begging and pleading for the past few days. It's been a bit pathetic really. By the way, you have the dubious honour of being the only person I've told, so keep it hush-hush will you', she added. 'Why can't they just own up to it and go? Why do I have to make the decision? Look, I'm sorry to drop this on you. It's a Saturday

184

afternoon and all you want to do is play a round of golf and relax and here I am dumping the sordid details of my private life in your lap. I'm sorry.'

Kate looked at her in all her vulnerability and made a decision.

'David has been having an affair for years', she stated matter of factly.

'What?', said Rachel incredulously, momentarily distracted from her own misery.

'Yes. He visits her pretty regularly, usually when he tells me he's out running.'

'I don't believe it! I mean, I mean, I don't doubt what you're saying, but David? How can you tolerate it?'

'I simply do not care', she said calmly. 'We haven't had sex for years. Frankly, I'm not even sure if he has sex with her, not that I would mind. I never found him attractive, not in that way anyway.'

Rachel stared at Kate, stunned by what she was hearing. 'My God, I had no idea.'

'I thought it would've got out by now frankly, but at least he's discrete. I'd hate to have to deal with all the sympathy', she said before catching herself, 'I'm not trying to say....'. Rachel saved her the trouble of completing the sentence.

'I know what you mean. Every situation is different. I just don't know what to say, he just doesn't seem the type.'

'They are all the type', replied Kate. 'Most of them anyway. The only reason I married him was to make sure that Hugh was looked after. I wasn't going to end up with some navvy who came home smelling of tarmac and beer every night and having to wrestle the housekeeping money from him every Friday evening.'

'But why did you think that your choices were so limited? Look at you, you're gorgeous, you're smart.'

'Things were different then. You've got to remember, I come from a very different world to you. My life was very different to your's. I wish I knew then what know now though. Anyway, my situation is what it is and I've no complaints. Hugh is doing well and that is all that matters, all that's ever mattered, so you have absolutely no need to be concerned for me. It's you that has got a decision to make.'

Rachel sighed heavily. 'I'll never be able to trust him again. That's what worries me. How can remain married to a man that I don't trust?'

'You've the kids to consider too.'

'I know, but to end up in your situation? I mean, I'm sorry, that's not what I wanted to say. I wanted to have a full, loving relationship, you know, a soulmate, or at least someone I could fucking trust.'

'I know what you mean. As I said, my priorities were different, and you know, I'm not at all unhappy. I can't say that the thought of David crawling all over me is much of a turn on and if he's got someone who thinks it is, then good for him, good for them both. Hugh's almost ready to go off on his own. I might take another look at things when he's flown the nest, who knows?'

'You seem so calm about it, so relaxed'. She started weeping again. 'I just want to go back to the way things were', her voice almost petulant.

'I can't tell you what to do love, but I will support you whatever you decide, you know that.'

'I know', she said with a tight - lipped smile, 'thanks'.

'Hello Mrs. Gallon', said Richard making a detour across the lounge of the Club. As with most of Hugh's friends he had a crush on Kate.

'Oh, hello Richard', she replied smiling, 'been playing today? And I've told you before, you can call me Kate.'

'No, I'm just in here looking for someone actually', he said peering around the room.

'Hugh?', asked Kate.

'No', he replied shaking his head.' 'Hugh's out somewhere with his new girlfriend.'

'His new girlfriend?', exclaimed Kate. 'What do you mean his new girlfriend? Who's his new girlfriend? What happened to Jane?' she asked growing slightly concerned.

'Oh, I don't know', replied Richard 'I've only just found out. We had a quick chat on the phone this morning and he didn't really go into any details.'

'Who is she? Do you know her?'

'I've never met her Kate', he replied blushing slightly, yet relishing this newfound familiarity. 'I don't know who she is', he said shrugging his shoulders.

'I thought he was supposed to be with Jane and the rest of your gang last night', she continued.

'That was the plan, but apparently he went out with some of his friends from work.'

'From work?', she exclaimed.

'Yes, it's all a bit mysterious at the moment.'

'How's Jane? Is she OK?'

'I haven't seen her Kate, I can't really say.'

'OK, Richard, you have a nice day', she said by way of a farewell, and he took the hint and departed. 'News to me', she said looking at Rachel.

'That's when you know they're growing up I suppose, when you're not the first one they tell their news to.'

'Yes, indeed', replied Kate thoughtfully, a fleeting sense of foreboding rippling through her. 'Well, they were never really suited, I thought. I mean she is a lovely girl and very pretty, but she was very straitlaced. Not a bad thing of course, but Hugh's got a bit of a wild streak in him, which I've done my best to curb by the way.'

'He's bloody gorgeous Kate, they're going to be forming a queue! They're at that age where they're just finding out what they want. I wouldn't even try to keep up with him if I were you and let's face it, once he goes off to university you wouldn't be able to if you tried.'

'You're right', said Kate resignedly, 'but it just seems pretty sudden, that's all and it does feel a bit strange not being involved somehow', she held her palms up towards Rachel as if toward off the inevitable rejoinder, 'I know, I know. It's really none of my business, but even saying that feels strange. 'Some of Hugh's decisions are none of my business', she repeated to herself as if to test her response to its brutal significance, to inoculate herself against this assault on her maternity. 'Where does it go, eh? Doesn't seem like two minutes since I was wiping his bum', she said, attempting to lighten the mood. They both smiled as if to conclude the matter, but Kate had glanced into the abyss and had seen the bleak, intransigent void that awaited her when Hugh began his own separate, independent life in earnest.

When measured against results all the sacrifices that she had made had been proved well worth enduring. She had spent almost twenty years living outside of herself, her every decision made for the betterment of another, but what was left for her now that this guiding purpose had run it's course? She felt ill - equipped to negotiate the future which loomed before her, and a great fear began to take shape. She abruptly turned from its cultivation to a misery that was not her own.

'Anyway, back to more pressing matters: you and Trevor?'

CHAPTER THIRTY

The taxi pulled up outside 'The Harp' and Hugh leapt out, the renewed surge of excitement at the prospect of meeting Clare again competing with an intense wave of guilt as he contemplated his earlier conversation with Jane. An inner voice was whispering to him, telling him that perhaps he had acted too hastily in jettisoning her on the basis of what was in reality no more than a blurred recollection of a drunken night out. He entered the pub and ordered a drink. He checked the clock. He was fifteen minutes early.

As he stood at the bar waiting for her to arrive his anxiety increased a notch. Perhaps Clare had dismissed the previous night's arrangements as a drunken miscalculation and was at this moment sat at home with her friends giggling at the thought of him taking them seriously. He checked the clock. The bar was beginning to fill. He took another drink and checked the clock again. He glanced around the room and tried to distract himself by attempting to conjure up the sense of nostalgia that he'd experienced the previous day, but he couldn't bring his attention to bear with sufficient focus. His stomach was churning. He smelt the beer to check that it wasn't the cause. He heard the door open, and his head spun around to see who was entering, but it wasn't her. He turned back to the bar and took another drink. He checked the clock again. She wasn't late yet, he noted trying to reassure himself and looked at the clock again, cursing the hands for moving so slowly.

Then he heard the door swing open again and his eyes darted in the direction of the sound. Suddenly there she was. She paused as she crossed the threshold and rummaged through her handbag, her eyes focused on its contents, then she looked up to the room and glanced around. Finally, their eyes locked, and she smiled at him with a warmth that made every cell in his body quiver with excitement. He tried to collect himself as she approached, but he could not dilute the joy that beamed from his face. There was no point in trying to contain the breadth of his smile because he knew that his eyes were in on the job too.

'I thought that you weren't coming', he said, unable to take his eyes from her, surprising himself in his openness about his anxiety.

'Well, you thought wrong', she replied pertly and, as if distracted, reached out to flick some small particle of fluff sitting unnoticed on his shirt. His heart raced in response to the casual intimacy of the gesture. She looked him squarely in the eyes and smiled once again, her gaze evaporating the distance between them. She turned briskly to the bar.

'What would you like?', she asked.

'I'll have a pint please. Of Guinness', he replied. She placed their order and they stood there waiting in silence, both watching the barmaid going about her business. His eyes repeatedly flit in her direction seeking out momentary glimpses of her until she turned her head and caught his surreptitious glance upon her. She held his gaze for the smallest of moments and smiled before looking back towards the barmaid. Then he felt her hand reach out and gently enfold his and she turned her face towards him wearing a look which spoke to his soul: 'I know, don't worry, I feel the same way too', and smiled.

They collected their drinks and sat down Just as Spencer walked through the door with a couple of companions who Hugh recognised from the previous night. Hugh nodded in acknowledgement and turned back to Clare.

'Does he work with you?', she asked as she raised her drink, looking towards Spencer.

'He does, but he's a trainee site agent, a kind of supervisor.'

'Hmmm', she replied thoughtfully. 'He's a big lad, but he's a bit flabby, isn't he. Doesn't really look like a building worker. Not like my big, strong man', she said, her eyes twinkling. Do you mind me calling you that? 'My man.'

'Of course not', he replied, 'I love it.'

She looked down own at her hands nested in her lap. 'Saying it seems so strange and so natural at the same time. I didn't even know who you were this time yesterday and today it feels like I've never not known you.' She started laughing and turned to him. 'I was so nervous about coming to meet you today. I thought that you might not come. I mean, we were both drinking last night, and I never even once asked you if you had a girlfriend.'

'Well, I certainly do now', he said and smiled at her. He couldn't see anything to be gained from going into the details of his parting with Jane. She was unimportant to him now and what had Frankie said? 'The whole truth just mixes things up'.

'I know exactly how you feel', he continued. 'I've never felt like this before.'

The afternoon moved on. Clare asked him about his work and he answered her questions, fleshing out his limited experience of the job, but he didn't see the need to mention that he had recently completed his A-levels and was planning on going to university in a few months' time. Why complicate matters at this point, he thought to himself, enough of the truth will do for now, the whole truth could wait. He didn't want to scare her off.

He persuaded himself that this omission wasn't an attempt to hide anything from her, it was simply that these aspects of his life weren't included in the natural flow of conversation. He would not have felt any discomfort at discussing other areas of his life, but they skipped over their respective work situations so quickly that it simply didn't occur to him enlarge upon his future plans in any detail.

They decided to move on elsewhere and Clare suggested 'The Prince Of Wales' public house not far from where they were. They left the pub hand in hand by way of Spencer's table and Hugh informed him of their plans and suggested that they might return later. The moment that they outside the doors Clare wrapped her arms around him and pulled him towards her.

'I've been wanting to do this since I first saw you today', she said and kissed him hard on the lips. They held the embrace for a few moments until a loud tutting noise from a customer entering the pub caused them to disengage, both slightly embarrassed.

'Later', she said holding his gaze and took his hand and led him along the footpath. He let her hand drop and wrapped his arm around her waist and pulled her closer to him, all the better to feel her body against his.

They walked to the next pub located only fifty meters or so along the way and ordered their drinks at the bar. No sooner had they completed their order than Frankie appeared beside Hugh and greeted him with an enthusiasm that belied the fact that they had parted company only a couple of hours ago. Hugh introduced him to Clare and Frankie insisted that he pay for their drinks and that they join him at his table where Mandy was sat waiting for him to return.

'So how long have you been working with Gene and Danny?', Hugh asked once they were all gathered around the table.

'Oh, about nine or ten months. I'd come up here from London with another gang, two brothers, but they ended up knocking shite out of one another so that was that.' He quickly turned to Clare. 'Sorry about my language love', he said sheepishly.

'Don't worry about me', she replied laughing, 'I've heard worse.'

'What about me, you bastard', said Mandy nudging him in the ribs with her elbow, 'don't I get an apology?', her giggles adding to Clare's.

Frankie smiled and turned back to Hugh. 'After that gang fell apart someone in the pub told me that Gene was looking for a man, so here I am. He's a good worker, he knows the game inside out and easy enough to get along with. Well, if you don't go ruffling his feathers that is', he said in reference to this morning's spat. 'You know he used to be a priest. Trained to be one anyway, so I heard. He met the wife, ditched the collar and came over here.'

'Oh, that's so romantic!', cooed Clare.

'Really!', exclaimed Hugh, his interest piqued. 'How interesting. Where is he today? Doesn't he bother with the beer?'

'He might have an odd one now and again, but his wife's a poorly woman. They had a kid years ago, so I heard, but the poor child died and so it's pretty much fallen on Gene to look after her. And he's good at it too. Straight home after work, no messing about. He'll be with her now. Nothing's too much trouble for her.'

'Oh, that's sweet', said Mandy.

'What about the other bloke, Danny? He looks like a bit of a hand full. What happened to his eye?', asked Hugh.

'Looks like and is', replied Frankie smiling ruefully. 'He's only been with us for a few weeks, but I've known of him for years. Now he is a hard-core long distance man. Every yard you go into there'll be some one that knows him or knows of him. A dangerous man to get on the wrong side of too, but you can see that by looking at him. He seems like a proper gentleman to me. I've heard a few rumours about the eye, but I don't know that I'd want to ask him the truth of it myself.'

'He doesn't say much, does he', observed Hugh, 'I mean, I don't know him that well of course.....'

'True, he's no loud-mouth, but when he does talk you'd better listen. He was known for fighting the travellers for money. He'd fight them two at a time from what I hear, but then again, if I believed half of what I heard I'd be twice as thick as I am now', he said smiling. 'I worked with a fellow a few years ago that told me he was living with some travelling woman down in the Black Country somewhere, but he's from around here so I'm told, or he used to live here years ago anyway. Gene reckoned he was doing a big road widening job with him when he was a young lad. One day the lads turned up for work and he was nowhere to be seen, just gone. Some woman involved. But, you know, that's the craic with a long distance man. Here today, gone tomorrow. He had the full set of bulbs then though, according to Gene. I heard a bunch of the travellers ambushed him and made an awful mess of him, took the eye clean out of his head, pickaxe shafts, the lot. They fucked off back to Ireland after that, so they weren't totally stupid, but I hear that he managed to get hold of a couple of them over the next few years. Didn't end too well for them.'

'Why is it that you lads are so interested in bloody fighting', said Mandy turning from Frankie and looking at Clare and shaking her head in disapproval. 'Give me a lover rather than a fighter any day', she added. 'Am I right Clare?'

'What's wrong with both?', she answered, smiling. 'I like to know that a man's a man, that he can protect me. I mean, nobody wants one of those idiots that's scrapping all the time, walking around with a chip on their shoulder, but it's nice to know that if it comes to the crunch, he's not going to be hiding behind your skirts.'

'Yeah, I suppose so', replied Mandy airily, 'but blokes make such a big deal out of it: this one punched that one and that one punched this one...'

'It's just a man thing, I suppose', said Clare.

'Well, just so you know, I'm far more of a lover than I am a fighter', said Frankie winking at Mandy.

Gene walked into the bedroom carrying a tray on which rested a small plate decorated with a thin slice of ham and a tiny mound of mashed potatoes. He set the plate down on the table next to the bed and put his hands under Cora's shoulders and lifted her up so that her back was supported by the headrest of the bed. He looked down at her. 'Comfortable love?' She smiled up at him and he turned and picked up the tray and flicked down two plastic legs from its underside and placed it across her lap. 'You'll like these, straight from the allotment, smothered in butter', he said smiling at her.

'Ooooh, they do smell nice', she replied picking up the fork awkwardly from the tray and looking up at him, her face aglow with excitement, like a child about to open a birthday gift.

'Don't worry if you can't finish it all love, just eat what you can'. He looked down at the meagre quantity of food set out for her and felt an ache of weary sadness. The frequency of these reminders of her decline did nothing to lessen their cruelty as they hammered away relentlessly at the same undefended place in his heart.

He sat on the chair next to the bed, ready to take satisfaction in her enjoyment of the food, but as she raised the fork to her mouth her entire body seemed to spasm and the fork dropped from her grasp and clattered onto the plate beneath. Her eyes rolled and her head lolled to one side. Her body spasmed again, juddering as if she was being rattled from the inside out. Then her eyes opened, wide and afraid. 'What was that Gene? What's happening to me?' Then it came again. Her shoulders seemed to fold in on themselves and she clutched at her chest, her head bowed as if to hide her pain. She let out a low groan and her hands fell from her breast and lay motionless in her lap, her head rolled to one side. He stared at her transfixed, his jaw slack and his eyes staring uncomprehendingly.

'Cora?', he whispered as he rose to his feet. 'Cora?', his voice stronger as he grasped her by her shoulders pushing her back all the better to look into her face. Her head slumped to one side in a slack, unnatural motion then rolled, her scrawny, sepia throat arched, the parchment-like skin taut, her unseeing eyes turned to the ceiling.

'Cora! Cora! Wake up! Wake up!', he pleaded shaking her wildly, his voice ragged with desperation, her body little more than a bundle of rags in his hands. He cupped the back of her head in the palm of his hand and looked into her untenanted eyes. 'I'm sorry love, I'm sorry. I didn't mean to hurt you. I'll be more gentle, more gentle', he whispered feverishly as he clasped her to him, rocking to and fro, tears cascading down his cheeks. His eyes locked shut and he turned his face upwards as if to give space to the terrifying roar of anguish which exploded from him, a futile effort to send his soul to join her's.

CHAPTER THIRTY-ONE

'Look, I'm going to have to get home', said Hugh looking down at Clare as they lay together under the duvet, her head on his chest. 'I haven't been spoken to my family since Thursday night. They're going to wonder what's going on.'

'We can meet later. You can pop back here any time you want, if you've got nothing better to do, that is', she said playfully.

'I'll have to check my diary', he replied grinning. She wrestled the pillow from beneath him and began hitting him with it.

'Don't push your luck, Mister', she replied smiling and he immediately enfolded her in his arms. 'I'm sorry, it was a bit crass of me.'

'Crass?', she repeated, her eyebrows raised in confusion as she enunciated the sound. Where do you get all these words from? You don't talk at all like the other building workers I know.'

'It just means that it was a silly, childish thing to say.' He pulled her closer to him. 'I can't believe where all these feelings have come from', he said earnestly, looking into her eyes. 'I've only known you for two or three days and it feels like we've been together forever. I've never felt like this before for somebody.'

'I know', she replied. 'It's wonderful, isn't it. The first time I saw you I just knew that you were going to be mine, even though you were just stood there gawping at me as if you'd never seen a girl before', she said smiling as she caressed his chest.

'I know', he replied, 'I was just drawn to you. I was a million miles away, just daydreaming. Something in my unconscious just responded to you and then when I saw you looking at me, I just thought 'wow! And then when you were dancing....you just blew me away.'

He looked over at the clock. 'I'd better go. They'll be worried', he said leaping out of bed.

'I'll make a coffee while you're getting showered', she said as he crossed the short distance to her tiny bathroom.

He returned to the room five minutes later, his freshly scrubbed skin contrasting sharply with the odour of beer clinging to his shirt. He made a mental note to change as soon as he got home.

'Well, it was a good afternoon, wasn't it? Frankie's good company. He's a funny bloke', he said as she lay in bed looking up at him, her mug clasped between her hands.

'I preferred the night-time to be honest. Or is that just me being crass?', she asked looking up at him and smiling. She reached out and began gently stroking his arm from the bed. He smiled back and leant down and took the cup from her hand before kissing her. 'They can wait a bit longer', he said.

He arrived home to an empty house. He'd expected his mother and father to be home from Mass some time ago, but he assumed that it wouldn't be long before they returned. The smell of the Sunday roast permeated the house reminding him of how hungry he was. He was upstairs changing his clothes when he heard the front door open, quickly followed by his mother's voice. 'Well, I'd better get it over with', he thought to himself and went down to greet them. His mother and father were chatting in the kitchen when he appeared at the bottom of the stairs.

'Oh, look who it is', said his mother immediately breaking off her conversation with David. 'And where have you been, Mr. Mysterious? I hear that you and Jane are no longer an item'.

'Oh really?', interjected David, noting that Kate had neglected to inform him of this. 'When did that happen?' In the absence of an answer, he continued. 'She's a very good-looking young woman, that one. You won't find a replacement for her that easily.' Kate glanced over at him, her eyes narrowed. He was unsure if the implied rebuke was designed to punish him for commenting on Jane's looks or the presumption that she was the best that Hugh could hope find in the way of girlfriends. Both, he concluded.

'Just ran out of steam that's all. Plus, I've met someone else.'

'Oh, yes?', replied David, 'that was fast work'.

'Oh, and who's the lucky lady?', asked Kate

'You wouldn't know her. She's not from around here', Hugh replied.

197

'Oh', replied Kate thoughtfully, 'where's she from then? How did you meet her?'

He decided that honesty was his best option. The more evasive he was, the more suspicious his mother would become, and what did he have to be evasive about anyway?

'I met her in a pub actually. On Friday after work.'

'Oh really? Which pub was this then?', Kate asked, managing to disguise her eagerness to know everything there was to know about this girl.

It's called 'The Harp', or something like that', he said causally and walked over to the fridge and opened the door to inspect its contents. 'What time's lunch mum?', His attempted at changing the subject was a complete failure.

''The Harp'!', exclaimed Kate, 'is that dump still open?', she asked turning to David. 'Why were you in that mucky old place?'

'We went after work actually and it's not at all mucky. We had a great time.'

'Really? I can't imagine Richard and Simon would've enjoyed it much.'

'They didn't go', he replied.

'And this girl. You met her in there?'

'I did.'

'A St. Ann's girl, I wonder?'

'Don't be a snob, mum.'

Kate turned and looked at David. 'Have you got anything to say about this?'

'About what?', he replied, half-smiling and somewhat relishing the fact that this might be one of those rare occasions where the golden boy was on the receiving end of her disapproval.

'About the fact that he's socialising in that kind of place, if you want to call it socialising.'

'Tut tut Kate', David admonished. 'Didn't your mother and father used to drink in there years ago? I know mine did.'

'It was more respectable then', she snapped. 'I mean', she explained looking at Hugh, 'it wasn't as rough in those days. I've heard some very frightening stories about that place, the customers always fighting, and the women, my God!'

'It was exactly like that when our parents used it, wasn't it?', added David, his voice ringing with confected innocence in his attempt to appear helpful despite his complete awareness that he was being anything but, certainly as far as Kate's anxiety was concerned. 'Well, perhaps not the women, but I've heard more than one tale about the police having to send half a dozen constables to wrestle your father out of the place.'

'It's that bloody job, isn't it?', Kate expostulated before turning to the oven and opening the door to check on the progress of the meat sizzling within. 'Well, I don't like it', she said, 'don't come running to me if you get a bloody nose. It's not like the golf club, you know', she said looking pointedly at David who cleared his throat and slunk off into the lounge pleased at his tiny victory.

'Exactly. It's not the golf club', countered Hugh, 'and if, in the unlikely event I was to get a bloody nose, I would hardly come running to my mother for help now would I', he continued indignantly and followed David into the lounge.

'Hang on a minute Dad, why did they need six constables to get Grandad out of the pub?', he asked enthusiastically. David ignored and him and turned on the television.

Kate took the meat from the oven and sat it down on the kitchen surface and looked out through the window in front of her. She felt a sense of unease ripple through her. She didn't know what to do about this turn of events or if indeed there was anything she could do. All she knew was that she didn't like it. It would be helpful if Hugh brought this new girlfriend to the house, she mused looking down at the meat. Sunday lunch perhaps; that might give her something to work with. A plan afoot she stabbed the carving fork into the joint and lifted it into an awaiting dish and carried the meat into the dining room.

CHAPTER THIRTY-TWO

Monday morning found Frankie feeling rougher than usual, but despite his hangover he had arisen half an hour earlier than usual to accommodate the walk to the meeting point. His first job of the morning would be to organise a new pick-up point with Gene to reflect his change in living arrangements now that he had found his way into Mandy's bed. He hadn't waited long before the waggon appeared and pulled up beside the pavement, the engine mumbling, ready to continue its journey. He hopped in and waited for the waggon to pull away, but it remained stationary at the kerb. He looked at Gene for an explanation as to the delay. Gene's face was pale, a bone-grey tincture colouring his skin that served to emphasis the watery redness of his eyes.

'Cora died on Saturday afternoon', said Gene gravely without turning his eyes away from some unseen object in the distance. A few moments of silence passed while Frankie processed the news.

'Jesus Christ, I'm sorry to hear that Gene', he replied. The silence returned until finally Frankie turned to him. 'What the fuck are doing here man?', he asked, trying to direct the conversation towards more familiar, practical talk. 'You can't be thinking of going into work, surely not?'

'No. No, I'm not', replied Gene distractedly. 'I just wanted to get the waggon to you and let you know the craic, that's all. Just drop me off at the yard I'll get myself a taxi back home.' replied Gene a dazed look about him.

'Fuck that', said Frankie. 'We'll just pick up Danny and then drop you back at the house. Don't give it a thought.'

'You're going to need another man', he replied.

'Forget about that', replied Frankie. The rest of the journey passed in silence, Frankie being unsure of what to say and Gene recognising that there was nothing to be said. They collected Danny and headed towards Gene's house.

'No yard today?', asked Danny. Frankie looked to Gene to answer the question, but the man seemed wholly detached from world around him. Frankie turned to Danny.

'Gene lost his wife over the weekend', he said solemnly.

'Oh', said Danny gravely and turned to face Gene. 'I'm sorry about your loss. If there's anything I can do you know that you just have to ask.' Gene turned to face him, pressed his lips together in an attempt at a smile and nodded almost imperceptibly.

The uneasy silence resumed until they arrived outside of Gene's house. He eased himself out of the waggon and was about to shut the door before seeming to recall something. 'Just so you know lads, the funeral'll be on Friday at St. Anne's. There'll be a bit of a spread afterwards in the Irish Club. Friday's a bad day to miss work, I know, so don't worry if you can't make it.'

'Of course we'll make it', replied Frankie.

'We'll be there', echoed Danny. Gene nodded and turned into his garden, slouching up the path to his front door, his shoulders sagging, his footsteps heavy and laboured.

'Jesus, he looks a beaten man', said Frankie.

'He does indeed', sighed Danny. 'Anyway, we're going to need another man.'

'I think I might know someone', replied Frankie, 'that's if they haven't set out from the yard yet.'

They arrived at the yard and Danny began loading the waggon. Frankie approached Fletcher who was standing by the side of the cabin riffling through a bundle of technical drawings. 'Have you seen the snagging gang around?', he asked and Fletcher, clearly irritated by the interruption, nodded briskly in the direction of the mechanic's shop, a large, flimsy-looking metal structure adjacent to the office set-up.

Steve, Gary and Hugh were stood in a loose semi-circle watching the mechanic as he repaired the engine of the waggon that had delayed their departure that morning. 'How are you now Hugh', Frankie called out as he approached the group and without waiting for an answer, he approached Gary and with a sideways nod of his head he indicated that he wished to speak to him in private. They walked a few meters away from the small group.

'Look', he said, 'we've just found out that Gene's wife died over the weekend. Now that's bad enough news I know, but it leaves us a man short. I was out with young Hugh there on Saturday and he said that he was a bit underused with your gang.

Now he wasn't saying anything against you lads, not at all, but he's young and full of beans and I just wondered if you'd miss him for the week until we get sorted. You know the craic yourself; it's not easy finding lads at short notice.'

'Well, I'm sorry to hear about Cora', replied Gary sadly. 'That'll be a blow for Gene alright. I remember her from forty years ago in 'The Harp'. What a live wire she was then. A fine woman indeed.' His thoughts appeared to drift before finally returning to the moment. 'Yes sure, take the lad', he said hurriedly collecting himself. 'I don't know why they put him with us anyway, two men in a snagging gang's plenty.' Frankie nodded and they both turned and walked back to the disabled waggon.

'You're coming out with us today', said Frankie looking at Hugh, 'if you're up to it of course.'

Hugh smiled. 'Where's the van?', he asked excitedly.

'Follow me', answered Frankie and started walking back to the waggon before stopping and turning to Gary. 'The Funeral's on Friday.' Gary nodded in acknowledgement.

'Who's died?', asked Hugh.

'The wife of the old fella who works with us, you know, Gene. His wife.'

'Oh, that's sad news', replied Hugh, 'and we were only talking about him on Saturday weren't we, him giving up the priesthood for her.'

'Well, his God's punishing him for that now. The fella's a wreck', Frankie replied emphatically. 'I've said it before and I'll say it again, blokes end up getting far too involved with these women and the next thing they know is that they've got a ring through their nose and they're getting lead about like a bull at market', said Frankie. Hugh bridled but held his counsel. 'A man's got to stay in control of himself. There can only be one boss in that yard', Frankie added conclusively.

That was enough for Hugh.

'Well, from what you said he made a pretty big sacrifice for her in the first place, and they've obviously been together ever since so it was clearly worthwhile to him', replied Hugh, the vulgar simplicity of Frankie's argument grating against him. 'The fact that he was prepared to devote so much of his time to her during her illness, that sounds to me like he loved her, and what's wrong with that? I think your theories might be leading you astray you know Frankie. Might be worth taking another look at them.'

'Shite talk', Frankie replied briskly, flicking his head skywards in a gesture of dismissal, like a petulant pony. He turned to Hugh with a sly smile on his face, a mischievous look in his eye and a conspiratorial tone in his voice. 'It's that young Clare, isn't it?', he said, 'all this love talk bollocks. She's got you wrapped up like a fresh kipper!', his smile dissolving into laughter as his hands began swirling through the air in front of him as if he were priming an orchestra as he broke into song. 'Oh I love you my darling and my love is true...'

Hugh leapt upon him and grabbed him around the neck, playfully putting him in a loose headlock and made as if to punch him. Frankie broke free easily, laughing uncontrollably, joining Hugh who was doing much the same.

'Ah, now I know your soft spot', said Frankie amidst his giggles. 'It'll be poetry and flowers all the way for you now boy! Big boxes of chocolates the size of that compressor there', he said nodding towards a machine the size of a small car, 'and then it'll be 'I love you sweetheart do you love me too?''

Hugh was now bent almost double with laughter as he listened to Frankie's increasing absurdities as they both stumbled towards the waggon. 'Back again?', asked Danny casually to Hugh as he turned from having heaved a huge flagstone onto the back of the waggon. Hugh and Frankie ceased laughing immediately upon hearing his voice and stood tall and serious like two errant infantrymen confronted by their sergeant.

'We'd better get out sharpish if we want to make a few quid today', Danny continued and walked around to the driver's side of the waggon, the slightest of smiles playing across his face.

They landed at the job and got set up. Frankie picked up the hammer at the head of the track and squeezed it into life, loosening up the backfilled earth which marked the spot at which they'd finished digging on Friday. Hugh stood at the side of the trench, shovel in hand, ready to dig out a space in the trench for him to occupy. The ground was soft on that stretch of footpath and so yielded easily under the hammer blade. For the next few hours, Hugh saw little other than the piles of debris that fell from the constantly renewed face of the trench and heard nothing but the roar of the compressor on the road beside him and the violent rattle of the hammer above him. It was if he were a piston embedded in the midst of some terrible machine shuttling the earth from the trench minute after minute, hour after hour as he raced to keep up with Frankie who gave no quarter to Hugh's inexperience as he worked determinedly to extend the length of the trench, inch by gruelling inch. Hugh had quickly fallen into a rhythm, knowing that a silent hammer was making no money and recognising that it would come to a stop only if Frankie was getting too far ahead of him. His hands were on fire and a vicious ache gnawed at the muscles in his lower back and calves. Sweat ran into his eyes. He envied Frankie. Just a push of the hammer blade into the capitulating tarmac followed by a swift flick of the wrists and the debris was delivered into the path of the shovel man. He was yet to realise that it was only Frankie's physical strength, his experience with the tool and the forgiving ground that made his work appear effortless.

He arrived home ten hours later in a state of near exhaustion. He hurt in the same places as he had done that first day out with Gary and Steve, but the pain was far more extravagant. The blisters had returned, shearing off the temporary callouses that had formed at the bridge of his palm. New blisters appeared too around the base of his thumb and the back of his neck was crimson with sunburn. His calves cramped. He had been emptied out of energy, used up, but fortunately he had managed to disguise the worst excesses of his pain from the other two. Rather the pain than the humiliation of being told he wasn't up to the work, he thought. He headed immediately for the shower then, having cleaned off, filled the bath in the hope that the warm water might ease the spasms in his leg muscles. He lay in the warm water for half an hour until his mother called him downstairs for supper. He dried himself off, dressed and went downstairs. His father was already sat at the dining table. His mother ferried supper to the table and then sat down herself and they all began to eat.

After five minutes of silence, David spoke.

'Oh', he said to Kate, 'I forgot to tell you. Cora Joyce died over the weekend.'

'Oh no!', replied Kate sadly placing her cutlery down onto the table giving the news her full attention. 'She was a lovely woman, a real bundle of energy. She was friends with my Mum years ago. I haven't seen her in ages, but I'd heard that she was ill. Gene told you, obviously.'

'No, actually not. I heard it from one of the agents. The funeral is on Friday.'

'He'll be lost without her. He's had a lot to put up with that man. First his little girl, now Cora. Mum told me that they were inseparable those two. He was a priest at one time, I heard. I think he left to marry her. Where's the funeral?'

'The usual', he replied. 'Bloody inconvenient time for it though. Every gang in the yard will take half a day off on Friday'.

'David!', Kate exclaimed. 'Is it all just pounds and pence with you?' In response he raised his eyebrows as if to indicate that the question did not merit a spoken answer.

'Did you know her husband mum?', asked Hugh.

'No, not really. I knew who he was. I knew Cora when I was young though. I remember she worked at the hospital with my mother years ago. She used to give us sweets when we were kids. She was a bit nuts, but in a good way. A lot of fun. He always struck me as being a bit dour, not on her level at all, but it just goes to show that you never know what draws people together.'

'Why are you so interested?', asked David.

'I'm working with his gang this week while he's off work.'

David's shoulders tightened and he turned to look directly at Hugh, a grave expression on his now ashen face.

'You're working with Frankie and his mate?', he asked coldly.

'Yes.'

'Who told you that you could do that?', snapped David. 'What about the fucking snagging gang?'

'David! Language!', exclaimed Kate.

'Frankie just asked me if I wanted to work with them and I said yes', his father's aggressive tone startling even Hugh. 'They had a word with Gary and he said he didn't really need me. It was boring with the snagging gang anyway. I was just stood around watching them most of the time.'

David glared at him for a moment, his lips pressed tightly together, and returned to his food. Kate and Hugh shot questioning glances at each other, both confused as to the cause of his sudden anger.

205

David's thoughts were tumbling over one another as he raced to find a way out of this appalling situation. It was fucking ridiculous to have let Greene anyway near the yard, he thought to himself, just asking for trouble. And now this. Fucking ridiculous. What was he thinking listening to that half-wit Jones? It was all Jones' fault anyway. Well, he was going to take control of the situation now. Greene had to go. Simple as that. He'd sort it out tomorrow.

Hugh was already out on site when David arrived in the yard the next morning. Jones was not on the gantry as usual but instead was down amongst the men on the floor of the yard, his huge chest puffed out like a bantam cockerel's and his chin raised imperiously as he strutted between the rumbling waggons issuing threats and insults as he went, fully aware that the news of his recent victory over the Mulligans would now be known to all. He had made it his business on the night of the confrontation to broadcast the news far and wide as he caroused the pubs and bars of the city, the tale becoming more elaborate and dramatic with every pint of Guinness he consumed. By Monday morning it was indeed common knowledge within the yard, but his success did nothing to stimulate admiration amongst the men. Instead, the pomposity of his current display only further intensified the disdain in which he was generally held and further enriched the collective hope that he would someday meet his comeuppance.

David caught Jones' eye and nodded his head to indicate that he wanted to speak to him in the storage space on the first floor of the portacabin, the only private space in the structure. Jones had expected that he would be eager to hear a full breakdown of his encounter with the Mulligans and he had given some thought during the drive to the yard that morning about how to present it to him in the most self-aggrandising terms possible. He smiled at David in an almost regal gesture of acknowledgement and ambled across the yard languishing in the warming prospect of praise to come. He fully anticipated that David would lionize him, would shower him with congratulations and laud him with well-deserved praise; there may even be a pay rise in the offing. Amidst the tedious drudgery of life, it was moments such as these which gave the common people the opportunity to witness him elevated to his proper level, he thought, to his rightful station in life. On top of this, it would send out a bright and clear signal that he remained a force to be reckoned with, a signal that the likes of Danny Greene could not ignore.

David Gallon made no secret of his admiration for fighting men. It was inextricably bound up with the culture and the history of the work and seldom was this aggression more celebrated as a virtue than by those who had no hope of participating in it. David Gallon had few illusions about his own physical prowess, but he was always eager to fete those who had acquired a reputation of being ready and able to settle matters of dispute on the cobbles. Jones was acutely aware that he had obtained his current position partly on that basis, though he had managed to persuade himself that Gallon had also recognised the depth of his intelligence, him being an intelligent man himself. Jones presented himself to the waiting Gallon preening with undisguised self-regard.

'How the fuck is it that Hugh is out working with Danny Greene?', barked Gallon making no attempt to restrain his temper. 'For fuck sake, you're supposed to be the senior agent here. Why the fuck are you deliberately trying to make us both look like fucking idiots?', Jones was aghast, disoriented. He struggled to co-ordinate his thoughts.

'What do you mean he's out with Greene? I put him with Gary. You saw me put him with Gary. We agreed', he replied in almost imploring tones, his self-confidence evaporating in an instant.

'Well, he isn't with fucking Gary now', David continued bitterly.

There was too much happening for Jones to immediately comprehend, and he stuttered and mumbled as he rummaged through what he was pleased to call his mind for a coherent response, his eyes darting left and right, deliberately avoiding looking at Gallon.

'We could just let them go. Put Hugh back with Gary, Sack them all', he proposed with increasing desperation.

'And how would that look, eh? Sacking a gang the day after the ganger man's wife dies, and a well-known man at that.'

'We could just put Hugh back with Gary then?', Jones suggested weakly, clutching at straws, desperate for something of use to contribute.

'No, Hugh wouldn't do it and it'd attract a lot of fuss, a lot of talk. Anyway, there all self-employed men, we can't go dictating who is and isn't in any gang.'

'Look, Gene's only going to be off for a week and its Tuesday today and the funeral's on Friday. He's only going to be with them a couple of days. Maybe it's just a mountain out of a molehill? I mean neither of them know anything anyway, do they?', Jones knew that he was taking a risk referring to the fundamental issue, even indirectly, but he had to draw on all of the resources at his disposal if he was to avoid being held responsible for the current debacle. David looked pensively at Jones then turned his gaze to the floor, contemplating the option.

'We just should've never given him the start. Just asking for trouble,' he murmured to himself.

'Look', interjected Jones, 'if you'd have knocked him back when everyone was looking for men, then it would've looked bad. People would've put two and two together and come up with five, you know that. I mean did you want all that again?'. And it would've got out, mark my words. navvies are the biggest gossips in the world, you know that.'

'OK, OK. I get your point', replied David, slightly calmer after exhausting his anger on Jones. 'Some perspective is what's needed. You're fight. It's only a couple of days. Let it run its course.' Jones could see by Gallon's worried expression that this temporary fix didn't resolve his underlying anxiety and, having skirted around the historical problem decided to take the opportunity to confront it head on.

'Now I say this only to try and help you, but what's the worst-case scenario, that it gets out? Who really cares after all this time? I mean, I don't want to get involved in your personal business, but does it still matter?'

Gallon rounded on him, his faced flushed with temper. 'Does it fucking matter? Of course it fucking matters. Do you think I'm prepared to put up with that kind of humiliation whether it was twenty minutes or twenty years ago? I have a reputation to maintain in this city.'

'You're right. I didn't mean to bring it up. I'm sorry. I was just trying to help', replied Jones sheepishly. He knew that he'd overstepped the mark and he couldn't decide whether Gallon's face had coloured as a consequence of his anger or his shame at having to acknowledge the existence of the fundamental problem.

'Ok, we don't need to discuss this any further. We'll just have to play it by ear. This time next week Gene will be away from those two gobshites and in the meantime I'll think of a pretext to put Hugh back with Gary. End of story.' Jones could detect the note of wishful thinking in Gallon's tone.

'You're absolutely right', he said reassuringly.

David scowled at him and left the room. Jones remained stationary in the centre of the small space, his teeth grinding together like tectonic plates, his small, pig – like eyes frantically darting around the room searching for a distraction which would deliver him from the rage welling within, but he could not contain it's enormity. He seized upon a broken whacker plate leant against the wall of the cabin and, raising it above his head, he hurled it out through the door, roaring ferociously as he did so. It flew through the air before it hit the floor of the yard with a dull, heavy thud and skidded along the compacted earth kicking up a trail of dust as it did so before finally coming to rest. It was fortunate the yard was empty. Weighing in excess of two-hundred pounds, the whacker would have shattered the bones of anyone caught in its path.

David heard the roar coming from below and jumped from his chair and raced to look out of the window of the office. He caught sight of the whacker as it came to rest in the centre of the yard. A malevolent smile crept over his face, and he returned to his desk.

CHAPTER THIRTY-THREE

As the week progressed Hugh's musculature slowly adapted to the elevated demands of price work. His body continued to ache in unexpected places, but his hands were becoming more resilient. The skin that had been shorn off his knuckles and fingers where he'd grazed them on the walls of the trench was starting to thicken and become coarser and the calluses on his palms were showing signs of returning. Most importantly, he had recognised that the key to keeping up with the frantic pace of this work was to ensure that he maintained his energy levels throughout the day. It astonished him that neither Frankie nor Danny appeared to eat very much. Sandwiches in the morning, sandwiches at lunchtime; this seemed standard sustenance for them and sufficient to fuel their day, but he needed many more calories and when time allowed, he would retreat to the waggon to bolt down huge mouthfuls of food raided from his parent's fridge. He kept alert too, noting what was going on with the job at every stage in the process and paying particular attention to the conversations between Frankie and Danny when specific problems were being discussed.

Although Danny had been in the gang only a short period of time, it was clear that he had assumed the role of ganger man. This didn't appear to rankle with Frankie in the least and he accepted Danny's seniority as a matter of course. The fact that Hugh and Frankie were working in close proximity at the head of the trench meant that they were able steal brief snippets of conversation throughout the course of the day.

The only complaint Frankie ever made in connection with Gene was that he wasn't very talkative. Frankie understood the reasons for Gene's focus on the job at hand, but he himself was a garrulous man by nature and he had an inexhaustible supply of anecdotes at his disposal. Hugh listened with rapt attention as Frankie regaled him with stories detailing the exploits of other long distance man such as himself and Danny, men who were known in yards and on sites across the country. Hugh was enthralled, such stories echoing the tales his grandfather had told him, stories which in his mind had taken on the status of myths and of guideposts.

The tale which particularly captured Hugh's interest was his account of Danny's confrontations with the Mulligans. This was a tale Frankie enjoyed telling too given his status as an eyewitness to two of its three instalments. He also recognised that he'd be telling these tales for a long time to come, and he wanted to ensure that he'd embedded every detail of these encounters into his memory.

He had to be careful in the telling of it though as Danny would occasionally wander up the track to discuss some aspect of the job with him and Frankie correctly assumed that he would not have been pleased to find him telling tales, no matter how flattering. And, of course, the tale was a flattering one: how, without fanfare or bluster, he had rescued Gene; how with a calm ferocity he had stood up to the three Mulligans and finally, how he had confronted the entire gang on their own territory and emerged unscathed. Hugh soaked up every detail, his admiration for Danny growing with every fresh revelation. 'Now here was a man my grandfather would have respected', he thought to himself.

Frankie was a natural storyteller, and he painted a picture rich in drama not entirely untouched by exaggeration. His own role in events was somewhat amplified, but not so much as to diminish Danny's central contribution.

'The guy came from nowhere', he said to a riveted Hugh, 'it all happened like that', he said snapping his fingers. 'One minute Gene's trying to get us into the yard and the next this awful beast of a man's trying to hoist him out of the window! Well, straight away I tried to lean over Gene to give this bloke a couple of shots, but Gene was having none of it. He was trying to push the lad away with one hand and holding me back with the other. I mean, if Gene wasn't such an ox of a man, I'd have been all over the kid myself. He was lucky Danny got to him first really.

And then there was the time when me and Danny were in the yard that day and the three of them pulled in. Jesus Christ, you should've seen the cut of 'em. A monstrous vision it was. A brutish crowd altogether. Well Danny sorted the first of them pretty sharpish, but I always knew that he would. I wasn't even paying that much attention really, but when I saw the other fella coming at Danny with a pickaxe shaft I took the head off our's pretty quickly and went straight for him, but Danny called me back, said it was his fight which was right and so I left him to it.'

Hugh had been giving Frankie his full attention, but as the tale had progressed and Frankie's stated role within the unfolding series of events had emerged, his scepticism grew.

'I thought you said the other day that you were a lover not a fighter?', queried Hugh looking directly at Frankie who quickly averted his eyes and looked down the length of the trench behind Hugh.

'Enough of this talk anyway', he replied hurriedly, 'Danny's coming. He wouldn't want us talking about him behind his back', and with that he squeezed the trigger of the jack hammer putting a stop to any further discussion. Hugh smiled and shook his head before resuming digging.

Frankie released the trigger silencing the hammer and looked down at Hugh. 'You want to stop that head shaking business you know, or it'll soon become a habit', he said smiling, 'you don't want to end up like Gene do you? The man's head's on a fucking spring', his laughter drowned out by the rattling of the hammer as he drove it down once again into the tarmac at his feet.

CHAPTER THIRTY-FOUR

They worked until midday on Friday and returned to the usual queue of hooting waggons all eager to get into the yard, unloaded and parked up as quickly as possible. Hugh was impressed at the number of men willing to sacrifice half a day's wages to attend the funeral and said as much to Frankie.

'Well, not many of the lads knew Cora, except maybe some of the old timers, but Gene is a well-liked man. He's been around forever', he replied. 'The lads'll want to show a bit of respect for his loss, you know.'

Hugh regretted the fact that he hadn't had the opportunity to get to know Gene better. Unlike his friends, who saw their grandparents, and elders in general, as being pretty much irrelevant to their lives, Hugh viewed them very differently. His own forebears had been fiercely proud Irish immigrants and he was aware that, in some hard to grasp but important way, he was at least in part heir to their culture, a culture whose echoes were to be found all around him: in the food he ate, the music he knew, the church he attended; in his very name. Although he did not fully know or understand the significance of these echoes they nonetheless resonated within him and he heard their call.

His grandfather, the stories of his own forebears, his own origins, was a tangible expression of a history which they both shared. This connection, common to many offspring of migrants, had encouraged Hugh to view the seniors in his community as custodians of a world gradually tipping into oblivion, a world which nonetheless continued to exert a spectral influence on his own. His grandfather had gone to great lengths to remind Hugh that he was part of a chain dissolving in time of which Hugh was simply the most recently forged link.

A substantial crowd was already gathered outside of the church dressed in dark, muted tones yet the mood was far from sombre. The fair weather encouraged the mourners to mill about greeting old acquaintances and sharing reminiscences about Cora. Hugh's mother and father were proving to be particularly popular and were approached by a steady stream of well-wishers and who interacted with them with great familiarity revealing to Hugh that his parents had a social hinterland far richer and deeper than he had hitherto recognised. None of their golf club friends were in attendance, he noted.

After fifteen minutes or so the mourners began funnelling through the ornate Gothic entrance into the half-lit space within. The Gallons seated themselves on a pew close to the altar, Kate being the only member of the family to genuflect prior to doing so. Hugh hadn't been to mass for years but was immediately whisked back to his childhood by the pungent odour of incense hanging in thin wisps in the air and the low, plangent organ music brooding from the gallery above. They sat in respectful silence interrupted only by traces of whispered conversations and embarrassed coughing which reverberated from walls elaborately decorated with luridly painted panels depicting the Last Passion of Christ.

The organ music grew louder as the priest emerged from a side entrance to the chancel, took up his position in front of the altar and looked down the central aisle of the nave to where pallbearers were emerging from the entrance to the church carrying Cora's coffin on their slow progress towards the bier placed in front of the altar.

The more dutiful of the congregation took to the hymns with a pious enthusiasm and their combined voices filled the space with a heightened sense of communion, conferring upon the occasion a rich sanctity. It came as a surprise to Hugh how much of the structure of the service that he had absorbed as a child: when to sit, when to stand, when to kneel, when to respond to the solemn offerings of the priest who, when the time came, spoke fondly and at great length about Cora. The time for holy communion approached and Hugh was unsure as to whether or not it was appropriate for him to receive. He turned to ask his mother for guidance and was taken aback to see a look of dumbfounded alarm on her face.

'What's up mum?', he asked concernedly, 'what's the matter?'

Upon hearing his voice Kate appeared to collect herself and turned to him and snapped. 'Nothing's the matter. You shouldn't be talking during the service', she scolded. He turned back to the priest confused at his mother's uncharacteristic burst of anger.

Moments earlier Kate had been surveying the attendees trying to identify who she recognised and who she didn't, who had aged well and who had not, what the women were wearing and other such matters. Funerals were one of the rare occasions where she had the opportunity to meet friends and acquaintances from her old life. The church was full of people that she hadn't seen or indeed even thought of for years as increased social mobility had caused old acquaintances to disperse, relinquishing the low-grade housing that they had occupied as immigrants, and children of immigrants, to the next wave of hopefuls. She found such occasions gratifying. They gave her a sense of achievement. She was one of the winners. She lived in a beautiful home, drove an expensive car and was married to a successful local employer, but most of all, her son was tall and handsome, well balanced and happy and on the brink of a university education, a life full of promise in front of him. Ironically, she found funerals life-affirming events: looking at her peers, being reminded of the awfulness of her start in life, she felt vindicated; her decisions had been the correct decisions even though the robed adjudicator declaiming from behind the altar might not agree. But who cared about him, she thought? She had sacrificed enough. She had paid a price and the final reckoning was her's alone.

This feeling of self-satisfaction gave her a slight energy lift and she picked up her hymnal and joined the singers in the congregation in giving voice to some ancient, mournful dirge warning of the perils of straying from the path of righteousness. She had been singing this hymn since she was a child and thought no more about its meaning now than she had done then. Her glance continued to drift across the ranks of the assembled flock as she mouthed the pious lyrics of the hymn. Her eyes rested idly on a figure to her left in a pew at the other side of the church, her angle of vision preventing her from fully making out his face. Despite this she felt a vague sense of recognition and her gaze lingered upon him, her attention half-focused on waiting for a change in his posture or a backward glance which might confirm if he was someone known to her. She did not have to wait long. The hymn came to an end and the members of the congregation sat back down as one. The figure turned slightly to ensure that his pew was free of bibles and hymn books before setting himself down and it was at the moment that she recognised him: Danny Greene.

Her heart rate leapt immediately, and she felt her draw drop and her eyes widen. David nudged her thigh and she realised that she was the only member of the

215

congregation left standing after the hymn had ended. She lowered herself slowly onto the pew not taking her eyes from the back of Danny Greene's head. Panic and confusion engulfed her, and she tried to master the frantic swirl of thoughts cascading through her mind. She turned her gaze back to the altar. She must be mistaken, she thought with some relief: it just couldn't be him. She tried to reason away what she had seen: Why would he be here? He may have been friends with Gene all those years ago, but to the extent of staying in touch with him? How? These men didn't write letters to one another. It just didn't happen. But it had to be him. She glanced at him again impatiently shifting her body trying to improve on her angle of vision. David nudged her again: 'What're you doing, you're fidgeting like a kid', he whispered with some irritation.

What the hell was he doing here after all these years? There was no reassuring answer to this question. She tried to persuade herself that it had been a case of mistaken identity. She had only seen his face for a fraction of a second and there was absolutely no reason why it would be him, not after all this time. And the eye patch? He never wore one of those. She took some solace from this, but not much. Hugh crashed into her thinking with some inane question, and she angrily dismissed him and then felt immediately guilty. 'Oh my God', she thought, 'Hugh!' and she became acutely aware of David sat next to her, his thigh pressed against her's in the cramped pew.

The priest indicated that communion was about to begin, and the members of the congregation began slowly making their way up to the altar. She didn't move her gaze from Danny, willing him to stand up and move down the pew towards the central aisle so that she could get a clear view of him. He finally arose and turned to his right, his full face turned towards her. She could be in no doubt. It was him.

She implored herself to calm down. She knelt at the pew and held her hands together as if in prayer, all the better to disguise the maelstrom raging in her mind. Had David seen him? It suddenly struck her that the whys and wherefores were irrelevant at this point; all that mattered was what Danny Greene's presence would do to her family. The possible threat to the domestic status quo galvanised her thinking. She had to tell David and immediately, whatever the consequences. This was going to open old wounds, deep wounds, but he had to know.

Now that she had at least the semblance of a plan she calmed down a notch or two. The shock had subsided, and her practical instincts kicked in. There were questions that needed to be answered, but for now David needed to be made aware of the situation. She leant over to him and whispered in his ear. 'We need to get out of here now. This instant. I'll tell you why outside.' David looked at her, his confusion evident, but he could see by her ashen complexion and her resolute tone of voice that her demand would tolerate no opposition. Anyway, he was relieved to escape from the tedium of the service. Then she turned to Hugh. 'Look, you're going to have to find your own way to the wake. Your father and I have got to go somewhere.'

The Mass was coming to an end and the priest was delivering his closing blessings as the opening bars of the final hymn began to resound through the church. She realised that if they didn't leave now then they would have to wait until the coffin had been carried out of the building and she would then be trapped in the general throng shuffling their way to the exit, with the possibility of being waylaid by old acquaintances wanting to gossip and chit-chat. Worst of all was the possibility of confronting Greene. She shuddered in anticipation of this dread prospect and ushered David out of the pew, genuflected and made her way quickly towards the exit.

'What's going on?', asked David as she strode towards their car. She didn't answer. She arrived at the car and turned to him.

'Quickly, come on. Get in.'

'What's the big hurry?', he said seating himself in the vehicle.

'Look, I don't know how to tell you this gently, so I'm just going to come out with it. Danny Greene is in the church.' She looked at him expecting to see his version of furious anger, but to her astonishment he simply sighed heavily and looked down at the steering wheel.

'I know', he said.

'You know? You know?', she replied, her confusion returning. 'What the hell do you mean 'you know'? How long have you known?'

'He's been here for over a month.' Kate looked at him uncomprehendingly. 'He's been working for us'.

'What do you mean he's working for us? Am I dreaming here?', she asked, almost to herself. She seemed to right herself and she turned back to him. 'What's going on here David? What the hell is going on?'

'He just turned up at the yard one day as part of a gang. Just showed up. What was I supposed to do, send him packing? How would that've looked? It would've had the same effect as confirming all the rumours?'

'How?'

'If I'd have not set him on people would have asked why and we all know that there's a ready-made answer to that question.'

'You should've just sent him away.'

'Where to, eh? There are other firms in this city you know. I can't banish him you know. You're putting this to me as if it were my fault. Let me remind you that it was me who had to bear the innuendo, the gossip and the rumours. It was me who had to tolerate the fucking humiliation', he roared smashing his fist down on the steering wheel.

'Ok, I see. You were put in a difficult position', she said in an attempt to placate him. 'I can see that. Let's not lose sight of who's the problem here. I'm sorry. I overreacted. Look, I know it's difficult for you, I really do, but there are other people to consider, aren't there?'

'Oh, the golden boy you mean.'

'Yes', she said sternly, her conciliatory tone evaporating, '*our* son.'

'Our son', he said sighing.

'Let's go home', she said. 'We can't possibly take the chance of bumping into him at the wake', she shifted her position in the seat and turned to him, a flinty expression on her face. 'I mean, can't you just get someone to frighten him off or something, just tell him to go. What about that big gorilla Jones; he's got to be good for something, surely?'

He turned to her and stared questioningly, his eyebrows raised.

'I know', she said sighing resignedly. 'He's not going to run from anyone. I'm just grasping at straws. Let's get out of here before the church starts emptying.'

CHAPTER THIRTY-FIVE

A peculiar feature of wakes is that, while they are occasions upon which to mourn the passing of a cherished family member, a respected friend or a barely known acquaintance, they are not typically gloomy or solemn gatherings. Certainly, there are pockets of grief, but this sorrow tends to be restricted to those most directly affected by the recent departure. Wakes are social events and, once commiserations have been offered, a general spirit of gaiety takes over. The event becomes an opportunity to catch up with people unseen for years, to update and be updated on births and deaths, to moan and to grumble about work, spouses and children and to settle old scores. And of course, to drink. Cora's funeral was no exception.

Gene had made arrangements for Cora to be buried in the cemetery in her hometown in Ireland and it was his intention to travel back with the casket later that day. The last thing he wanted to do was to socialise. He had dutifully greeted and thanked members of the congregation for their attendance at the Mass as they had left the church, but it was clear to all that he was broken man. He had barely eaten since her death, and it showed. His face was as grey and as clammy as putty and his suit jacket hung loosely from his shoulders. It was noticed by more than one of Cora's friends that his breath was infused with the odour of whiskey. The wake was to be held at the Irish Democratic Club, a local social Club which had been a popular family venue for forty years or more, but which had fallen into a steady decline from which it had little hope of recovery. Nonetheless, it served its purpose a venue for christening parties, wedding celebrations and, as in this instance, wakes.

Danny, Frankie and Hugh arrived at the Club together. Frankie had spoken to Gene on the telephone the previous day and Gene had told him that he would spend at least a week in Ireland, but that they should not rely upon him returning to work any time soon.

'I think that could be him done you know', said Frankie as they made their way to the Club. He didn't look well at all today. He's lost a good bit of weight too.'

'Aye', replied Danny solemnly.

Hugh noted what was being said and reminded himself to redouble his efforts at work in order to maintain his position within the gang.

They could hear music spilling from the open windows of the Club as they approached and as they entered they could feel it, that and the thrum of two hundred chattering voices filling the space. Frankie and Hugh had arranged to meet their respective girlfriends here and Hugh was pleased to observe that they were already sat together chatting.

They ordered their drinks and negotiated a route through the standing crowd to the table. Clare rose immediately and wrapped her arms around Hugh's neck, almost spilling the drinks he was carrying, kissing him full on the lips.

'What about me?', said Frankie looking down at Mandy in mock expectation, 'don't I get the big hello?'

'Leave that to the kids, eh?', she replied smiling before turning to Clare and mouthing 'only joking' to her. Danny, who had insisted on buying his own drink, sat down at the table and Hugh was surprised to note that he had set a fruit juice down in front of him.

'Not drinking today Danny?', he asked.

'No, I've a few things to do this afternoon. I just wanted to go to the church to pay my respects.'

Hugh was disappointed at this news. He had hoped that a few pints and a relaxed mood might encourage Danny to open up about his own past, a past from which Hugh might extract lessons as to how to shape his own future, his understanding of it its possibilities not yet having been sufficiently fed by his own experience. He had witnessed at first hand the deference that Danny was shown by the men in the yard, a deference almost approaching awe and Danny's refusal to follow even the basic orthodoxies of navvy life further intrigued his young mind. It wasn't simply his fearlessness that Hugh had come to admire, but his independence, his causal insistence on following his own path, the fact that he appeared so self-contained.

Hugh was becoming more and more dissatisfied with the future that appeared mapped out for him: university, career, mortgage, marriage, kids, retirement, death. It all seemed so compartmentalised, so predictable. He need only to look at his father's life to know that he didn't want this for himself. His father had followed all the rules, participated in all the expected patterns of behaviour, had structured his life in all the prescribed ways. He had, in effect, done what he had been told to do.

Hugh's grandfather had filled his young mind with stories of a kind of life that was defined by rebelliousness, independence, freedom and possibility, a life in which a man was dependent on no one, beholden to no one, but to live this kind of life a fellow had to be a certain kind of man: bold, strong, tough, detached. These were the qualities Hugh had seen in his grandfather and they were those that he was coming to see in Danny too.

He had long ago recognised that his father was not the kind of man he wanted to be and the older he got, even the nominal regard he might have had for him had quickly vanished. In fact, most of the adult males he had any dealings with, which typically meant either teachers or his friends' fathers, were just the same. The all seemed owned either by their wives, their jobs or their lifestyles, they were the *obedient* men. He had no intention of being an obedient man.

In picking up a shovel he had quickly come to believe that he was coming to a world that was authentic, a life which was stripped down to its essentials, and it was the work of a man to confront this unvarnished reality. From all he had seen and heard, Danny embodied the qualities which his grandfather had so admired and so it seemed natural to Hugh that he should look to Danny as he had once looked to his grandfather, as a guide. He had no doubts that the long distance nan's life was not an easy one, but he was beginning to see in it a route to authenticity.

An Irish music band had been assembling on the stage as they had arrived and their first number exploded into the room in a raucous mix of fiddle, banjo and accordion. The younger men and women immediately flooded to the edge of the small stage on which the musicians stood in a cramped huddle each one having barely enough room to extract a tune from their respective instruments. Soon the audience had moved back from the edge of the stage to create the boundary of a semi-circle within which mourners jigged and reeled in wild abandon, much as Cora would have wanted them to do.

Danny left after ten minutes citing the level of noise in the place and upon his departure Clare remarked to Hugh on the resemblance between him and Danny before pulling him up from his seat and towards the makeshift dance floor. As they arrived, she pulled off her shoes and passed them to Hugh to hold before squeezing through the perimeter crowd and hurling herself into the dance.

The wake continued in an uproarious fashion. The music was loud and the conversation raucous. Having consumed their fourth or fifth drink Hugh rose from his seat and stated his intention of going to the bar, but he was immediately pulled back down into his seat by Clare who insisted on buying the round of drinks herself. Hugh tried to persuade her otherwise, but she was quick to point out that she had not bought her share that day and that she had no intention of being a kept woman, a justification which caused Mandy to smile wryly.

She had been gone for around ten minutes when Hugh heard her voice rising above the general din. She sounded angry. He quickly jumped to his feet and hurriedly pushed his way through the crowd to the bar. She was in the midst of an argument with a man who Hugh didn't recognise. Hugh looked down at her feet and the cause of the argument became clear: there had been a collision of some kind which had knocked the tray carrying the recently purchased drinks to the floor. The argument appeared to hinge on who was responsible and as Clare seemed perfectly in control of the situation he did not intervene, instead he stood there in silence and waited for tempers to subside. However, the culprit was clearly not used to women talking back to him and was growing increasingly irate before finally losing patience and swearing at Clare and shoving her shoulder causing her to stumble backwards. Clare steadied herself and glared at the man in stunned silence. Murmurs of disapproval arose from the small crowd of spectators and the assailant turned to leave the bar correctly guessing that he had overstepped the mark.

Hugh took Clare by the shoulders, looking intently into her eyes, asking her if she was alright. She didn't immediately respond to him but upon fully recovering from the shock of the assault, she hurled a tirade of abuse at the departing assailant before collecting herself and quickly confirming to Hugh that she was unhurt. The attacker turned and shot a tirade of insults in her direction, his outrage preventing him from acknowledging Hugh's presence at her side. Hugh was like a scrap yard guard dog let loose from its chains and he leapt at the man gripping him firmly around the throat, slamming him viciously into an adjacent wall before rifling his fist into the man's abdomen.

'You better get yourself off', snarled Hugh through gritted teeth, his eyes blazing with rage. A couple of the men in the small crowd of spectators separated him from the now panic-stricken assailant who collapsed on the floor the instant that he was released, his face twisted in pain.

'He's not worth it lad', said one the small cluster of men who had briefly restrained him as they released their grip. 'He's learned his lesson. Don't get yourself barred for a jackass like that.' The assailant clambered to his feet and scrambled towards the door, chased off by jeers from the remaining spectators. Clare moved towards Hugh and put her arms around his waist, pulling him towards her and staring into his eyes.

'Thank you for sticking up for me', she said in a low voice, 'no one's ever done that for me before.' He had never felt so masculine before, so utterly male. He smiled back at her.

'Let me get the drinks next time, eh?'

They returned to the table. 'Was that you causing all the shenanigans at the bar?', asked Frankie and Hugh gave him quick account of events. 'I wouldn't worry about it', replied Frankie, 'It won't be the last flare up of the day', and smiled knowingly.

'I don't want you getting involved in any of that nonsense', added Mandy, 'I don't like it.'

'Nor do I', added Clare, 'but you can't have grown men pushing women around, it's just not on.'

'That's different', said Mandy enthusiastically nodding in agreement.

The undertaker escorted Gene into his office and invited him to sit down at his desk. He positioned himself so that he was facing Gene and carefully examined a collection of documents, selected two and passed them to Gene.

'I'd be grateful if you would just sign these where they're marked, please. Just for the transfer of the deceased.' Gene bent low over the papers, scribbled his name and passed them back. The effort in completing this task seemed to exhaust him and he sighed and glanced indifferently around the room. 'You're free to spend a little time in the chapel of rest if you'd like. We won't be going in there for half an hour or so', murmured the undertaker solicitously.

Gene nodded slowly in assent and arose from his seat with considerable effort and looked through the open door of the undertaker's office towards the chapel entrance beyond. His back was bent and his shoulders rounded as he ambled towards the entrance. The door was ajar and he gently pushed it open. The chapel was dimly lit; the smell of candle wax and incense hung in the air. He glanced around the room hoping to find something to distract him for a moment, anything that would delay turning his attention to the coffin. A bible was propped open on a small table covered in a delicate white cloth and two large ecclesiastical candles flickered in the semi-darkness. He pulled up a chair and placed it next to the coffin, its faux brass handles glimmering sheepishly in the muted half-light.

He stretched his arm along the top of the box and rested it there. He turned his red-rimmed eyes to look at the cross affixed to the coffin lid and murmured quietly. 'What now Cora love, what now?', and slowly lowered his eyes to the floor.

CHAPTER THIRTY-SIX

Frankie had been proved right. There had been a further couple of scuffles as the afternoon progressed and, as Frankie was acquainted with at least one of the participants, he took great delight in furnishing Hugh with the backstory to this confrontation. This was immediately followed up by a more general survey of the fighting men in the yard, of which there were a surprisingly large number. Frankie's natural talkativeness grew more expansive with every pint he consumed, and he found an engaged and appreciative audience in Hugh.

Clare eventually grew tired of Mandy's inane conversation and after waiting for a natural break in Frankie's monologue, turned to Hugh. 'Are you stopping at mine tonight?', she asked hoping to distract him, a saucy smile intimating the prospect of pleasures to come.

'Of course, I am. I'll just have to let them know at home.' He got up and made his way to the telephone. His mother answered. 'I'm not going to be back tonight mum', he said, assuming that this was sufficient information.

'Where are you?', she asked.

'I'm at the Irish Club, you know, for the wake.'

'Where are you stopping tonight? I haven't seen Richard or Roger at our house for a couple of weeks. They were never away up until you stared this job. Is everything OK with them, I mean, you haven't fallen out with them or anything have you?'

'Oh, no. Everything's fine. I've just been too tired to meet them during the week and I was with Clare all weekend.'

'I see. And when are we going to meet this Clare that you appear to be sacrificing your friends for?'

'I'm not sacrificing my friends for anyone Mum. She's just a really nice girl.'

'What's her surname?', she enquired lightly. 'Where does she live?'

Her name's Clare O'Brien if you must know. She's got a flat above the taxi office on Grape Road.'

'I'm just interested, that's all. Is that a crime?', replied Kate making a mental note to dig into Clare's background. 'Look', she continued, changing the subject. 'I hope that you're not making a habit of spending your time in those kinds of drinking establishment. They're very rough you know. I don't like the idea of you being there if the truth be known.'

'Don't worry mum, I can look after myself'. This was not the answer she wanted to hear.

'It's not about that. You're still a young lad. I don't like you hanging around with that kind of people, you've got a different life to lead.'

'Don't be such a snob mum. They're your people remember?'

'We can talk about this later. Just be careful', she admonished. 'Do you hear me?', she added.

'I will', he replied and said goodbye.

Clare was growing more affectionate with each passing drink, and very soon she was nestled up against him. 'Do you like stopping with me?', whispered Clare as she kissed him provocatively on the neck.

'I love it', he replied enthusiastically.

'You can stay anytime you want you know. It's not a special treat. I love waking up next to you. I love falling asleep beside you. I just love you altogether, I think.' She said, surprising herself, and staring directly into Hugh's face to judge his reaction. After all, it was the first time that either of them had actually mentioned the word itself.

'I love you too', he said gravely, and they peered into one another's eyes.

'Jesus Christ, will you stop!', exclaimed Frankie, 'all this lovey-dovey bollocks, its curdling my beer!'

'Leave them alone', said Mandy. 'They're young. Let them enjoy it. Take no notice of him Clare.'

The two young lovers smiled at one another and turned to face their friends. Frankie caught Hugh's attention and nodded his head in the direction of the lounge area. 'Jones has just walked in', he said. 'That'll be bad news for someone.'

'Why? I know he's a bit loud, but I found him OK', replied Hugh.

'He's going to be OK with you, isn't he? You're the boss's son.'

Frankie's remark immediately caught Clare's attention. 'You're the boss's son, but he's a big shot, isn't he?', she asked looking at Frankie. 'You never told me anything about that. I thought that you were just a normal working lad!'

'It never occurred to mention it', Hugh replied. Clare looked away. He realised his explanation was a weak one.

After a moment or two of silence she turned to him. 'Why would you hide your background from me Hugh? Don't you think I'm good enough? Or do you think that I'm the kind of girl who's just interested in squeezing money out of blokes?'

He stared blankly at her. He wasn't expecting such direct questions and his embarrassment and confusion prevented him from providing her with an immediate response. He hadn't intended to deceive her; he just hadn't got around to telling her yet.

'He's loaded, isn't he?', she repeated, turning to Frankie once again.

'He won't be short of a few bob, I would've thought. Lives in a big mansion up around the park.'

'Jones is a bastard', he continued recognising that he had said too much and wanting to change the direction of conversation as quickly as possible. 'I mean it. He won't be in here for a social call, that's for certain.'

'He'll be here for the funeral, won't he?', replied Hugh hoping to follow Frankie's lead onto safer ground. Clare remained silent.

'He'll have come to the church for that maybe, but he's not in here to drown his sorrows.'

Frankie glanced across the table at Clare. He could see from the expression on her face that she was not yet done with Hugh. He didn't want to have to witness any further confrontation, so he stood up and offered to go to the bar. Mandy, similarly aware of the tension simmering between the young lovers, offered to help him with the drinks leaving Clare and Hugh alone at the table. Clare turned to Hugh. 'Why are you doing this digging work then if your dad's the boss? Shouldn't you have an office job, something easier?'

'Well, I'm not doing this permanently, you know. I'm supposed to be going off to college, at least that's what my parents think, but I've been planning on having a year off to go travelling.'

'College? You're going to college?', she said in astonishment at this fresh revelation. 'You've got all the exams for that? And what do you mean by 'travelling', like a gypsy, 'travelling' as in being a traveller?'

He smiled. 'No, travelling as in travelling around the world. Yes, I did my exams. I did pretty well actually.'

'Oh, I see', she replied, a disconsolate look on her face. 'When are you doing this travelling?'

'I haven't decided yet, probably later this year.'

' And how long will you be gone for?'

'Oh, a year, I suppose', he replied casually trying to make light of the plan.

Clare peered down at her lap, lost in thought. Hugh sat motionless unsure of what to say, detecting a change in her mood and knowing that his words were responsible. After five minutes of this silence Clare reached down and gathered her handbag from the floor and stood up, glaring down at Hugh.

'So', she said, a hard edge to her voice, 'I've learned a lot today. It seems to me that you're just a posh boy slumming it with the riff-raff until you decide to take off to your big, flashy university or spend a year flying from beach to beach, eh? And why not find yourself a silly working lass to pass the summer with. I mean, you can just dump her when the real fun starts, can't you? Who'd care? I mean, what's she in comparison with all those posh young student girls, eh?'

Hugh tried to protest, but Clare was having none of it. 'To think I trusted you', she said, 'I thought you were different, but you're just the same as the rest of them. Say anything you think you have to get a girl into bed.' Her disappointment was rapidly turning to anger. She fell silent and shook her head. 'I can't believe I fell for it', she muttered under her breath and turned to leave.

Hugh jumped to his feet and grabbed her by the arm to prevent her from departing. She came to an immediate halt and stared fixedly at his hand grasping her arm. 'You're hurting me', she said. 'You're not that much different from that lad earlier are you, eh?'

With that he immediately let go of her and she turned and strode towards the door. Frankie and Mandy returned to the table bearing drinks and sat down.

'Where's Clare?', asked Frankie.

'She's just gone, just walked out', replied Hugh shaking his head uncomprehendingly. She didn't even give me chance to explain. She just left', he replied disconsolately.

Frankie tried to lighten the mood.

'Fuck me', he exclaimed, 'ten minutes ago it was all hugs and kisses and staring into one another's eyes, and now they're not even talking to each other! Fucking hell, spare me this love's young dream shite. It'd wear a man out trying to keep up with it. I'm off to the toilet', he said standing up from the table, half recognising his own part in provoking their argument and wishing to steer clear of any recriminations.

Hugh and Mandy sat in silence and after a few minutes had passed she eventually took pity on him.

'Look Hugh, she's only a young lass. She'll be back. You know, when lasses start having feelings for a bloke it changes things. They want to feel that you're being honest with them, totally honest. The truth, the whole truth and nothing but the truth as they say.'

'I would have told her about my dad, about the trip, university, all of that. It just never came up,' he replied scratching around for a justification.

'Well, they all seem like pretty important things not to have cropped up in conversation', she stated flatly. 'You can see why she thought you were avoiding them, especially the stuff about you going away.'

Hugh signed in recognition at the truth of Mandy's point.

'Look, all you need to do is to talk to her, just tell her the truth. It's obvious that she likes you, but you've got to be straight with her.'

Hugh nodded in agreement. 'She seemed pretty angry', he replied barely disguising the note of anxiety in his voice.

'She's going to be. What do you expect? Imagine if you'd accidentally found out something which completely changed your opinion of her? You can blame Frankie and his big mouth for that. No, you can't', she said correcting herself, 'you've no one but yourself to blame, but we've all had a drink and beer does tend to light a fire under things. Just give her a bit of time. Where is he anyway? He's been gone a while', she said feeling that she'd said all that was needed to be said to Hugh.

Frankie was at the urinal when he heard the door open behind him. He turned around to see Jones filling the doorway. 'Get the fuck out', he barked at the customer stood next to Frankie who immediately zipped up and hurriedly tried to negotiate his way past Jones' immobile bulk. Jones didn't take his eyes off Frankie. 'Now', he began, 'no doubt you've heard the tittle tattle about my run in with the Mulligans. Didn't work out well for them, as I'm sure you know. Now, I asked myself, why was it that the Mulligans came all the way down to the yard looking for The Bull? Then it occurred to me: the little chat I had with Frankie boy the other week. You, through the goodness of your heart, took it upon yourself to fill them in on our little conversation, eh?'

'What are you talking about?', replied Frankie, trying to mask his anxiety with a thick coating of resistance, 'I said nothing to them. I don't even fucking know them.'

'Oh really', replied Jones with growing malice, 'you were seen up at 'The Prince of Wales' the week before. I can just see you now, dropping a few choice words into their ears to stir up a bit of bother to entertain you and the boys, eh'. He started slowly rolling his shirt sleeves up.

'I was up there with a girl. She's out there now. Go ask her', he replied, his fear growing.

'I'm not interested in talking to your floozies', he said with disgust. 'I can just imagine it: 'Colm Jones is stirring up a bit of trouble between you and that Danny Greene, I hear. Tells me you're going to give Greene a hiding, I hear', he rasped, his anger becoming more apparent. 'I didn't know that you Mulligan lads were at the beck and call of Colm Jones. Nobody likes to be used to do someone else's dirty work, now do they? It was a good job that they picked on the wrong man when they picked on me, but for all you knew I could've come right unstuck, eh?'

'You're talking shite Jones. I told you, I don't even know the Mulligans.'

'Oh really? Yet you were living with one of the cousins not so long back.'

This was news to Frankie, but he couldn't discount the truth of Jones' assertion. He'd been with so many women in the past ten months he didn't remember all of their names. He might not even have asked them for their surnames. He recognised that there was no point in trying to educate Jones.

'I'm not listening to this bollocks', he said and made his way towards the door, far more in hope than in expectation. As he approached the exit, Jones lashed out, crashing his fist into Frankie's face, snapping his head backwards. The flesh below his right eye split immediately, opening up a scarlet furrow from a which a spurt of blood exploded sending a fine crimson mist into the air. Frankie rocked backwards and Jones caught him again, the flesh of Frankie's nose spreading under the weight of the blow. He fell backwards into the urinal, senseless. Jones glanced down at Frankie lying prone amidst the foul-smelling liquid and yellow cubes of disinfectant and his face contorted into a mask of disgust: 'Good enough for you', he spat dismissively and returned to the bar.

Mandy turned to Hugh. 'Just nip into the gents will you, make sure he hasn't slipped and cracked his skull open', she said light heartedly. Hugh was grateful of the opportunity to leave the table for while he recognised that Mandy had the best of intentions in attempting to console him, he also detected a note of reprimand in what she had to say and this reminder of his foolishness irked him. He walked towards the toilets in a state of distraction, preoccupied with finding a way of making things right with Clare.

As he pushed the door open, he saw Frankie prostrate and he sped over to him and pulled him out of the latrine, disregarding the liquid that drenched the right side of his body. 'Wake up Frankie, wake up', he said and began shaking him by the shoulders. Frankie regained consciousness and struggled unsteadily to his feet looking confusedly at Hugh.

'What happened?', asked Hugh looking around frantically. Frankie looked into the mirror and saw the blood and the twisted remnant of his nose. 'Did you fall? Collapse? What?', asked Hugh trying to obtain information from Frankie in case he needed to call for medical attention.

'No', he replied, rocking back and forth then resting his hand on the sink to steady himself. 'I had a bit of as run-in with Jones. Didn't work out that well for me', he smiled weakly then staggered backwards as a wave of pain hit him and he grasped at the sink to steady himself.

'Jones! Why? Why were you fighting Jones?', asked Hugh, his confusion mounting.

'Well, it wasn't really a fight if the truth be known', Frankie replied and with that he turned and vomited into the sink. He turned on the taps and splashed water over his face to wash away the blood that was streaming from his nose and from the gash below his right eye.

'You're going to need some stitches in those cuts', said Hugh. 'The one below the eye looks deep. Why did he hit you?'

Frankie relayed the details of Jones' tete-a-tete about the Mulligans seeking out Danny. 'He thinks that it was me told the Mulligans that Jones was putting it about that they were going to clobber Danny. They obviously don't like their name being used to threaten people, not unless it's them doing the threatening. Anyway, obviously they came unstuck, but Jones thinks I put them onto him.'

'And did you?'

'Did I fuck! I've no interest in getting involved with them Mulligans. I don't even know why Jones told me when he could've gone straight to Danny himself.'

'Maybe he was scared of going straight to Danny?'

'Seems that way. If you ask me, he was just looking for someone to punch. He's the kind of fella that gets the migraine if he doesn't give someone a shot every couple of months', he said trying to smile and wincing at the pain.

There was a knock at the door closely followed by Mandy's voice.

'Are you in there Frankie? Are you alright?', she called tentatively.

Hugh went to the door and let her in. She looked at Frankie and flew to him pulling up smartly when she inhaled the stench rising from his clothes.

'Oh my God, what happened?', she asked standing away from him.

I slipped', he said sarcastically.

'We're going to have to get you to the hospital with that eye', she said.

'I'm not going to any hospital', he replied and looked at Hugh, 'would you see if there's any plasters behind the bar?'

'Frankie, that needs stitches', replied Hugh gravely. 'I can't believe Jones has done this. I thought he was a good bloke. I'm going to have a word with my father about this.'

'Fuck that', said Frankie adamantly, 'don't do any such thing. This is between me and Jones, nobody else.' He quickly spun around and once again vomited into the sink.

'Come on', said Mandy, 'I'll get you home. You need to get cleaned up.'

'I'll ring a taxi', said Hugh, 'I'll tell them to meet you round the back, so you don't need to walk through the bar. You might as well leave now before anyone else comes in. The taxi won't be long.'

Hugh called the cab and said his goodbyes to Frankie and Mandy. He toyed with the idea of going to Clare's flat but decided to follow Mandy's advice and let matters cool down. He would visit her in the morning he decided. It occurred to him that a slight diversion would take him past 'The Harp' on his journey home. 'One for the road', he thought to himself.

The pub was still quite busy when he entered and he made his way to the bar and ordered a drink. Jenny served him.

'How's that tosser Frankie', she enquired as she was pulling his pint.

'Oh, he's OK, you know, not much change.'

'That's his problem', she snorted as she placed Hugh's drink on the counter. He picked the drink up and surveyed the bar looking for somewhere to sit. He noticed a space next to The Professor and walked over to the table, nodding at him before sitting down. He didn't know The Professor very well, but they had developed a habit of acknowledging one another when their paths crossed at the bar.

Hugh sank heavily on to the backrest on the seat and once again went over the conversation with Clare. His foolishness was becoming more apparent to him the more he considered his decision not to be fully open with her. He cursed himself for taking Frankie's ridiculous advice about not disclosing the 'whole truth', yet despite this he found himself being forced to recognise that there had been a whispering voice in the back of his mind encouraging him to present himself to Clare as a young navvy, this version of himself being the more obviously adult one, the more conspicuously male one. He sought out the origin of this voice and it led back to his grandfather.

It seemed ridiculous when he reflected on it now, not that he'd actually made a specific decision not to tell her about his 'real' life, the life he was expected to live; he had just avoided doing so. He had no intention of continuing with the pretence, indeed, he couldn't see how he could even if he wanted to. The reality was that beneath this silence, he had wanted to tell her that he had a university place; he wanted her to be proud of him.

'So, you're the scion of the House of Gallon?', asked The Professor jolting Hugh from his train of thought.

'Sorry?', replied Hugh turning towards him, not quite catching his meaning. 'Scion' it means 'heir'. You are David Gallon's son, aren't you?'

'I am', replied Hugh, surprised at the deep, cultured tone of the Professor's voice. It seemed somehow out of place in the rough setting of the tap room of 'The Harp'.'

'I used to teach your father. Years ago now, of course. When he used to attend the grammar school.'

'St. Michael's?', replied Hugh.

'Is there any other?', replied The Professor, 'for a good Catholic lad, that is', and he smiled ambivalently. 'He can't have been much younger than you at the time. What're you twenty? Twenty-one?'

'No', replied Hugh. 'I'm eighteen. I went there too actually. Just finished my A-Levels.'

'Yes, David Gallon', he said thoughtfully. 'Decent student. Rather a quiet boy, as I recall. I must say, you don't resemble him much. I've seen you in here a couple of times, but I can't for the life of me remember seeing any other St. Mick's lads in here before. Not really their territory. And I think I've seen you in working clothes too. The plot thickens, I say to myself. Has your dad got you out doing a shift or two, making you pay for your keep? I must say that wouldn't have surprised me with your father's father, but of course that wouldn't really have been David's *metier*.'

'You could say that', replied Hugh. 'And what's a St. Michael's teacher doing in 'The Harp'. Not really their territory, is it?'

The Professor chortled. 'Touché!', he replied. *'Ex*-teacher, might I correct you. The answer to your question is a long, complicated and ultimately tedious one, so I will spare you the boredom of having to listen to it. I would imagine that you're working over the summer, unless your A-levels went disastrously wrong, of course, in which case let me wish you well at the beginning of what I hope will be a long and auspicious career of digging down deep and throwing well back!' And with that he raised his glass.

'You were right the first time', said Hugh smiling, intrigued by his new companion.

'And how are you finding it? Bit of a change from what your used to, I would imagine. Who are you working with?'

'It is, but I really like it. I mean, it was hard at first, but now I love it. Out in the fresh air, hard, physical graft, it just feels good. I'm working with Danny Greene and Frankie Conroy. You must know Frankie. Everyone knows Frankie.'

'Yes, of course. I know Frankie very well', he replied. 'And Danny too, to a lesser extent. I know *of* him, of course, but everybody knows *of* Danny. You're with two very capable lads there. You do well to keep up, if you don't mind me saying.'

'I try', he replied.

'Well, you're a big, strong lad at the prime of your youth. If you couldn't do it now, then there wouldn't be much hope for you a few years down the line. Now there's a toast if ever there was one. Let us drink to the 'prime of youth' and he raised his glass, spilling some of the contents onto the table. Hugh quickly lifted his glass and made a brief contact with The Professor's before glancing around to ensure that no one was watching them.

'That's the irresistible progress of genetic inheritance for you.'

'Now, it's funny that you should mention that', said Hugh, 'I'm very interested in biology. I did it at 'A' level actually. I was talking about this exact same thing with my girlfriend, my *ex*-girlfriend should I say, a couple of weeks ago. I'm not so sure about the inevitability bit. I mean look at my dad. The jackhammer would throw him all over the place. I don't think he's ever picked up a shovel.'

'Hmmmmm, yes, your father..........', he observed cryptically. 'Well now, hold your horses', he continued. 'It's not quite as simple as a one-to-one transfer, you know. Surely you recall from your biology class that for a genetic trait to pass down a little bit of luck is required, you know, two dominant genes must be at play. Perhaps that just didn't happen with your dad.'

'It certainly didn't', replied Hugh. 'Any sentence with the words 'dominant' and 'David Gallon' in it has got off to a bad start if you ask me. He's not really a dominant personality.'

'And that bothers you?', asked The Professor.

'It doesn't *bother* me, really. It's his problem, isn't it? I mean, it's not very inspiring if that's what you mean.'

'Oh, I'm sorry you feel that way', replied The Professor. 'A young lad needs a role model, an example to follow. It's crucial. Very important for the transmission of knowledge, lessons from a life well lived and so on, or not as well lived as might've been hoped perhaps, as seems more often to be the case. In any event a young man needs a paradigm. They crave it.'

'I've always got my grandfather for that', replied Hugh. 'You might've known him, Joe Hanlon?'

'Ah Joe', he replied thoughtfully. 'He was certainly an erm.....' The Professor paused as if searching for the right descriptor '.......an *interesting* character', he continued satisfied that he had found an adjective which satisfied his desire for diplomatic response.

'Interesting? What does that mean?', replied Hugh, his voice carrying a slight note of indignation at The Professor's care in selecting a description of his grandfather. Hugh was unused to hearing his grandfather described in anything less than glowing terms within the family.

'Oh, don't get me wrong', replied The Professor hurriedly. 'I didn't know him intimately, but I knew him well enough to recognise that he was a rather complex character. Not the usual run of the mill muck savage. Very intelligent, very charismatic. I always thought that he was in the wrong line of work, frankly, deserved much more out of life. It must have been very frustrating for him.'

'What do you mean? In what way?', replied Hugh not entirely placated.

'You've got to remember that Irish lads in those days didn't have anything like the opportunities they have now. The proverbial deck was stacked against them.'

'He was a tough man though', replied Hugh.

'Oh yes', continued The Professor laughing, 'he was certainly that, but of course old age puts paid to the warrior. He would've been far more than that had the times been a little kinder to him.'

Hugh had never heard his grandfather being spoken about in such a considered way before. The reality was that he hadn't even spoken to that many people outside of the family who actually knew him. Yet there was something in The Professor's tone, in the words he chose, which concerned Hugh, nothing he could put his finger on and certainly nothing nakedly disparaging, but The Professor seemed to have reserved to himself a full and frank account of his true opinion of Joe Hanlon. Hugh pushed these thoughts from his mind: he had more pressing matters to consider.

CHAPTER THIRTY-SEVEN

Hugh woke up the next morning in his own bed. His first thought upon opening his eyes was of Clare and a slow panic rippled through him as he recalled the events of the previous day; her disappointment, her anger. He tried to quell this restless anxiety with reason and rationality: he had been an utter fool to follow Frankie's advice so uncritically, that was indisputable. Why had he looked to Frankie as a source of guidance, he asked himself. It was stupid of him, juvenile.

He had never set out to deliberately deceive her. How could he? He wasn't going to lie her about his situation, his father was too well known; she was bound to learn the truth at some point. In any event, the fact remained that they had only had a couple of dates and the matter simply had not yet arisen. He wasn't even aware of Clare's own family circumstances. As to the trip he was considering, well, he thought, what was stopping her from joining him?

On top of this, she had reacted pretty swiftly and dramatically; she hadn't given him the opportunity to explain himself, she'd just stormed out and in doing so she had compared him to the low life at the bar who he had defended her against earlier in the day. That was too much, he concluded, his feelings of despondency and alarm now replaced by indignation. How dare she be so unreasonable, so utterly irrational. He lay on the bed trying to nourish his indignation; better that than the panic that had greeted him upon awakening, but he knew that it was futile. He could not rid himself of the memory of the wounded look in her eyes, the anguish in her voice, the decisiveness of her departure.

The clock read seven thirty. He knew it was too early to call her, but he picked up the receiver anyway only to immediately return it to its stand. His mouth felt dry and he decided to get up and get dressed. He ambled downstairs and into the kitchen. His mother was sat at the kitchen table with his father who was eating breakfast. His mother stood up and, after wishing him 'good morning', offered to make him a coffee. Hugh slumped into a vacant chair.

'So', she said, handing him a mug, 'who is this Clare that seems to be taking up so much of your time then?'

'Do we have to talk about that now?', he whined.

'I was just asking, no need to bite my head off', his mother replied with a smile, sensing that Hugh was not in the best of humour.

'We've only been on a few dates', he replied, introducing a little warmth into his tone by way of apology.

Kate immediately recognised the change of tone for what it was and decided to put it to good use.

'And what does she do, this girl?'

'She works at the nursery on Dean street'.

'Is it serious?'

'What do you mean 'serious'?'

'You know what I mean. Are you keen on her?'

'Well, if you must know, yes I am. I like her a lot.'

Kate considered his response in silence.

'You want to be careful, you know. A lot of girls will try to trap a lad like you.'

'What do you mean, 'a lad like me'?'

'Well, you're a catch, you've got a bright future ahead of you. If you don't mess it up that is.'

He looked at her not entirely sure of what she meant. 'I'm not going to mess anything up. I just really like her. She's not the same as the girls we know.'

'I bet she isn't', replied Kate, sarcasm evident in her tone.

'I can't believe how snobbish everyone is.'

'I'm not being snobbish, love. I just don't want you to get distracted, that's all. You've got big, new experiences coming up, far better than anything that's happening here, and I don't want you to miss out for any reason, that's all.'

'I'm not going to miss out on anything'.

Kate turned to David who had been sitting quietly through the conversation.

'Have you got anything to say David?'

'He's just got a new girlfriend, that's all. I don't know what the fuss is about to be honest.'

She gave him a hard look, brief enough for Hugh to miss, but definite enough for David to recognise that this was not the answer she wanted from him. Kate couldn't quite put her finger on why she sensed danger, but she did, and she wanted her husband to confirm its presence too. She could tell that her boy was infatuated with this girl, and it worried her.

'When are we going to meet her then?', she continued changing her tone, trying to keep it as light as possible. Why don't you bring her for lunch tomorrow?'

'OK, I'll ask her', he said, knowing that he wouldn't, not yet anyway given that technically, their relationship could be regarded as finished. His restlessness had returned. He got up from the chair, collected his coffee and went back up to his room and picked up a book in the hope that it might distract him from thoughts of Clare. He fell onto his bed and flipped through a couple of pages before causally dropping it onto the floor. He got up and listlessly toyed with a couple of small dumbbells that had languished unused in the corner of his room for two or three years. He soon grew bored of them.

He showered and dressed and returned to his room, took another book from the shelf in his bedroom and once again slumped onto his bed. He flicked through its pages and, finding nothing to distract him, again cast it aside. He stood up and walked over to the window and peered idly out through his bedroom curtains into the spacious garden at the rear of the house. His mother had hired a local gardener who was currently down on his knees in one of the flower beds that bordered the lush, expansive lawn. He happened to turn around just as Hugh was peering down at him. Hugh quickly closed the curtains and threw himself back onto his bed. He lay there for a while and began to grow drowsy. It came as a relief to feel the tension and anxiety draining from him and he allowed himself to drift off to sleep.

He awoke with a start and fumbled for the clock. It read nine thirty. He quickly swung his feet onto the floor and telephoned Clare's number. The call was answered almost immediately.

'Hello', he said, his voice almost a whisper.

'Hello Hugh', she replied. Her voice was even and strong.

'I think we need to talk about, you know, things', he offered.

'I think we do', she replied, retaining her matter-of-fact tone.

'Shall I come around?'

'No, not here. Let's meet somewhere neutral. How about 'The Pond'?'

'The Pond' was a small artificial lake ringed by a belt of shallow woodland close to Clare's flat, a relic of former glory days when the area was home to wealthy local mill owners, their spacious Victorian villas long ago converted into cheap bedsit apartments. Hugh readily assented. The sound of her voice had banished every last vestige of his earlier attempt to rationalise himself out of the situation he had created. All he wanted to do was to see her, to smother her with apologies and to win her forgiveness.

'When?', he asked hurriedly. 'I can leave right now'.

'OK', she replied' 'I'll see you there in half an hour. I'm not dressed yet.'

A picture of her naked body flashed into his mind, and he dismissed it immediately, embarrassed by his own superficiality.

'OK, I'll see you there.'

He waited for her to hang up and rushed down the stairs, garbling out to his mother that he was going out as he passed her in the kitchen. He mounted his bicycle and sped out into the fresh morning air, exhilarated by the possibility of redemption to come.

He arrived at the entrance to The Pond, a magnificent set of heavy yet ornately designed Gothic gates erected at a time when the city had a bolder, more confident view of itself. The roads had been quiet which had given him the opportunity to burn off the adrenaline-induced energy tingling through his limbs as he contemplated the conversation awaiting him and as a result he arrived ten minutes earlier that he had expected.

He waited impatiently, unable to still himself, striding to and fro across the wide expanse of the entrance, rehearsing his apology, trying to calibrate it so as to preserve as much personal dignity as possible. The minutes dragged by as if each one weighed a ton and then he saw her on the other side of the road, and it seemed like nanoseconds had fluttered by since he'd arrived at the gate. His adrenaline surged again and he resisted the urge to smile at her, not wanting to appear as if he was diminishing the gravity of the matter at hand.

She crossed the road and he walked down the pavement to greet her, inwardly cursing the lack of time he'd had to consider what he was going to say, his facial expression serious to the point of solemnity.

241

'Sorry I'm late', she said smiling briefly.

'Oh, no problem', he replied. They walked in silence through the entrance gates, a cloud of nervous apprehension enveloping them both and they continued onwards ascending the tarmacked pathway toward the lake at the top of the hill.

They walked in silence, both staring at the pathway ahead. Two or three minutes passed before either of them spoke.

'How did you get here?', Clare asked and in her tone was a cautious politeness as if she was addressing the question to someone whom she barely knew, which, all things considered, was not entirely inappropriate given the short length of time since they had first met.

'I cycled', Hugh replied and suddenly came to a stop, an anxious look on his face, before pivoting towards the gate and sprinting back down the hill to retrieve his bicycle, left forgotten and unattended outside the gates. Moments later he reappeared pushing the cycle at his side as he ran up the hill to re-join her.

She smiled affectionately and shook her head. 'What're we going to do with you, eh? All this talk about travelling around the world and you can't even get from your house to The Pond without almost losing your bike.'

He looked into her eyes and smiled, and she held his gaze. They had returned to one another.

'Look', he said, 'I don't care about the stupid trip, I don't care about university. You're the only one I care about. Nothing does or will ever come before that. I just got carried away with things, you know, with us. It just never occurred to me to mention anything, there was just so much other stuff going on.'

She linked her arm through his and they continued their walk up the hill. 'I know', she replied with a sigh and glanced up at the pale blue heavens, her eyes searching the emptiness as if looking for guidance.

'Your life just seems so different from mine', she began. 'I think that was it, the shock of finding that out all in one go. It just knocked me for six. I mean, look at how we met. Look at where we were, who you were with, how you were dressed. Everything. I mean, what was I supposed to think?'

'look, I ….', he interjected urgently.

'No, wait. Let me finish', she said calmly but insistently, needing to be heard.

'My mum and dad were disasters. He was an alcoholic who came and went as he pleased. He was a navvy too, by the way. He'd only turn up at the house when he ran out of money, or money enough for the pub anyway, and when he was home he'd just make everyone's life a misery. He was a bastard', she said bitterly. 'My mum, well, she was just ground down by it all. She ended up on the drink too. That's why I got out as soon as I could.

I never bothered with school. Oh, I went, occasionally', she said and smiled at him, 'but it was just somewhere to go. I remember me and my friend turned up late one morning and they told us that everyone was doing an exam and that we should be in there with the rest of them. We never went back after that. But that doesn't mean I'm thick you know', she added a hint of defiance in her voice, 'I just haven't got the certificates and stuff. And now here I am', she continued, coming to a stop, 'in love with you, someone I barely know. Where did that come from?', she asked, a look of bewilderment on her face. 'Your family's got all this money and this, that and the other and you're off to university or wherever. You're going to be gone, that's all that matters to me.' She turned to him, confusion etched into her delicate young features. 'What are we supposed to do, just have one of those summer romances?', she asked. 'No, I can't do that', she said as if to herself, shaking her head and looking away. 'Not with you. Not now.' She continued walking. Hugh followed her in silence.

They crested the hill and joined the footpath which skirted the edge of the lake. It was almost deserted save for an old man walking his dog in the distance and a young woman pushing a baby carriage along the pathway at the other side of the water. They stood in silence listening to the gentle morning breeze wafting through the tall trees, their leaves trembling, whispering to the morning with parched tongues.

Hugh turned to her. Ten minutes earlier he had seen her as a wild, passionate, slightly intimidating beauty, funny and engaging, independent and bold, but now he saw someone else in her, someone he wanted to protect, to nourish. He had never *cared* so much for another person. He wrapped his arms around her waist and she moved into the embrace and then stopped abruptly placing the palms of her hands on his chest and looked directly up at him.

'It's not a sob story you know, what I've just told you. I manage well enough. I mean, the flat isn't great, but it's a start. I'll do better, I know I will.'

'I know you will too', he said emphatically, 'but you'll do better a lot quicker if there's two us trying.'

Her eyes sparkled and she reached up and cradled the back of his head, pulling him down to meet her lips.

CHAPTER THIRTY-EIGHT

Hugh was waiting outside his house when the waggon pulled up on Monday morning. Frankie was barely recognisable. The right side of his face was swollen and coloured with the tones of an artist's palate, screeds of yellow fading into green fading into blue and then violet. The laceration below his eye gaped obscenely, the leaflets of skin pulled apart by the distorted contours of his face. His nose bent unnaturally, curving at an angle that almost made Hugh shudder. He got into the waggon unsure of how to react to the vandalised face next to him. The best he could muster was to ask if Frankie was feeling alright.

'About as well as I look', he replied, the accompanying smile quickly replaced by a wince.

They continued the journey to Danny's pick-up point in silence. Hugh was astonished that the man was even considering going into work given the carnage that Jones had wrought upon his face. They pulled-up and Danny got into the waggon. He took one look at Frankie and immediately instructed him to turn off the engine.

'What the fuck happened to you man?', he asked incredulously.

'You know Jones told me that the Mulligans were coming for you, well maybe they weren't. It looks like Jones was just using their name to put the frighteners on you. Anyway, they came looking for him instead. He blamed me for that, thought that I'd told them that he was bandying their name about.'

'Jones did this?', Danny replied angrily.

'Aye', but I don't want you getting involved on my behalf. It'd only make me look like an even bigger ass. I mean it Danny, I don't need anyone to fight my battles for me', his words deliberate and conclusive. Danny looked straight ahead, his face stern, his good eye narrowed. Hugh could hear his breathing deepen.

'OK, I understand, but I may have my own business with Jones, so if anything does happen with me and him don't confuse the two.'

'You know yourself Danny, I'd rather lose on my own than have it said I need another man to do my fighting for me.'

'Aye, I know. But first things first, you're going not anywhere near that yard until you've been to the hospital. That wound needs stitches. I mean it', he said authoritatively.

'It'll be fine', replied Frankie.

'Look, I don't want to fall out with you Frankie, just trust me, your face needs putting back together.'

Frankie realised he'd lost this argument and headed off in the direction of the hospital.

'Make sure you get it sorted now. Whatever work we do today, we'll split three ways so don't worry about the money. I feel bad about this. Don't make me feel any worse.'

'Aye, but no rare up with Jones, OK?', replied Frankie.

They pulled up outside the Accident and Emergency Department of the local hospital and Frankie took himself inside. Danny took his place in the driver's seat and they and they headed for the yard. Their journey continued in silence, but Hugh felt a change in the mood in the cab, a tension that filled the cramped space of the cabin like light. He looked at Danny. He could sense the colossal effort that Danny was putting himself through to restrain himself in preparation for their arrival in the yard and their inevitable encounter with Jones.

'Are you going to say anything to him, Jones I mean?', asked Hugh tentatively. 'I know you told Frankie that you wouldn't, but you seem pretty wound up. I mean, I am too. Frankie had warned me about Jones and I defended him. I had no idea that he was such a bully. I mean, why would anyone hurt Frankie? Jones is a bastard', he concluded bitterly.

'I won't do anything. Yet', replied Danny. 'Frankie's got too much respect for himself to ask another man to fight his battles for him. You're no kind of man at all if that's your game.'

'But Frankie can't do anything. I mean, he's not really a fighter, is he?', asked Hugh.

'He's not, but that's not the point. Sometimes you've just got to take a beating like a man and accept it for what it is. If you're half-patient you'll often as not get your chance somewhere down the line and when you do, you've still got your self-respect. Running off whining looking for someone else to do your dirty work for you, that's no way to go on. Own the fucking thing's what I say. There are some things that can't be farmed out.'

Traffic in the yard was thinning out as the waggon made its way through the gates and they had little difficulty in parking up where they needed to be. Hugh glanced up at the gantry as he exited the waggon. Jones was still up there bawling out abuse to the stragglers still in the yard. As he walked around the waggon Jones called out down to them

'Where's your third man, the blackguard? Had a little accident, did he? Slipped in a puddle of his own piss I heard', and with that his raucous laughter echoed around the yard.

Danny didn't even look in Jones' direction and instead carried on with the tasks at hand, but it was too much for Hugh. He stopped what he was doing and strode towards the staircase.

'Remember what Frankie said kid', instructed Danny as Hugh flew past him, racing across the yard and up the staircase. He had no idea what he was going to do or say but lurking in the back of his mind was the realisation that, as the boss' son he could get away with more than the average man in the yard. He reached the top of the stairs and was greeted by a smiling Jones.

'How are you lad', he said warmly, 'only a bit of fun, eh?'

'I'm doing a lot better than Frankie fucking Conroy', replied Hugh sternly. Jones' expression changed immediately. The smile was dropped to be replaced by a hard, cold look.

'Look lad, you're new to this game and you'll be out of it in a month or so. It's a rough game full of rough men and it might look a bit harsh coming from your world but take my advice and don't get involved in things you don't understand. This is a man's business; we don't do debating clubs and that studenty shite here. I don't want to fall out with you, but I'm telling you, keep your fucking nose out. You hear me now?'

Hugh waited for him to finish.

'You're a bully. I understand that clearly enough', replied Hugh looking Jones in the eyes.

'Go in and whine to your father if you want', Jones replied, flinching at Hugh's insult, 'but he's not going to give a shite, especially since it didn't happen here.' Hugh stood glaring at him. Jones sighed and decided to change tac, resuming his earlier friendly tone. 'Look lad, you're in with a bad lot there, especially Greene. You go on about me giving Frankie a couple of well-deserved slaps, but Danny Greene is a fucking animal. Well known for it. Do yourself a favour and go back with the snagging gang. I mean, look at you, you've only been out with them for a couple of weeks and you're trying to put fight on me, and we both know that's not the best idea you're going to have today.'

Hugh faced Jones, fully aware of his own ineffectiveness in the face of the colossus before him. His heart pounded in his chest like the piston on a jackhammer and his muscles fizzed with unused energy. His biology classes had shown him that these feelings were something to be embraced: they were fuel, not fear. He looked Jones squarely in the eyes: 'You're just a bully Jones. A big, thick, useless bully.' He turned to descend the steps. Jones watched him leave. 'Cheeky, spoilt young wanker', he thought to himself, 'if he was any other man's son he'd be bouncing down those steps on his head.'

Danny was waiting for Hugh in the waggon. They pulled out of the yard and after ten minutes or so Danny turned to Hugh.

'You looked like you were giving Jones a bit if a talking to', he said with a hint of a smile.

'I just told him that he was a bully, that's all, which he is. I didn't do anything wrong, did I?', replied Hugh, quickly looking at Danny for reassurance.

'Well, you're right about The Heifer, but if I were you, I'd take a step back and let them sort it out between themselves. There's nothing wrong with you telling Jones what you think, but as I said it's not for you to go hurling punches at him. It won't be the first time Frankie has had a couple of shots and it won't be the last. It's just part of the game. He'll get over it soon enough.'

Hugh felt a rush of unexpected pride at the notion that Danny seemed to be implying that he might be viewed as a credible challenger to Jones. This feeling didn't last long though. Fast upon its heels came the realisation that in all probability Danny was merely being charitable in his estimation of the likely threat that he posed to Jones, a sentiment disguising a caution. This stung in direct proportion to the warm rush of satisfaction he had felt moments earlier.

They continued their journey in silence. Finally, Hugh turned to Danny. 'Jones said that I ought to go back to the snagging gang. He thinks that you're a bad influence.'

Danny let out a roar of laughter the like of which Hugh had never heard from him before. 'A bad influence, eh?', repeated Danny between claps of laughter. 'He might be right', he said as his unexpected mirth subsided. 'A bad influence…..in this line of work. Now that's one for the book', he murmured to himself, finally regaining his usual composure.

'Well, what do you think?', asked Danny. 'I can tell a fighting man from the other side of the street', he said, his gaze remaining on the road ahead, 'and I was keeping an eye you up there with Jones in case things got out of hand. He's twice the size of you, but you didn't seem afraid of him. It seems to me that you're well able to look after yourself. The bad influence must've already crept in from somewhere if you ask me', he said with a smile.

Hugh felt exhilarated. He almost reddened. The countless anecdotes that his grandfather had regaled him with as a youngster had invariably lauded the qualities of the fighting man and in doing so had elevated these faceless individuals into titans occupying an exulted place in Hugh's imagination. They had become anonymous beacons illuminating the path to manhood, figures to admire, to emulate. And now a man who might have fallen straight out of this pantheon was recognising in him this very quality, treating him as a kindred spirit. He felt recognised. His energy levels surged, and he had an intense feeling that at that precise moment that he had passed from boyhood to manhood.

Words surged out of him carrying thoughts, feelings and intuitions that had been whirling within him for months, but which were alien to those who inhabited his other life, words that would frighten them, that they would not understand, but now at last here was someone who would hear him. 'I've never been afraid of fighting', he said to Danny. 'I mean, I don't go looking for trouble or start it just for the sake of it but I'm not going to cower for anyone. I suppose it's about defiance as much as anything and sometimes physical force is the only way to put that defiance out into the world. It's about not being afraid, not being weak, just standing up for yourself and that's what being a man is all about, isn't it?', he said turning to face Danny for the first time in the conversation. 'Did you know the word 'violence' comes from Latin?', he continued 'It means to be full of strength and that's mental strength not just physical. A man has to be strong in his mind, in his character or else what is he? Just someone to be kicked around? He's no good to anybody if that's all he is. I'm not saying that fighting solves everything because I know it doesn't, but there are some things that only physical force can put a stop to. It's just hard-wired into what we are as animals, as men. But the thing is, where I come from, everyone is afraid to get involved, so they look down on it as something that only stupid people do. My friends are terrified of engaging in anything like that. I mean, a couple of weeks ago I had to save my mate from getting beaten up. He was just allowing himself to be punched, frozen with fear. I couldn't understand it. They don't fight because they're frightened of getting hurt, but even when they are getting hurt, they still don't fight, even to defend themselves.'

'Jesus, you've got a lot to say, that's for sure', replied Danny turning to smile at Hugh. 'I've never known a fighting man give that much thought to it, but I suppose that's one of the benefits of a proper education. Remember, people from your world think differently, that's all. They don't have to deal with the likes of me, or Jones or the Mulligans, or they think they don't anyway, but what they don't realise is that the world's a dangerous place and all their nice words only protect them from people like themselves. There's plenty out there that don't give a shite about all that fancy talk.'

'Jones said that you were well known as a fighting man or at least words to that effect. A few people have said that actually, said Hugh tentatively.

'You know for all the roughness of the men at this kind of work they do like to gossip', replied Danny.

'Is it true? I mean, you certainly do look like you can look after yourself. I don't mean that in a bad way, I mean..........'

Danny looked at him with a quizzical half-smile on his face, surprised at the directness of the question.

'Have I been a fighting man? You could say that, I suppose, but there's no novelty there. As I said, it's a rough job. The work itself toughens you up. There's no shortage of fighting men around, especially if there are a few pints involved.'

Hugh tried a risky gambit.

'Is that how you lost your eye, in a fight?'

'You're not short of questions, are you?'

'I'm sorry', replied Hugh sheepishly, 'I didn't mean to pry, I mean I didn't......'

'Well, it wasn't so much of a fight', interrupted Danny mercifully, sensing Hugh's discomfort. 'It was more of a massacre, but I've managed to get a hold of most of the culprits over the years.'

'Most of them?', enquired Hugh.

Danny ignored the question and pulled the waggon into the side of the road. 'Well, here we are. Let's get stuck in', he said.

Hugh had arranged to meet Richard that evening and was eager to share his news. He had much to tell him. Hugh had rather jokingly suggested that they meet at 'The Harp' and much to Hugh's surprise Richard had agreed to the proposal.

He and Danny had finished work in good time allowing Hugh to get to the pub in advance of Richard's arrival. He wasn't going to test Richard's fortitude any more than necessary given his unexpected concession in agreeing to meet there, a fortitude which would have been severely strained if he'd have been obliged to hang around the tap room of 'The Harp' alone. Hugh was on his second pint when Richard joined him at the bar. Hugh ordered a drink for his friend. Richard surveyed the tap room. 'So, you've finally found time for your old pal, eh, after numerous failed arrangements. It's a bit basic in here, isn't it?', he observed before picking up his drink.

'Well, it's certainly not on a par with the lounge of the golf Club', replied Hugh.

'No, it certainly isn't', replied Richard emphatically.

He took a step back in order to get a fuller look at Hugh. 'Well, well, you do look the very image of a young Irish navvy, fresh off the boat', he said. 'Big boots, mud-spatterd in all the right places, but does the crack of your arse show when you lean down to pick stuff up from the floor?', he said smiling.

'Now, now, don't take the piss. They don't take kindly to posh kids criticising their sartorial imperfections in here, you know', replied Hugh nodding to a passing acquaintance.

'Actually, you look good. Have you put some weight on? You look thicker, more solid', continued Richard quickly glancing around to ensure that he hadn't been overheard as they moved from the bar to a table.

'I've been eating like a horse actually and I've definitely gained some muscle. Beats the gym.'

'You've got a tan as well, lucky you. Now, you can promise me I'm not going to get beaten up in here, right? I'm viewing this visit as a sociological experiment, an exercise in field work. I'm not here to provoke the indigenous population. Everyone's been asking about you since you rejected civilisation and went native you know. Oh, and I saw Jane at the weekend.'

'And?', asked Hugh indifferently.

'She's started going out with Brandon Lewis.'

'That gobshite?'

'Gobshite?', repeated Richard slowly, considering the sound as he might a strange artefact. 'What strange new words you've learned in this new land.'

'You know what I mean. He is a bit of a dick.'

'You're not entirely incorrect, but clearly Jane doesn't think so.'

'Well, that's fine. Not really any of my business now, is it?'

'It is not. So, what about this new girl that you're seeing. When do I get to meet her? She must be something special if you've neglected your friends for her.'

'She is. She's vivacious, gorgeous and she has her own flat. She'll be here shortly.'

'Her own flat? You shit me not! Oh, by the way, I saw your mother the other day too at the golf Club. You know, where the civilised people go to relax. She gave me the third degree about you. She doesn't seem overly happy with how you're spending your time. Have you told her about the gap year stuff yet?'

'I'm thinking about dropping the idea', replied Hugh.

'Well, that's a controversy narrowly averted. She'll never know how close she came to the fear and anxiety that is a parent's experience of their child's gap year'.

As he was saying this another young man arrived at the table and greeted Hugh. 'She seems to think that you're spending too much time in here too. Don't know whatever gave her that idea....', he continued, his eyes following the recent visitor to the table as he returned to the bar.

'It's OK in here. I like it. I mean, it's very different to where we usually go, and I accept that it can be a bit rough sometimes. All that's true, but I feel very comfortable in here. It must be the influence of some kind of spooky atavistic call of recognition.'

'Well, you certainly seem well known. Here's another one', observed Richard nodding his head in the direction of an approaching visitor. Hugh swivelled around in his chair. It was Spencer. He smiled in anticipation of his greeting, but Spencer had something quite different in mind.

'Who the fuck do you think you are talking to my uncle like that?', he bawled at Hugh. 'Just because you're the boss's lad, eh, think you can come on all high and mighty?' He was now stood over the seated Hugh, 'Think you're fucking big shot, eh?'

'Calm down, calm down', said Richard rising to his feet. 'I'm sure this is just a simple misunderstanding.' Spencer had had clearly already wound himself up as a prelude to approaching the table. He glared at Richard.

'And you can shut the fuck up, you posh cunt', he snarled. Richard visibly withered under Spencer's gaze and resumed his seat.

Hugh had been caught off guard by Spencer's unexpected aggression and it took him a moment or two to get a grip of the situation, but it was clear to him that this interaction was only going to end one way. He rose to his feet, a grim look on his face. 'Get the fuck out the back', he growled at Spencer.

'What are you doing Hugh, don't get involved', pleaded Richard rising to his feet again only to be sat back down again by a menacing glance from Spencer.

'Really?', said Spencer sarcastically you want a fucking taste, do you? Come on then', and he turned in the direction of the rear exit to the pub.

'My God, how utterly predictable', said Richard, an exasperated expression on his face. 'You're not really going outside with him?'

'You just wait here Richard', replied Hugh as he rose from his seat and walked towards the door.

'Fuck that, I want to watch', replied Richard taking a hurried gulp from his drink and leaping to his feet.

Spencer had obviously briefed his friends as to his intentions in approaching Hugh and they followed Richard as he headed outside. Spencer was sat on an empty beer cask casually smoking a cigarette which he flicked to one side as Hugh emerged from the door. Hugh and Richard stood by the door as Spencer's friends filed past them and gathered around their champion.

Hugh took a couple of steps forward to the centre of the yard.

'Come on then, let's get busy. Get your arse over here', he said calmly looking at Spencer who emerged from the cluster of men accompanied by a chorus of grunted encouragement.

The two combatants took up their positions facing one another and as they did so one of Spencer's friends took it upon himself to officiate and, much to Richard's relief, explained to all assembled that the fight was to be resolved between the two men at either side of him and that no one else should involve themselves either to help or to hinder.

Spencer was eager to put on a show for his friends and immediately began issuing wild threats to Hugh, forewarning him of the horrors to come. His ranting increased in intensity, spreading to his associates like a contagion and they bawled out instructions and advice to him as to how he should best proceed. Richard began to wonder at what point the gang would lose control and pounce on him as the first course. Hugh stared at Spencer unconcerned by noise surrounding him, waiting for Spencer to make a move. Just as his tirade appeared to be reaching its peak Spencer dropped his right shoulder in preparation to throwing a punch. He was too slow and too clumsy. Hugh immediately dispatched a straight right to his jaw sending Spencer staggering backwards like a drunkard into the arms of his waiting friends. One look at him told them that he was out cold, and they lay him down on the ground and glanced at one another unsure of what to do next. Spencer was several years older than Hugh and had a burgeoning reputation of his own to cultivate and this fight was expected to be a straightforward matter for him, hence his attempt to milk the preamble and frame the fight as dramatically as he could, all the better to bejewel his inevitable victory. He began moaning and a couple of his friends leant down to help to raise him from the tarmac, but it was clear from the dazed expression on his face that any further contribution from him was out of the question. The remainder of the group wandered listlessly back into the pub, a couple of whom patted Hugh on the shoulder to congratulate him.

Spencer's brother was one of the men steadying him as he tried to regain his senses and the swift defeat of his sibling's pretensions caused him to disregard the impromptu referee's rules of engagement. Without warning he fell on Hugh like an avalanche. He was considerably heavier than Hugh and he clearly had no other plan than simply to throw himself at him. Hugh felt a dull shock as he hit the tarmac, a bright flash sparkling through his consciousness as the back of his head collided with the ground and he felt the dead weight of his attacker upon him. He realised immediately that he had to manoeuvre his way out of his vulnerability and this he did in moments, gripping the man's shirt and utilising the strength in his shoulders to twist his body from under the weight bearing down on him. Within seconds of the attack Hugh was in the dominant position. Spencer's brother began to flail wildly while Hugh positioned himself on his knees to bear down on his trunk. Hugh sensed that the lad was panicking and that he would run out of energy very quickly. He did so in moments and began gasping for air. For the first time made eye contact with Hugh.

Hugh raised his right fist above the man's face.

'Pay attention fat boy', he growled. 'I could break your face open with this', he said flicking his eyes towards the fist hovering menacingly above his attacker's face, 'but I'm going to let you up and, trust me, if you try any funny business I will fucking hospitalise you. Do you understand?' The assailant nodded vigorously.

Hugh rose to his feet in one swift movement and turned to face the disappointed aggressor who struggled onto one knee and sucked in mouthfuls of air before staggering to his feet and stumbling back to his remaining friends.

Richard looked at Hugh. 'Well, another pleasant evening at the local, eh?'

Hugh smiled.

'Not my fault. Very brave of you to hang around though.' They walked back to their seats in the bar.

'Does this happen every time you come to this pub?', Richard asked.

'No, not at all. There's just some stuff being going on at work. Spilled over a bit.'

'So that's just one unending round of larks and high jinks too, eh?'

'Not exactly Richard. Take a look at this.' He rummaged in his pocket and drew out his wallet, plucking a small, printed sheet of paper from within and passing it to Richard.'

'Where am I looking?', he asked peering down at a pay slip.

Hugh pointed to a figure.

'You can't be serious', Richard said in astonishment. 'You get paid that much for one week's work? That's a man's wage!'

'Its hard work, you know. Took me weeks and a lot of pain to adjust to it. The gang I'm in share the money equally. If you don't pull your weight, you get booted out. I was just lucky that I got in with a good gang. And they're good blokes too.' He decided that it was unnecessary to go into any details about Frankie's recent misadventure given what had just happened. 'One of them is a really interesting bloke, Danny they call him. Tough bloke, but really smart too.'

'How about getting me a job there', asked Richard only half-jokingly.

'Trust me, you wouldn't thank me for it. In fact, it would probably mean the end of our friendship', he said smiling. 'You just haven't got the navvy genes. Look at my hands', he said turning his palms up.

'Bloody hell, they're like leather. Those callouses!', said Richard in astonishment.

'Everyone earned', he replied. 'Oh, here she is', he said looking over Richard's shoulder and smiling broadly.

Richard spun around following the direction of Hugh's gaze. Clare breezed into the pub, her hair causally swept away from her face, her eyes focused squarely on Hugh and her smile radiating warmth and affection. She glided past Richard taking no notice of him and wrapped her arms around Hugh. 'Oh I've been missing you today', she said gleefully and cupped his face in her hands, kissing him on the lips.

'This is Richard', Hugh announced to her looking at his friend and flushing slightly.

'Hello Richard', she said enthusiastically. 'He's told me a lot about you.'

'Hello Clare, likewise', he replied smiling broadly.

Clare asked if anyone wanted a drink and took herself to the bar to place her order. Richard watched her go turned to Hugh.

'My God', he exclaimed in hushed tones, 'she is gorgeous. And you met her in here? I need to take up boxing lessons and start coming in here more often. I mean it, she's stunning.' Hugh smiled, trying to restrain his pride.

'And you say that she's got her own place too?'

'She has indeed', he replied.

'You seem to be leaving us mere juveniles behind, don't you?'

'I do feel different, to be frank. I just seemed to have slotted into this world', he said.

'Well, it's your father's world too I suppose, at least the work part of it', suggested Richard.

'No, no it isn't', countered Hugh immediately. He sort of hovers above it peering in from a distance. He wouldn't last two minutes if his little wings gave out and he found himself in the midst of it.'

'Well, it seems to suit you anyway. Particularly Clare. I'm not surprised that you've put the travelling plans on hold.'

'Did I hear that right?', said Clare as she placed the drinks on the table. 'You're not abandoning me to go off to Timbuktu?'

'I was going to tell you later', he said smiling up at her.

She shrieked and threw herself on him, smothering him in kisses, her joy evident. After a moment of two this euphoria she sat down next to him. 'I've been worried sick, you know', she said turning to Richard, then embraced Hugh again, barely able to contain her excitement.

'Well, I feel honoured to witness such obvious romantic joy!', said Richard raising his glass. The contented couple raised their own to meet his.

'Excuse me boys, I've just got to go to the ladies', said Clare.

'She's certainly a far cry from Jane, I'll give you that. A great deal more……..ebullient, shall we say.'

'I'm in love mate', replied Hugh candidly, 'and before you comment, it's not just because of the sex, although that's out of this world. She's a wonderful girl in so many ways. As I said, everything's spot on right now. I'm really enjoying the work, the lads I work with are great and I've got more money than I know what to do with. And, to top it all off, there's Clare.'

'Well, I have to say, you look really well. You looked tanned, you look fit. You seem a bit different too, maybe is just the regular sex', he said enviously.

'I might just carry on with this work instead of travelling in my gap year. It'd put a ton of money in my bank, and it means I can stay with Clare.'

'What do you mean, 'stay with Clare'? Move in with her?'

'You can move in with me any time you want', said Clare causally as she resumed her seat next to Hugh. 'You're there often enough, anyway.'

'You have an excellent sense of timing Clare', said Richard and she smiled at him.

'No offence but aren't you a bit young for all this cohabitation business?', asked Richard.

'Well, you've got to start sometime', replied Clare, turning to Hugh and smiling.

CHAPTER THIRTY-NINE

Frankie was waiting for them at his pick-up point the next morning. The kaleidoscopic bruising had faded somewhat along with the worst of the swelling, but his right eye was underscored by a ragged black scar. The knotted sutures which held his face together formed a raised filigree of flesh which marked out areas of damage like fine barbed wire.

Hugh was surprised to see him. He had assumed that Frankie would want to avoid Jones, but clearly not. His mood was improved too, or at least he made an effort to make it appear so. Hugh ran through the events of the previous evening not wanting either of them to hear it from a third party. 'Well, we could be driving a different waggon tomorrow', said Frankie when Hugh finished his tale.

'What do you mean?', asked Hugh.

'We might get run off the job', he replied.

Danny, who had remained silent during the course of Hugh's account, turned to them both.

'Look, if men were going to get the boot for a bit of a rumpus in the pub, then the entire game would come to a stop before the end of the week and from you've said it was him that started it anyway.'

'And I do suppose you might have a bit of pull with the boss man too. Well, we'll see soon enough anyway. At least you came out of it a bit better than me, anyway', said Frankie smiling.

It hadn't yet occurred to Hugh to consider the wider implications of the fight in terms of his relations with Jones and, more importantly, his father. He'd been distracted by Clare's enthusiasm for the idea of their moving in together. His first instinct had been to agree with Richard; they were way too young for such an arrangement, but the more he considered the prospect the more attractive it became. He was certainly earning enough money to support them both and he would have be living independently once he went to university anyway. He would hardly decline the opportunity to share a flat and a bed with a girl then.

He looked from Frankie to Danny. These men were free to do as they please. They rolled the dice every morning they got up. They were free, well at least Danny was, he concluded. Frankie seemed to spend his life bouncing from woman to woman in search of what he thought would be an easy life. That wasn't freedom, not really. That was just a failure to take responsibility for himself, to rely on someone else to make a life for you. Just another door into the jail house.

Danny on the other hand seemed completely self-possessed. He did what he wanted, when he wanted. He was the author of his own life; no responsibilities, no commitments; a man amongst men, respected by his peers and beholden to no body. That was the way a man should live, he concluded. But then there was Clare to consider. This conflict unnerved him.

They had been allocated a new street to work on and this had been accompanied with instructions that they should work strictly within the confines of the official regulations, which meant that all signs and barriers had to be in place, that they complied with official start and finish times and that they strictly adhered to all health and safety rules. This degree of adherence to official working practices was only insisted upon when men were set to work in the more salubrious areas of the city. Experience had taught the agents at GCE that the wealthier the neighbourhood, the more likely were its residents to complain of any inconvenience caused to them, real or imagined. The gang ensured that the site was set up in textbook fashion and once that was done, they waited in the waggon for twenty minutes until eight o'clock, the official start time.

Hugh mulled over the implications of Clare's offer for most of the morning, his body now so accustomed to the dynamics of his work that he had little need to focus his attentions on them. His mother would be set against it of course, but the move seemed to him like the natural thing to do. His reverie was interrupted by the arrival of his father on site, an almost unheard-of event. It was Frankie who spotted his car pulling up behind Hugh and he stopped the hammer and nodded towards it. 'He must be awful pissed off with you if he's come out on to site to deliver your bollocking.'

David didn't get out of the car, but instead wound his window down and hammered the horn to attract Hugh's attention. Hugh laid down the shovel on the footpath and walked reluctantly towards the inevitable dressing down.

'What the bloody hell's going on? Fighting again, eh? What is wrong with you, its every other week! Doesn't bode well for your future career, does it? Why're you getting involved in things that don't concern you? This is man's business, it's not for you to stick your nose into.' Hugh bridled at the implication.

'You're talking about Spencer, I assume. I had no choice in the matter. He started it.'

'Listen to yourself. You sound like a five-year-old: 'he started it', repeated David dismissively. 'I can expect that kind of behaviour from Spencer because he's a half-wit, but you're supposed to be the golden boy, according to your mother anyway. I've a good mind to sack you. That's what your mother wants, by the way. Anyway, make sure that you're at home tonight, she wants to speak to you.'

'About this?', he asked cautiously.

'This and some other matters', and with that he drove off.

Hugh walked back to the trench. He doubted that his father would sack him, not because of the fight anyway, but he knew his mother would be furious.

'Jesus, look at the face on you. Anyone'd think you'd been given a bollocking by the Pope himself', exclaimed Frankie, his attempt at laughter quickly converting to a yelp of pain.

'Serves you right', said Hugh as he jumped down into the trench.

'So do we need another man?', asked Frankie dabbing the wound with his fingers to check if it had started bleeding again.

'Not yet', replied Hugh, 'but we might do soon enough if you insist on trying to infect that wound.'

Frankie quickly pulled his fingers away from his face and was about to start the hammer when he nodded towards one of the houses adjacent to the track. Hugh turned his head towards the object of Frankie's interest, a woman making her way down the driveway of a large, handsome Victorian villa. She was dressed in an expensive, three-quarter length bathrobe, the collars of which she held together with her right hand clearly anxious to prevent her voluminous breasts from spilling out into the morning air. She was tall and slender with shoulder length blonde hair, her long, toned legs carrying her along with a causal elegance. Frankie let a slow, soft whistle. 'Jesus Christ', he exclaimed under his breath. The woman sauntered to the bottom of the driveway and made directly for them.

'Good morning gentlemen', she said in a crisp, polished tone as she approached them. 'I realise that this work is necessary, but how long will I have to tolerate this chaos and disruption?', she asked casting her eyes along the wrecked footpath.

'Oh, we'll be gone in a couple of days', replied Frankie rising to exhibit his full height and wiping the right side of his face in an attempt to disguise his wounds, a gesture which did little more than emphasise their presence.

'Cable TV, isn't it?', she asked glancing at the grab waggon unloading its cargo of stone aggregate.

'Indeed it is', answered Frankie, 'but don't worry. We'll be leaving your part of the street spick and span before we leave tonight.'

The woman turned to Frankie, nodding her head briskly as if confirming that this was a promise that she would hold him to. Then, as if noticing him as a person for the first time, she stared directly at Frankie's scarring.

'My word, you have been in the wars, haven't you?', Frankie smiled self-consciously.

'It was an accident. I tripped and fell. It happens in this line of work.'

'How clumsy of you', she replied brusquely and peered closer at the suture work that framed his eye.

'They haven't done a very good job of knitting it back together again, have they?' She raised her hand as if to touch it and then hesitated before explaining to him that she was a doctor. He nodded his permission for her to proceed. She cupped his right temple and used her thumb to press gently on the skin around the lesion.

'Not a good job at all, I'm afraid. Where did you have this done?'

He answered her.

'Come with me', she ordered, turning back towards the driveway. 'There are a great deal of rather nasty pathogens lurking in the soil you're digging up and apparently smearing yourself with', she advised Frankie. She continued striding towards her house and, after a few steps, looked behind her to confirm that Frankie was following.

He remained rooted to the spot.

'Come on, chop chop. I don't bite'.

Frankie looked down at Hugh, his expression amazed and overjoyed. He raced after her, catching her as she turned into the driveway.

Frankie was in the house for around ten minutes before he re-emerged and came striding down the driveway, his chest puffed out and an enormous grin on his face.

'You look pleased with yourself', said Hugh, 'don't tell me you've got a date with her.'

'I wish I could say it was so', he replied picking up the hammer, 'but even a master like me needs a little more time to work his magic. I do have a plan though. As tidy as the front garden is, the back one's a tip. It needs digging over for starters. She has some old gardener that comes in once a week, but he's not up to heavy work, so I said I'd do it for her this Saturday, you know, as a payback for looking at the old scratch.' He pointed to the area around the scar which had been liberally coated in some kind of gel.

'She's a fine - looking woman that one and I think that she's single too. She must be, no self-respecting man would leave his woman to sort out a back garden like that on her own', he continued.

'A bit ambitious of you Frankie, no? I mean she is a doctor besides being gorgeous', said Hugh, a smile playing across his face.

'You cheeky bastard', replied Frankie, laughing and then once again gritting his teeth in pain. 'Oh, we had a nice little chat me and her while she was doing her thing. She was going to make me a pot of tea you know, but I wouldn't hold you lads up more than was necessary. It'd be a fine old thing though if I could warm me feet up against her hearth on a winter's night.'

'No offence to Mandy, but it'd certainly be a bit of a promotion, don't you think?', replied Hugh.

'Maybe, but it'd be well deserved', he said winking a Hugh, 'very well deserved', before squeezing the hammer back into life.

CHAPTER FORTY

Hugh walked up the driveway of his parent's house that evening with a lively sense of trepidation buzzing through his mind. He wasn't in the least bit concerned with the prospect of a further rebuke from his father, but his mother was a different matter. Her disapproval was a rare phenomenon and was not to be taken lightly. He tried to steel himself against the oncoming sermon with the thought that he was a man now, he did a man's job and, as such, the occasional crossing of swords with co-workers was to be expected; it was simply part of a man's world that women would never understand.

As he rehearsed his argument, he could not help but recognise that perhaps it wasn't as persuasive as he'd hoped it might and his reluctant entrance into his mother's domain seemed to undermine his confidence in its validity completely.

He walked through the kitchen and the absence of the sounds usually playing around the house at this time, the clattering of pots and pans, the TV wittering away, idle conversation floating through the air, served only to enhance his disquietude. As he entered the lounge he saw why: his mother and father were sat in grim silence awaiting his arrival. 'This is going to be fun', he thought to himself as he sat down.

'I think we know why we're here', began Kate. 'I have to say Hugh that I've been hearing a great deal regarding your antics recently and frankly I'm not at all impressed.'

Hugh looked accusingly at David who didn't appear particularly focused on the matter at hand now that his mother had taken the lead on the basis of information David had provided.

'And don't look at your dad as if he's to blame', said Kate the mention of his name causing David to emerge from his reverie. 'I've heard a few things from a number of different sources, for your information. You're never out of one of the roughest pubs in the city, you're going out with some girl we've never met, older than you, doesn't live at home, God knows what her background is, and now the fighting issue has raised its head again. And I bumped into Jane last week and she told me all about the incidents at the party and in the car park of the shopping centre. Yes, I know about those too.'

In the absence of any suitable alternative course of action Hugh simply sat in silence, waiting for the reprimand to run its course. Kate sensed that her approach wasn't having the desired effect and she softened her tone.

'Look darling, we just want what's best for you. I've discussed it with your father, and we think it was probably a mistake you starting that job. This fighting business, it goes against everything you've got in store for you. Certainly, get a part-time job, but that dirty pub and this girl you're seeing, we think that you should put them behind you. I mean, you never know, girls can be devious.'

David shot a glance at Kate as she uttered these words.

'You've had a go at being a navvy, which is fine, but now it's time to move on. In fact your father insists on it', she said looking pointedly at David.

Gallon felt her glare burning into his cheek.

'Yes, I insist upon it', he confirmed half-heartedly.

'You insist on it?', repeated Hugh. 'What does that mean? That you're going to sack me? For what? You'd be a laughing-stock', he continued, his confidence increasing now that his father was his adversary. David didn't reply. This was exactly the argument he'd used to Kate when she had proposed this course of action earlier in the day.

Kate was growing increasingly anxious as she felt her authority over the situation beginning to dwindle. She knew her son had a defiant streak, and she was reluctant to put its limits to the test, but she had a deep sense that there was something more at stake here than just which pubs he chose to use or what girl he chose to date. She decided to broaden the context, to try put matters in their proper perspective.

'Look, I know that the work and everything that goes with it is novel, a new set of experiences, new people, new places, new challenges, but you're going to get all of that when you go to university, and without all this bloody fighting', she smiled indulgently, hoping to lighten the mood.

Hugh decided to be bold.

'About that, I've been thinking of taking a gap year. I'm surprised Jane didn't mention that to you too given how much else she'd had to say.'

'What?', his mother exclaimed, a horrified expression on her face. 'You can't do that', she cried out. Then, unexpectedly, David made an unprompted contribution.

'You know, it might not be a bad idea. See the world', he said turning to Kate, a questioning look on his face.

Kate looked from David to Hugh, utterly mortified, trying to work through the implications of what she'd just heard.

'But, erm', Hugh interjected, his confidence steadily growing,' I don't mean that I'd go travelling, I'd stay here and work, get some money together.' His mother looked at him in open-mouthed horror.

'You can't be serious?', David asked, half-smiling.

'That's insane love', said Kate, almost beseechingly. 'Who gives up a place at university to go digging the roads? It's ridiculous.' She looked beyond the room lost in thought, trying to grasp the gravity of what she was hearing.

'It's not ridiculous, it's fucking stupid', replied David scowling, his earlier indifference now hardened into indignation at the thought of Hugh not only hanging around his house for another year, but now also his place of work.

'If you do that you'd better find yourself somewhere else to live', he spat decisively.

Kate's head spun and she stared directly at him. 'I wouldn't go that far David.'

'I would, and I will. It's about time he grew up instead of playing at being an adult. Think about somebody else for a fucking change.'

'David, language!', barked Kate sternly. She felt that matters were spinning out of her control; she turned to Hugh. 'He doesn't mean it love, he's just worried', her voice imploring, desperate.

Hugh didn't meet her eyes. Instead, he turned to David, his own sense indignation rising. 'If that's what you want, that's what you'll get'.

He rose to his feet and made for the stairs.

Kate's eyes followed Hugh. 'You've gone too far David', she said weakly.

'What other sanction do we have? Stop his pocket money?' He'll stay on the couch at one of his mates' for a couple of days then he'll be back, tail between his legs.'

Kate knew that it wouldn't be that simple. She looked at David anxiously and ran to the bottom of the stairs.

'Hugh, come down', she said warmly. 'Things have just got out of hand. You don't need to go anywhere.'

She waited for a reply. The house remained silent. Hugh appeared at the top of the stairs carrying a holdall crammed full with clothing. He looked down at the suddenly diminished figure of his mother at the foot of the stairs and then descended and walked past her without acknowledgement, not daring to witness the look of desperate sadness etched onto her face.

He mounted his bicycle and he was at Clare's flat in twenty minutes. He knocked and waited for her to appear. When she opened the door he remained on the doorstep paralysed by a sudden sense of sheepishness. Clare looked at him, confused by his silence.

Finally, he managed to speak: 'I've moved out. Can you put me up for a couple of days until I make some arrangements?'

She flung her arms around him with a yelp of excitement.

CHAPTER FORTY-ONE

The gang had continued working on the doctor's street for the remainder of the week, moving further away from her house with each passing day, forcing the track onwards. Nonetheless, she would toot the horn of her Mercedes sports car as she passed Frankie in her usual course of toing and froing from her house. Every passing blast of acknowledgement would leave him as excited as a puppy and he would commence babbling about the golden future that awaited them both.

Saturday morning could not pass quickly enough for Frankie. 'Come on Hugh', he said more than once 'we've got to get done sharpish. I've got a doctor's appointment you know', and he would grin widely at what he took to be wit. It wasn't a particularly amusing remark the first time he'd said it and it did not grow any funnier with repetition. At break time he could barely contain his excitement. 'Oh, it'll be the high life for me soon enough. No more jackhammer for this bonny lad. I'll have hands like a lawyer's in six months', he said looking at his thickly calloused palms.

'I'd lower your expectations a bit, if I were you Frankie', cautioned Hugh. 'You're a navvy going around to do a bit of gardening work for a doctor. Free gardening work. You don't even know the woman's second name and you're already planning how you'll celebrate your tenth wedding anniversary with her. I'd bring myself back down to earth if I were you.'

'He's not wrong', added Danny. 'She's not one of these young bar girls, you know.'

This counsel had no effect. As far as Frankie was concerned, it was a testament to the universal appeal of his good looks and athletic physique that even so elevated a woman as she would fall for him and, more importantly, open the doors of her life to him. As far as he was concerned, it was only a matter of time before she would be asking him to move in and shortly thereafter questioning the wisdom of his continuing to work when he could be spending so much more time with her instead.

As per their agreement, he found himself knocking on her door at two o'clock on Saturday afternoon. She invited him in, but he looked down at his muddy boots and reluctantly declined, cursing himself for the lack of foresight which deprived him of the opportunity to take in the lay of the interior of the house and instead he proposed that he follow the pathway to the garden at the rear. She offered to make him a cup of tea which he gratefully accepted, and she disappeared into the house closing the door behind her. He was further encouraged when she emerged from the back door holding a tray upon which rested two cups of before sitting herself down beside him at the garden table. She explained to him what she wanted doing and Frankie immediately noted that he could spin this work out into at least two visits if necessary.

'Why doesn't your husband do it?', he asked casually in the midst of their conversation, hoping to disguise the fact that for him this was the key question asked specifically to elicit from her whether or not there was in fact a husband around the place.

'Oh, I've been divorced for a couple of years', she answered casually. 'He wasn't really the physical type anyway. He would've just paid someone to do it'. Frankie took encouragement from this, priding himself that he was an exemplar of what she had referred to as 'the physical type' and, quickly capitalising on his insight, he rose to his feet stretching out his arms and arching his back in preparation for the rigours ahead, a display which would have made him a laughing-stock if he'd have performed it on site.

'Well, I'd better get started', he said, not noticing the barely suppressed smile creeping across her lips as she observed his warm-up, quickly hidden behind her teacup. He ambled over to the garden shed and pulled open the door and squinted into the half-darkness within and selected the tools necessary for the job at hand and then pulled his T-shirt over his head and hung it on the corner of the shed door. It was certainly hot enough for him to work bare chested and he wanted to satisfy himself that she would have an opportunity to take in his well-honed physique.

He turned to look back to the table and was pleased to see her still sitting there sipping on her tea. 'You carry on', she shouted to him across the garden. 'I'm just going to enjoy the sunshine for a while.'

'Just going to enjoy watching Frankie', he thought to himself and ensured that he didn't stray far from her line of sight. After around ten minutes he heard an unexpected voice and turned around to see what he assumed was one of her friends greeting her from the driver's seat of an expensive convertible which was slowly coming to a stop at the head of the driveway.

'Good morning Susan, thought you'd be out here topping up your tan', said the expensively dressed arrival as she emerged gracefully from the vehicle and sat herself down at the garden table. They chatted out of Frankie's earshot for a moment or two before they both arose and entered the house. It was definitely a minus point that she hadn't introduced him to her friend he noted, but a minus point amidst what he took to be an avalanche of positives compared to which her lapse of etiquette fell away into insignificance. He spent the first ten or fifteen minutes getting stuck into the work; he was eager to display his energy and to get some blood pumping into his muscles, all the better to entice her.

Susan's friend sat down at the large, oak kitchen table. 'He's well put together', she observed with a smile. 'Where did you find him?'

'Ditch digger. Working outside of the house. That's why I was waiting for you in the garden. Thought you'd like a gander. Well-made, isn't he?', she replied laughing. Her friend got up from the table and took a surreptitiously look through the kitchen curtains.

'I'm a sucker for a bit of rough myself', she replied, 'though they can get a bit clingy if you're not careful.'

'He's like a dog on heat that one. Couldn't wait to get his shirt off to exhibit his wares.'

'Well, he divested himself of the wrong item of clothing if that was his intention', she replied, and they both cackled with laughter.

'Are you going to dip your toe?'

'Haven't decided yet.'

With that Frankie appeared at the open kitchen door his lean, athletic torso glistening with sweat. 'Talk of the devil', Susan exclaimed. 'Do come in. More tea?', she enquired.

'I won't muddy your floor', he replied, noting her friend and calculating that her presence would not be conducive to the woo he intended to pitch. He surveyed the kitchen noting its dimensions and made a rough calculation of the size of the interior of the house on that basis. 'Fuck me, this would suit me down to the ground', he thought to himself.

'I've got to shoot off in about half an hour', he said, 'but I can finish off tomorrow, if you want.'

'Are you sure? Oh, thank you so much. That would be great', replied Susan.

'OK, then. I'll be here early, so don't panic if you hear a bit of movement in the garden.'

'I might be still in bed when you arrive, so feel free to wake me up if you need anything', she said glancing slyly at her friend.

Frankie smiled broadly and said his goodbyes in a state of high optimism as to how his life was set to unfold.

CHAPTER FORTY-TWO

'She couldn't take her eyes off me', said Frankie to The Professor in the pub later that afternoon only entering once he had confirmed that Jenny was not working behind the bar.

'Jesus, even her mate gave me the once over with her eyes. I'm telling you now, that is one fine woman. She way she talks, the smell of perfume off her, Jesus, she's a class act. And I'm back there again tomorrow.'

'And what do you think is in it for her Frankie?', enquired The Professor removing his spectacles and looking at Frankie square in the face.

Frankie returned his look with genuine astonishment. 'Isn't it obvious?', he replied indignantly.

'Do you think that you've got much in common, shared interests and such? If she's a doctor, she's going to be very well educated. No offence intended Frankie, but you wouldn't describe yourself in those terms, would you?', he replied a slight smile playing across his mouth.

'No, I wouldn't', he replied, 'but that doesn't matter. You know as well as I do that the women do take to me, most of the time, if I behave myself, that is. And I'm going to behave myself right with this one. I've no intention of rocking the boat at all. Keep her happy in the cot and Bob's yer uncle, as they say.'

'I'd go steady, if I were you. It might not be that straight forward, you know.'

'If you'd have seen the way she was looking at me you'd know. She was almost drooling at the mouth, she was.'

'Well, good luck to you then. You've been around women long enough to know, I suppose'.

'This is the one I've been waiting for', he said rubbing the palms of his hands together excitedly. It almost makes getting those few shots from Jones seem worthwhile.'

The Professor looked askance at him and shook his head.

'So, what are you going to do?', asked Rachel sympathetically as she refilled Kate's wine glass. Kate had spent the previous hour detailing the circumstances leading up to Hugh's departure and she had drunk far more wine than usual in a bid to smother the anxiety that had emerged every time she considered the matter. She had thought about nothing else all week. At first, she had blamed David and had lashed out at him verbally which had not helped matters, serving instead only to increase her sense of isolation. She could not help but feel that he was gratified that Hugh was out of the house. She had recalled that when news of Hugh's exam results came though, David's principal concern was steering him towards universities at the other end of the country and emphasising how important it was that he used this as opportunity to develop his independence. Now she wanted to blame David for Hugh's departure and had sought to do so, but she knew that the matter was not that simple.

'What can I do?', she replied. 'David said that he'd be back in a couple of days wanting his laundry doing, but that hasn't happened; I knew it wouldn't anyway'.

'Have you thought of going to see him yourself, talk to him?'

'There'd be no point. I know how stubborn he can be. Plus, he's got that girl. What young lad would leave that? I gave his father a note to pass on to him. It just told him that he was welcome to come back anytime. What else could I say? The house is very quiet without him though', she said turning her eyes to the floor.

'Can't David speak to him? He's his father after all.'

'No. That wouldn't help. They don't get along. Never have, you know that. I think David is pleased that he's gone to be honest', continued Kate sadly.

'Don't say that, Kate. It's his son, of course he's going miss him.'

Kate stared down at her glass and twisted the stem anxiously. She seemed on the brink of saying something, so Rachel remained silent giving her the time to collect her thoughts. Then Kate began quietly sobbing, her shoulders jerking slightly as she tried to contain her emotions and she raised her hand to shade her eyes as if from the sunlight. Rachel immediately moved to her side and put her arm around Kate's shoulder. 'Oh Kate, he'll be back', she said soothingly. 'He's just trying to be the big man, you know what they're like. Come on darling, this isn't like you.'

As soon as she felt Rachel's arm around her shoulder, Kate mastered herself. Straightening her back she wiped away her tears with her hand.

'David's not his father, not his real father, I mean', she said.

Rachel leaned back almost imperceptibly, a look of astonishment on her face.

'What?', she said aghast, 'but of course he is.' She caught herself immediately, recognising how ridiculous her remark was.

'What do you mean? Who is the father then?'

'It doesn't matter. It's just not David.'

'Does he know?'

'Yes, he does. He's always known.'

Rachel collapsed back into the sofas if to absorb the shock. 'Does the real, I mean the biological father know?'

'No, he doesn't.'

'I don't know what to say. Obviously, Hugh doesn't know.'

'No, he doesn't, and he doesn't need to know either. Ever.' She looked at Rachel with a severity that demanded her absolute compliance.

'Of course, of course', blustered Rachel with utter sincerity, 'but how did it happen?'

Kate looked at her with raised eyebrows.

'I mean what were the circumstances? Did you have an affair?'

No. It wasn't anything like that. I've known David forever. I used to see him regularly at church when we were young believe it or not and I knew that he was infatuated with me. To be perfectly honest, everybody knew he had a thing for me. I mean, if you want me to be even more honest everybody had a thing for me at that time and everybody knew it. I was simply born lucky in that way. I never took much notice of it until other people did. The poor lad couldn't disguise it. He'd go weak at the knees if I so much as looked at him. My father was insistent that I should marry him. Never shut up about it.'

'What did your father have to do with it?', exclaimed Rachel, a look of indignation on her face.

'You'd be surprised', replied Kate. 'I told you, mine was a very different world from your's. Him and David's father went way back, old country way back. You know it wouldn't have surprised me if they'd made some kind of deal, some kind of gentleman's agreement.'

'Gentleman! Ha!', snorted Rachel.

'I know, I know', but it was a different world then. *They* came from a different world.'

'Anyway, I fell in love with someone else. Proper hook, line and sinker stuff, like you do when you're that age, when you know nothing. One thing led to another, and I got pregnant.'

'The father?'

'I didn't tell him. I just broke it off. I didn't want him to know.'

'But surely he would've found out, I mean people talk.'

'Don't they just', she replied bitterly. 'He didn't take it very well, the poor, poor man', she said, her gaze lost to the distance. 'He must have hated me so much after that.' With this acknowledgement she tilted her head back, closing her eyes and moaning as if she'd been physically wounded, for the first time allowing herself to acknowledge the pain that she'd caused him. She cradled her face in her hands and sobbed without restraint, her body convulsing in an agony of recognition. She looked at Rachel imploringly, her face ashen, as if her friend could grant her forgiveness.

'I had to do it. I just had to. I had no choice.'

Rachel took Kate in her arms and held her until she had exhausted herself. After a minute or two of agonised sobbing Kate sat up, rested her elbow on her knee, holding her forehead in her hand, the last of her tears falling onto her lap.

'He, the father that is, he just disappeared after that'.

'Look, I don't mean to pry, but what was so wrong with him? I mean, why didn't you have the child with him if you loved him so much?'

'It was a hardest thing I've ever done, but he just couldn't offer the life I wanted for my kid. I mean I loved him: I loved him! I loved him! I loved him!', she cried exuberantly as if the memory once uncovered had to be exalted, and then she sighed once again, 'but I had to be strong for the child whatever it cost me. He hadn't had a great life himself the poor man, kicked from pillar to post by his father, out working on building sites from when he was old enough to pick up a shovel. He worked at a fairground at one point. He was a rough lad himself, on the surface I mean, but he was so tender with me, so gentle and kind. It broke my heart to do that to him, but I had to, I just had to.' With that the tears returned, and Rachel embraced her again. 'Go on dear, let it out.'

After a minute or so of this catharsis Kate began to collect herself. Rachel rustled in her handbag and passed her tissues to dry her eyes and her cheeks. Kate leant back into the sofa, exhausted.

'So, David?', asked Rachel.

'I told him the truth. I told him that I was pregnant. He knew the child wasn't his, of course. We hadn't done anything like that. I told him that I'd marry him, but it would have to be soon. It was a take it or leave it offer.'

'Wow! That was bold of you.'

'When I look back now, I can't believe that I had the nerve, but it all seemed inevitable. David wasn't much in the looks department, I suppose, and I knew that he was there for the taking. I don't think he'd ever had a girlfriend up to that point. I just took a chance and he went along with it. I used him, let's say it as it is.'

'And he accepted Hugh as his own, obviously?'

'He tried, but there was a lot of gossip when Hugh was born so soon after the wedding and that really got to David. I mean, everyone knew who Hugh's father was. I mean it really got to him. You know what they're like about the whole 'manhood' thing. Perhaps you don't. It's different in that community. David had a loose enough grip on it anyway, even then. He'd had a difficult relationship with his father too, been a late developer, that kind of thing. He was incredibly sensitive to what people thought of him, still is really, and that definitely affected the way he dealt with Hugh. I mean, he wasn't nasty to him or anything, I wouldn't have stood for that', she said decisively, 'but it affected him in ways only I would notice. As far as anyone else was concerned, there didn't appear to be a problem. The thing is, he's back in city, the father that is. He's been back for a couple of months.'

'Bloody hell! Have you seen him, spoken to him?'

'I saw him at funeral recently. I didn't speak to him. I couldn't speak to him. I haven't been able to bring myself to think of him for almost twenty years. That was the only option, block him out totally, but the thing is I've been seeing so much of

276

him in Hugh as he's got older. Oh, I've tried to ignore it, but I can't help it. I knew his father's face better than I knew my own. Sometimes Hugh will just glance at me with a certain expression on his face or just scratch his bloody head in a certain way and I see his father. I just feel like a complete bitch. The same day I saw him, at the funeral that is, I even tried to get David to use his influence to scare him away, make him leave the city. My God! What have I become! What kind of person am I? I've ruined the lives of three of the most important men in my life', she said turning to her friend in an agony of confusion.

'Anyway, fortunately he didn't see me at the funeral, thank God', she continued, her soul fatigued by the wearying effects of resignation, 'but it's not that simple. Hugh is now working with him, and he thinks that there's nothing like him.'

'Bloody hell! That is ridiculous Kate!', Rachel exclaimed. 'How have you people allowed this to happen? I mean David, of course.'

Kate ignored the implication.

'It's horrendous. Everything that I've worked for, all the sacrifices I've made have come to nothing. It's like God is punishing me for having the gall to think that I had a say in what would happen in the future.'

'Hindsight is a wonderful thing I know, but you should never have let Hugh work for David. I mean that's where it all started, right?'

'Well spotted', Kate replied flatly, 'but to be honest I'd hoped that he'd get fed up with it after a month, but he was brought up with these stories from his grandfather, my father', she added, 'and that man was a sweet talker if ever there was one, a natural salesman or thought he was anyway. I suppose he was just selling himself, his past, his life, to the lad, trying to glamorise it all, trying to win him over. The thing was he didn't need to.' She sighed heavily. 'Glamourise', she repeated the word sarcastically. 'Glamourise' being ankle deep in freezing water in a muddy trench in the middle of winter with the rain pissing down on your back for ten hours earning as much in a week as a lawyer earns in an hour sat in a warm office? I suppose it shows the extent of his persuasiveness, that he could only convince a kid of the value of that experience. Christ knows he didn't have much success with the adults.

I honestly thought that nonsense had gone in one ear and come out of the other, but it had obviously got stuck somewhere in between. He was obviously a bigger influence on him than I'd thought. I'd hoped that David would've been a guide to him, you know, the way that fathers are supposed to be, but he never had the strength of character, never had any character at all really. Oh I don't know what goes on in a boy's mind. I really thought I did...'

'I don't know what to say', replied Rachel.

'There's not a lot to say. I've spent my entire adult life trying to protect my son, trying to give him the tools to protect himself, and the first chance he gets he runs headlong into the fire with his eyes closed hoping for the best on the advice of an old, drunken failure who wasn't fit to lace Hugh's boots, and would've said so himself if he'd lived long enough and stayed sober for long enough to do so. It's heart-breaking.'

CHAPTER FORTY-THREE

Frankie arrived at Susan's house at seven thirty the next morning. His plan was to work for an hour and then wake her up. She had seen what his body had to offer and as far as he could tell she was well pleased with what she had seen. He took the view that if her friend had validated his appeal then he was as good as resident in the grand house before him. He worked for a little longer than he had planned as the relative coolness of the early morning had prevented him from generating the glossy coating of sweat which would display the contours of his tanned musculature to full effect. He was starting to develop a thirst when he heard a knocking on the window in one of the upstairs rooms. He looked up and saw Susan standing there. She was wearing a thin summer dressing gown causally tied at the waist. He wondered for just how long she had been watching him. He waived back smiling and resumed his work.

Within minutes she was in the garden barefoot, the robe draped around her like an afterthought.

'Would you like to come in for a cup of tea', she enquired smiling broadly.

'I would indeed', he replied and followed her along the garden path up to the house, utterly engrossed by the alluring lines of her shapely frame. He pulled off his boots, revealing freshly laundered socks, before entering the Kitchen and sat down at the table as she attended to the kettle.

'This'll be routine soon enough', he thought to himself, nestling into the chair and surveying the room. 'Where's your friend today', he asked, not that he was particularly interested in her whereabouts, but as a conversational gambit the enquiry exploited the small patch of common ground they had available to them.

'Oh, she'll be at home, I suppose. She took a bit of a fancy to you', she said turning around and smiling at him. Frankie smiled sheepishly, trying to imitate modesty before deciding upon a different approach.

'And why wouldn't she?', he said, a mischievous smile spreading across his face. Susan brought two cups of tea to the table and sat down. As she did so, her robe fell open slightly to reveal the dusky globe of her left breast. 'Oh, sorry', she said causally and pulled the wandering curtain of fabric tightly across her chest.

They engaged in small talk about the garden for a while before she asked to examine his face. She peered at the pale scar tissue developing around his eye. The bruising was subsiding.

'You're going to have a nasty scar there, you know', she said thoughtfully. She stood up and walked around to him. 'Stand up', she ordered, 'let me get a better look'. She held him by the shoulders and tried to pivot his body in the direction of the morning light cascading in through the French windows. She adjusted his position slightly but didn't look at his face, instead her eyes rested on her hands, tiny on the broad beam of his shoulders. 'My, my you are a well-made fellow, aren't you', she said lowering her hands to gently squeeze his biceps. It was only then that she looked into his face, her lips parted. He was looking at her intently. 'I am indeed', he replied, almost whispering, 'in many ways'.

Her hand went to the back of his head, and she brought his lips down to meet her's.

CHAPTER FORTY-FOUR

Frankie was in joyous spirits in the yard on Monday morning eagerly relaying the events of the previous day to acquaintances in another gang. Hugh and Danny were loading the waggon having long since wearied of his exuberance. However, it wasn't long before Frankie's high spirits soon came to Jones' attention

'Hey punchbag', he bellowed down to him from the gantry, 'stop talking shite and get that waggon of your's washed down before you leave this fucking yard. Just because you live like a pig in shit doesn't give you the right to let company property get into that kind of a state. Get it cleaned.'

Frankie looked up at Jones.

'Good to see you answer to your fucking name, punchy', roared Jones and threw his head back in laughter. Frankie returned to the waggon. Danny was scowling up at Jones whose laughter came to an abrupt end when he caught the malevolence in Danny's glare, and he turned and entered the office. Frankie looked at Danny.

'Don't go getting involved in anything with that useless fucker because of me.'

'Who said it was because of you?', replied Danny.

'That fat bastard can't piss me off today. I am the man of the moment', he said. 'Did I happen to mention that I hit the jackpot with the doctor yesterday?', he asked, winking at Hugh.

'Yes, you did', replied Hugh, 'on several occasions and in alarming detail.'

'Well, all of this will soon be a thing of the past', said Frankie sweeping his arm in front of him. 'A new life awaits!'

'He needs a good crack', Jones observed looking towards David.

'Who is it this time?', replied David wearily.

'Greene', replied Jones gruffly, monitoring David's response with great care. David dropped his pen onto his desk and leant back in his chair as if considering what Jones had just said.

'You've grown quite ambitious since your run in with the Mulligans, eh?' Jones bridled at the implication that he was lesser man than Greene. 'Anyway, a little bird tells me that you got the wrong man when you hammered Frankie.'

'What do you mean?', replied Jones, his inclination towards anger tempered only by his deference towards his boss.

'Frankie didn't tell the Mulligans you'd been using their name against Greene at all. It was Greene himself. Went straight into 'The Royal' on his own and confronted them once he'd heard the tale. I mean you wanted him to find out, didn't you? Why tell Frankie otherwise?'

'I was trying to help you. You wanted him gone, right?'

'Maybe you knocked out the wrong man, that's all', replied Gallon feigning indifference.

'What's changed? I could've done him when he first arrived, but you didn't want that, did you?'

David had been returning to his decision to keep Danny Greene around ever since Hugh had left the house. No doubt Hugh's departure was matter of public knowledge by now and God knows what people were saying. Kate had been a picture of despondency, snapping at him as if he'd driven the kid out, yet it was him that had provided them both with a roof over their heads, lifted them out of the gutter and in return had received nothing but disrespect from him and a begrudging gratitude from her. It was clear to him that Kate and Hugh were the core of the family and that he was merely a convenient add-on kept around for solely material purposes and to deflect damage to her reputation. God knows he'd done that, he thought, more absorbed the damage than deflected it in fact.

He'd seen Greene in Hugh's features immediately despite Kate's strenuous denials. Nonetheless, the reality was that he was unable to bond with the kid although he had convinced himself that he had worked hard to disguise it. Those were the days when he would have done anything for Kate. She was his joy and his motivation. He adored her. And then there was the gossip, the gossip and innuendo. Even his father had quizzed him about it. His final words on the subject still echoed in his memory: 'fuck me, if you can't even sire your own kid what kind of man does that make you, eh?'

At the root of all his problems was Danny Greene a man who'd left city as soon as the going got tough, albeit with a little encouragement, leaving everyone else to clean up his mess. And he, David Gallon, had dutifully done so. For years he had viewed Greene's departure as the cause of his joy, but as Hugh matured and grown more distant, he had taken his mother with him. David increasingly came to see himself through his father's eyes. 'What kind of man am I that I can't sire my own child?' he would ask himself in the dark, sleepless hours of the deep night. The answer did not please him. The home he'd created was no more than a cuckoo's nest. Greene had made a fool of him, and he had no reason to make a secret of it. For all he knew, Greene could have been spreading the truth of his paternity all over the city. Why, Hugh was even working with him! Working alongside of him! How could he have been so stupid, allowing himself to be pushed into corner in order to keep a lid on things when everybody knew the squalid truth anyway and, moreover, everyone believed that he was ignorant of the fact that they knew. A double fool. He'd been a running joke. Well, not anymore.

'To be honest', he said turning to Jones, his tone softening, 'and I don't mean any disrespect by this, but I just got the feeling that perhaps you didn't want to fight him you know, with his reputation, and, well, your history with him. We've been friends for years and I didn't want to put you in that situation.' He knew Jones' vulnerabilities and his little speech had been designed to excite the most sensitive of these: that of being made into a lesser man by a greater one. His entire persona was a fiction extrapolated from his size, bulk and aggression. It was a fiction which he maintained and embellished every waking moment. Most of the time Jones allowed himself to be convinced by it, but David knew where the cracks were located.

'You didn't want to put me in that situation!', replied Jones, utterly aghast. 'Fucking hell David, I'd fight that man on a daily basis as a job if I could. I know he's got a name and all that, but I'd break him in two, you should've known that. Fucking hell!', he exclaimed finally, his tone of exasperation confirming to David that he had indeed prized open the fissures in Jones' self-esteem.

'Ok, I'm sorry then', replied David, 'calm down.'

Yet beneath his bluster Jones knew that Greene was a force to be reckoned with, a formidable opponent and, all things considered, he would have much preferred that the prohibition preventing any confrontation with Greene would have remained in place. Greene presented a significant threat, not just to how he was perceived around the city, but to how he viewed himself. It was a fight that he couldn't afford to lose; his carefully crafted sense of himself would be in jeopardy. And what exactly was Gallon playing at? Clearly something has happened, circumstances have changed, but how? Gallon was, to all intents and purposes, inviting him to fight Greene, no, goading him to fight Greene. He had left him with little choice in the matter. Either confront him or lose face. It was that simple. He felt a shot of adrenaline as the realisation matured, but no immediate sense of fear. He took some comfort from that.

CHAPTER FORTY-FIVE

Kate pulled up outside a row of scruffy, dilapidated shops located in one of the less desirable areas of city. She parked her car on the main road not trusting the grim-looking side streets that peeled off from the main thoroughfare. She sat for a moment and recalled these roads from her youth at a time when they were clean, safe and buzzing with energy, the homes of hard-working families suffused with a sense of community, now they were disordered to the point of dereliction, a motif for this area of the city.

She reached into her handbag to retrieve a piece of paper with an address scribbled on it and peered through the windscreen of her car trying to identify whether or not the shops were numbered. They weren't. She got out still clutching the piece of paper and, after wandering up and down the strip of shops, discovered an old, worn plate affixed to the weathered façade of a hairdressers indicating the street number of the building. She counted forward and found the property that she was looking for; a taxi office above which Clare's flat was located.

She walked to the rear of the row of shops. The narrow, cobbled backstreet was unkempt and malodorous, rubbish strewn across its length, a cat prowling tight up against the bleak stone walls eyeing her suspiciously. Each shop had a small backyard, and she could hear the frantic barking of an angry dog behind the tall, wooden gate of one of the buildings further down the alley. She hoped that this was not the entrance she was looking for. She finally located the gate she was looking for, the building number emblazoned in emulsion across the rotting timber. A rickety wooden staircase led to a cheap, paint-starved door. She ascended the staircase carefully and knocked, not expecting the doorbell to work.

Clare answered the door.

'Hello', said Kate, 'I'm Kate, Hugh's mother. I wonder if we could talk.' Clare stared at her, surprise stealing her tongue.

'Hugh's not here, he's at work', she mumbled finally, hoping that this statement of fact would bring the visit to a close.

285

'Actually, I'd like to talk to you, if you've got the time', said Kate, smiling reassuringly at the girl. Clare hesitated for a second before realising that she had no choice but to invite Kate inside.

The door opened directly into the lounge. The room was small and cheaply furnished, but it was clean. Kate entered glancing around the room and made to sit down on a sofa, but then quickly stood up and asked Clare for permission to do so.

Clare nodded briskly, 'of course, please do', she said slightly embarrassed that her permission was sought by the woman whose unexpected presence made her feel so utterly at a loss. Kate sat down as Clare hurriedly gathered a pile of clothing dumped on the sofa next to where Kate had seated herself. Kate watched her as she did this, smiling at Clare as she returned an apologetic glance. Kate's heart leapt when she saw a couple of Hugh's shirts amongst the bundle.

'Laundry day', said Clare blushing slightly. 'Would you like a coffee?'

'No, thank you', replied Kate. 'I'd like to talk to you about Hugh'.

'Ok', said Clare and she sat down on the chair opposite Kate, setting the laundry down on the floor beside her. There was less than a meter between them.

'First of all, I want you to know that this is not about you', said Kate, 'not in the slightest. I don't know you, even though I did ask Hugh repeatedly if we could meet you', she said, shaking her head and sighing slightly in momentary exasperation at her son. 'I've got nothing against you as a person. Nothing. The truth is, when I started going out with Hugh's father his mother was dead set against me, so I know what that feels like, and I do not want you to feel that way at all.'

Clare relaxed slightly, inwardly recognising that Kate was trying to make the conversation as easy as possible for her, the rehearsed quality of her opening speech suggesting to her that perhaps Kate was a little anxious herself.

'I'm really worried about Hugh', she continued. 'Not because he's with you', she added hurriedly, 'but because of the turn his life has taken recently. I don't think it's for the better. All the drinking, the fighting and now this decision to delay going to college. He was brought up with all this talk about the navvy lifestyle, you see, the tough guys, the devil may care attitude, the whole macho culture of it and I blame my father for that, filling his head with all that nonsense. I mean, his own father's not like that at all, quite the opposite in fact. Hugh doesn't realise that men like my father came from a different world. My father would have been mortified to think that Hugh wanted to go back to that, especially when he's got such a bright future ahead of him. I mean, I can understand the novelty of it all, but I'm just worried that he's going to do something that he can't undo.'

Clare had been listening attentively. 'I am on the pill, if that's what you're worried about', Clare stated baldly. It was Kate's turn to be taken aback. This was her principal fear, but she had decided that it was perhaps unwise to broach it directly at this point, so she was relieved that Clare had the intelligence and sensitivity to address it for her.

'That's reassuring', replied Kate eager to pass over the matter as quickly as possible now that the required confirmation had been received. 'I'm just worried that he'll get distracted by the quick money, the freedom, the lack of responsibility, you know. He' still so young, I mean you both are. All this business about taking a year off. It just seems crazy to me, and to work on the roads? The blokes he seems to admire would give their right arm for a chance like the one he's been given.'

'I understand what you mean, from a mother's point of view', said Clare. Kate's frankness had gone a long way to putting Clare at her ease; at least she didn't have to deal with an angry, belligerent mother who blamed her for corrupting her cherished son.

'But from what I know, he's been planning this year off business for ages. He was going to go travelling with his ex-girlfriend, Jane is it?', Clare enquired tentatively.

'Yes, I know', Kate replied with a sigh.

'He asked me to go with him and I told him that I couldn't. I don't want to be away from home for that long living in grotty hostels. On top of that, I really like my job and I want to keep it.' This fresh revelation stung Kate, the realisation that Hugh's life had dimensions from which she was entirely excluded. On top of this, a girl who Kate barely knew was now in a position of greater influence over her son than she was.

'Look Mrs Gallon, as I said, I can understand your worries, but honestly, I can't tell him what to do any more than you can and even if I tried, he'd probably just do the opposite anyway. He can be very stubborn.' Kate smiled at this girl's understanding of her boy.

'OK then, I'd better be going, I don't want to take up any more of your time', she said standing up. 'If nothing else, at least we've got to meet at last. Kate reached into her handbag and pulled out a small notebook. She scribbled her contact details before tearing off the note and passing it to Clare. 'Here's my number. Let me take you out to lunch next time and I promise, no more serious stuff', she said smiling as she passed the note to Clare who returned her smile as she took the scrap of paper. 'Erm, just before you go', said Clare a little sheepishly as Kate was opening the door, 'what was Jane like?'. Kate smiled inwardly at Clare's little pang of jealousy.

'Not a patch on you love', she replied as she walked out of the door. 'Use that phone number.' It would do no harm to keep her on side, thought Kate.

CHAPTER FORTY-SIX

Despite Jones' earlier attempts to humiliate him Frankie had been in high spirits all day. It was a fool's errand on Jones behalf anyway: Frankie was well liked amongst the men and the beating he had received had only attracted sympathy for him and caused the prevailing hostility towards Jones to intensify. There had been more than one man mumbling over a pint that Jones was due a comeuppance, but so far no one had put themselves forward as the man for the task.

'Oh, she had a body like a goddess', said Frankie silencing the hammer again.

'Yes, you've said', replied Hugh from the trench, 'several times'.

'We were like beasts of the field', he continued.

'Yes, you said.'

'And the house, it's a fucking mansion, man.'

'Yes, I've seen it remember?', replied Hugh, hoping that Frankie would glean from his tone of voice that he was wearying of his tales of his sexual exploits. He did not.

'You see', he said looking earnestly at Hugh, 'I've been building up to this for years. That's why I've stayed a single man. I was due a woman of quality.'

'You deserve neutering', said Danny as he walked up towards them, smiling. 'How far do you want to go today, do you think we'll make it to the road crossing?', he asked Frankie. They both peered ahead calculating the distance and the time it would take to complete the remaining sixty or so meters of track. As they were considering this a large BMW car pulled upon the road behind them. It looked suspicious parked in such an isolated spot, thirty or forty meters away from the nearest house. Two large, tough looking men emerged from the vehicle and walked towards them. 'Now then, a couple of Mulligans', said Frankie under his breath. As they got closer Danny recognised the older of the two men from the pub.

'Don't panic', he said, 'I know one of them', said Danny reassuringly.

'How are you Danny', said the more familiar face.

'Good enough Tony', he replied.

Hugh looked up from the trench, uncertain as to how the situation would develop. He adjusted his grip on the shaft of the shovel in the event that he might need to use it for purposes other than that for which it had been designed. 'I've got some news for you, but I'll be honest, there's more than one way for you to take it.'

'Speak away', said Danny. Hugh could see the growing tension in Frankie's face and felt a twinge of anxiety himself as he considered the threat that these two gorillas posed, yet Danny seemed perfectly relaxed. Hugh drew confidence from his demeanour.

'You might want to hear what we've got to say in private.' The speaker appeared grave, but unthreatening.

'Will what you have to say change depending on the size of the audience?', asked Danny causally.

'No, it won't', came the reply.

'Well then, talk away.'

'OK, first things first. You know we came unstuck with Jones. Everyone knows we came unstuck with Jones', he said pointedly looking at his companion, one of the gang that had been so sorely beaten, 'so you know that we've got an axe to grind with him and you might want to think about that when I tell you what I know.' Danny listened. 'The night you lost the bulb', he said nodding towards Danny's eye-patch, 'I heard it was half a dozen of them jumped you. I happen to know that it was Jones that put them up to it.'

'Is that right?', said Danny becoming noticeably more attentive.

'Look, I know how it sounds, but I know that you're not stupid. I've a cousin of mine coming from across the water at the weekend. He'll tell it to you right. Once you've spoken to him you can make your own mind up; it's up to you. And look, this whole carry on started with a game of 'he said this and he said that', people getting other men to do their dirty work for them, so we know how that goes. Listen to this man, if what he says is any good to you, fair enough. If not, enough said on the subject. My father would've wanted to help you with this, so that's why I'm sticking my nose in, if you want to know.'

With that they turned and walked back to their car. Danny watched them leave, deep in thought. This was the first occasion that the either Frankie or Hugh had heard any reference made to Danny's eye in his presence and it left them feeling somewhat uncomfortable. They looked at one another, each one unsure of what to make of the encounter.

After a moment or two's silence Frankie spoke: 'what do you reckon then?'

'I think we'll probably make the crossing, don't you?', replied Danny.

Frankie looked at him with a puzzled expression on his face.

'No, I meant the Mulligans', added Frankie.

'Hmmm….', mused Danny, 'hard to know', and with that he walked back down the track to resume his work. Frankie looked at Hugh and shrugged his shoulders before picking up the jack hammer.

'So, do you have a doctor's appointment tonight?', asked Hugh deploying the already stale play on words that Frankie had become so fond of in order to move conversation on from Danny's inscrutable reply.

'Not officially, but I left one of our shovels there just in case I needed an excuse to go back. Thinking ahead, you see. I've been doing this for a long time, you know', he said smiling at Hugh before squeezing the hammer into action.

CHAPTER FORTY-SEVEN

David arrived home that evening to find Kate languishing on the couch. 'No supper this evening?', he said walking into the lounge.

'I'll put you something on now', she replied, raising herself up from the sofa as if it cost her a great effort to do so. It had been an emotionally exhausting couple of days and she was feeling frayed, run down.

'I went to see Hugh's new girlfriend today', she said as she entered the kitchen.

'Oh', came the reply.

'Oh?', is that the best you can do?'. She heard him sigh from the kitchen.

'OK, what did she have to say?', he replied, dutifully entering the kitchen and crossing his arms as he stood there waiting for her to speak.

'I know that at the back of it all you're pleased he's gone', replied Kate testily, 'but you might show a little more interest in the fact that our son is out of control, on the brink of wasting his life.'

She waited a moment or two for a reply and then looked around to see him standing in the doorway.

'Our son?', he asked raising his eyebrows to emphasise the note of scepticism in his voice.

'Yes, our son', she replied defiantly.

'It seems to me that what's bred in the bone comes out in the marrow.'

She glared at him.

'And what do you mean by that?', she asked her anger rising.

'Well, the father was just a common or garden thug, wasn't he? But that was more to your taste then, wasn't it.' She picked up one of the onions lying on the work surface and hurled it directly at him. He ducked, the missile barely missing him. He looked at her impassively and turned to go back to the lounge. Kate's anger had reached its peak and she strode into the lounge.

'He was more of a man than you ever were. He wouldn't sit in silence while some arsehole was insulting him, insulting his wife, his people.'

'Oh the bloody golf Club thing again, eh?', replied David, shaking his head, his own temper rising. 'Yep, he's certainly some man alright. I suppose that's why he's living in rented accommodation above a grotty, old pub. That's why he bums aimlessly around the country, battling it out with other no-mark thugs like himself. That's why he works for me!', he bellowed. 'And how much of a man was he when your father ran him out of city, eh, when your father sent him scurrying off like a frightened kitten?', She looked at him uncomprehendingly.

'What do you mean? What's my father got to do with this?', she asked, her anger replaced by confusion.

'I'm surprised that you didn't threaten to break Hugh's girlfriend's legs if she didn't clear out, or did you? That seems to be your family's preferred method of dealing with what you consider to be unsuitable romantic associations', replied David bitterly.

'What the hell are you talking about?'

'Don't you think it was a bit of a coincidence that Greene got his beating and disappeared just after you got pregnant?'

'Stop talking in riddles and spit it out. What're you trying to say?'

'It was Jones that organised the beating and, wait for it, under instructions from your dear old, departed father. He wasn't about to see you getting married to a rough and tumble young navvy, was he? Sound familiar?'

She looked at him in disbelief before dropping into a chair.

'It was your father who wanted rid of Greene, and he got Jones to organise it for him. They gave him a right hiding, so I hear. Might even have gone a bit overboard, but you know what Jones is like. Now I come to think about it, perhaps that's where he left his eye, who knows with a bloke like Jones? And you thought Greene had left because you rejected him? How romantic', he said laughing disdainfully. 'He left because he knew his life wouldn't be worth living if he stayed.'

She was bewildered. 'My father did that?', she asked of no one and memories of that awful night came flooding back to her: she had told Danny that they could no longer be together, that her feelings for him had dwindled and that she could no longer maintain the pretence of caring for him. It had broken her heart to do so and for months afterwards the look of betrayal and despondency with which he greeted this revelation would haunt her thoughts and dreams, her feelings of guilt, shame and loss driving her to the edge of physical illness. It was only the thought of the child growing within her that helped her to cauterise this wound and push the guilt deep into her soul.

She did recall hearing that Danny had been badly beaten up the day after she had broken up with him and she had assumed that he had drunk too much and got himself into trouble. She had held herself responsible for that too which had only added to her misery.

This new revelation reignited her guilt and she felt overwhelmed by shame: ashamed for the way that she had treated him, ashamed for the manner in which her father had treated him; ashamed to her very core. She stood up and wiped away the tears that were edging from her eyes and without looking at David, walked out of the house.

David watched her leave making no attempt to stop her.

'I've given those two the best of everything', he thought bitterly, 'and it's still him that's the star of the show. A one-eyed has-been with fuck all! And the way he walks around that yard, my fucking yard, as if he owns it.' He recognised that he was ratcheting up his temper, but the trajectory seemed unstoppable. How dare she compare him to that loser, that wastrel, that uneducated bruiser. He had nothing better to do with his life than to come here to stir up forgotten troubles. And who's the intended victim? Why him of course. Who else? Once the story got out, he'd be the laughing-stock of the place, humiliated once again.

Greene had to be got shut of and that was that, and the more painful his departure the better. He took comfort from the fact that he'd already primed Jones. Perhaps he should've just let him lose on Greene that first day. So, it might have got people talking, but it would have been ancient history by now. He would have to work on Jones, which wouldn't be too difficult he thought, after all, that's what he was there for, but it wouldn't do any harm to breathe a little harder onto the kindling.

CHAPTER FORTY-EIGHT

Hugh had hardly got his boots off before Clare was skipping around him in a state of high excitement. 'Oh my God, your mother was here, your mother was here!'

'What? When?', he exclaimed, looking up at her in surprise as he sat on the steps trying to unravel his laces.

'She wanted to talk about you, about your future.'

'And?', he asked, standing up to look at her directly. Clare recounted the main points of the conversation.

'She's really worried about you, you know.'

'That's what mothers do, they worry', he replied.

'I mean it. Maybe you should talk to her.'

'Why? So I can listen to why I should go to university, why I should get a job stuck in a suit and tie for the next forty years, why I should be more like my dad? I want a life like Danny's, or someone like that. You should've seen him today', he said excitedly, 'that bloke has got nerves of steel. Nothing seems to frighten him.'

'Him again? I'm talking about your mother', she said somewhat testily. 'To be honest, I liked her. She seemed nice.'

'I'm sorry love', he replied his tone designed to soothe the slight irritation in her voice. 'I'm really glad that you like her, but just don't want the kind of a life she expects me to live. I don't want to be tied to something I can't escape from.'

'Like me?', she asked quietly.

He looked up at her. 'Don't ever think like that. I'm escaping to you, not from you.'

She smiled warmly at him. 'Let me wash your back', she said leading him into the shower.

Danny dropped Frankie off outside the doctor's house and this time he was prepared. He carried a small holdall in which he had packed a change of socks and underwear along with his toothbrush and shaving tackle. Usually, he would take up residence with almost immediate effect– a couple of boozy nights out arranged consecutively he found worked best, and the next thing he knew the lady in question would be asking him he wanted for dinner that evening. Susan didn't seem the boozy type though and the pubs he was familiar with were certainly not her territory. No matter, he thought, I've got this under control.

He strolled confidently up the driveway and rang the doorbell. No answer. He rang again. Susan's car was parked in the driveway, so she was definitely at home. Finally, the door opened. 'Oh, it's you', said Susan slightly surprised. 'I wasn't expecting you.'

'I left one of my tools here', he said smiling broadly. She glanced down at her watch. 'OK, I've got half an hour', she said, 'come in.'

CHAPTER FORTY-NINE

Hugh and Clare were sat with The Professor in 'The Harp' on Saturday afternoon and Hugh was eagerly relaying to him details of the conversation between Danny and Tony Mulligan which had taken place earlier in the week, explaining that Danny was due to meet with the Mulligans again later that day. The Professor was listening avidly when something distracted his attention. He looked at Hugh and nodded over his shoulder to indicate the presence of someone behind him. Hugh turned and saw his father walking towards the bar. He immediately caught his eye and to his surprise David broke into a warm smile.

'Bloody hell, that's my dad. What's he doing here?', he said his brow furrowing as he turned to Clare. He stood up and joined David at the bar. 'Hello', he said coldly. 'What can I get you?'

'Hello Hugh', exclaimed David with considerably more ebullience than was usual when greeting his son. 'I'll just have a half a pint of Guinness please'. He appeared to be in good spirits.

'Bloody hell', he said looking around the bar. 'It's been a long time since I was last in here. Hasn't changed much in fact I think The Professor was sat in exactly the same place as he is now', he chortled and raised his glass to The Professor who was looking in his direction.

'What are you doing in here?', asked Hugh, a note of suspicion in his tone.

'Well, that's not very friendly now, is it? I just passing on the way to the golf club and I thought I'd pop in and see how you were, clear the air a bit.'

'Has my mother put you up to this?', Hugh replied.

'Oh no. Certainly not. She's not talking to me at the moment actually. Look, I've been giving the matter some thought and it's obvious that you're very committed to the new job and we've never really got around to talking about it. I was just interested in how you're getting along with it, that's all. I'm mean, not wanting to pull rank or anything, but it is my firm, remember.

You seem to be getting on particularly well with Frankie and Danny. You do well to keep up with the pace; you're in with one of the better gangs there. I must say, I wasn't best pleased about the beating that Jones gave to Frankie, to be honest. A bit over the top, but you know Jones. Bit of a monster', he said chuckling. 'It happened in here, didn't it?' Hugh remained silent as David continued. 'I mean, I could understand him and Danny fighting given their errrmmm, how to put it.......... rather dramatic past.' He cast a brief, surreptitious glance at Hugh over the rim of his glass as he raised it to his mouth.

'Danny? What dramatic past?', said Hugh his attention duly engaged.

'Oh, you wouldn't be interested, ancient history and all that. Old men's tales', he said smiling briefly. Hugh sensed that he was being reeled-in but he was intrigued to find out why.

'So, what's the tale then?', he asked unable to resist the bait.

David appeared to give the matter some thought. 'Well, it was quite heavily rumoured that it was Jones who cost him his eye, but rumours are rumours. Just gossip. I don't take much notice of that kind of nonsense myself.'

'Why would he do that?', asked Hugh eagerly.

'Oh, I don't know. I asked him about it years ago, but he told me he knew nothing about it. The story was that he had some assistance so I could see him denying it for that reason alone. These fighting men and their pride, eh? Threatened to thump anyone he heard pushing the rumour, but if you ask me, it wouldn't surprise me if Jones was hedging his bets, you know, keeping the cat in the bag, as it were. He's a crafty one', said David smiling inscrutably.

Hugh looked away all the better to process this information and David again shot a sideways glance towards him to confirm that Hugh was indeed considering what he had just told him. They chatted for a few minutes more and Hugh brought him to meet Clare. David greeted her perfunctorily and then left almost immediately afterwards claiming that he had a meeting to attend at the golf club.

Danny entered 'The Royal' and scanned the crowd looking for the Mulligans. It didn't take him long to locate them and he went directly to their table.

'How are you Tony', he said, 'you've got someone who wants to talk to me.'

'Sit down. Let me get you a drink', came the reply.

298

CHAPTER FIFTY

Hugh leapt into the waggon on Monday morning eager to share the information his father had provided with Frankie. 'Turn the engine off', he said. 'Look, I heard something over the weekend about Danny, something important.'

'Oh really?', said Frankie somewhat distractedly.

'It's about the time he lost his eye.' This caught Frankie's attention:

'Go on', he said his interest fully ignited.

'I've found out from a totally trustworthy source that it was Jones who organised the beating that Danny got.'

'Jones?', exclaimed Frankie.

'Yep. The thing is, I don't know whether I should tell Danny or not.'

'Who told you?', asked Frankie.

'I can't say, but trust me, I heard it from someone who knows.'

'To be honest kid, I wouldn't tell him unless you can provide a name. Otherwise it's just gossip, and dangerous gossip at that.'

Hugh sat back and considered his options. Frankie started the engine and they set off. 'I can't believe that doctor', said Frankie changing the subject to reveal his true preoccupation. 'I went around to her house on Saturday and we did the business, then she asked to me to leave straight afterwards. She had somewhere to go, she said. That's not how it works. She should've been pleased to have me for the weekend. I can't understand it. I wonder if she's a bit thick? I'm going to have to go see her again and tell her the way this thing works.'

'And what way's that then?', enquired Hugh tartly his eyebrows raised, feeling somewhat irritated that his news had been side lined.

'Well, she needs to know when she's got a good man and treat him right.'

Hugh chuckled, shook his head and returned to his own preoccupations.

They collected Danny at the usual spot. Hugh decided to wait until they got to the yard to share his news him which was just as well as Frankie spent the entire journey discussing his confusion over the doctor's behaviour. Danny paid no attention to Frankie's lament and appeared more withdrawn than usual. When they arrived at the yard Frankie was the first out of the waggon. Danny was about to follow him when Hugh asked him to wait.

'Look', he said, 'I might be none of my business, but I heard something over the weekend which might interest you. It's about what happened to your eye.'

'OK', said Danny, 'Speak up.'

'I was told over the weekend that it was Jones who organised the group of men that jumped you.'

'And who told you that?', asked Danny his tone of voice indicating more of a general curiosity than the impassioned grab at information that Hugh was expecting. He was beginning to feel a little deflated that his news had twice been greeted with such little enthusiasm.

'My father told me.'

'Your father?', said Danny and grunted. 'My misfortune seems to be a popular topic of conversation at the moment. It's the same news I heard over the weekend.'

Danny peered through the windscreen of the waggon and stared up at Jones grandstanding from his usual position on the gantry. Hugh detected an in increase in the depth and speed of Danny's breathing then, without word to Hugh, he leapt out of the waggon leaving the door swinging behind him and strode towards the staircase.

'Hey, fat man', Danny roared at Jones, 'get your body down here now because if I have to come up for you, I'll throw you off the fucking gantry.' Jones stopped in mid-bellow, and he scoured the yard for the source of these threats quickly identifying Danny. This was it, he thought, the time has come.

'Are you talking to me you one-eyed fuckdog', he bellowed in response and turned to make his way down the stairs. David was in the office. He had been anticipating this exchange, or a version of it, and Greene's initial broadside had sent a warm rush of satisfaction shooting through him. He sat back in his chair and waited for Jones' inevitable response and when it came, as it had to, he smiled to himself and got up out of his chair and made his way to the gantry. Jones was half-way down the stairs when the office door swung closed behind David. He looked down into the yard and saw the men rushing to form a semi-circle around Danny as he waited in silence at the bottom of the stairs for Jones to descend.

'What's all this shouting about?', bawled David. 'Jones get the fuck back up here, this is a place of business, not a bloody pub car park'. Jones stopped in his tracks and turned to look up at David and then, his eyes ablaze, turned to look down at Danny before reluctantly turning to ascend the stairway. When he reached the gantry, David addressed the yard. 'If there's any fighting to be done, it'll here on Saturday afternoon, right? One o'clock sharp.'

Jones turned once more and looked down at Danny. 'Don't have me coming looking for you now, you one-eyed cunt!', he barked down at him, a menacing smile playing across his fleshy lips and with that he turned and walked into the office.

David followed him in. 'Jesus Christ, we've got a half a dozen councilmen arriving for a site inspection this morning. Now, wouldn't that've looked great, eh? You and Greene tearing lumps out of one another in the yard?'

'You wanted it to happen, didn't you?', said Jones his previous aggression quickly turning to confusion.

'Yes, but not first thing in the morning in the fucking yard when we're expecting visitors! Anyway, now that it's been announced there'll be a yard full on Saturday to watch you annihilate him. Won't do any harm to let the word get around, build up the spectator numbers. He won't be able to show his face around this city once you've put him through his paces, eh?' David rubbed his palms together excitedly before slapping Jones on the back and returning to his seat.

The crowd in the yard began to break up as the men returned to their various tasks, sharing opinions on what they had just witnessed and speculating on the likely outcome. Danny turned and walked a pace or two as if to re-join his gang before spinning around and leaping up the staircase. Hugh raced up the steps behind him. Danny barged into the office sending the door crashing against the wall of the portacabin.

'Now then fat man, enough of this public shite. Come with me now and let's get this sorted', he erupted. Jones rose to his feet and looked at David partly for permission, partly for reassurance. David stood up from his desk.

'It's not happening until Saturday Danny, just accept that. I'll not have any of that nonsense on my premises today otherwise the police will be involved, OK? I don't know what this is about and I don't want to know, but if you've anything to sort out you can do it here at the weekend when there's nobody around to interfere, right?'

Hugh was standing in the doorway panting, staring at his father, utterly confused. He didn't understand why David was lying. His father knew exactly what this was about. Danny was lost in thought for a moment. 'Stay out of my way until the weekend, fat man', said Danny acidly and walked out with Hugh close on his heels.

CHAPTER FIFTY-ONE

Frankie had remained at the waggon barely noticing the events unfolding around him. In addition to his reluctance to offer himself as a potential target for Jones' rage he remained preoccupied with the confusing turn of events with the doctor. He attempted to discuss the matter with Hugh several times during the course of the day, but Hugh was immersed in the excitement of the morning and distracted by the prospect of the confrontation to come and as a result the two men spent the entire day talking past one another. Frankie had never experienced this kind of uncertainty before and as the day progressed he grew increasingly fraught.

By the time the shift came to an end Frankie had made up his mind to visit Susan's house and settle the matter once and for all.

Hugh arrived home that evening eager to share news of the day's events with Clare. At first, she was caught up in his excitement without paying much attention to its cause, but as the evening wore on and Hugh continued to labour the theme she became increasingly concerned. Clare had given much thought to Kate's anxieties surrounding Hugh's preoccupation with fighting and his growing tendency to define himself in terms of it. She reminded herself that he had been involved in two confrontations in the short period of time that they had been together albeit neither of which had been of his making, but still......

'Look I know that you've got yourself all wound up about this business with Danny, but I'm not sure that I want you to be there', she said to him tentatively.

'What?', he exclaimed turning to look at her with an incredulous look on his face, 'not go? Are you out of your mind? Why wouldn't I go?'

'These things have a way of getting out of hand and I know that if Danny gets into trouble you'll try and help him; I mean, it's obvious that he's your bloody hero. I mean, you talk about nothing else.'

'My hero? What're you talking about?', replied Hugh, a slight irritability creeping into his voice. 'Just because I respect the bloke all of a sudden he's my hero. That's ridiculous.'

'St. Danny of the Trench', she said dismissively. After a few moments of silence she decided to change her approach and softened her tone. 'I just don't want you to get involved. I don't want you getting hurt.'

'I'm not a child, you know', replied Hugh indignantly. 'I can look after myself.'

'I know you can against lads of your own age', she said in a conciliatory tone, 'but these are big, strong blokes. I mean, Danny lost his eye and according to you he can look after himself. I mean, he lost an eye', she repeated emphatically, 'is that being able to look after yourself?'

'Well, I'm not leaving my mate to deal with this on his own and that's that', he replied as if that were his final word on the matter.

'Look love', she said softly, cradling his head in her hands before kissing him. 'I keep saying, these are big blokes. You're only a teenager. I think that you're having yourself on a bit, I mean you're just putting yourself in harm's way.' As these final words left her mouth she knew that she had overstepped a mark and she instantly regretted it.

'Just a kid, am I?', Hugh snapped. 'Well you won't have much use for me here then, will you', he continued as he leapt up from the chair. 'Just for your information I'm not frightened of any of them. None. At least Danny Greene shows me some respect which is more than you're doing'. With that he pulled on his boots and walked out of the flat slamming the door behind him.

Clare watched him go then sank down into the sofa and began sobbing. This was their first argument since they'd started living together and this in itself was enough to upset her, but she was now genuinely worried about the risk he was exposing himself to. She was also deeply disappointed that she could not make him see why she was worried. It was if the vulnerability he would not recognise in himself had been transferred to her: she felt alone and powerless. She recalled that she had Kate's number. Perhaps his mother and father might be able to talk some sense into him. She was a little uncomfortable calling his parents when his mother had only recently visited her for the same reasons, but perhaps his father could exert some influence after all everybody involved worked for him, he was the boss. She fumbled in her handbag looking for the scrap of paper on which Kate had scribbled her number and dialled it nervously, unsure of how Kate would react. She suspected that Kate might hold her partially responsible for the danger Hugh was placing himself in, but it was a risk that she was prepared to take.

Kate answered the telephone and Clare began explaining to her that she had argued with Hugh but was soon weeping into the telephone, much to Kate's alarm. Kate tried to calm her down and finally Clare was able to communicate the basic facts of their argument to her. Kate insisted that she come to Clare's flat immediately and hurriedly left her home. She arrived around twenty minutes later, an anxious look on her face. Everything Clare told her seemed to increase Kate's anxiety. 'He's not going to listen or me or his father; he'll just do what he wants', said Kate finally, equal measures of resignation and frustration in her voice.

'It just seems ridiculous that two grown men are arranging to have a fight and I just can't see why Hugh is making such a big deal about it. He's been talking about nothing else. I don't want him involved in all this, I mean, he's just a lad. He's too young. They treat this fighting business as if it was a sport, but it's not: people get seriously hurt. I mean look at this Danny bloke. He lost one of his eyes in a bloody fight and Hugh seems to see him as some kind of God. I don't know what I'm more worried about, what Hugh'll do if Danny wins this stupid fight or if he ends up losing it. What is it with these men? Can't Mr. Gallon speak to this Jones bloke, get him to call it off?', Clare asked, 'can't you?' she continued, grasping at straws. Kate shook her head.

'I doubt that there's much David could say. He'll probably be as eager a spectator as any of them, and Jones is just a thug; he lives for this kind of thing.' They sat in silence, their anxiety deepening. After a minute or two Kate seemed to arrive at a decision. 'There is one chance. I don't think that it will work, but I could give it a try', she said pensively.

'What's that?', asked Clare.

'I'm afraid I can't say yet Clare, just leave it with me', and with that she stood up and made her farewells reassuring Clare that she would contact her if she made any progress.

CHAPTER FIFTY-TWO

Frankie walked up Susan's driveway before coming to a stop as he reached the house, noting the presence of an unfamiliar car parked in the driveway. It half occurred to him that it was too early in the day for morning visitors and this recognition served only to add to his discomfort. He could not escape the feeling that he was being forced to engage in an act of supplication and this did not sit at all well with him. He could not fathom why he was having to work so hard to get what he wanted. Women adored him. They always had. The women he selected should be appreciative, they should recognise that they were favoured and behave accordingly. In any case, he thought in an attempt to reassure himself, these initial stumbles were matters that they would laugh about in the years to come as no more than her playing hard to get. He knocked on the door and waited impatiently for her. After what seemed like an eternity the door was eventually opened by a man wearing nothing but jogging pants, his torso exposed.

'Can I help you?', the stranger asked. Frankie was taken aback. The man was not wearing anything on his feet.

'Is Susan at home?', he asked trying to peer over the stranger's shoulder. The man did not answer him and instead turned around and called out Susan's name. Without looking back at Frankie, the man walked into the lounge.

Susan appeared a couple of moments later wearing only a bathrobe, which disconcerted Frankie even more.

'Oh, hello', she said without using his name, a tone of disappointment in her voice. 'What can I do for you?', she asked moving over the threshold and closing the door behind her.

'Who's he?', asked Frankie indignantly.

'Oh, that's Nigel, he's my boyfriend', she replied causally.

Frankie looked at her in astonishment. 'Your boyfriend?', he exclaimed. 'What do you mean 'your boyfriend?' She looked at him with a faux quizzical expression on her face.

'You need me to explain the concept of 'boyfriend' to you?', she said dismissively, her impatience apparent.

'But I thought I was your boyfriend', he mumbled confusedly. Susan let out an involuntary burst of laughter and then immediately collected herself.

'Oh no, whatever gave you that idea? We shagged a couple of times, but so what? You thought that you were my boyfriend? How quaint', she said smiling patronisingly. Frankie stood in silence facing her incapable of fully grasping the import of what was being said to him. Finally, the reality of the situation began to filter through to him.

'Does he know?', asked Frankie gesturing with his head to behind the door.

'Oh yes, of course he does. He likes to hear about my little flings.'

Frankie stood there, transfixed, staring at her. 'Well, if that's all', she said briskly, 'I'd better be getting back.' Franky remained on the doorstep as she closed the door unable to fully comprehend the horror of what had just taken place. He turned as if in a trance and made his way back down the driveway, not knowing where the path might take him.

CHAPTER FIFTY-THREE

Kate's eyes flickered anxiously towards the telephone as they had done every few minutes over the course of the past half an hour. A tumble of thoughts had been rolling through her mind each one presenting a new reason against doing what she was about to do, but she was out of options, and she knew it. She picked up the receiver only to replace it back into its cradle. Finally, she steeled herself and picked up the phone again and called 'The Harp'.' A woman answered; Kate asked to speak to Danny Greene.

She heard what she thought was a door being opened and someone shouting for Danny. Her mouth was dry, and her heart was beating like a hummingbird's, adrenaline careening through her veins.

'Hello?', came the voice on the other end of the line, its deep cadence sending a shock wave rippling through her body and sending her thoughts into a maelstrom of swirling confusion. She had planned and re-planned what she intended to say, but all had flown from her mind upon hearing his voice. She couldn't bring herself to respond.

'Hello?', came the voice again.

Finally, she gained sufficient mastery of her emotions to respond. 'Hello Danny. Its Kate O' Hanlon', she said in a voice that was almost a whisper. A heavy silence greeted her announcement. 'Hello?', she repeated as if testing that he was still on the line.

'Hello Kate', came the reply, grave and distant.

'Look Danny', she continued, 'I know that it's been a long time, but I'd like to talk to you.' The silence returned engulfing her as if it were an abyss.

'What would you like to talk to me about Kate?', he asked eventually, his tone level and matter of fact.

'Not over the telephone', she replied. 'I can pick you up if you want. We can go somewhere for a coffee.'

She could almost hear him thinking. Finally, he replied. 'OK, let's say thirty minutes?'

Once the call was over Danny stood there motionless his gaze directed at the telephone but his mind spinning in numerous directions at once trying to make sense of the conversation that had just taken place, the speaker he had just engaged with. For almost twenty years her memory had been circling his life like a ghost, sometimes looming in close to its centre, sometimes hovering at the periphery at such a distance that she could barely be detected, but she was always there. The voice he had just heard somehow seemed to him less real than the memories with which he was so familiar.

His legs felt weak, and he sat down heavily on the steps behind him. He speculated briefly on what she might want to talk to him about before recognising the pointlessness of the endeavour. He stood up and slowly ascended the stairs and entered his room before opening the door of the ancient mahogany wardrobe and reaching in to retrieve his jacket. As he pulled it from its hanger, he caught a glimpse of his reflection in the mirror attached to the inner panel of the wardrobe door. He raised his hand to his face and gently touched the scar tissue under his eye patch. He pulled on his jacket and made his way downstairs. Better be waiting for her, he thought, rather than put her through the trial of coming into the pub and having to ask for me. That would certainly get idle tongues busy.

He stood at the corner of the street away from the entrance to the pub and took deep draughts of the fresh evening air and tried to reorientate himself towards the oncoming world. For twenty years Kate had lived for him only in his memory, an ethereal, intangible presence. Embellished with all of the virtues of abstraction, she had achieved a certain perfection in his mind, untouched by the corrosive coarseness of the living world. The memory of her had been something that he could cleave to at those times when he sought comfort or solace. He never gave any thought to the brutality of her rejection; indeed, he had banished the fact of it from his mind, even less did he speculate on the reasons for her turning away. For him the end of the relationship was simply that: it was a cessation after which there was nothing. One minute the world was full of light and hope; the next it was not. That was it. It was as if a god had spoken and in his mind, he could exert as much control over this change in his affairs as he could over a shift in the weather. Her words of rejection did not corrupt his love. She had told him what she wanted him to know and, just as it was her love to give, it was also her's to cease giving, but equally what he had retained of her, of their time together, she could not take back, and that was his vision of her. This vision belonged to him alone and he shielded it with great care all the better to ensure that it was preserved untarnished in his memory. In so insulating this vision of her he had banished all consideration of that day from his thoughts, from his memory.

As he stood there waiting for her to arrive, he was seized by the sudden realisation that this vision was now in jeopardy; it was too susceptible to the world, too vulnerable to her presence. Yet test it he must. It was inconceivable that he would decline to see her, to speak to her, utterly inconceivable. The Kate he would meet tonight, he told himself, was not *his* Kate, not the Kate of his vision. That Kate was gone. She had vanished that day as if under the command of a dark magic and now all that remained of her was preserved within him.

He waited for around ten minutes before she pulled up at the side of the road next to him in a large, expensive-looking sports car. The passenger side window descended slowly, and Danny peered into the vehicle to confirm that it was her inside. He nodded briefly at her as he caught her eye and he pulled open the door of the car and eased himself in. He sat there waiting for her to speak his hands cradled in his lap. He didn't turn to look at her. The interior of the car was suffused with the smell of her perfume. 'Hello Danny', she said her tone a mixture of warmth and anxiety, 'you look well.' He turned to face her, exposing the eye patch.
'Really?', he replied not disguising the sarcasm, his defences marshalled and alert. She returned his glance with a weak smile.

She had considered a hundred openings to this conversation, but they all fell away unable to support the weight of the moment. There were too many things to say, too many apologies to make and too much forgiveness to ask for. Yet none of it counted now. It wasn't about her; it wasn't even about Danny. It was about her son. Their son. She started the car and they drove in silence for around ten minutes until she found a secluded place to pull up.
'I want to talk to you about Hugh', she said turning to him.
'Hugh?', he replied somewhat taken aback.

'I'm worried about him', she continued, her anxiety evident. 'I don't like the turn his life has taken. Before he started this job, he was just a normal kid looking forward to going to university. He had a world of opportunity open to him, a lifetime of opportunity, but he seems to have fallen through the ice with this bloody digging carry on. It was supposed to be a chance to earn a bit of money, but now he's submerged in it. He's drinking far too much, he's getting into fights and now he tells me that her doesn't want to go to college, he wants to be a navvy instead.'

'That's a stupid decision', Danny replied immediately, 'but why are you telling me, it's not my business what your son wants to do?'

'Well, from what I gather it seems he very much admires you. You're the big hero at the moment. You know what young lads are like at that age, they're impressionable, they look for role models. According to his girlfriend, it's Danny this and Danny that. I mean, this trouble you've got with Jones for example. Apparently, he talks about nothing else. I don't want him to be involved Danny. It's dangerous for a young, headstrong lad. I thought that you might speak to him.'

'How is he involved?', he asked, disconcerted that she had penetrated so deeply into his personal business, embarrassed that the upcoming fight indicated how little progress he had made in his life. He tried to move the subject away from himself.

'Why can't his father speak to him?', he asked.

'That's a part of the problem. Look, this is private family business, so please keep it to yourself. He doesn't get on with his father. He doesn't respect him. He was brought up with stories that glamorised the navvy lifestyle and he wants to be a part of that nonsense.'

'Glamorise?', said Danny incredulously, 'how could you glamorise ditch digging?'

'I don't know. Maybe 'glamorise' is the wrong word, but he seems to think that this digging business is man's work and of course he's at an age where he wants to be seen that way, as a man. He's looking for a route to adulthood, I suppose, for what he thinks are manly attributes.'

'What's all that got to do with me? I mean, I like the lad, but he's not going to listen to me even if I knew what to say to him, even if I had any right to tell him how to live his life, which I don't.'

'That's just it. You're probably the only person who he would listen to at the moment. You seem to be the one he's latched on to.'

'So, what you want me to say to him is something along the lines of 'I've had a shitty life, made some stupid choices, so don't do what I've done, don't be an idiot, is that it?'

'No. Look', she replied, sensing his rising indignation, feeling its justification. 'I don't pretend to know what your life has been like and I'm not going to make any judgements on it. All I'm asking you is to speak to him and let him know that he has other options, that this lifestyle isn't all long summer days and big cheques at the end of the week.'

'Look, its none of my business what the lad does and frankly, as I've said, I don't have the right to tell anyone how to live their life. It seems from what you've said that he knows what's on offer at the university and he's made his choice. There's nothing else for me to say. I'll bid you farewell Mrs Gallon', and with that he turned to open the car door. Kate flicked a switch and all the doors of the vehicle locked simultaneously. Danny turned to her with a confused look on his face. 'What're you doing?'

She sat there for a moment in silence, staring forward with a grave expression on her face as if steeling herself.

'I had no intention of telling you this when I asked to meet you tonight, but it seems now that I have no choice.' She paused and took a deep breath before turning to him. 'Hugh is your son', she said and lowered her eyes unable to look him in the face.

'What're you talking about?', said Danny his eye narrowing as he scrutinised her face as she turned away. Then he snorted lightly and smiled. 'You're scraping the bottom of the barrel now, aren't you?'

'It's true', she replied flatly. 'I ended our relationship the day I found out that I was pregnant', and she buried her gaze in her lap unable to look at him.

'You were pregnant?', he murmured to himself in disbelief, his attention thrust back into the memories of that forbidden day like a talon into an open would. 'What? But why?', he stuttered unable to assimilate what she had said to him. She turned to him, his face suddenly ashen, his features twisted into a mask of confusion and torment. For a the briefest of moments she once again saw the small boy she had seen in his face those many years ago, a boy alone and vulnerable. Her heart felt as if it was being wrenched from her body as she realised that it was her that was once again the author of this man's misery. Yet despite this second thrust of the dagger here she was prevailing upon him to clear up a calamity of her own making.

After a moment or two of silence he turned to her. 'I don't believe you. Open these fucking doors before I kick them off their hinges.'

'Danny, believe me it's true', she implored. 'I mean look at the boy. It's undeniable. Why do you think I'm here asking you this? 'Danny could not deny the honesty present in her eyes, and he sat in silence unable to fully absorb what he was being told.

'Why didn't you tell me? We could've made it work.'

'No, we couldn't Danny', she replied as if exhausted, worn out, 'not in the way I wanted.'

'The way you wanted? What about what I might've wanted?'

His question went unanswered, and they sat in brutal silence 'Hugh is my son?', he whispered out loud. 'Does Gallon know?' he asked, his voice harsh.

'He does.'

'Hugh?'

'Of course not', she replied.

The silence returned. Danny looked at her directly. 'So, if you didn't have this problem with Hugh then you'd never have told me, I'd never have known that I was a father?'

Kate remained silent. She didn't answer him because he wasn't strictly presenting her with a question. She could feel his indignation flooding the car and she didn't blame him. 'And you're telling me this now in the hope that I might help you manipulate the lad out of doing something that he has chosen to do, but that *you're* not happy with, right?'

'It's not about manipulation, it's about proper parenting', she said trying to muster some dignity in the face of the truth in his accusation.

'So, when you've failed as a parent because your kid isn't doing what you want them to do, you try to totally upend my life in the hope that I can help you feel like a better mother?', he replied bitterly.

313

'You know I loved you Danny, but we had nothing to offer a child. We were just too young.'

'You mean I had nothing to offer, right?'

She looked down at her hands again.

'So, you sold my right to be a father to the highest bidder, eh? You denied him a father and me a son. Yet despite all this, all the lying, all the pain you've caused, here we are, him in a trench holding a shovel looking up at me working a jackhammer.'

CHAPTER FIFTY-FOUR

Kate stared at him, the full truth of her situation falling down upon her like an avalanche. She may have been a curator of secrets, but he was the author of revelation. In a couple of quietly spoken sentences he had brought forth the futility of her life's work, had shown her how nature would insist upon having its way against the schemes of those who would try to subvert its itinerary. The recognition felt like a blow to her solar plexus, but she would not be defeated: nature spoke through her maternity too. She decided that she would deal with the meaning of this revelation later. She had more urgent business before her.

'He has options Danny. Surely, you want him to have an easier life than you've had?'

'You knew what my life had been like', he said. 'I could deal with my father, with my upbringing. He was just an animal, he knew no different, but you gave me hope, you gave me another way. Then just like that', he said snapping his fingers, 'you just cast me down as if I was nothing, as if what we had meant nothing. How was I supposed to make sense of that? How? The plans I had for us, the plans *we* had for us! It's a brutal thing to rob a man of hope. I don't deny it was your's to give and to take back, but it's not a small thing to give a man a future and then steal it away from him. And now the dreams you have for your lad are scattered and you want me to help you to put them back together again? After what you did to mine? You destroyed my youth and not satisfied with that you come to try to wreck the time I've got left?

A malevolent look crept over his face and his voice grew sinister. 'What if I tell him? What if I tell him and ask him and that girl of his to come away with me? There's work all over the country. How would you feel about that, eh?

She shielded her eyes with her hand. A shudder ran through her as she recognised that the power Danny held over Hugh, that the power she had hoped to exploit could quite easily be used to pull Hugh further away from her. 'I did what I thought was best for Hugh, as I'm doing now. Do you think that I wanted to bring this up at this time in our lives, that I wanted to hurt you either then or now?'

315

"Want' has got nothing to do with it', he replied bitterly. 'You've done it clear-eyed and wide awake, both then and now. My happiness, my feelings are just an acceptable cost to you, right?'

She bridled at the accuracy of his estimation of her thinking, but she would not allow it to distract her from her purpose.

'The fact is that he is your son', she continued, 'and you have the power to guide him towards a better life than you've had. Can't you see that it's as much your responsibility as it is mine to see that the lad's happy?'

Danny let out a snort of indignation.

'You seem think that just because you're married to a local big-shot you can manipulate people into doing what you want, eh? How do even know what you're saying is true? For your information I don't, but one thing I do know for certain is that that you'd say anything or do anything to get that lad out of the trench, that's clear enough. The truth is that my feelings would be the least of things. We've both seen that before. Now open this fucking door before I kick it off its hinges.'

She flicked a switch and he pushed the door open and got out of the car. She watched him walk off into the night, her sense of hopelessness and guilt intensifying with every step he took away from her. As he vanished into the darkness, she yearned to call him back, to beg for his forgiveness, to plead with him for a chance to undo the damage that she had wrought in this man's life, this man that she had loved, the father of her child. Even if in her anguish she had called out to him she knew she would not be believed, and she could not blame him for his doubt. She sat in the car and stared bleakly into the night.

Her body convulsed and tears surged from her eyes, the pent-up guilt and shame of eighteen years flooding out of her. She felt her life careening far beyond the scope of her control and she thrashed the steering wheel of the car with clenched fists in a fit of rage, frustration and self-recrimination until she fell back into the seat exhausted.

A leaden sense of powerless threatened to overwhelm her, but she resisted its weight with an icy defiance. Perhaps she could not exert control over Danny or Hugh, but she did remain mistress of herself. She needed to act in her own interests now and that would begin with recognising her marriage for the sham that it was and asking David Gallon for a divorce.

CHAPTER FIFTY-FIVE

Danny was waiting at the usual collection point the next morning. He had barely slept the night before and he remained dazed by his encounter with Kate. He hardly noticed that Frankie had arrived fifteen minutes late at the pick-up point. Frankie pushed open the door of the waggon and lurched out almost stumbling to the ground before righting himself and throwing the keys to Danny. Without any further ado he turned his back on him and staggered down the footpath in the direction from which he had come. Danny called after him, but he was too preoccupied with his own concerns to pursue him when Frankie did not answer. He got into the waggon and immediately bridled at the smell of alcohol Frankie had left behind him and drove to the next pick-up point, the turmoil in his mind intensifying as he came to a stop beside Hugh, unsure of how to react given that the young man he was looking at might well be his own flesh and blood.

'Where's Frankie this morning?', asked Hugh smiling as he climbed in.

'He showed up late and just slung the keys at me and headed off without a word. Judging by the stink in the cab he was still drunk from last night', Danny replied his eyes averted, resisting the temptation to scrutinise Hugh's face for signs of resemblance.

'That's unusual for him', replied Hugh, 'I've never known him miss work before.' He was secretly gratified that Frankie wouldn't be around as it would give him the opportunity to discuss the forthcoming fight with Danny rather than spend another day listening to Frankie bemoan the doctor's lack of appreciation for the masculine virtues he believed he so obviously embodied.

They drove into the yard in silence and both men went about their work. When Hugh had first started with GCE his presence in the yard had gone largely unnoticed other than the occasional casual reference to him as the boss' son. His lack of personal significance within the pecking order had been further confirmed by his inclusion within the ageing snagging gang, a conspicuous anomaly for a lad of his age who, had he been any other man's son, would have been expected to put his youthful vigour to more productive use in the trench.

However, this had changed when he had teamed up with Danny and Frankie, men who were well-respected within the yard, Danny particularly so, and he had further added to his reputation as a result of his altercation with Spencer. He had now acquired a degree of notoriety amongst the younger men in the yard who began relying on his presumed familiarity with both combatants in the forthcoming fight.

That morning he had no sooner stepped out of the waggon than he was approached a by wiry, diminutive figure who looked to be in his late twenties, a man who Frankie had previously picked out to Hugh as being one of the fastest shovel men in the yard. He bustled towards Hugh his shoulders rolling, absent mindedly kicking stray rocks across the ground, a highly charged bundle of energy of a man. 'So is yer man eating well', he asked twitching his head in the direction of Danny's back as the big man disappeared behind one of the parked waggons to locate their compressor.

'I don't know', replied Hugh a little nonplussed. 'I'd suppose so.'

'He needs to be getting plenty of steak into him, plenty', emphasised the animated little man, his words spilling out of him so quickly that they almost merged into one. He raised a huge, sinuous hand wrapped around a paper package dripping red.

'Give this to him', he said briskly. 'It's a good bite of sirloin. Tell him it's on me, Davie Flynn.'

'You're giving him a piece of meat?', enquired Hugh a surprised burst of laughter escaping from him unchecked by his deference to such seasoned digging men.

'I am indeed and what's so fucking funny about that?', replied Davie indignantly raising himself to his full height and puffing out his tautly muscled sparrow chest. 'There's money spent there you know', he continued, 'good money. I'd be happy enough to see it on my plate of an evening.'

'Look, I'm not trying to offend you. I was just a bit surprised that's all', replied Hugh in an attempt to placate the benefactor he had unintentionally annoyed.

'Yeah, well', replied Davie sceptically, narrowing his eyes as he stared at Hugh. 'That bastard Jones gave my old father a mighty beating years ago and as much as I'd like to return the favour myself, I'd be no match for him. The old Heifer's just too big for a bantamweight like me, but yer man over there', he said looking in

Danny's direction, 'he's a different story. I can see the savage in him as clear as day and I don't want him to flag for want of a decent feed when the times comes.'

Hugh nodded in acknowledgement and took the sodden parcel from his outstretched hand. As he reached down he couldn't help but notice the incongruity of the enormous gnarled fingers squeezing the once rectangular package into a bow shape, fingers which looked as if they belonged to some huge tree-dwelling creature whose mode of locomotion consisted in swinging through the branches of a remote pre-historic forest. 'Remember, tell him it's from Davie Flynn, right', and with that spun on his heels and hastened back the way he had come launching stray stones into near orbit as he went.

Danny came into view dragging the enormous compressor behind him and Hugh flung the package onto the seat of the waggon and rushed behind the machine and began pushing.

'You've just had a gift off one of the lads', he said to Danny as he heaved his shoulder into the back of the compressor.

'Oh yes?', Danny replied.

'Davie Flynn's given you a piece of steak to help you to keep your strength up for the carry on with Jones.' Danny's shoulders jumped slightly as he let out an amused snort.

'The rock-kicker Flynn, eh?', he said his back still facing Hugh. 'He'll take someone's eye out one of these days', he continued. 'Decent enough of him though, I suppose', he said as he leant down and attached the compressor to the hook at the back of the waggon.

Although Danny was not exactly unfriendly towards his colleagues in the yard he could hardly be described as sociable, eschewing as he did the idle chit chat that was common currency amongst the men, much to Jones' annoyance. Yet he was not disliked. This aura of detachment further augmented a presence already acknowledged as being stern and forbidding for here, as with every yard he walked into, his reputation had preceded him.

The general consensus was that Danny would repay the countless threats and insults that Jones had hurled down from the gantry over the years, that he was finally over-matched. Yet Danny was not the first challenger to Jones' dominance within the yard, but none of these earlier pretenders came with Danny's pedigree or his chilling air of invincibility. Jones' history of bullying, aggression and general disrespect for the men under him had set down deep roots of resentment within the yard and the prospect of him meeting his comeuppance against Greene had been widely discussed and was eagerly anticipated amongst the gangs. His behaviour in the days preceding the fight had been carefully scrutinised and it had been suggested more than once that his swagger was infused with greater purpose than before and his tirades from the gantry were filled with greater malice, signs which the older men took to be indications of his growing anxiety at the dethroning to come. It was also noted that he descended into the yard with considerably less frequency than was his earlier habit. These observations were shared, analysed and argued over by the men, sometimes a little too enthusiastically by some, but all were nonetheless united in their conviction that The Heifer was ready for slaughter.

Hugh relished the growing sense of anticipation within the yard and basked in the reflected glory owed to his privileged association with the popular favourite. There was no doubt in his or anyone else's mind that Danny would prove to be the victor despite Jones' size advantage. The sight of Danny striding across the yard, flag stones sat atop his boulder - like shoulders, his torso heavy and lean, had persuaded everyone in the yard that his physical strength was more than a match for Jones'. But more persuasive was his face, a dark mask of brooding aggression made more alarming by the rough-cut patch of leather shrouding his missing eye, a grisly token of the stakes he was willing to play for. Whenever he emerged from the waggon eyes would follow him warily as if he were some dread ahistorical presence cast amongst them, bent on destruction.

Word of the upcoming fight had spread around the pubs of the city like news of a monarch's death. Jones had a few reluctant advocates, typically men who he had previously beaten or humiliated and who wanted to preserve a shred of dignity by emphasising his non-negotiable invincibility. The older men had persuaded the younger of the inevitability of the outcome with rumoured tales of Danny's past exploits. A few of these anecdotes were outright fabrications told to aggrandise the teller, most were embellished to a greater or lesser degree, but all were designed to elevate Danny to the status of an almost mythical avenger brought forth to rid the city of the scourge of Jones and were told with such passionate conviction that they quickly convinced minds eager to see Jones brought low.

Over frothing pints and rattling jack hammers the general drift of conversation was beginning to turn away from the outcome of the contest and towards how Jones would deal with defeat. The commonly held view was that shame and disgrace would compel him to leave the firm, maybe even the city. This prospect alone had made Danny every man's hero and newest best friend, although most of his advocates had never so much as met him. For those more determined to increase their social capital simply nodding to Danny in the yard was sufficient yarn from which to spin the pretence of a life-long friendship.

Frankie did not appear at the pick-up point for the rest of the week and Hugh had spent a couple of evenings scouting around the pubs looking for him more eager to talk about the forthcoming confrontation than he was to discuss his plans in connection with a return to work, but all to no avail. He could not be found in any of his usual haunts. By Friday evening Hugh was becoming concerned. He had learned that Mandy had kicked him out of her house and that he had been barred from several pubs as a result of his drunken misbehaviour.

Hugh had been approached by one of the drunks in the last pub he had visited on Thursday evening and been told in a manner which almost defied intelligibility that he should try The Pond, which came as a surprise to him. His anxiety regarding Frankie's whereabouts had escalated to the point where he was prepared to undertake what he half thought would be a fool's errand and pay a visit to the suggested location.

Hugh scouted the open expanse of field and copse for half an hour before he spotted a gathering of itinerants, some standing and talking in a small group, others sitting or sleeping on the ground against a low wall marking off the perimeter of the park. All were drinking from bottles or cans of assorted alcoholic beverages. As he approached them, he was obliged to divert his path around two of the company who were engaged in a clumsy, uncoordinated tussle. Hugh stood for a moment and watched as one of the men freed himself and staggered backwards. His opponent made a lunge for him, and they again proceeded to grapple with one another clutching at the loose rags that hung from their bodies in a perverse and disordered dance.

Then Hugh caught sight of Frankie sitting against the wall, his face glistening with beer-sweat and grime, his unshaven chin bubbling with acne. He called his name and Frankie glanced around in a confused stupor. Hugh approached him.

'Bloody hell Frankie, what's going on?', he asked looking down at the dishevelled figure.

Frankie looked up through narrowed eyes.

'Jesus Christ! it's the boss's son!', he exclaimed and immediately attempted to rise to his feet but as he did so he fell backwards against the wall and then onto the grass. Hugh reached down to pull him up at least far enough that he could resume his seated position against the wall. As he did so he almost gagged at the odour rising from him. Frankie looked up.

'Hey, its Hugh, hello Hughie!', he croaked with false amiability. His eyes rolled in his head.

Hugh sat down next him careful to maintain his distance.

'So, what's the craic Frankie?', he demanded. 'You look like a mangy dog and you smell like rat puke.'

Frankie ignored the question and began croaking out an Irish song, grinning at Hugh who listened impatiently for a moment or two. 'Look at the state of you, what're you doing to yourself?' Frankie stopped singing and looked down at his vomit-stained shirt and made a slow, half-hearted attempt to brush away some the accumulated filth that was smeared across it. He turned to look up at Hugh and broke out in sobs, turning away from him and nestling his chin in his chest.

'I'm fucked man, I'm fucked', he whimpered dropping his eyes to the ground, tears rolling off the end of his nose.

'What do you mean you're fucked?', asked Hugh caught between compassion and irritation.

'I'm fucked', he reiterated as if this brief self-diagnosis contained all the information necessary to answer Hugh's question.

'OK, we've established that, but why are you fucked?'.

'That doctor made a complete cunt outta me. She just used me then gave me the boot.'

'Well, no offence, but isn't that exactly what you tend to do with women?'

'That's the whole point', groaned Frankie, '*I* do it. Not them. Me.'

'Well, you've obviously met your match. Why are you making such a big deal out of it?'

'What am I good for if I can't get the women I want? Good for nothing that's what. Women have always wanted me. You know old Frankie's plan, find one with money and Bob's your uncle. Set for life. No more jack hammer ringing in your ears, no more ripping your knuckles to bits on the side of the trench, no more getting drenched for ten hours a day in the middle of winter and no more moving around. I'm sick of it. City after city after city', he said exhaustedly. 'No roots, no future, never around long enough to know anybody. I'm just sick of it. This long - distance man shite, there's nothing good about it, just bouncing from city to city, not known to anybody, not knowing anybody. A stranger everywhere you go; forgotten the day after you leave. The one thing I was good at was women. Now, I could rely on that', he said smiling, crusts of dried saliva accumulated at the corners of his mouth. 'It gave me a future. Now it only works with women just like me. They can't give me what I want. Most of them haven't two pennies to rub together themselves. What's wrong with these rich women? They must be soft in the head. I mean, she had another fella there when she could've had me!', he exclaimed, astonished at his own revelation. 'She just fucking used me and threw me onto the shit-heap', he said bitterly before softening his tone. 'Maybe that's where I belong after all.' With that he began singing again as if this outburst of self-pity had never happened.

'Where have you been living, you look filthy', asked Hugh.

'Oh, here and there, you know. The weather's been fine. You don't notice the cold with a drop or two of the good stuff in you. These are great lads', he said, a sweep of his arm indicating the group of drunks around him, some asleep on the ground, others arguing incoherently. 'I've done it before.'

'Look, I can't put you up at Clare's. It's too small. How are you for money?'

Frankie reached into his pocket and pulled out a crumpled wad of notes, the majority of which fluttered to the floor attracting the interest of a couple of the itinerants standing nearby. Frankie showed no interest in picking them up and Hugh had to reach down to the ground and retrieve them. He counted a little short of three hundred pounds.

'Why are you sleeping out here when you've got all this cash in your pocket?'

Frankie looked down at the money in Hugh's hands as if he was seeing it for the first time.

'Come on', said Hugh reaching out and taking Frankie by the arm, 'Let's see if we can find you a room.'

'I'm all right where I am', said Frankie angrily pulling his arm free of Hugh's grip and snatching the bundle of notes from his hand. 'You get back to your big fancy house and your rich Daddy.'

Hugh looked down at him as he pushed the crumpled notes into his pocket and turned to leave completely dispirited at what he had seen and heard, unwilling to argue with his friend in his current shambolic state.

'Ey!', cried Frankie as he walked away. Hugh looked back expectantly hoping that he might have had a change of heart.

'You can tell Danny that they pulled Gene's body out of the river Moy in Mayo last week. They don't know if he fell in or ......what.' Frankie looked away his expression bathed in melancholy.

'How do you know?', asked Hugh.

'I just fucking know, alright?', he replied bitterly looking at Hugh an indignant expression on his face. 'Do you think I'd make it up?' He turned away and resumed his song, his rolling tears clearing tiny pale pathways down his filthy cheeks.

Hugh returned to Clare's flat to find her asleep on the sofa. She had been waiting up for him but as the night had drawn on, she had been defeated by fatigue. She had recently taken on a second job and regularly worked longer hours than even Hugh did. She was ambitious and more than willing to underwrite that ambition with hard work and self-sacrifice.

He carefully sat down beside her so as not to disturb her rest and gently stroked her hair. As he did so a loose strand caught on one of the rough callouses that now armoured his palm and he attempted to unhook it. Clare stirred her from her slumbers, and she reached out to him, her eyes still closed, and pulled him down to her. Their kisses were warm and affectionate, and he took an unexpected depth of comfort from them.

She asked him drowsily where he had been and he explained to her that he had been out looking for Frankie, but for reasons inexplicable even to himself, he didn't want to tell her that he'd found him just yet. All he knew was that he didn't want to revisit that experience while the memory of it was so caustic. The meeting with Frankie had soured something within him. Seeing the physical condition he was in, the fragility of the ties that bound him to reality, brought home to him the extent to which these long distance men he had recently so admired were walking a tightrope over a bottomless abyss of loneliness, isolation and despair with drink as their only safety net. What had someone once said? 'You're only a stride away from the park bench in this kind of work.' He shuddered slightly as he recalled Frankie's tears and quickly purged the memory from his mind.

'I hope he'll be OK', murmured Clare before yawning deeply and pulling him closer to her.

'So do I', replied Hugh.

CHAPTER FIFTY -SIX

Friday was to prove to be a strange, unsettling day for Hugh. The morning had begun with him relaying the news of Gene's death to Danny who greeted it with a casual resignation bordering on indifference, an attitude which came as a surprise to Hugh. He wasn't expecting a grand exhibition of grief from Danny as he understood that he didn't know the man that well and, in any case, the grim asceticism of his character would have precluded this, but during the time that they had worked together Hugh had that that he had caught glimpses of aspects of his personality which suggested the presence of greater depths of feeling than he was prepared to exhibit, but perhaps he was mistaken, he thought.

'Best place for the man', was Danny's only rejoinder.

The mood in the waggon was not much improved when Hugh relayed the details of his encounter with Frankie. Danny seemed to maintain his grim indifference commenting only that Frankie wasn't the first and wouldn't be the last navvy to meet a similar fate. Then suddenly as if seized by a fresh imperative he turned to Hugh.

'It's a filthy fucking job is this', he growled, his good eye narrowed into a malevolent slit. Hugh shuddered slightly, his body betraying him, for the first time feeling the initial tremors of Danny's anger. 'Any man with half an ounce of sense would throw his boots into the nearest fire and throw his shovel as far as his arm would let him.' He sighed heavily and shook his head, the initial rumbling seeming to subside and to be replaced an exasperated fatalism. 'Every fucking day the same: dig it out, fill it in, dig it out, fill it in. Every trench no different from the last. No wonder the boys turn to drink. They're watching their lives disappear one shovelful at a time and there's fuck all they can do about it except get mad drunk and beat the shite out of one another. And all this talk about hard men, that's the fucking worst of it', he snorted derisively. 'Nothing but tales told by jackasses to please donkeys', he sneered. Hugh sat in confused silence dumbstruck by the sudden vehemence of Danny's outburst. He turned his head to gaze out the passenger window, seeing nothing, frantically trying to make sense of speech he had just listened to.

'Hard men, eh?', Danny continued, his voice coming to Hugh as if from afar. 'Let me show you what it costs to have a starring role in a jackass' tale. Look at me', he barked suddenly. Hugh's head immediately swung back to look directly at Danny, the blood draining from his face and his pupils dilating.

Danny raised his hand to the back of his head and loosened the knot in the thick leather cord that held his eye patch in place. The covering fell away and into his lap and Danny looked directly at Hugh. A veil of skin had been grafted onto the upper part of his forehead and pulled taught across the void where the eye should have been, unnaturally white in colour, thin blue veins pulsing angrily below its surface such as might be found on the translucent body of a subterrane grub. The border where it married in with the skin overlaying the cheek bone was signalled by a livid purple ridge of scar tissue which ran in an angry crescent from his nose up swooping up his temple at coming to a stop at his hairline. Danny shuddered involuntarily at the grotesqueness so suddenly revealed.

Danny lightly scratched the skin covered depression where it joined the upper part of his forehead before causally pointing to the catastrophe where his eye had been. 'Pretty as a picture, eh?', said Danny sardonically. 'That 's why I have to wear the home-made patch, they don't do 'em big enough at the hospitals', Hugh winced. 'Part of the price you pay for a starring in their stupid fucking stories, for being a big shot fighting man', he said bitterly and looked away in disgust and then with practised dexterity made a loose knot with the ends of the strap before pulling it back over his head and tightening it.

Hugh had no idea what to make of this outburst and the expression fixed on Danny's face clearly indicated that further enquiries would not be welcomed. A terrible thought edged its way into Hugh's mind: was this anger designed to mask Danny's pessimism about likely outcome of his forthcoming confrontation with Jones? Was fear at its root? He dismissed the idea as preposterous and, as if to reassure himself, cast a brief sideways glance in Danny's direction taking in his boxer's frame, his tree-trunk neck and the brooding, uncompromising expression on a face, incapable of wearing the pall of fear, or so Hugh wanted to believe.

The two men worked separately for most of that day. Danny had decided to concentrate on remedial tasks on the basis that, if these weren't done, they wouldn't be paid for any of the work completed that week. Hugh was surprised at this decision as snagging work was usually undertaken on Saturday mornings, but he acknowledged that perhaps Danny had decided to complete these small jobs on a normal working day in order to leave the morning of the fight free. In any case, the vehemence of Danny's recent outburst convinced Hugh that perhaps it was preferrable that they worked separately on this occasion.

'This time tomorrow we'll know the result, not that it's in any doubt', said Hugh excitedly to Clare as he sat down to supper that evening. She sighed and put her knife and fork on the table beside her plate and looked directly at him, her voice taking on an earnest tone.

'Look, I know that this fight nonsense is a big deal for you. I mean you've talked about nothing else all week, but it's all getting a bit worrying Hugh. I mean, the idea of a man fighting to protect someone is a good thing on the surface, I suppose, but two men trying to hurt one another over some silly argument, I mean really hurt one another, there's nothing good about that at all, all that blood and pain, it's just awful. I mean, look at Danny's face, his eye. Really, when he looks back, don't you think he believes that he would've been better off just not fighting and keeping his sight, his eye? What's so important that you lose your eye over it, just some argument in a pub?'

'It wasn't like that', replied Hugh. 'He was attacked by a group of blokes he had to defend himself.'

'OK, but it's because he's the kind of bloke that he is that he got attacked in the first place. I mean, look at your dad. He knows how to behave. You don't see him rolling around in the mud trying to knock the hell out of another bloke, do you? It just seems undignified for grown men. I think it's a bit stupid that they can't just sort out what they need to sort out without knocking lumps out of one another. It's a bit childish. It shows a lack of maturity if you ask me.'

'What are you talking about?', Hugh replied light heartedly trying to deflect the gravity of what she was saying with a smile. 'You seemed pretty impressed when I grabbed that lad in 'The Harp''.'

'That was different. He was being rude and nasty and I'm a girl. I can't start punching men. The thing is you fellas like to fight for the sake of it and you don't stop to think about the risk, about the consequences. The more I think about it, I just don't like the idea of you fighting anyone for any reason', and with that she reached out and cupped the side of his face in her hand, staring intently into his eyes, searching them.

'Hugh', she said softly, 'I love you and I can't bear the idea of anyone hurting you or spoiling this lovely face of your's', and with that she kissed him tenderly on the lips.

'You sound like my mother', He replied unsettled by the stubborn logic of her little speech. 'And it's not fighting for the sake of it', he countered wanting to redress the silence that had fallen upon him when Danny had made a similar point, a failure that had rankled with him. 'It's just in our nature as men to defend those we care about, things that are important to us. It's so basic to what we are it's almost a defining feature. Fair enough, it's a double-edged sword. Defence is just the reverse side of attack, but that's exactly it: it's a dangerous world because *people* are dangerous. No matter how we gloss over it and try to pretend that we're all kind, sophisticated and clever. Folk don't recognise how insulated they are and how fragile that insulation really is. We're just a species that fights just like all the other animals and a man that doesn't recognise that has got a problem. It's a basic anthropological fact that people are too afraid to recognise.'

'I don't know about any anthropofology or whatever', she countered,' but maybe your mother's onto something. You keep telling me that you don't want to be trapped like your dad, that you don't want the career, the mortgage, the kids. Well, to be honest it sounds to me like you just can't accept responsibility. You seem to think that being a man is all about being a tough guy, being free to do what you want when you want. Well, it's not. I'm sorry, but that sounds a lot like what a kid might think. Don't get me wrong a cowardly man is no man at all, I accept that, but there's more to be being a man than just standing toe to toe with a bloke in a pub car park. It's about taking responsibility for yourself, for your wife and your family. It's about not putting yourself first every time.' She looked down at her plate. 'It worries me a bit, you know. The things you say you don't want are exactly the things I do: a nice house, nice kids, a decent job.' She turned back to face him. 'I mean what kind of future do we have if you want to end up like Danny or Frankie? Do you really think that they're happy men? Alright, they might not be tied down as you put it but why is that such a good thing? I mean, you talk about being tied down as if it was some horrible punishment, but I see it differently. It's about being connected, being attached, being rooted in things that mean something, things that you care about and love. That's what makes us free you know, being in each other's lives, having possibilities in front of you. Blokes like Danny are the ones that are really trapped, stuck in their own little worlds, lonely and uncared for.'

'Phew!', he breathed out between pursed lips, his eyes wide, 'you've said a lot there. I didn't realise that you'd thought about it so deeply', he replied.

'I've had to', she replied. 'Look Hugh', she continued, 'I've told you before I want to make something of my life. Maybe it's because I'm older than you or because I come from a different background, I don't know, but what I do know is that a person has got to face up to reality and take responsibility for getting what they want because no one is going to give it to you. It's a struggle, I know that, and I do want a man by side to do it, someone to share the struggle, someone who's not afraid to face the world on its own terms and make the most of what it's got to offer. I know that's you', she reached out and place her hand over his clenched fist resting on the table and squeezed it tightly to reassure him. 'All this tough guy stuff has its place, but there's more than one kind of fight and there's more than one kind of courage and being a man is recognising that and doing what's necessary.'

'I get what you're saying', he replied cautiously not wanting the conversation to tip over into an argument. 'I'm not trying to say that being a man is just about being a tough guy. I know it's more than that. It's about respect. Perhaps it's because we're men that we can see that things can get ugly fast, I don't know. I was really interested in biology at school, and you know that it's a scientific fact that men are more aware of threats than woman, that women are generally more trusting than men. It's a hormonal thing, men are driven by a hormone called testosterone and women by something called oxytocin. It's not as simple as that, of course, but you get my point. I'm not saying that you're wrong Clare, but maybe men just look at things differently, that's all.'

'I don't know anything about that', she replied, 'but as you say, it all seems a bit too simple an explanation to me. All I know is that I love you and I don't want to see you getting hurt'.

'I understand that and don't think that I don't appreciate your feelings, but a man has to show the world that he's not afraid, that he won't be trampled on, and what Danny's going to do tomorrow is exactly that. He's just a man standing up for himself, that's all. Can't you see why that is something to respect, to admire?

Clare sighed. 'Well, I hope he doesn't let you down, if that's the way you think, but whether he wins or loses this bloody fight, he'd be more of a man in my eyes if he just walked away from the whole stupid situation.'

CHAPTER FIFTY-SEVEN

Hugh awoke early the following morning to the sound of Clare showering. She had agreed at short notice to work an extra shift and he crawled out of bed in order to make her a breakfast of cereal, toast and coffee. The salutary effects of the previous night's conversation were still at play in his mind, and he had concluded that it would be unwise to make any further reference to the fight until he found answers within himself to the questions Clare had raised. As troubling as these questions were to him, they had caused his admiration for Clare to grow for although there was a gap of only three years between them, he could not help but recognise that her level of maturity was under - represented in this age difference. Her strength of purpose, her depth of understanding and, most of all, her vision of what she wanted from her life made him shudder when he compared it to his own vulnerable certainties in the face of a future hurtling towards him at a dizzying speed.

They ate breakfast together and chatted. Their mood was light, both of them carefully avoiding any reference to the previous night's conversation, yet despite his diplomatic resistance to discussing the fight that afternoon Hugh's mind was bubbling like a steaming cauldron. Clare finished eating and glanced up at the clock and leapt up from her chair, quickly kissed Hugh on the crown of his head before rushing out through the door.

Hugh got up from the table and turned on the small TV in the corner of the room, but soon grew bored with what was on offer. The newspaper proved equally ineffective at distracting him and he glanced around the small room looking for something, anything, to take his mind from the weary passage of time as it slowly dragged itself towards twelve o'clock when he could head off down to the yard. He pulled out the vacuum and began cleaning the flat. Then he showered. He dressed and came back into the room and turned on the TV again and laid down on the sofa and dozed off into a fitful sleep.

He awoke with a start and immediately sought out the clock: ten thirty. He sighed with relief as he contemplated the unthinkable disaster of sleeping beyond one o'clock.

His restlessness got the better of him and he couldn't remain in the flat any longer and decided to walk down to 'The Harp'. Standing outside the pub waiting for the doors to open would be a novel experience he thought, and no doubt one that his mother would greet with horror and disapproval, but he had already drunk cider with Frankie at seven o'clock in the morning in the yard, so starting drinking at eleven would hardly be the peak of his supposed moral corruption, he concluded and headed for the door.

The walk killed a further twenty or so minutes and was he surprised on his arrival to find the place open and busy with customers. All the talk was of the approaching fight and the air was full of excited chatter as to the expected outcome. He was surprised to see so many strangers in the bar and he took their presence as an indication of how far word had spread across the city. As he waited to be served, he reflected on Clare's views on how pointless and juvenile the whole business of fighting was. She just didn't get it, he concluded. He glanced around him and saw the excitement etched on the faces of the men crowded into the pub, the atmosphere suffused with an air hatched from a deep ancestral past, charged with an ethereal distillation of something brutal yet necessary. He understood her point about a man needing to take responsibility for his family, but he also acknowledged to himself that she didn't grasp the importance that men attach to being their own last resort, their unwillingness to be trampled underfoot. This, he felt, was something essential to what it was to be a man, this willingness to fight to preserve his dignity and self-respect, brutal and basic as it may be, was also fundamental, a defining characteristic accumulated over the ages.

These were the lessons he had learned from refining his grandfather's lessons through the filter of his own predispositions. Today's fight was emblematic of this. It wasn't a sporting event, nor was it was a game; there were no rewards nor prizes nor accolades; the result would leave the world untouched. What was at stake for these two men was their self-respect. The Giant against the Cyclops, he thought to himself and smiled. As much as he had grown to detest Jones, he could not deny him credit for facing Danny Greene, a fearsome challenge that few men would dare to confront.

He had persuaded himself that Danny's outburst of the previous day was simply an assault on the gossip mongers, the tittle-tattlers, the weak men who took vicarious satisfaction from achievements that they were unable to attain for themselves. He chortled lightly to himself when he recalled that he has almost considered attributing Danny's speech to nervousness or anxiety. He had come to realise that Danny Greene was a man untouched by such fear, a man who was the absolute incarnation of what his grandfather had taught him: a man in whom courage, integrity and self-reliance were folded together into a dynamic and resolute physical force in the world, a fighting man. In Danny Greene, Hugh saw all that his father was not. He saw a man to emulate. He felt an irresistible recognition surging within him that his fate was somehow intertwined with Danny's. His pulse raced at the prospect of the glory to come.

He was distracted from his ruminations by Davey who appeared in front of him as if from nowhere. 'So you gave him that steak, right?,' he asked shifting his weight from one foot to another in a half dance as his body tried to dissipate the incessant flow of energy bubbling through his wiry little frame. Just as in their previous encounter in the yard, he enunciated the words of his question so briskly that it was difficult for Hugh to disentangle the individual words from within the humming stream of sounds that flowed from him.

'Yes er, yes I did', he replied finally.

'Good, good. Oh, he's going to batter him from one end of the yard to the other. I can't wait. I just can't wait', he continued excitedly, a bright smile blossoming on his face. 'No man deserves it more. No, no man deserves a good battering than Jones. Beat my father up. Left him in an awful state. I might've told you.'

'Yes, you did', replied Hugh, quietly amused at Davie's attempts to constrain the volcanic wells of energy straining for escape within him.

'I'd do it myself you know, but he's too big. Just too big', he continued looking down at the floor as if in lament for the trick nature had played upon him. 'I'd just love to do it myself. Love it!, he exclaimed, 'but he's too big, but anyway your mate'll knock the big ole' Heifer senseless. I just can't wait to see it, just can't', and with that he was disappeared into the crowd, his departure signalled with as much ceremony as his arrival.

Hugh looked around the room and caught the eye of The Professor who beckoned him over to his table.

'So, the big day, eh?', he said when Hugh finally settled himself down next to him.

'Indeed it is', replied Hugh.

'Well, there's been talk of little else in here for the past few days. No doubt Danny is your choice as the victor?'. Hugh nodded enthusiastically. 'I hope you're right', The Professor continued. 'I'm sure that Jones would be absolutely insufferable if things went his way today particularly after his triumph over the Mulligans, but I'm with you.: Danny Greene all the way!', he exclaimed raising his tightly clenched fists in a gesture of triumph. 'I've had quite a number of little talks with Mr Greene while he's been living here. Interesting chap, you know. Doesn't take one long to forget about his reputation when one is talking to him, but there is something inscrutable about him all the same, something behind the rather terrifying exterior, something deep. I can't put my finger on it. That's why it's inscrutable, I suppose, eh?', he said chortling to himself. 'I remember speaking to Frankie a while ago about him. I called him the exemplar of the *viri pugnator,* the Fighting Man, but I do think that I may have misjudged him. He's quite a learned man, you know. Very well read. Knows his *Homer.*

'What?!', exclaimed Hugh, his astonishment shaking him down to his boots. 'Danny Greene reads *Homer*?, He asked.

'And why wouldn't he?', enquired The Professor with mild indignation, 'because he's a navvy and navvies aren't supposed to read books?'

'I just never knew', replied Hugh blushing slightly.

'Well, did you ever think to ask him?', the lightly scolding tone not yet entirely abandoned.

'No. No, I didn't', replied Hugh, his thoughts racing back to the night in the pizza restaurant when he had berated Jane for exactly the same kind of arrogance that he was guilty of now.

'Hmmmm', intoned The Professor contemplatively, noting Hugh's presumption but suspending judgement on it. 'Well, if it's any consolation, you're not the only one guilty of underestimating Mr. Daniel Greene. As I said, I had thought of him only in terms of the *viri pugnator*, but I was wrong. Of course, I amended my original characterisation as I learned more about him, as one should do of course', he continued with minimal pomposity.

'To continue with the classical theme, Danny Greene seems to me to most embody the Greek quality of *Andreia*. I suppose that's a foreign idea for you is it not, coming as you do from a science background?', he asked raising his eyebrows in a subtle gesture of disdain as he hesitated before enunciating the word 'science' as if the sound of it left a bitter taste in his mouth.

'You would be right', confirmed Hugh smiling at The Professor's small academic conceit.

'Do allow me to enlighten you then young man. *Andreia* denotes a much richer quality than that embodied in the word *pugnator* which, if you would have followed a more enriching course of study, you would know means 'fighter or warrior.'

'Get on with it', said Hugh laughing, 'stop showing off.'

The Professor added the sound of his own laughter to Hugh's.

'When I say 'richer' I mean that it involves more than just a willingness to fight, although that's part of the meaning too but in some ways you might not expect. In essence, *Andreia* means manly courage or manly spirit, not only to challenge the behaviour of other men, but also to confront one's own foolishness, one's own vices or ignorance. It denotes the courage to accept oneself on one's own terms without the need for the approval of the herd. It also designates a willingness for, even a love of, toil and effort, interestingly enough. In fact, the great Cicero talks of Hercules as embodying the spirit of *Andreia* in the course of his many labours along the path to wisdom. Aristotle said it was about finding the right course between cowardice and rashness, about knowing when to fight and when not to, irrespective of provocation, taking a wider perspective on matters. I mean, you don't hear about Danny being rash with his fists, do you? There always appears to be a good reason for him to raise them and I can't think of any man less dependent on the approval of others, can you? But interestingly, while *Andreia* extols the courage to fight when necessary, the quality is compromised by acts of anger or bullying or self-serving

337

aggression. Yes' he concluded contemplatively, 'the more I think about it the more the word seems to fit Danny Greene.'

Hugh was deeply engrossed in what The Professor was saying but before he could respond they were approached by one of the men from the yard, Georgie Moore, a stout, ginger-haired grab waggon driver with a crimson complexion and thick, almost purple lips, conspicuous evidence of the toll his colossal over-consumption of Guinness was having on his heart.

'How're you now young fellow', he bellowed at Hugh and continued without waiting for a reply. 'Myself, I can't see Jones lasting five minutes against that rough looking beast of a mate of your's, eh?', he half stated, half enquired.

'Oh, he'll beat him', replied Hugh casually. 'I don't think anyone doubts that', he continued with the confident tone of an expert.

'But within five minutes?', the man pressed, the bright red skin on his face appearing to be stretched to breaking point by the thick layer of fat beneath it.

'I don't know about that. Jones is a big lump of a man. Dangerous too. I'm sure Danny will use his head.'

'Oh, so longer than five minutes you think?, you see Albert over there is taking wagers', he said nodding pointlessly in the direction of the crowd surrounding them, 'whether Jones'll go down in five or ten or by God fifteen minutes and I know you and Greene are the best of mates.'

Hugh felt a sudden glow of pride.

'I wouldn't say we're the *best* of mates exactly', he replied modestly, 'but we are in the same gang. He's a sound man. Now that I come to think about it, I wouldn't be surprised if he came out all guns blazing, you know. He's not going to waste his time playing around with Jones when there's a few pints waiting to be drunk', he said despite knowing that Danny wasn't a drinker.

'I get ya', replied Georgie winking at Hugh and scurried off into the crowd to place his bet.

Twelve thirty arrived and the tap room began emptying as the crowd made its way to the yard. Just as Hugh was about to quiz The Professor further on his Classical interpretation of Danny's character they were joined by a couple of the younger lads from the yard, Paul and Luke.

'Come on Hugh. Let's get going', said Paul, 'what are you dawdling for?', and he turned from the table and made his way towards the door.

Hugh rose to his feet and looked down at The Professor who appeared to be making no effort to move.

'Not coming?', asked Hugh.

'Oh, I don't think that it'd be worth the walk for an old man like me', he said and smiled enigmatically.

'Suit yourself', replied Hugh, 'but I want to talk to talk to you about this *Andreia* stuff later', and finished his drink before hurrying across the room to join Luke.

'Well, I'm surprised that you're here to be honest', commented Luke as they followed Paul outside. 'I'd have thought you'd be with your mate getting him warmed up and stuff, you know, like a Second or whatever they're called.'

'Are you serious?!', exclaimed Hugh. 'Danny Greene doesn't need a Second. This isn't a boxing match you know. This is bare knuckle, blood and guts, last man standing stuff. Danny Greene is a very good friend of mine, and I can tell you now that if he needed a Second, which he doesn't, then it'd be me in his corner. Me and Danny go back a long way.'

Luke looked at Hugh silently assessing his age. 'Really? A long way, eh?', he said sceptically.

Hugh realised that he'd overstepped the bounds of credulity. 'Well, a good while anyway. I've known him long enough to know that he's the best man in the yard. I mean how many men have had the balls to face Jones over the years? Not many and I've heard and those that did, well, it didn't end well for them. You've got to have heard the stories about Danny, everyone's heard those.'

'Yeah, but they're just stories aren't they. Look I'm not saying that they're not true', he followed up quickly not wanting to appear as if he was impugning Danny's reputation.

'Well, what're you talking about then?, replied Hugh indignantly. 'He sorted out three of those Mulligans in the yard on his own. Four if you count the first lad that had a go at Gene. I'll tell you what', he said noticing the bookie who Georgie had mentioned earlier.

'Albert, come over here a minute', he called out to the back of a figure a few yards in front of them.

A fair - haired man of around sixty years minced his way towards Hugh smiling broadly, wearing a battered Trilby hat and a pale flannel suit liberally decorated with ancient splashes of a Guinness - like residue.

'What can I do for you gentleman?', he asked, his tone sprightly and frank.

'I'd like to put a bet on Danny Greene to win within five', said Hugh with confidence, casting glances at Luke as he did so.

Albert smiled as widely as his mouth would allow revealing two gold false teeth where his canines had once resided. 'Certainly, young man', he replied and reached into his inside pocket and pulled out a small well-used flip over notebook attached to which was a small pencil.

'Hugh Gallon, isn't it?', he asked scribbling his name in the notebook. Albert was a man who made it his business to know everybody's name.

'And how much would you like to wager today young Sir?'

Hugh reached into his pocket and to his horror discovered that he had only brought ten pounds with him.

'A tenner', said Luke guffawing, 'Bloody hell, you haven't got much confidence in your mate, have you?'

Hugh felt a dual pang of anger and embarrassment and turned to look enquiringly at Albert who immediately spoke out. 'Oh, I'm afraid that we don't offer credit Sir', he said disapprovingly pre-empting what he anticipated would be Hugh's next question, 'but I couldn't help but noticing that watch on your wrist. Looks like a very interesting piece. Very interesting indeed. Might I have a quick look over it.'

Hugh looked down to the ground, a distinctly uncomfortable feeling washing over him, anticipating what was coming next.

'Let the man have a look at the watch!', exclaimed Luke. 'He'll give you a fair price won't you Albert.'

Albert nodded enthusiastically almost toppling his hat from his head.

'You said Danny was a certainty', continued Luke looking directly at Hugh. 'What've you got to lose, eh? I mean, he wouldn't be right impressed if he thought his best mate wouldn't risk an old watch on him beating Jones, would he?'

Hugh's dilemma was that it wasn't an old watch in the sense that Luke had intended. The time piece was indeed antique and had been bought by Hugh's grandfather at an exorbitant price during one of his rare periods of temporary affluence. Kate, despite her youth, had recognised the uncertain fate that awaited the watch so long as it remained attached to her father's wrist and had taken the piece from him when he had arrived home one night in a state of almost imbecilic drunkenness, and she had found him languishing in a comatose state on the sofa. Joe had awoken the next morning to discover an unadorned wrist and all hell immediately broke lose, with what scant furniture they possessed being upturned, carpets being torn up from the floorboards and much roaring and cursing echoing through the small terraced house and spilling out into those at either side of it for good measure.

Kate lay in bed smiling mischievously to herself, the sheets pulled up to her chin, while her father raged below, the watch safely ensconced in her underwear drawer, a location which her he would absolutely never investigate. Joe trawled every path he might have taken from whatever pub he might have visited the night before, his memory eroded by drink and anguish, and of course he found nothing. He never bought another watch after this loss, such was his grief. He did get himself good and drunk again later that day though, lamenting the bitter fate which awaited all those foolish enough to become attached to the baubles and accoutrements of personal aggrandisement.

Kate had held on to the watch for years, resisting all temptation to pawn it or to sell it no matter how great the need, and when she married such temptations vanished anyway. In her youth she would look at it occasionally, the cool stylishness of its design entrancing her and reminding her that despite her drab life of grind and of dirt there was a world beyond her own full of elegance, wealth and sophistication. The watch was her link to this world. As a child she would peer into its polished, gleaming face and see reflected the image of a woman with infinite wealth at her disposal.

She had finally parted with the watch when she presented it as a gift to Hugh to celebrate the joint occasions of his examination success and his eighteenth birthday. He knew only that it had been his grandfather's watch and he had treasured it accordingly oblivious to its monetary worth.

Albert took the watch from him and reached into his jacket pocket and pulled out a jeweller's eyeglass which he jammed into his eye socket. He twisted and turned the watch in his be-ringed fingers, examining it this way and that, bringing it to his ear and rattling it before turning to Hugh, the eye glass still secured below the rim of Trilby.

'I can give you two hundred quid. Final offer. Two hundred', the almost servile *bon homie* of a few moments ago was now gone to be replaced with a cold, hard seriousness etched into his expression as deeply as it was into his voice.

'And I'm going to give you two to one on Danny Greene same as what I gave everyone else.'

'No you didn't', interjected Luke, 'you gave me three to one.'

Albert scowled momentarily and turned to Hugh. 'Alright', he said to Hugh reluctantly, 'three to one, but if it's a no contest or the fight doesn't go ahead for whatever reason then the stake's mine. OK?'. He turned away muttering to himself just loud enough for Hugh and Luke to catch what he was saying. 'I'm shooting myself in the bloody foot here. Stupid man Albert, stupid man.'

Hugh looked at Luke for reassurance. This was his first ever wager. Luke nodded encouragingly.

'I mean, Danny can't lose', Hugh said in reply to the gesture, persuading himself that that the bet was a sound one. 'Done!', he exclaimed turning back to Albert. 'But make sure nothing happens to that watch. I mean it', he said directing a look laced with menace at the bookie.

'OK, OK, nothing's going to happen to your stuff', he replied nervously as he pocketed the watch and turned to re-join the stream of people making their way to the yard, a look of smug self-satisfaction on his face.

'Well, you've just made yourself a nice few quid there my friend', said Luke smiling. 'Beer on you later?'

'All you can drink', replied Hugh.

David Gallon had the foresight to clear the open expanse of the yard of compressors and waggons which were now parked around its perimeter. At the very centre of the yard a number of traffic cones had been arranged so as to loosely demarcate the area where the fight would at least begin, no one knowing where it would eventually come to an end, and hundreds of men were now milling around this space or stood in groups chatting as the hour approached. Hugh and his friends worked their way through the crowd to find themselves a place to observe the action close to the makeshift ring. Hugh looked around expecting to see Danny already there but he was disappointed. He instinctively looked down at his watch to confirm the time and was instantly reminded of his wager by the pale watch-shaped outline of the watch on his otherwise tanned wrist.

He turned to Paul and asked him the time.

'Ten to one', came the reply.

'He'll be in no hurry', Hugh reassured himself, murmuring recollections of his recent conversation with Danny beginning to stalk him from afar.

Then Jones emerged from the office and walked to the edge of the gantry, his head held high in an almost regal gesture of disdain, gripping the guardrail with surprisingly small hands as he surveyed the scene below him. He was greeted by a chorus of boos and imprecations from the men each one relishing the opportunity to hurl insults at Jones from within the relative anonymity of the mob. David joined him on the gantry.

'Don't take any notice of these halfwits, Colm', he said smiling down at the men before eventually turning to Jones and clapping his hands together to show his support.

'I've spotted a few that I'll be talking to later', replied Jones menacingly. 'I can't see Greene', he said scouring the yard.

'He'll be wanting to make a grand entrance at the last minute, no doubt. He always struck me as a bit of a poseur what with that bloody eye patch. Looks like something from the stone age', replied David.

Jones turned and started descending the stairs and with each step he took the volume of the curses hurled at him diminished. He stepped onto the floor of the yard and all was quiet save for a low thrum of muttered conversation. A channel immediately opened up before him leading to the small circle of cones at the centre of the yard and he sauntered towards it, a faint smile on his face dislodged only when he caught the eye of one of the men who had so recently berated him. To this man he issued a malevolent scowl.

Jones arrived at the centre of the yard and looked around him. 'Anyone here taking bets', he bellowed. Albert replied nervously.

'Erm, I am Mr. Jones.' Jones walked a couple of steps to the edge of the crowd to join him and, after a brief exchange of words and cash, he waived a makeshift betting slip in the air as he turned to ensure that everyone in the crowd could see it.

'The easiest five hundred quid I ever made! Now where is the bollocks', he bellowed as he rolled up his shirt sleeves and looked around the now cheering crowd.

'Where the fuck's your mate?', asked Luke turning to Hugh.

'What time is it?', he replied.

'It's five past one.'

Hugh looked towards the gate. There was no sign of Danny. 'He's delayed, that's all', he said, the quiver in his voice and his rictus grin which accompanied it indicating that even Hugh was doubtful as to the truth of the explanation. Hugh felt a tap on his shoulder and spun around half expecting it to be Danny wanting to push his way through, but instead it was Davie.

'Where the fuck is he?', he demanded.

Hugh turned away from him unable to provide an answer. He stared into the crowd and caught Georgie's eye. 'Where's yer fucking mate then, eh?', he bawled out across the ring, his complexion now taking on a puce colour in his anger, and he flung his betting slip onto the floor and turned to push his way through the crowd towards the gates.

Jones was now parading around the ring his confidence rising. 'Where is the wanker? I'll tell you where, he'll be sat at home shaking like a shiteing dog. The man's shivered out', he cried. 'All talk!' Jones spotted Hugh in the crowd. 'Where's your mate, eh? What kind of man is he, eh? He's a coward, that's what'. Jones' ebullience knew no bounds as he circled the perimeter of the circle. 'Anybody like to step in at short notice?', he cackled jubilantly, overfed on self-satisfaction.

This proved too much for the assembled men. Not that all of them were afraid of Jones, and indeed a few of them might have been persuaded to take

Danny's place, but they were instead disgusted with the fact that Jones had been allowed this moment of glory, and that Greene had handed it to him. The men started drifting off. 'So much for that shivering mate of your's', commented one as he passed Hugh on route to the gate. The remark did not register with Hugh. He was unable to properly grasp what had happened. His mind rushed through an entire list of reasons as to why Danny hadn't turned up, knowing in his heart that each one failed to make the grade as a convincing explanation.

'Known him for years, eh'?, said Luke dismissively, 'well, he can't have thought much of you leaving you stood here waiting like a prick with the rest of us', and headed off towards the gate.

Hugh looked around and saw a small group of men talking and nodding towards him as if it were him that had been found out to be a coward. Shame and confusion were devouring him. He had to get out of the yard as quickly as possible. He walked briskly towards the gate with his head lowered not wanting to make eye contact with anyone and almost collided with Jones who had installed himself directly into his path.

'If you see your mate, that cowardly piece of shit, you can tell him that he's done here, right? And if I see him around myself, I'll just come out throwing.' Hugh stared at the ground unable bring himself to look up at Jones. It was if he were carrying Danny's shame. 'And what're you going to do with yourself now?', Jones continued. 'I haven't seen Frankie in the yard all week, so that's him sacked too which means that you've no gang left. You'd better speak to Daddy, see if he can get you back with the snaggers, but if you'd take my advice, you'd just forget about this work altogether. It isn't for you posh kids. Get back to your books and leave this carry on to the men', and with that he barged through Hugh as if he wasn't there almost knocking him to the ground.

Hugh exited the yard and wandered aimlessly though the streets utterly confused, demoralised and humiliated. Danny had been a coward all along. He was filled with self-recrimination as he realised that the man whose example had come to inform his decisions about who he was and who he wanted to be was a fraudster, a pale impersonation of a man. All the talk which elevated him above the common crowd had been predicated on exaggeration and falsehood and he and everyone else had fallen prey to a myth that they themselves had helped to create. But hadn't Danny warned him of this the day before? Weren't these revelations a simple warning against reliance on these myths? Hugh couldn't summon the energy to even attempt to answer these questions. He was beset by a shame that curdled within him, a shame born of his own naivety. His grandfather's talk belonged to a different time, a different world and he hadn't had the sense to see this. He had never felt so naive, so childish, so removed from adulthood. He grappled with the reality that both Danny and Frankie had proved to be cowards in their own ways, and he'd fallen for their nonsense like a gullible child. The myth of manhood that had been passed down to him by his grandfather and so utterly embodied in the person of Danny Greene was little more than a fiction which served only to reduce men to the status of animals able to compete with one another only on the most base level.

Perhaps Clare had been right, he thought, her sense of what of what it meant to be a man was certainly a far richer and more fertile one than that offered by the bleak, lonely life of the long distance men. Clare! Her name exploded through his mind as if his drifting thoughts had triggered a short fuse. How was he going to explain Danny's cowardice too her? How could his justify his reliance on an image made of dust?

He felt himself flush with embarrassment as he recalled the almost child-like enthusiasm with which he had relayed news of the fight, how he had lauded Danny, how he had talked of nothing else for the past week. In fact, she had painted a picture of the immaturity of the entire situation, hadn't she? Then he felt a wave of panic flood over him. How would she respond when he revealed to her that his understanding of the world had been so wrong, now that he was shorn of his delusions he could no longer maintain the attitudes and behaviours which flowed from them? Would she still want him? Would she want Hugh Gallon the eighteen-year old student?

CHAPTER FIFTY-EIGHT

Hugh's desultory meanderings had inadvertently taken him close to his mother's house. He suspected that his father would still be with Jones at the yard, so he decided to take the chance and head in the direction of home. When he arrived at the house his father's car was nowhere to be seen. He sat on the doorstep and removed his boots. He looked at them and shook his head in disgust before rising to his stocking feet and walking over to the dustbin. He lifted the lid and dropped the boots on top of the rest of the rubbish and then entered the house. His mother was sat on the sofa flicking though a magazine as he collapsed into an armchair, a look of sadness and resignation etched onto his face. She looked up and knew that her son had returned to her.

'What's up lad?', She asked recognising his pain. 'Fallen out with Clare?'

'No', he replied, 'but she might be falling out with me. This whole navvy business', he said shaking his head in disgust, 'what a waste of time. It's just full of thugs, wasters and frauds.'

'Well don't worry about Clare', she replied reassuringly, 'take it from me, she won't be falling out with you any time soon as long as you haven't done anything silly, that is. You'd do well to keep in that young lady's good books. Smart as a whip and lovely looking too. So, what's happened at work?'

'Oh, I'm finished with it. I've no one to work with anyway. One of the lads in the gang has gone completely off the rails and the other one, that Danny bloke, he's just disappeared. He was supposed to be having this big fight with Jones. Turns out that Jones was part of a gang that cost him his eye years ago, but this Danny guy didn't have the guts to face him.'

'What do you mean 'disappeared'?', she asked with conspicuous urgency.

'He's just gone. Didn't show up at the yard for the fight with Jones. I don't think that he'll be showing his face around this city again. What a complete fraud *he* was. I'd trusted that bloke and he was a complete waste of time. They all make a big deal about fighting men, even granddad, but it's all rubbish, all talk', he said despondently and rummaged in the magazine rack next to him and turned to her. 'Can you remember where I left the university prospectus?'

'Yes, it's in your father's office. I'll get it for you', she said hurriedly and rose to her feet grateful for the opportunity to take in what she had just been told. 'Oh, and a package arrived for you this morning. Feels like a book', she said collecting the parcel from the table before tossing it to Hugh.

Hugh tore off the wrapping paper to reveal a worn copy of Homer's '*The Odyssey*'. He looked through the wrapping paper but couldn't find a card or any other indication of the identity of the sender.

Kate entered the office, quickly closed the door behind her and fell into a chair and began sobbing, deeply and convulsively. She couldn't fathom whether this uncontrollable out-flooding of tears was a reaction to Hugh returning home or because he had found his way back to his proper path. Both, she concluded. Then as quickly and as unexpectedly as they had begun her tears ceased and she wiped her eyes with the palms of her hands and laughed as if suddenly reprieved from an awful and devastating fate. She breathed a deep sigh of deliverance and leant back in the chair, the brief outburst of emotion leaving her exhausted, but before she could fully languish in the reassuring warmth of her relief the thought of Danny Greene exploded in her mind like a sonic boom.

She was immediately filled with a swirling confusion comprised of guilt, gratitude and pity. Ultimately, Danny had trusted her and accepted that Hugh was his own flesh and blood. He had denied himself a son's love and respect and forsaken his most valuable asset, his reputation, in order to give the boy a future. Her tears came again, but this time they burned with acid self-recrimination. This was the second time that she had used him as a sacrifice to Hugh's future, a man who she had renounced and who had every reason to despise her had come to her rescue when she was drowning in despair. She recalled what her father had done to Danny, what he had done to Hugh, and cursed him, but most of all she cursed herself for failing to appreciate the rough nobility of Danny Greene and the life they might have had together.

She looked around the home office with its expensive furniture and tasteful decorations and then out through the windows onto the manicured lawns and carefully tended flower beds at the back of the house and for the first time she recognised what she had lost. She had abandoned the love of an honourable man and deprived her son of a father who he could respect, and for what? Some nicer furniture, an impressive address, an expensive car? She leant forward and with a cry of frustration swept her arms across David's desk sending the various items that sat on its surface crashing to the floor. Then she promised herself with a resolve locked into her soul that she would find Danny Greene and repay him for his sacrifice.

She stood up from the chair, dried her eyes and took a deep breath before returning to the lounge.

'What was that banging Mum', asked Hugh.

'Don't worry about that', she said dismissively, 'I want you to know that I'm divorcing your father', and as she uttered these words a fiery light glistened in her eyes.

CHAPTER FIFTY-NINE

The yard had pretty much cleared of men and Jones sat in the office rocking on his groaning chair, his ebullient chatter echoing around the place, yet he remained mindful of the need to keep his sense of relief under control and prevent it from escaping into the euphoria it demanded. Spencer prattled on enthusiastically, pestering Jones with questions about the non-fight until the last remaining vein of tension running through Jones' centre caused him to snap at his young nephew who then turned to the recently arrived Fletcher, regaling him with an extended description of an event in which Fletcher had insufficient interest to attend.

David sat behind his desk keeping his own counsel, but all the while noting Jones' glee. He had congratulated Jones sufficiently he thought, and there was no need for him to get too effusive, after all, there hadn't been any actual fisticuffs and it wouldn't do to let Jones get too carried away with himself anyway. Nonetheless, Greene was finally out of the picture, and, by way of a bonus, he wouldn't have Hugh moping around the house or loitering around the yard making a fool of himself. All together it had been an excellent day.

He stood up from his seat and turned to Jones. 'Right', he said decisively, 'it's time for me to be off. The missus wants a serious talk with me', he said emphasising the word 'serious' and raising his eyebrows and shaking his head dismissively. Jones smiled indulgently. 'Bloody women, eh?'
'It'll be about Hugh wanting to come home now that he's out of work, no doubt. Well, it's my bloody house and she'll do what she's told. There's going a to be a few changes around the place now that he's out of the way, so she'd better get used to it', the events of the past few days furnishing him with a new sense of domestic self-confidence. He patted Jones on the shoulder as he left the office.

Jones was in the process of gathering his things to leave when the telephone rang. Fletcher answered it and during the course of a brief conversation he jotted down an address on the notebook in front of him before returning the receiver to its cradle. 'Look, I'm sorry to tell you this', he said looking at Jones, 'but that was the police. You're needed out on site. Something's happened. There's been some kind of accident. They asked for you by name.' Fletcher reached out from behind his desk and held the piece of paper out for Jones.

'Five minutes later and I'd have been gone', said Jones irritably as he snatched the note from Fletcher's hand. He didn't recognise the address at first glance, but Fletcher gave him a couple of landmarks to aim for and after a drive of twenty minutes or so and a stop for further directions, he found himself outside a row of derelict houses in a run-down, largely abandoned part of the city.

He pulled-in to the kerb noting with some irritation that the road ahead of him was blocked-off. He picked up the note to confirm the address and got out of his car. He stood on the pavement and looked around, confused. There was nothing to see here he concluded and he was about to return to his car. Suddenly, he heard movement behind him, and he turned as quickly as his bulk would allow. Streaming out of the abandoned house behind him were ten members of the Mulligan gang, each one holding either an iron bar or a pickaxe handle. Before he could recruit himself, the Mulligans had surrounded him, hemming him in against the door of one of the abandoned terraced houses which fronted onto the pavement. His eyes cast around frantically for an escape route, but there was none. The Mulligans fell upon him like wolves.

The train eased to a stop and Danny stood up from the stiff platform seat and made his way towards doors as they slowly parted, his rucksack slung over his shoulder. He adjusted the leather eye-patch which lent his face a savage, unforgiving look; his thick, calloused fingers surprisingly deft in the touching of it, and boarded the train. They were looking for men in the south, or so he'd been told.

The well-healed crowd sat in attentive silence as the hostess began her introductory remarks from the lectern positioned on a raised dais at the head of the plush function room of one of the city's better hotels.

'And so ladies and gentleman, we come to the final award of the evening, please show your appreciation for the two thousand and seven winner of the Women in Business Awards, Clare O'Brien of *Tiny Tots Nurseries Limited*'. A polite ripple of applause spread around the function room as Clare stood up from her seat at the rear of the dais and collected a small plaque from the speaker and took her place at the lectern.

'Thank you ladies and gentlemen, most generous of you. First of all, I can't take sole credit for this award. *'Tiny Tots Nurseries'* began as an idea which quickly became a passion, but it would've gone nowhere without the confidence and support, and let's not forget money, provided to me by my friend and business partner, Kate O'Shea, and so it is my pleasure to accept this award on behalf of us both. Stand up Kate, let them see you', she said smiling broadly. Kate reluctantly rose from her seat at one of the expensively adorned dining tables and lifted a flute of champagne. Applause broke out again and Clare returned to her seat.

'Thank you Clare', said the hostess resuming her position at the lectern 'Well ladies and gentlemen, that brings tonight's proceedings to a close. I'd like to thank you all for attending and please give all our winners one final round of applause.'

Kate turned to Hugh who was seated beside her and whispered to him. 'We opened nursery twenty-three last week, you know. Or rather Clare did.'

'Well done', he replied. 'As I've said before, a very wise investment on your behalf. You always recognised something in her, even when we were a couple', replied Hugh.

'I certainly did. She always had a spark of something that and I was just happy that the divorce gave me the money to back my confidence in her. On the subject of divorce, have you heard anything from David lately?'

'No', replied Hugh dismissively. 'I told you, I got a missed call from him about eighteen months ago, but I didn't return it. We haven't got anything to say to each other frankly. I mean, if I saw him, I would say hello of course, but there's not much chance of that happening given that I live at the other end of the country. Did you know that it's been over ten years since I've seen Clare for that matter. I think the last time was at your house and that was before the kids were born'.

'Did Samantha and the kids get off OK? I know that she was looking forward to the break'

Hugh looked at his watch. 'They'll be arriving at the villa about now', he replied. 'I dropped her and the kids off at the airport this morning before setting off here.'

'And you're going out when?', asked Kate.

'I'll join them in a couple of days. I'm looking forward to getting away myself.'

'I bet you are. Well, no one said that being a doctor was an easy life, eh?', she said smiling at him.

With that Clare arrived at the table.

'Hello Hugh', she exclaimed. 'I saw you from the lectern. So pleased you could make it. It's lovely to see you. It's been years'.

Hugh rose from his seat, and they embraced.

'It's lovely to see you too Clare. I was saying to Mum that it's got to have been ten years?'

'At least', replied Clare. 'You're looking well.'

'And you don't seem to have changed at all. A bit more expensively dressed perhaps', he said smiling.

'Well, business is good. No time for anything else though. I'm still on the look-out for Mr. Right after too many Mr. Wrongs. Present company excepted of course', she said with a wink and a smile and with that she sat down next to Kate before putting her hand to her mouth to muffle her voice.

'I bloody hate these things', she whispered, 'but you've got to do them. All hand shaking and business cards. Boring as hell. I'm glad this one's in the old hometown though and I can actually spend some time with my old mate', she said squeezing Kate's hand. 'As you know, I don't get much chance to get back.'

'Nor does Hugh', replied Kate in gentle admonishment.

'Come on Mum, you know I do my best. You were at our's only last month.'

'I know', she replied smiling, 'just teasing.'

'Look', said Clare, 'why don't we get out of here, go somewhere else? It's still early. People are drifting off anyway.'

'Sure', replied Hugh. 'Where do you have in mind?'

'Oh, I don't know. It's been years since I socialised here', replied Clare glancing at Kate for a recommendation.

'Don't look at me', she replied, 'I don't come into the city at all. I'm much too happy in my little village.'

Hugh smiled and shrugged his shoulders.

'I'll tell you what', exclaimed Clare, surprised by the novelty of her own idea, 'let's go to 'The Harp'!'

''The Harp'! That old hovel? Really?', asked Kate sceptically. 'Is it still in business?'

'Funny you should mention that place', said Hugh. 'I passed it on the way in here. I was astonished to see the doors open and frankly I did get a slight twinge of nostalgia myself.'

'Well, that's it! 'The Harp' it is for a trip down Memory Lane. Any objections?', asked Clare.

'But none of us have been properly inoculated, unless you've got your kit with you Hugh?', said Kate.

'Mother! Don't be so snobbish', admonished Hugh.

'Leave it to me', said Clare. 'I'll organise a taxi.'

Half an hour later the cab pulled up outside 'The Harp', its exterior of Yorkshire stone glowing a warm yellow under discretely housed spotlights hidden beneath the bright green signage advertising its name.

'Hmmm. Looks like it's had a bit of a makeover', said Kate peering through the window of the taxi. 'It's even got hanging baskets.'

'It's a popular place', interjected the taxi driver as he collected the fare from Hugh. 'They do lovely food I hear, but it's a bit expensive for us taxi drivers', he continued as he looked disappointedly at the money Hugh passed to him noting that he hadn't included a tip.

The first thing that struck them as they entered then pub was that the dividing wall between tap room and lounge had been taken down and the pub was now one large open-plan space. It was barely recognisable from the venue they had each expected. The carpets had been pulled up and had been replaced by glossy timber flooring which had a large green shamrock embossed into its surface in front of the highly polished bar. The artificially distressed walls were adorned with framed pictures of Irish poets of days gone by and in a niche above the bar was a small harp whose maple frame shone under a golden spotlight. The bar was full of seated patrons, some eating, some sipping from wine glasses, all were well-dressed.

'My, my', said Kate as she sauntered towards the bar, 'haven't things changed in here. What a pleasant surprise'. She placed their order.

'It's one of those Irish theme pubs, it seems', observed Hugh glancing around before nodding towards the back of the room, 'that's where you danced the first day I met you, remember?', he said looking at Clare.

'I do indeed', she replied wistfully.

'And over there', he pointed looking at his mother. 'I remember sitting there as a child with my grandfather'.

Kate looked towards the area of the pub that Hugh had indicated and as she did so her attention was caught by something else instead.

'My God!', she exclaimed, 'take a look over there, by the fire reading a newspaper'

Hugh and Clare turned as one.

'It can't be', said Kate.

'I think it is', replied Hugh.

'I recognise him', added Clare. 'Isn't that The Professor?'

'Yes, it is. I can't believe that he's still alive. He was an old man when I was a young one', added Hugh.

They collected their drinks and walked towards his table.

'Now then', said Hugh by way of introduction. 'I wonder if you remember me?'

The Professor looked up as if startled and peered first at Hugh, then at Kate and finally Clare.

'I see an O'Shea, a Gallon and an O'Brien before me. Am I mistaken?'

They looked at one another in surprise and admiration at his powers of recollection.

'Sit down', he continued, 'sit down. It's not often I see people from the old days in here and even rarer do I see those from the old, old days', he said peering at Kate from over the rim of his glasses and smiling.

'How are you said Kate. You're looking well. What age are you now?' She couldn't help herself but enquire.

'I'm eighty two', he replied, 'and I don't look a day over eighty three. I put it all down to carrot juice', he said raising a glass half filled with bright orange liquid. 'They get it in specially for me you know. They're very obliging. I'm like one of the ornaments in here, one of the artefacts', he said nodding towards a shillelagh hanging on the wall opposite. 'They allow me in to add a bit of extra character, I suppose.'

'So, where's everyone else? It's a very different clientele the last time I was in here', asked Hugh glancing around the room.

'Oh, they all went years ago. People moved on in the natural course of things and no one came to replace them. The Irish lads just stopped coming over to England when their economy picked up. Plus, the council finally demolished all the back-to back housing and made an attempt at gentrifying the area. I mean, look at this place, as gentrified as can be.'

'But you're still here', added Hugh.

'I am indeed, largely because I haven't touched a drop of the hard stuff for years.'

'Now', continued Hugh, 'as I recall, you very much kept yourself to yourself in the old days, never really paid much attention to the gossip going on around you', said Hugh slyly winking at his mother, 'but do you know what happened to any of those lads, Frankie Conroy for example?'

'Ah, Frankie boy', replied The Professor. 'As a matter of fact, I did hear a whisper about him a few years ago. I heard he had rather a bad accident while he was working in the Midlands somewhere, fell foul of a Great Awakener, you know cut into an electric cable, but the upside was he received quite a significant award of compensation as a consequence. From what I gather he's married with a couple of children and he is, like myself, a tea-totaller, which is ironic given that I hear he owns an off-licence.'

'What about Danny Greene', interjected Kate. 'Whatever became of him?', her question was expressed with such an intensity that both Clare and Hugh turned to look at her.

'Danny Greene. Now that is a name from the past alright. A very unusual man, Mr. Greene. Not at all what people thought.'

'I really looked up to him when I was a teenager', said Hugh.

'You bloody idolised him!', added Clare.

'I know. I thought that he was some kind of superhero. I wanted to be just like him. My grandfather had brought me up on tales of these rough, tough navvy men and Danny Greene was just the embodiment of it all. He left town under a cloud though, remember? Shattered a lot of illusions for me when he did that, but I suppose it was for the best. It made me grow up really.'

'Of course it was for the best', added Kate. 'Look at you now. You had us all very worried over that summer you know.'

'I still think about him sometimes, especially during the winter. I'll be driving along in the car and I'll see lads knee deep in a trench out in the cold, the wind and the rain and I remember how lucky I am. So, what became of him?'

'I haven't heard anything about him for years to be perfectly honest,' replied The Professor, 'I would imagine that he'd be well past his prime for that kind of work now, but you never know with men like him. Life dealt that man an unfair deck.'

'Well, he wasn't as tough as he thought he was in the end, was he?', said Hugh as he rose to go to the gents.

'No one is, I'm afraid', replied The Professor wryly.

Kate watched Hugh disappear through the door and quickly turned to The Professor. 'How would a person go about finding him, Danny Greene that is, if they really wanted to?'

'Oh, I don't know Kate. It's been such a long time since I heard anything of him', he replied. 'Short of pulling up at every roadside gang you see I don't know what to suggest.'

''I've tried that', she said quickly.

'Then keep on. You never know where these long distance men will show up.'

Clare looked at Kate with a quizzical expression. 'I'll explain all one day, but just not now', said Kate. 'Neither of you need mention my interest to Hugh, OK?'

'Of course not', replied Clare even more confused.

'Let me see what I can do', said The Professor smiling sagely at Kate 'I've got a book full of phone numbers at home. Who knows what a few calls might turn up.'

Kate smiled warmly at him and scribbled her telephone number on a beer mat and passed it to him. 'I would very much appreciate that, thank you.'

Hugh returned to the table and sat down. 'I think I was a bit harsh on Danny just then. You know the day before he left we were talking in the waggon and he seemed to be trying to tell me something. It was a strange conversation. He showed me the scar tissue under his eye patch, an appalling bit of surgical work by the way. It was if he was foreshadowing something. In retrospect, I thought he was afraid, and I think I was right, but it wasn't himself that he was afraid for. For some reason, I think that he was afraid for me.'

'As I said, he was a most unusual man', added The Professor and glanced towards Kate who lowered her eyes. 'He'll be around somewhere, no doubt.'

This is a country of streets and of highways, of carriageways and footways and the digging goes on and on. The road is never ending for the long distance men.

THE END

Printed in Great Britain
by Amazon

42275241R00209